EARLY
ONE
MORNING

EARLY ONE MORNING

VIRGINIA BAILY

virago

VIRAGO

First published in Great Britain in 2015 by Virago Press

13 5 7 9 10 8 6 4 2

A CIP catalogue record for this book is
available from the British Library.

HB ISBN 978-0-349-00648-2
C FORMAT ISBN 978-0-349-00649-9

Typeset in Bembo by M Rules
Printed and bound in Great Britain by
Clays Ltd, St Ives PLC

Papers used by Virago are from well-managed forests
and other responsible sources.

MIX
Paper from
responsible sources
FSC® C104740

Virago
An imprint of
Little, Brown Book Group
Carmelite House
50 Victoria Embankment
London EC4Y 0DZ

An Hachette UK Company
www.hachette.co.uk

www.littlebrown.co.uk

In memory of my father, Peter Baily

ONE

ROME, OCTOBER 1943

A young woman marches briskly down a Rome street. Her coat is tightly belted, a scarf is wound around her head and a large cloth bag is slung slantways across her body. Over her arm she carries a smaller bag, containing her purse with a few lira in it and her papers – her identity card and ration book. 'Chiara Ravello, spinster,' the card declares and gives her address as Via dei Cappellari 147, flat number 5. She has no umbrella against the steady rain falling out of the dark sky, an unrelenting downpour that will continue for hours, as if complicit in the day's events.

Within fifteen minutes of the phone call summoning her – 'Mamma is sick,' Gennaro had said – she was out of the door. That she is decently dressed at all, given her speed and the fact that her sister, Cecilia, followed her around the apartment, getting in the way and asking fatuous questions, is a minor miracle.

'Who was on the telephone?' This at the bathroom door as Chiara splashed water on her face. 'Why are you getting dressed? It's only a quarter to six.' This as Chiara fetched her

1

stockings from the rail in front of the stove and tugged the damp resistant things up her chilly legs.

The rain has pervaded the inside of the apartment; a faint fog seems to hang in the kitchen air.

'You can't go out without a petticoat.' This as she pulled her red woollen dress over her head and buckled her belt. Then, rallying, 'Shall I make you a coffee?'

Finally, while Cecilia rinsed out the pot at the sink, Chiara had a second to think what might be needed: to don her coat and scarf, and to locate that extra bag in case any-thing could be salvaged, to consider and discount taking her bicycle on the grounds that it would take too long to man-handle down the stairwell and it would be quicker to walk. Gennaro's bar on Via del Portico d'Ottavia was less than a kilometre away.

At the kitchen door she turned to say she had to go and saw that Cecilia had stopped, was standing with the empty coffee pot dangling from her hand, her mouth open. Chiara knew Cecilia had remembered that there was no coffee in the house, that there had been no coffee for over two months. She knew too that the memory had stirred up all that went with that knowledge: the bombs, the deaths, the Nazi occupation, everything that collectively Chiara referred to in her own head as 'the rubble'. On another day she would have comforted her sister, but not today.

'I won't be long,' she said.

'Don't go out,' Cecilia said, in her little-girl voice.

'Oh, for the love of God,' Chiara shouted and she was out the door, her boots clattering on the stone stairs but not loudly enough to drown out her sister's wail.

At street level, she thought better of it and ran back up the two flights. 'Get dressed. Pack a bag with warm clothes.'

The dithery, wilting look that made Chiara want to slap her into awareness came over Cecilia's beautiful, doe-eyed face. 'Is it a holiday?' she asked.

'Yes. We're going away,' Chiara said. 'Pack a bag for me too. I'll be home in a couple of hours, or less.' She showed her on the clock. 'I'll bring you back something special.'

'Shall I take my sewing stuff?'

'What you can fit in. Not the machine.'

'I'll put in a blanket each.'

'I'm sorry I shouted.'

'I won't tell.'

Whom Cecilia thinks she might tell is a mystery.

The street is dark. A curfew operates now, and the street lights are not lit. Chiara's feet are damp, her boots leak and she slips on the wet cobbles. When she gets to the corner of Campo dei Fiori, she pauses. The first glimmers of this grey dawn that have not yet found their way down into the narrow shaft that is Via dei Cappellari illuminate a deserted square. It is six o'clock on a Saturday morning, and the market should be setting up. The statue of Bruno Giordano is the only human form to be seen. She glances up at him, solemn, hooded, portentous, as if there might be comfort to be had. She shivers.

She crosses the square by skirting its edges, hugging the buildings. The streets have been emptier since the Nazis took over. As during a bad weather warning – earthquake, snow or landslide – the people of Rome huddle indoors and go out these days only if it is strictly necessary. Always, at night, there are the sounds of sporadic gunfire. There are stories of people being stopped arbitrarily, lined up against walls and marched away, to be interrogated in buildings newly occupied and adapted for the purpose, from where screams can be heard.

3

Later, families are summoned to collect mangled bodies. This is not new; it went on throughout the years of fascism, but it has reached a more terrifying dimension, now that Rome has been declared an open city. It is no longer possible to stay safe by keeping your head down. There is a confusion about sides and allegiances.

Halfway down Via dei Giubbonari, Chiara turns right into an even narrower street, a route that will bring her out farther down the main road, away from the principal junction. She does not know what she is going towards, only that her help is needed and that, whatever this new trouble, it is happening in the old Jewish quarter. If it weren't for the gold levy that the Nazi command imposed on the Jewish population of Rome a few days ago, she might not now be so sure that the location of Gennaro's bar, in the ghetto's main thoroughfare, is significant.

Fifty kilograms of gold. She had helped organise and collect donations – rings and lockets, old coins and cufflinks. She would even have contributed her father's signet ring, but it wasn't in the jewellery box where she kept it. Afterwards, after the officials had weighed the gold and pronounced it sufficient, she had found the ring wedged in a gap between the tiles on top of her dressing table. She had been glad not to have had to give up this ring that had belonged to her dear father, five years dead.

Babbo, she thinks, her precious father, and she reaches for a comforting memory of him, but instead an image appears of Carlo, her fiancé, who died only a month later. A grief so strong wells up in her that she whimpers. Loneliness travels through her like cold in her bones.

With the gold collection, they thought they had pre-empted further trouble and bought the Jews of Rome some peace. But

4

now, she thinks, her steps slow with the rain tumbling down on her, what if an error in the counting has been uncovered? What if the Nazi booty is short by ten grams? By the weight of a ring? She shakes her head, her scarf sodden against the back of her neck.

She hurries on. It might not be anything so serious. She might be tormenting herself needlessly. And at least she will get a proper cup of coffee at Gennaro's.

She emerges at a small intersection where there is a patch of grass out of which a lone plane tree grows. She has it in mind to take cover under this tree and assess the situation. There is nothing to assess. Or she has no way of assessing whatever there is. The main road, Via Arenula, is silent and empty. She loiters underneath the tree, clinging to its protection. She is still on 'her' side. By stepping off the kerb, crossing the road, she will enter another world. It is as if the walls that used to surround the ghetto half a century earlier have been rebuilt. They are invisible, but they exist.

She still has the option of turning back.

She thinks of Cecilia. She visualises her listening to light music on the radio while she packs and then switching it off when the regular government communiqué comes on. In her mind she has her instead putting on the gramophone player and packing their cases to the rhythms of her song of the moment, sung by her new favourite matinée idol, Gino Bechi. They saw the film three times when it came out in March. 'The Road Through the Wood' is the tune playing in homes across Rome as people pack their bags, lock up their houses and flee the city. Why should she and Cecilia be any different? They are luckier than most. Their grandmother – their *nonna* – still lives up in the hills.

A far-off rumbling noise gets louder. She keeps close in to

the tree, envisaging a military vehicle. Then a bus with steamed-up windows rolls into view. There seems to be no one on board apart from the driver. A dog comes trotting down the road, stopping to sniff at odd pieces of boggy rubbish in the gutter. The municipal services have broken down, and the streets have not been cleaned for weeks. The dog wanders onto the pavement and cocks a leg against the tree.

Chiara looks for signs in these occurrences – the absence of passers-by, the fact that public transport is running, the glimmer of the paler patches on the mottled bark of the plane tree in the early morning light, the way the rainwater drips off the end of the yellowing leaves, the dog choosing this tree to urinate against – interpreting them as first one thing and then its opposite. Her consciousness flickers between extremes: that the message was wrong or misconstrued or a false alarm, and it is as normal a day as Rome gets to have these days, or that something untoward is taking place on an apocalyptic scale.

A bird squawks in the branches above her; a cold drop of rain lands on her nose. The rain has soaked her through, seeped up into her boots and down through her scarf to her hair, dampening her shoulder blades and the tender, chilly place between them. The rainwater gurgles down the drains, and she is standing as still as Giordano himself, frozen in stone. She wants to go home. She pictures a blue china bird with its head thrown back and its beak wide, perched on a windowsill. The view of the tower of San Lorenzo from the window, the pine trees of the cemetery beyond. Their childhood home.

Rubble, she thinks.

Across the road there is a movement. A man in uniform has appeared from out of the shadows of one of the streets leading into the ghetto. And with that sight, that reminder of

6

danger, doubt falls from her. She moves out from under the tree and steps off the pavement.

Mamma's sick, she thinks. That is what Gennaro said to her on the telephone. It's their code in case the line is tapped, but they hadn't worked out what the next part of the story should be.

And she is thinking, as she crosses the road, about what she will say if stopped. She can't say she's going to visit her mother, who died in the San Lorenzo bombing three months ago and wouldn't be living in the ghetto anyway. An old lady who does live in the ghetto comes into Chiara's mind. She doesn't know her real name but everyone calls her Nonna Torta – which might mean Granny Pie or Granny Wrong; both epithets would suit. She used to supply bread and pastries for the bakery in Piazza Guidia. The unleavened bread made with coarse, unhusked flour and used at Passover, the rye loaf with caraway, the plaited challah, the twisted loaf with poppy seeds, the nutty pastries filled with dried fruit, figs and plum paste. Priests and nuns had been known to come and queue for her famous wild cherry tart, and there were rumours that the pope himself had tasted it.

Chiara will say, if stopped, that she has heard Nonna Torta, an old friend of her grandmother's, is sick, and she is on her way to see whether there is anything she can do for her. Perhaps it is because she knows Nonna Torta's address that the old lady has presented herself in her mind. She is a regular at Gennaro's bar and lives in Via di Sant'Ambrogio, just behind. Or perhaps it is because Nonna Torta is indeed unwell, not sick in her body but wandering in her mind.

The soldier has taken up position against the side of the building. He ignores Chiara as she passes him. She understands that he is not there to stop people from entering the Jewish quarter but from leaving it. He has the spread-winged eagle insignia on his cap.

Terrible noises assail her as she enters the ghetto. Screams and bellows, metal sparking off stone. As she walks farther in, Chiara assembles everything she knows about Nonna Torta. The effort keeps her from crying out or running or reacting in any way at the sight of German soldiers stationed at corners, battering at front doors; the frightened faces at windows. From high up in buildings come shrill cries.

Nonna Torta wears her pinny at all times except on the Sabbath. She is bow-legged. Her hair is white as the feathers of a dove. She is a storyteller although she often repeats herself. Chiara finds her difficult to understand because she mixes in words and phrases from the Judaeo-Roman dialect. She has lived in the ghetto all her life and was born before Italian unification. She remembers the ghetto walls being torn down, back when she was a girl, and the place opening up. People moving out across the river to Trastevere, which was previously unheard of; before, the Jews had all been crammed in there together, cosy and separate. No change occurs without something being lost, after all.

The thought of Nonna Torta gives Chiara a frisson of hope. It is the thought of longevity, of lives lived out to complete their natural course.

When she turns into Via del Portico d'Ottavia, she falters. A column of grey-clad soldiers are lined up along the pavement, the officers standing at strategic intervals. One of them is addressing the soldiers, instructing them. Gennaro's bar is shut, locked up, the blind pulled down behind the glass. Beyond, where the Theatre of Marcellus looms up, massive and ancient as if untouchable, three lorries with dark tarpaulins are parked. Suddenly, the men all start to shout, a terrible bellowing roar that makes the hair on her body stand on end and the damp place between her shoulder blades throb. Just as suddenly, they stop. Then they disperse, in groups of two or three, disappearing down various streets of the ghetto. The few remaining ones take up position, some in front of the lorries, others at each of the tributary roads.

Chiara knocks at the door of the bar.

'It's me,' she whispers through the keyhole.

The blind lifts a fraction, and Gennaro's face appears, his eyes black and wild, his cheeks smeared with soot. He opens the door a crack, bundles her in and leads her through to the storeroom behind the bar where an overstuffed, pot-bellied stove belches out smoke. This is one of the places they keep the anti-fascist pamphlets that a team of volunteers leave around the city, moving quickly and as if they are going about their everyday business. There are several stores at different locations around Rome, and a printing press in a sound-proofed chamber behind a butcher's refrigerator in the Testaccio area.

Gennaro has been burning evidence.

'Can you get on with this?' he says, gesturing at the stove and the small mountain of leaflets next to it or strewn around the floor. He must have just swept them from the shelves. 'I need to get the bar open.' He makes a noise that could be interpreted as a laugh. 'Business as usual. Give the appearance of.'

'They're not here for us,' Chiara says.

'No,' he says. 'But still, we wouldn't want them to find all this, would we?'

'They're rounding up the Jews,' she says.

Then she notices the headline article on the uppermost pamphlet, written by a prominent Jewish intellectual. Like many, he had returned to Rome after Mussolini was ousted in

9

July and before the armistice was declared in September. In that brief period, when they thought that for the first time in twenty years they could say what they wanted, he had produced a flurry of articles. She wonders where he is now, and hopes he has got out of the city.

'You've got soot on your face,' she says to Gennaro.

He wipes it off with his sleeve, grimaces at her as if she is criticising him. It is hard to be kind when you're frightened.

'Go on,' she says and smiles. Her smile probably looks like a grimace too.

Gennaro has packed the stove too tightly. Chiara has brought the spare bag with some idea of rescuing pamphlets for another time, or for posterity, or for some other reason that had seemed compelling in the kitchen fog earlier. It escapes her now, when, like Gennaro, she urgently wants to obliterate all traces of them. She snatches up a long, slender piece of wood from the sack of logs and kindling, and jabs at the dense mass of smoking newsprint. The piece of wood snaps.

She casts about for a better tool, flings wide the half-open door of a cupboard and finds a metal dustpan and broom, a big bottle of pink liquid that might be a cleaning product or might be paraffin – should she pour it in? Would the whole building go up in flames? – and yet another pile of pamphlets. These date back four months, to the beginning of the summer, and feature a photograph of Mussolini addressing the crowds in Piazza Venezia, the people filling the square like ants, and a caption she can no longer read. A powerful, disgusting smell emanates from the cupboard. She pushes the door to, returns to the stove, armed with the dustpan, and pokes fiercely at the wodge of paper inside, trying to break it up. The stove is like a little animal that they have been force-feeding. It is starting to choke.

10

A vision of Cecilia as a child appears. She sits opposite Chiara at the table in the kitchen of their former home in San Lorenzo (*rubble*, Chiara thinks automatically). A steaming plate of tripe sits untouched on the red-and-yellow-checked cloth in front of her sister. Meat disgusts Cecilia, and offal most of all. With ham and mortadella, the kind of meat that is served in slices, she has developed a method of furtively scooping it into her lap, to be thrown away, hidden or devoured by Chiara later. It is the discovery of the hidden stashes of rotting meat behind the sofa that has invoked greater vigilance from their mother at mealtimes. Tripe stew in tomato sauce is too messy a dish for lap scooping but, in any case, their mother is in the room with them, or in and out at least, so Chiara cannot help.

'Eat up your food, Cecilia, or you won't grow big and strong,' their mother says, for the hundredth time.

Cecilia is constantly admonished thus. She must be nine or ten years old, Chiara thinks, after the onset of her illness but before that summer when a spate of uncontrollable seizures damaged her brain irrecoverably. As their mother comes to the table, Cecilia grabs a hunk of bread and stuffs the whole piece into her mouth. To show willing, perhaps. Her jaw clicks. She cannot move it to masticate and cannot get the huge unchewed lump down her throat. Her eyes are popping. Her face is going red. If she were a snake with a rabbit in its jaw, she would throw back her head and her powerful neck muscles would take over the business of swallowing. But Cecilia is not a snake. Her little neck cannot expand. Then Mamma is there, banging Cecilia's back, which doesn't work, then sticking her finger into Cecilia's mouth and hooking the mush out, which does.

Chiara uses the dustpan handle to hook the papers out of the stove. She lays them out on the floor, unpicks and loosens

11

the wad, then starts again, tearing the sheets into smaller scraps, stoking the flames. Their mamma was a demon for physical intervention in their maladies: greased fingers up the bottom for constipation, vigorous chest massaging with oil for colds, tincture of iodine slathered over cuts, methylene blue for sore throats. If poking and rubbing and the application of unguents, ointments and poultices didn't work, then you were malingering. If the malady continued or worsened beyond denial, then it was to the priest with you. She didn't believe in doctors.

Chiara is making progress. The stove is burning at full capacity, and she starts to warm up. Steam rises from her clothes. As she gets into a rhythm of tearing, shredding, burning, poking, she shuts her mind to the intermittent roars, to what might be going on outside. She is like an engine driver, stoking her little train, thundering down the rickety track. She needs to get to her destination. This is her job.

She clears the pile, sweeps up the debris and tips it in. She watches as the last scraps are consumed and then remembers the other stack in the stinking cupboard. The stench hits her anew when she opens the door. She lifts most of the pile of papers, which are pulp in her hands. When she stuffs them into the stove, a heavy, noxious smoke billows out. She wraps her scarf over her nose and mouth, soggy fragments of newsprint sticking to her fingers and catching around her wrists, and works at the damp mass with her improvised poker, forcing it to fragment. She coaxes a flame, then another. It catches fire.

She goes back to check she has cleared the cupboard. She peels a leaflet from the cupboard base and seems to see, for a fraction of a moment, two little green lights, instantly extinguished. She leans in, clutching her scarf around her nose, and the lights reappear. They are the eyes of a cat. A black cat with white paws, lying at the back of the cupboard, four or five tiny kittens at her breast. To one side, stiff and lifeless, lies the runt, the tiniest of creatures. Chiara sees that she has destroyed the cat's newspaper nest, her refuge, the home she has found for herself and her offspring. Now she pulls the last pamphlet out from under the family and takes their bed. The emaciated cat makes a sound, attempts to stand but lacks the strength.

Chiara picks up the runt's body with the last remaining leaflet and chucks it in the stove. She returns to look at the cat. She allows herself to contemplate the cat's life: running from dogs, skulking, roaming the city's ruins, scavenging for scraps. The brief wild moment when these babies were conceived. She ponders leaving the cloth bag as a bed for the animals. The cat is patently starving.

People are going hungry.

It is only a cat.

She wipes her face and hands with the end of her scarf and goes through to the bar. There are no customers. Gennaro has raised the blinds and set some tables and chairs out on the street, in the rain. Chiara looks out at the people there. She has never seen human beings being herded before.

'Coffee?' Gennaro says.

Chiara wants to go now, but she is overcome by a wave of nausea and her legs tremble. She steadies herself against the bar, turning away from the sights beyond the window.

'Please,' she says.

She stirs sugar in, three spoonfuls, and becomes aware that Gennaro is talking to her, telling her some tale. He is saying he didn't notice anything strange when he first arrived at the bar at five o'clock this morning. He had cycled in as usual from his home on the other side of the river. All the way, nothing strange, except that the river was swollen with all the rain. On Garibaldi bridge the rain had intensified, and he had paused to pull up his hood and adjust the bike light. He had been cycling slowly because his brakes didn't work very well.

He had stopped to buy some coal, and the chap there, whom Gennaro had known for years, a real busybody of a man who had his finger in a lot of pies, a lot, had told him that he had heard this great noise during the night, coming from the ghetto. A cacophony, he called it. Round after round of gunfire and explosions. Shouting and bellowing, just like they had been doing on the street when Chiara arrived. It had gone quiet again at about four in the morning.

Anyway, this bloke, Federico, had told him there wasn't any coal, and he didn't know when supplies would next come, so Gennaro had bought a bundle of firewood instead. It was a bit damp because of being tied on the back of his bicycle and that's why it was so smoky in the back room when he had first lit the stove. It wasn't even seasoned wood. But you had to take what you could get these days.

'Where do you get your coal?' Chiara finds herself asking, as if that is a more pressing subject than the night-time noises or what is happening outside in the street. 'Do you go to that place off Viale Trastevere?' She imagines for a moment that she is interested in the answer, that she will change her coal supplier.

A young man enters the bar. A soldier accompanies him but stops at the threshold, neither in nor out. Gennaro greets the man by name. Alberto. He puts his fibre suitcase down beside his legs and orders an espresso. The case is tied shut with a blue dressing-gown cord. His black scarf is neatly crossed at the front and tucked into the upturned collar of his shabby coat. His hair is flattened from standing in the rain. His face is pale, broad, unshaven. His cheeks hang slack, his full-lipped mouth slightly open. There is no conversation while Gennaro prepares the man's drink. The cup rattles against the saucer as he lifts it. He has to use both hands. His fingernails are dark with oil or dust.

Chiara's thoughts have become a case of ball-bearings, skittering and careering. She thinks about the treat she is going to take home to Cecilia and wonders whether perhaps Gennaro has something squirrelled away that she might do a deal on. Some biscuits perhaps. Or whether, if the buses are running, she could get up to Tor di Nona where the black marketeers trade and see if there is cheese to be had, or a tin of tuna or beans.

She tries to stay with these thoughts. They are comfortable. But then the flames licking at the kitten's lank fur are in her head and she questions whether it was actually dead. She is horribly present in this room, now, in this moment. It is as if the damp seepage that, despite the heat of the flames, persists in the hollow of her back, is not rainwater but something else, some residue from a deep pool of human pain. She has been dipped in it, and it coats her.

The man swallows noisily, puts his cup down on the counter and runs his hand along the wooden surface. He leans forward and, in a quiet voice, he asks Gennaro a question. He says, 'What are they going to do with us?'

Gennaro shakes his head.

The man looks around him, his gaze lingering on the tables and chairs. Chiara feels his eyes on her, but she doesn't meet them. The soldier at the door calls him. He picks up his bag and leaves.

Chiara follows him as far as the doorway and watches as he is escorted back into the line of people being herded along the street to the waiting lorries. The population of the ghetto – the old, the young, babies in arms, people on crutches, women and children – all shuffle towards the trucks in an almost-silent procession. Some of the very smallest among them are crying and griping, the way babies do, but the adults and the bigger children, the ones capable of speech, do not speak. There are some young men like the one who came into the bar, but not many.

'Where are the men?' she asks.

Gennaro comes to stand next to her. 'It's tobacco ration day,' he says. 'They'll have gone to get their ciggies.'

She glances sideways at him. 'What?'

His face is solemn. Streaks of soot remain in the creases of his jowls, accentuating their droop, as if he's been made up to look doleful. Can lives hang on so little as a packet of ciga-rettes? Chiara wonders.

'Yes,' Gennaro says as if she's spoken out loud. 'That's how it is.'

Some of the people still have their nightwear on underneath their coats. Most are carrying bags or have bundles strapped to their backs. They are being nudged along with the points of guns. On the other side of the line, two officers lean against the wall, chatting and smoking.

'What *will* they do with them?'

'They're probably taking them to a labour camp up north,' Gennaro says.

'Babies and old ladies in a labour camp?' Chiara says.

But now Gennaro is saying something about his mother having warned him not to open a bar in the ghetto, and how it used to be a pawnbroker's, and who was going to come here now, and how it will be blighted, and then, mid-sentence, he stops speaking and stands there, shame-faced. Then he starts

16

jabbering on again about nothing strange, he noticed nothing strange earlier, and again he stutters to a halt.

'They'll be back one day,' he says eventually. 'When this war is over.'

They watch as the last person in the line passes. Nonna Torta brings up the rear, swaying and muttering. She is in her nightdress and slippers with her pinny on top. She has no bag.

Across the way, the two Nazi officers are still talking, their backs resting against the stonework, each with the sole of his left foot, encased in its knee-high boot, flat to the wall in a dis-quieting but almost reassuring symmetry.

Gennaro is crying.

'Did you know you have a hungry cat and some kittens in your storeroom cupboard?' Chiara says.

'A cat?' he says. 'I'll take her some milk.' He goes back to the counter and bends down, rooting about. 'Got some little biscuits she might like,' he says and disappears into the back room.

Chiara steps out into the street and joins a small group of bystanders. She places herself at the rear beside a woman with unkempt grey hair who holds both hands to her cheeks as if she is resisting covering her eyes. Chiara too knows that she has to watch this whole spectacle. She has to bear witness. Then when she has borne witness, she can perhaps walk away; she can go back to her life. She can gather up her sister, and some rations and clothes, and she can leave this city and take refuge in their grandmother's house in the mountains and wait for the Allies to arrive.

Her mind flies away to the sheep in the meadow behind her grandmother's house. Always, all of her life, this field, the feel of it – the smell of the grass and the wild oregano that grows in the hedgerows; the clearness of the air, fresh and sparkling and brighter than the air in the valleys; the view of the other hills, the way they undulate away in all directions – all of this has been a comfort to her. The cleanness and the safety of hills: she longs for them.

The inhabitants of the ghetto have been corralled into a hollow in the road in front of the Theatre of Marcellus where the ground has been excavated. Elsewhere, from the direction of the river, comes shouting and the crack of gunshot, but these people, who stand waiting among the ruined, broken pillars, are hushed.

The tarpaulins on the sides of the lorries have been rolled up, and this now-homeless throng are made to climb aboard. The gap between the witnesses and the rounded-up Jews is widening. It's as if she is watching them across a swelling river.

A young family catches her eye. They are already on the back of one of the trucks and have managed to stay together. The father is intent, serious, handsome in his shirt and tie, suit and coat. He has a high forehead and his curly hair has been dampened down. He is the sort of man who might smoke a pipe, Chiara thinks, as her own father had done. And who might stick it in his mouth and suck on it while he was pondering a difficulty, then remove it to make a pronouncement. The sort of man who is not hasty in his judgments. Now he is trying to find a way of being the man of the family, of retaining some dignity. In his arms he holds a curly-haired girl, chubby-faced, with fat little wrists protruding from her big-buttoned coat, eyes sparkling as if this is an adventure. In between the husband and wife stands another, bigger child, a boy, perhaps seven or eight years old. He is clutching the sleeve of his mother's coat.

It is the woman who draws Chiara's attention. She holds a toddler, whose mouth is turned down, as if in parody of the

18

looks on the faces of the surrounding adults. The woman is better dressed than most and gives the impression of having chosen her outfit with care, not hurriedly throwing on whatever she could find in the frantic minutes before they were forced out of their homes. This woman wears pearl stud earrings and a dark-green hat on the back of her head. Her coat is also dark green, tightly belted. It is like a going-away outfit.

Perhaps, when the terrible hullabaloo was taking place at four this morning, she didn't retreat fearfully into the nethermost recesses of her apartment nor pull the blanket over her head, but dared to look out and saw the Nazi soldiers running amok. And when they interrupted their mayhem, instead of thinking it was over and going back to bed, she made her family get up and get dressed. She fed them bread and a hot drink. She packed their bags, one for each of them. This family, Chiara thinks, had been going to run, but they didn't do it fast enough.

The woman's eyes flick from side to side, searching the crowd. If the gap between the onlookers and the Jews is now a torrent, this woman is still searching for a bridge, a raft, a piece of flotsam.

Chiara is staring at the woman, and the woman's restless gaze finds her. Without taking her gaze from Chiara's, the woman bends down and unpicks her son's fingers from her coat, pushes him away. Chiara glances at the child, back up to the woman who is still fixing her steadily, down to the boy who has grabbed a different handful of cloth. Chiara focuses on the mother's fingers as she unfurls the claw of the child's hand, prising him off again. Chiara's eyes swivel between mother and son, but the woman never takes her eyes off Chiara. She grips the boy's shoulder, says something and the boy stands clear of her, hands dangling by his sides. The boy, the only straight-haired member of the family, is neatly turned out, grey shorts, socks pulled up, one knee scabby.

Then Chiara is shouting and pushing her way to the front of the small crowd, shrugging off a restraining hand that briefly rests on her arm.

'My nephew,' she shouts out. 'That's my nephew,' pointing at the boy.

'This child is yours?' the soldier who is directing operations at this truck asks in heavily accented Italian.

'Yes,' she says. 'My sister's.'

The boy wobbles on the edge of the truck, his face stretched, intense but unfocused. He is like the child made to stand on a stool at the front of the class, singled out for humiliation.

'Pass him down to me. Come to auntie, darling,' Chiara cries out.

Encouraged by the sound of her own voice – shrill, maternal, outraged – she keeps up the clamour, holding out her arms to receive him. Some of the people around join in. 'Pass that boy down,' and 'This is his aunt,' and even, from somewhere in the group, a man's voice, 'That boy is no Jew.'

A soldier of superior rank appears and demands to see Chiara's papers. She recognises him as one of the two that were leaning against the wall opposite Gennaro's bar. While he unfolds her documents, the boy is handed down. He is stiff and heavy. She sets him down beside her, pulls him tight into her flank, gripping his hand. She can feel the tautness in him.

She does not look at the mother again. She must not see doubt. She looks instead at the officer's face, lean and clean-shaven, up to his peaked cap, along to the tip of his revolver, down to the skull-and-crossbones collar patch. She notices the gold thread on his epaulette, and the stitching that has torn at some point and been resewn more clumsily in a different-coloured thread. The damp patch between her shoulders throbs, as if expecting a bullet. It will surely travel straight through to her heart.

'My sister,' she comments, staring at a trail of thread, 'is a seamstress. You wouldn't even see the stitches if she had done that mending.'

She knows he doesn't understand her. They are just words she sends out to try to pierce the bubble of silence that has descended on them like a solid-domed roof. A great emptiness fills her head as if she might be about to faint.

'Spinster,' the officer says, pointing to the word with his ungloved hand.

'He is my sister's boy,' she replies.

He looks at her and at the child. Is it enough that the words 'of the Jewish race' are absent from her documents? Chiara has never made the fascist salute. Even at school she managed to avoid it and has prided herself on this small act of tacit resistance. Now, though, she is wondering whether the moment has come, whether that would in some way settle the matter.

The truck engines start up and a cry is wrenched from the boy at her side. 'Mamma,' he screams and Chiara snatches him up, presses him into her chest.

He starts to kick her.

'Mamma. Mamma,' he screams again and again. It is all she can do to hold him.

She hisses into his ear, 'Shut up or the soldier will shoot,' and he goes limp against her, a dead weight. 'Can you give me my card, please?' she says boldly. 'I need to get him home.'

The driver of the second vehicle shouts something. He is ready to leave. The SS officer glances over at the lorry. His eyes

run over its occupants. And then he leans down and tousles the boy's hair.

'Be good for your auntie,' he says and drops Chiara's papers into the cloth bag hanging from her shoulder.

Out of the corner of her eye, she can see the boy's little suitcase up there on the truck next to where he had been standing. His clothes, his possessions, maybe a toy or a bedtime book. Something that was his. She can't have any of it. Not a single thing. Not a photograph. Not a vest.

The trucks pull away.

Chiara stands in a daze with the heavy child in her arms, his face pressed into her coat.

'Off you go,' the officer says, giving her a look that she doesn't understand. He raises his voice, addressing the whole crowd. 'Go away now,' he barks and claps his hands, in a theatrical gesture. The show is over.

Chiara moves away as quickly as she can, the inert child clutched to her bosom, his feet swinging into her knees with each step. She wonders whether she has suffocated him. She takes the road to the river, lurches along Lungotevere under the plane trees and, when she gets past Garibaldi bridge, she puts him down. He has left a trail of snot down the front of her coat.

'I want my mamma,' he says.

She looks at him. Small, defiant. Orphaned. Her knees buckle, and she puts her hand to the parapet. For the first time this morning, the sun comes out, giving the leaves above their heads an orangey-gold glow. Down below, a fallen branch bobs past on the engorged river. She steadies herself.

'I'm taking you home with me,' Chiara starts to say but stops and grabs at his clothing instead, because he is making a run for it. She hoicks him in close, crouches behind him, pins his flailing arms, shushes him. A label is sticking out from his coat collar. *Daniele Levi* she reads upside down. That will have to go. She wraps her arms around him tightly, there on the pavement, holding him still, binding him. She takes the end of the tag in her teeth and pulls at it, rips it free.

All the way home, Chiara drags the boy, kicking and shouting 'Mamma' until his voice is hoarse. If it were a battle of wills, he might have got away. His determination to run is at least as great as her determination to keep him. But it is a question of physical strength, and he does not have a chance.

By the time they get to Via dei Cappellari, he is silent.

Two packed suitcases are in the hall. Cecilia is sitting at her sewing table in the salon. She does not immediately look up. She is hemming a piece of fabric the colour of damson plums. The folds of the cloth ripple over the edge of the table, almost down to the floor, catching the glow from the watery sunlight at the window. She snips the thread with a pair of scissors, straightens up.

'Finished,' she says, and looks at them, over the top of her round-rimmed reading glasses. She stares at the exhausted, tear-stained child.

'Is this my something special?' she says to Chiara. Then, before Chiara can answer, 'Didn't they have any girls?'

TWO

There was the *before*: before Maria found the letter, or understood what it meant. That was etched in clarity, a sunshine time not appreciated then but revered in retrospect when it was forever gone. Everything with its shine and polish and sharply defined gleaming edges that reflected the light back at you. Then there was the *after*, when a fog had descended and the air was heavy with it, so Maria felt as if, just by breathing, she might be slowly drowning.

In the middle, at half past six in the evening, came the pit. To think about it was to have the sensation of falling backwards. Not to think about it – not to have it replay endlessly, not just in her head but in her being, as if she were caught in the beam of a strobe light that meted out white pain – was beyond her.

To the *before* time belonged her little sister, Nel, sitting on Maria's knee to have her hair plaited, their brother Patrick skating on yellow dusters up and down the hall, polishing the parquet to earn his pocket money. There was Tabitha, next-door's cat whom she was feeding while the neighbours were on holiday, chasing a butterfly under the lilac bush. There was a walk across the promenade to the newsagent on the other side of the lake to buy the *Telegraph* for her dad, and ice creams for herself and the kids. Flirting with the boy in the ice-cream van. There was Brian. He was a creature of the before time. Poor Brian. The whole family watching *Doctor Who*, Maria cross-legged on the floor, leaning against her dad's shins. The comfort of those legs in their brown-corduroy gardening trousers. Gone.

Maria had been waiting for Brian to phone. She was thinking that kissing him, or rather, being kissed by him – he was the first boy she had ever properly kissed – had been a teeth-clashing, spittle-infused experience. She was wondering whether snogging was necessarily like that or if it was to do with Brian's prominent teeth. There was a swollen rim inside her lower lip where his teeth had pressed into her. She ran her tongue along it repeatedly.

With exams looming, life and revision were all blurred together so that even there, sprawled on the beanbag under the stairs next to the telephone on a Saturday afternoon, she had a book propped open.

Lift me with thee to some starry sphere, she read.

She was doing Keats and the Romantic Poets for English Lit. She tried to imagine Brian lifting her with him to some starry sphere. A thought slipped in before she had time to shut it out: any version of a starry sphere that Brian could access might not be one she wanted to enter.

Patrick skated past.

'Oh, Brian,' he said, clutching his hands to his heart as he sashayed by. He was eight years old and thought himself a great wit.

'Shut up and go away,' Maria said. He shot the length of the hall to the front door, shimmied off his duster, turned and thundered up the stairs.

She had met Brian at a high school gig that she had gone to on the night of her sixteenth birthday with her friend Ed, and now Ed wasn't speaking to her. The band were sixth-form boys who played Led Zeppelin and Deep Purple covers. The lead guitarist had a trick of sliding to the front of the stage on his knees, and the singer shook his head about as if he had a blond mane like Robert Plant. The boys at that school weren't allowed to grow their hair.

Maria, wearing her new lilac loons and a striped, skinny-rib jumper, saw this boy out of the corner of her eye and kept looking at him until he glanced across. The band was playing 'Black Dog'. The boy, who had a feathery haircut like Rod Stewart's, down to his shoulders, couldn't keep away. She was like the woman in the song, dripping honey. She drew him to her, holding herself very still, her head slightly bowed, first looking at him from under her lashes and then down at the floor. He walked over and leant in close to be heard over the noise of the music. A hot tickle in her ear. He had to go back-stage, he said, because he was recording the band. She didn't catch why.

'Don't go away,' he breathed.

He disappeared through a door on the left-hand side of the stage, and Maria had stayed close by, full of promise and mystery, swaying to the music, but all the time with an eye on the door where the boy had gone. By the time he came out, her lift was waiting and she had to go. She had pressed her number, boldly, into his hand.

It had been three days before he had phoned.

'Brian,' she said to her mum when he eventually did. 'Why did he have to be called Brian? It's as bad as Trevor.'

27

'Good Irish name,' her mum said. 'Don't forget Brian Boru, the high king of Ireland.'

Maria's dad was Irish.

Lolling in the crunchy folds of the beanbag with Keats open on her lap, Maria thought about how she had liked Brian best in those three days, when she was in a kind of agony of expectation and waiting, thrilled with a yearning. When, closeted in her bedroom, she would play her mum's old jazz (she hadn't got any records of her own yet) on the portable stereophonic record player she'd had as a birthday present, and would practise kissing, using the back of her hand. This was before she had known that he thought novels were a waste of paper and that people who laughed at Monty Python were fakes, or that he was a first-year student at university, reading Chemistry, of all things.

In those three days, the squat green telephone on the shelf under the stairs had assumed a presence all its own. She had picked up the receiver often to check the ringtone was there, quickly put it back in case he had elected that very second to call, had found it engaged and given up for ever. She had offered up her equanimity and well-being to a ginger stranger in a school hall. As one might do, then, in the before time.

'Dress rehearsal,' Nel shouted down the stairs.

The kids were preparing the Fabulous Kelly Easter Rabbit Show to be performed on the landing on Easter Sunday after the treasure hunt. Maria was the compère.

The phone rang. 'Can you call me back?' Brian said. 'I'm in a phone box.'

'Someone get me a pen and a piece of paper,' Maria bellowed.

'Do you want to go to the pictures tonight?' Brian said. He wanted to see *Conquest of the Planet of the Apes* again.

Nel came hurtling down the stairs. 'Pat's doing a poo,' she said.

Nel was six. She liked to talk about bottoms, farts, poo, and had learnt to make a squelching noise with her hands. She snorted with laughter.

'Pen and paper, quick,' Maria said.

'Where from?'

'Mum's desk.'

Maria repeated the number in her head and listened to Brian tell her film times. Nel was taking an age.

'Quick, quick,' Maria shouted.

The line went dead. From the back room came a great clattering. Maria unfolded herself from the depths of the beanbag and went to investigate, muttering the number.

Nel was standing beside an upturned drawer, manila envelopes and pieces of paper protruding from beneath it. 'It wouldn't open,' she said. 'The drawer was stuck.'

'That's the one they keep locked,' Maria said. 'It's for important documents.'

'You said quick quick.'

'It must have been a bit broken already,' Maria said. 'Or Mum didn't lock it properly. Or,' she squeezed Nel's little bicep, 'you've got superhuman strength.'

Nel squealed and wriggled.

'Never mind. Let me phone Brian back and then I'll tidy it up.'

They went back to the hall and Maria dialled what she thought was the number. 'It doesn't work,' she said.

Nel was hovering helpfully near by. 'You said a seven at the end,' she said.

Maria, unconvinced, tried altering the last digit and this time it rang but no one answered.

29

'That's not right either,' she said.

She thought of Brian in the telephone box waiting for her call, hunching up his velvet jacket round his ears, turning his back to the irate queue building up outside. She imagined a battleaxe with a hairnet rapping on the glass. *Conquest of the Planet of the Apes* again, she thought. How desperately unglamorous.

'Never mind,' she said, 'I tried. He'll phone again.'

Nel ran off upstairs.

Maria slid her hand under the drawer and flipped it over, pushing the contents back into place. It was stacked with labelled manila envelopes. *Legal Docs* said the uppermost one. She flicked through. *Deeds, Certificates, Guarantees, Insurance.* She picked up the drawer, slotted it back into the desk and pushed it shut. As she turned away a piece of thin airmail paper lying on the carpet caught her eye. She picked it up and turned it over. It was a typed letter, dated just a week before, with a handwritten postscript.

```
                        Via dei Cappellari 147,
                          Int. 5, Roma, Italia


                           Signora Edna Kelly
                      41 Buttermere Avenue,
                                      Cardiff


                           17 March 1973


Dear Mrs Kelly,
   I write in reply to your letter
addressed to the occupant of the above
address. I am unable to pass on your
```

```
correspondence to Daniele Levi as you
request because I do not know his
whereabouts. He left a long time ago and
never gave a forwarding address.

                          Yours sincerely,
                 Signora Chiara Ravello
```

Who was this writing to her mother from Rome? She knew her mother had a sort of penfriend in Italy, from when she'd been an au pair there. Was it something to do with that? But her mum's correspondent was female, and this letter referred to a 'he'. She struggled to recall what her mum might have told her. Helen, the friend in Italy was called. She had married an Italian and stayed, but her mum had come home and married Maria's dad. Her childhood sweetheart.

Maria studied the postscript. The handwriting was angular and upright, written in black ink, with a fountain pen, not a biro, old-fashioned and somehow foreign. The letters were formed separately, a jerky, staccato style, as if the writer had never learnt joined-up script. Only the Rs in the middle of 'sorry' connected. They reached out to each other and then to the Y, with a curl first and then a bar across, like little bridges, holding the word together.

Sorry.

```
PS. It pains me to say. It is not known
if Daniele is alive or dead. So sorry.
```

She laid the letter back on top of the legal docs envelope and shut the drawer.

*

Pat and Nel were either side of Dad on the sofa so they could slide over the back and hide if they got scared, Maria on the floor at his feet, Mum on the armchair. The Saturday teatime *Doctor Who* ritual. A paper napkin and a side plate on each of their laps, a picnic spread out on the tablecloth in the middle of the carpet: open ham-and-mustard sandwiches and mashed-egg-and-cress ones made with crusty white bread from the bakery on Albany Road, jars of pickle, crisps doled out from a giant packet, an apple or an orange each, and a pot of tea.

Maria loved Saturday afternoon tea and had loved *Doctor Who* since it first started ten years earlier; she had been six, but Pat and Nel hadn't even been born then. Their first-ever television set was black and white. Now it was in colour. The Spiridons, spindly creatures enslaved by the Daleks, became fully visible when dead. Only then could their furry, floor-length purple cloaks be seen – cloaks the same colour, Maria observed, as her own crushed-velvet maxi coat.

'Would you rather have the power of invisibility or be able to travel through time?' she asked in the kitchen afterwards. She was washing the dishes while her mum cleared up and put things away.

'Time travel,' her mum replied straightaway.

'Where would you go?' Maria asked, swilling her hands about to froth the water.

'When would you go, that's more the question,' her mum replied. 'What era would you visit?' She stood next to Maria a moment, the bunched-up tablecloth in her hands, a faraway look on her face.

'I'd go to Rome in 1821,' Maria said, 'to Keats's house. I'd take modern treatments for tuberculosis, and then he would get better and write more poetry.'

'You'd need a nurse on board,' her mum said. '*Moi*,' she

32

added, patting her own chest and identifying herself as the nurse intended, in case Maria was in any doubt.

Maria watched her mum through the window as she shook the crumbs out in the garden. She was wearing the stripy pink-nylon overall she always wore to do the housework, buttoned up over her clothes. She returned, clipped a clothes-peg onto the crisp packet to keep the remaining crisps fresh, and went into the pantry.

'Would you go to Rome, Mum?' Maria said. 'Would you go and see Daniele Levi?'

The name had just popped into her head, but once she had said it, she wanted to say it again. She had to raise her voice because the clattering noise of jars and tins had intensified.

'Who *is* Daniele Levi, Mum?' Maria said.

The answer was silence. A sudden and localised silence in which Maria could hear the television from the front room and her brother giggling as he did when being tickled.

'Mum?' Maria said, half turning, her hands still in the warm soapy water.

The patchwork curtain that hung in front of the pantry instead of a door was still. The silence was of someone holding their breath. What came into Maria's head was that her mother was enacting a scene from *Doctor Who*, pretending to have been transported into another time dimension, and she nearly laughed. She drew her hands out of the bowl and wiped them down the front of her dungarees.

'Mum?' she said again.

Her mum burst out from behind the curtain. 'Where's your dad?' she said. 'I forgot to tell him ... I just need to ... We need ...'

Her face had assumed an expression that was like a smile but wasn't, and she offered this grimace to the part of the kitchen where Maria stood and then walked quickly out, closing the door behind her.

Maria took a step away from the sink and stopped in the middle of the kitchen, watching her parents in the hall through the frosted glass of the kitchen door. The glass distorted their outlines and smudged their movements as if they were under water. Her mum was speaking, grabbing at her dad's shirt, resting her head on his chest. He put his arms around her. He patted her back, twisting his head to look in Maria's direction.

Maria's grandad came into her mind. She remembered how, soon after he died, he kept appearing in her dreams. Not in a dynamic way, not as a protagonist, but as a silent bystander, attenuated and barely there. She'd wake up, glad to have seen him again but with the sad knowledge that, even in her dreams, she couldn't resurrect him. That to wish him alive again was to wish him the kind of posthumous life that Keats endured in those last months in Italy. There wasn't a time-travel machine and there was no going back.

She opened the kitchen door. She felt sick.

'Come into the back room, Maria,' her dad said in a quiet voice. 'We need to talk to you.'

'Go on, love,' he said to her mum, ushering her ahead of him. 'I'll get the kids to leave us alone for ten minutes.'

What had been unsaid for sixteen years and a month suddenly couldn't wait a minute longer. Her mother was bursting with it. She didn't even wait for Maria's dad to come back but simply blurted it out.

She told Maria that Daniele Levi was her father, her biological father. As she said the word 'father', Maria's dad came into the room.

Something jolted through Maria's body, as if she had a

skipping rope or a whip inside and it was being flicked. She thought she heard it crack. Her spine arched.

'No,' she said, looking at her dad.

'I'm sorry,' he said, 'we should have told you before.'

'No,' Maria said.

She was sitting on the edge of the swivel chair, the rim pressing into the back of her thighs, and she felt as if she were falling backwards, her back arching further, her legs flailing, an involuntary reverse dive from a high board.

They told her things; they held hands while they did it.

He loved her as much as Pat and Nel, he said, he always had, since he'd first set eyes on her when she was three years old. He had meant to tell her, they had meant to, always meant to, but it was never the right time, they loved her so much, she was their precious, pretty, talented girl.

'No,' Maria said, tumbling backwards and down, plummeting in free-fall.

The phone rang out in the hall, and they let it ring. Pat answered it eventually and shouted that it was Brian.

'Do you want me to go?' her mum said. 'I can tell him you're not well or something and that you'll phone him later.'

'No,' Maria said. She went into the hall.

'You didn't phone me back,' Brian said.

'No,' she said.

'Are you all right?' he said.

'No,' she said.

'What's the matter?' he said. 'Don't you want to see *Planet of the Apes*?'

'No,' she said.

'Something else then?'

'No,' she said. She replaced the receiver.

Her parents were waiting for her to return. She went up to

her bedroom, shut the door and pressed herself flat against it, the painted wood under her palms, her face buried in the folds of her dressing gown that hung from a hook. She was falling backwards and she was knocking forwards. The thud of her knocking head was muffled by the dressing gown. She wanted to be let out. Or to be let in. Out or in, anywhere but there. Where? There, inside her skin. Let me out.

The telephone rang again. There was a pain in her throat, an acid burning, and her stomach cramped. She clambered onto the bed, dragged the bedroom window open, stuck her head out and vomited onto the front path. She watched and heard it splatter. She couldn't sit down. She couldn't stand. She banged her head against the door again. There was nowhere to go.

They came and they tapped. One at a time. But she didn't speak to them and they went away again. A note was pushed under her door. She trod on it, grinding it into the carpet. Her non-biological father called up that they were taking the kids over to Gran's house and would be back in ten minutes.

'Yuck,' she heard Pat say, 'someone's been sick on the path.'

As soon as they'd gone, she pulled on her boots and jacket, rinsed out her mouth quickly under the cold tap and shot out of the house. She let herself into the next-door neighbours' with the key they'd left her. It was quiet and still in there.

She looked at the picture on the neighbours' wall, a winter tree against a swirling setting sun, gloopy lumps of oil paint, laid on thick, black and orange and red. A horrible, ugly, desolate scene. She touched the ornaments on the mantelpiece as if they might be fake, a porcelain shepherdess with her gold-tipped crook. Her coy partner kneeling, posy in hand.

She turned and ran from the house. She ran along the path beside the lake, up to the end and into the little wood there.

It was getting dark. No one walked there in the dark. She plunged off the main path into the undergrowth, crashing about between the trees, scratching her arms and legs on small branches, trampling white flowers under her feet so they sent out a strong, pungent smell. Jumping and stamping on the blooms, skidding on the mud beside the stream.

She heard a voice. 'Excuse me, miss,' it said.

And she ran away, along the lake, then up into the unlit back lanes, panting as if a wild beast were at her tail. She slipped back into the neighbours' house seconds before her parents' car pulled up.

They shouted so loudly for her that she could hear them through the walls.

THREE

Chiara reverently unwrapped her new purchase at the kitchen table. The man at the market had swathed the red glass bowl in layer upon layer of newspaper, assuring her that she had acquired a bargain. It was a piece of *murano sommerso*, an inner layer of crimson submerged in an outer clear layer. The crack in the base didn't detract from the beauty, only from the price, the man said.

She knew it was a sales pitch, but he needn't have bothered because she was going to buy it anyway. It seemed to her the colour of solace. The cat came slinking in, leapt onto the table, sniffed the bowl and purred.

'You've got your own bowl, Asmaro,' Chiara said, lifting him down. 'This one is just for me.'

The doorbell buzzed.

'Are you ready?' Simone said through the intercom. They were going to the cinema.

'Come up a minute,' Chiara said. 'I want to show you something.'

Down below in the street, Simone sighed. 'We'll be late,' she said.

It wasn't true. They had plenty of time, but Simone

wouldn't lightly undertake the stairs to Chiara's apartment. There had to be the promise of a dinner at least.

'I'll bring it down,' Chiara said.

She snatched up a piece of the newspaper to protect the bowl and was half out the door, keys in one hand and glass bowl in the other, when the telephone rang. She ought to get it because it might be the translation agency with another job. Or the publisher about collecting the page proofs of the book she had just finished working on. She dithered an instant, and the ringing stopped after only three trills. It couldn't have been important. She went on down.

Simone was peering into the window of the antique shop on the other side of the narrow street. The proprietor knelt there, arranging a standard lamp at an angle to a wing-backed armchair beside a shelf crammed with pieces of glass, costume jewellery, mosaic-covered ceramics. Clad in a green satin summer coat with a mandarin collar, her dyed chestnut hair held in place with a jewelled clasp, gem-encrusted ballet pumps on her feet, Simone would not have looked out of place in the window display. She was, as always, her own extravagant work of art. Just to see her there, in all her radiant and age-defying glamour, gave Chiara a warm feeling. To be bound up with this full-bodied, generous-spirited woman, this lover of abundance and outcasts, this relentless seeker of the bright side, was good for Chiara's soul. As it had been good for her father's too, back in the day. She wanted to hug her.

She stepped across, tapped Simone on the shoulder so she swung round, and clasped her in a one-armed embrace, the bowl held out at an angle, standing on tiptoe and burying her face in Simone's shoulder. Simone's perfume evoked roses and vanilla. Chiara was embraced in return, her hair ruffled and patted as if she were a small dog or a child.

40

'Hello, my dear,' Simone said. 'You're in a jolly mood. What's that about?'

Chiara handed over the bowl and, as she made her points, counted them off the fingers of her left hand with her right.

'One. The proofs of the book I translated have arrived and I'm really pleased with how it's turned out. Two. I'm down to five cigarettes a day. And three, this exquisite new bowl.'

Simone looked at the piece of glass.

'Actually, it's since I sent that letter,' Chiara said. 'I feel more spacious. As if I have discovered a chamber in my apartment I didn't know was there.' She drew a big square with the newspaper, as if creating the extra room in the air.

'What letter?' Simone said, without looking up. She turned the bowl over. 'It's got a crack on the bottom,' she said.

'I know it has,' Chiara said. 'The letter to the woman in England.' She tutted at herself. 'I mean Wales,' she said.

Simone raised her gaze. Her eyes swivelled from side to side as if she were reading an invisible noticeboard. 'No,' she said eventually, 'what woman?'

Chiara realised with a jolt that she hadn't told Simone yet. She had intended to, but not about the turmoil into which the letter from the woman in Cardiff had thrown her. Nor that it had awakened her ghosts from their slumber, the pair of them, Cecilia and Daniele, dropping with silent screeches from the hidden alcoves in the rooftops of her mind. Not that, no. But what she had done about it. How she had used it as an opportunity. Her measured response. She didn't need to tell Simone, in fact. This was about her, not Simone.

'Nothing,' she said. 'It was to do with a piece of work. I thought I'd told you.'

She had sat at the kitchen table and fed a piece of airmail paper into her Olivetti typewriter. With an eye for grammatical

41

accuracy, she had assembled words that were individually neutral into phrases that expressed her ignorance of Daniele's fate. When she had read it through, the tone had seemed too formal. It didn't acknowledge any of the sorrow or anguish that might accompany this uncertainty about a man and his life. She had added a handwritten note at the bottom, which included the word 'sorry'. She had resisted scrawling it a hundred times. Once was enough, if it was sincerely meant. She had refrained from even hinting at her own connection with Daniele.

There were only three overt reminders of Daniele still around the flat, and none that would be apparent to anyone else.

His leather jacket hung underneath a slew of other outdoor garments on the coat rail in the entrance hall next to the hatstand. It was like the jacket Marlon Brando wore in *The Wild Ones*.

The trivet he had made in metalwork stood on the work surface in the kitchen. She used it every day for the hot coffee pot.

The photograph of him was concealed behind one of her grandparents and stood on her bedside table. The design of the frame, an old-fashioned gilt thing from the flea market, allowed the pictures to slide in and out from the side and did not require the removal of the backing. She had only to turn the frame on its side and tap, and the hidden picture of Daniele would pop out. She liked to think of Daniele tucked in with Nonna.

She had gathered them up, these three things, wrapped them in brown paper and deposited the parcel out of the way in the junk room.

Chiara had taken the letter from the unknown woman in Wales, about whom she had deliberately and effortfully refrained from speculating, as an invitation to bid Daniele goodbye. The posting of those words, the physical letting go of them and their consignment to the wider world, had allowed her to feel that a knot that had been lodged behind her breastbone was starting to unravel. Daniele was gone. She had not seen him for a decade. She might never know what had become of him, but it was over. She had purposely shut a door that had remained propped open for too long.

'How much did you pay for this?' Simone said.

'Five thousand lira.'

'Shall we ask him what he makes of your find?' Simone said, with a nod at the antique-shop man.

'No,' Chiara said. 'Let's not.' She reached out to take back the bowl.

'Hang on,' Simone said. 'Let me have a proper look.'

While Simone examined the piece, turning it round in her hands and holding it up so it caught the light, Chiara read the crumpled newspaper page in which she had wrapped it. The right-wing bomber who had accidentally blown himself up on the Turin train was out of danger and had been transferred from hospital to prison.

'Whoever is with us awaits the moment to leap from the trench and into the fray, to strike, strike, strike,' was the slogan of his organisation, New Order. It might sound stupid, but it didn't stop them being dangerous.

She couldn't keep track of all the neo-fascist groups. It made her feel scared and hopeless about what was going on in society, but it didn't dampen this inner feeling of space and possibility. She might take up tango, she thought, tucking the paper under her arm and arching one shoulder in what she felt might be a tango pose.

'Do you know what this reminds me of?' Simone said. 'It's

the red lamp they keep lit in church to show God is present or the Eucharist is blessed or whatever it is.'

Chiara looked again at her new acquisition. Simone was holding it balanced on the palms of both hands, like a votive offering.

'Your mother's daughter, despite everything,' Simone said. 'Catholic to the core.'

'I am not,' Chiara said, offended. 'Actually, it's more like the light in a brothel. It's you who's seeing the sacred in the profane. Not me.'

Simone smiled. 'It's very lovely,' she said. 'I'll wait for you down here. No rush. I'm going to have a nose in the shop here. We're meeting Silvia and Nando in fifteen minutes.'

'Oh, are we?' Chiara said.

She had forgotten they were coming too. She carried the bowl back upstairs. She went slowly so as not to drop it and held the rail with the other hand because the stairs were steep and the stairwell dark. Her new-found spaciousness made her want to take deeper breaths, to fill her chest cavity with fresh air, which was how she had discovered that her lung capacity was reduced.

'Compromised,' old Doctor Bruni had said and then cackled raspingly as if he had made a great joke. He had a cigarette hanging out of the corner of his mouth at the time. He didn't seem to think her condition was anything to worry about but, still, she was trying to cut down on the fags. A wheeze that pooled at the bottom of her lungs wouldn't shift, and she wanted to be able to trot up the stairs again.

She placed the bowl on the shelf in the entrance hall. Now that it had been pointed out, she saw it was indeed the same colour as a sanctuary light. Religious red. But that wasn't why she liked it so much. It was reminiscent of something else. She groped about for what, and then it came to her. It was the lamp that used to hang in her bedroom when she was little. In their bedroom, hers and Cecilia's, in the San Lorenzo apartment.

The phone rang again. Even though Simone was waiting down in the street, Chiara decided to answer it this time. She was thinking about the red lamp in a sconce on the wall, and the way their mother would light the candle in it with a taper before they said their prayers. When she was very young she used to think it was a magic wand, that taper.

Distracted, she couldn't understand what the person on the other end was saying. A female voice, speaking in a whisper. 'Pardon?' she said.

'Do you speak English?' the woman said, in English. She had a young voice, very soft.

'Yes,' Chiara said, thinking it must be an offer of some work.

She didn't normally take on interpreting jobs because her spoken English wasn't nearly as fluent as her written, but she had just finished a book translation and there wasn't anything else on the horizon. At the other end she could hear the person breathing.

'I do indeed speak English,' Chiara added to encourage her and to demonstrate that she was up to whatever task. The doorbell buzzed.

'Are you Signora Chiara Ravello?' the woman said. She pronounced Chiara as if the 'ch' were soft, like 'church' in English.

'Chiara Ravello, yes,' she said with the correct pronunciation.

'I'm calling to ask ...' The quiet voice was almost obliterated by the sound of the doorbell again. Simone must be holding her finger on the buzzer.

45

'Wait one moment, please,' Chiara said. 'One little moment. I will return.' She put the receiver on the hall table and hurried to the salon window. 'Telephone call,' she shouted down.

Simone tipped her head back to look up and mercifully released her finger. She cupped her hand to her ear.

'I'm on the telephone,' Chiara shouted again, holding an imaginary phone to her face.

Simone flashed up the fingers of both hands.

'Yes, I'll see you in ten minutes in the piazza,' Chiara called.

Simone signalled her agreement and sailed off towards the square in her unhurried and stately fashion. Two young people on bicycles rattled past speaking loudly. 'It's anarchy,' one of them said. They passed either side of Simone, talking over the top of her head, skimming her sides so that she wobbled a moment like a big old hull buffeted by the wake of speedier craft. There was barely room for three abreast in the narrow street.

Chiara returned to the telephone and picked it up, putting the receiver to her ear. 'Hello,' she said. 'I can hear you now.'

The line was dead.

She decided, as she moulded her hair into place and applied some lipstick, that what she would say to Simone was, 'You will be pleased to know that I have finally closed a door on the past. I am no longer waiting for Daniele to reappear or mooning over my lost boy. I am entering a new phase. So, let's talk about him, not in a maudlin way, but about the good times.'

Or words to that effect.

But, instead of the good times, what came to mind was an image of Simone's grim face as she eyed Daniele. And he, fourteen and newly lanky, lying on his bed with that skullcap perched on the back of his head and a sort of sneer on his face.

'What's got into you?' Simone had said.

'Ask *her*,' he had replied, glancing at Chiara, crowding in behind.

The skullcap had an edging of red and purple embroidery that might well have been hand-stitched. The first time Chiara saw him wearing it, she thought that it must have come out of the treasure chest, the great oak sideboard in what they still called the chickens' room. But it was odd, a skullcap. It jarred. Then, when she commented that it looked like one of those caps the Jewish men wore for prayer, he told her he had got it from the synagogue, and she had felt the first flutter of fear.

'They have these hats in a basket by the entrance, for men who have forgotten their own. *Kippeh*,' he said, reaching up and taking it off his head. 'It's called a *kippeh*.'

'I didn't know you had been to the synagogue,' she said carefully.

'You do now.' He twirled the hat round on the end of his finger.

She thought, He knows. How does he know? Don't be silly. He couldn't know.

The file containing all the scant documents she had relating to his family was hidden between the mattress and the springs of her bed.

'I've been exploring my Jewishness,' he said.

She nodded dumbly, afraid to speak.

'How come we never go to the ghetto?' he said.

'Why would we?' she managed to say, as lightly as she could.

She went to check that the file hadn't been moved. Until she heard his voice at the door, she hadn't realised he was behind her.

'What have you got there?' he said.

There was nothing she could do. She had always intended to tell him, sooner or later, when the time was right. That was why she had kept the file. She wouldn't have chosen this moment, but it seemed the moment had chosen her. She had thought he had some notion already, and she owed it to him or what was it, she couldn't really remember now her reasoning and justification, but anyway, the time had come. Perhaps she just wanted to unburden herself of a secret.

He sat beside her on the bed and he seemed all right. He said he was. The relief was immense.

Then he went out to the shop for her, to buy some pasta, and he didn't come back for two days.

He had been lying there in darkness until they had blundered in and switched on the light, she and Simone, not knowing he was there, that he must have come home while they were out searching.

'Where have you been?' Simone had said. 'Why didn't you at least telephone? We've been out of our minds with worry.'

He shrugged, then made a dismissive noise, indicating that he wasn't going to tell them where he had been; that it was no business of theirs.

'You're an ungrateful little shit, sometimes, you really are,' Simone said to him.

'Yes, that's me. Ungrateful piece of shit,' he had replied and he had raised an eyebrow at them both as if he didn't care at all.

And Chiara had never explained to Simone, either at the time or afterwards, what it was that had sparked his disappearance. She had let Simone think whatever she thought, that he was just wayward.

She should have destroyed the file and kept her mouth shut.

She shook her head. She searched for some happier Simone–Daniele moments and an array presented themselves: the nuns, the chicken on the balcony, the gladiator shield, the jigsaw, that day in the park. They were all from early on. She remembered the very first time they had met, Simone and Daniele. There, on a street in Trastevere in 1944, waiting in a line outside the horse-butcher's. She and Daniele back in Rome from the hills, two little scavengers in a city of scavengers. They had eaten risotto bianco together, and a slow-cooked horsemeat stew.

The memory of that day, of Daniele sitting on Simone's lap and the way she had murmured something in his ear, reminded Chiara anew of Simone's capacity for acceptance. Daniele could be difficult, errant, absent, but Simone did not take it personally. When he had first discovered drugs and Chiara had panicked, Simone had turned up with a present for him, a battered second-hand trumpet.

'Perhaps this will keep you out of trouble,' she had said.

His first public performance was at a Christmas concert in the pontifical college. Chiara was nervous. She didn't think he was ready. It was mostly a carol concert, but a short jazz section had been inserted in the middle. Daniele's solo came at the end of this. He stepped forward. He was fifteen and by then he was wearing his hair slicked back. He kept his eyes down, raised the trumpet to his lips and blew. The noise it emitted was raucous, cacophonous, all the notes jangling. He played with a wild abandon, bending his knees and puffing out his cheeks. Chiara felt her face freeze into a mask of humiliation. Was he deliberately playing the wrong notes? Sabotaging the performance? When he finished, there was a silence in the hall.

Then Simone leapt up, clapping and shouting 'Bravo' and stamping her feet.

Chiara, after a second's delay, followed her lead and as the two of them clapped and whistled, a smattering of other people, perhaps thinking that they must have witnessed something avant-garde and not wanting to seem philistines, joined in. Up on the stage, Daniele looked at the audience for the first time and gave a little bow. His face was flushed and his dark eyes shone.

'You liked my improvisation then?' he said afterwards.

'Breathtaking,' Simone said. 'Keep shaking us out of our complacency.'

The phone rang again.

'Signora Ravello?' It was the same person as before. 'I'm sorry to bother you,' she said in her papery voice. 'I think you knew Daniele Levi.'

Chiara's head thumped. She turned so her back was against the wall for support.

Knew. Past tense. Was he dead then? He must have gone to an English-speaking country, and now he was dead. Of course he was dead. What use pretending that she hadn't suspected as much? No matter the damage done, he would have contacted her if he were alive. Ten years and never a word. Was it an overdose? Or had he had an accident? But he was dead and this was . . .

Who was this? This was the British police or some other official who had traced her. How? Because on his identity card or another document, she was listed as his next of kin. Of course.

No, that couldn't be it. Because on his identity card, his name was Daniele Ravello but this person had said Levi. Daniele Levi.

Her heart trembled.

'Yes,' she said, cautiously.

There was a great release of breath at the other end of the line. 'Oh,' the woman said.

Let him not be dead, let him not be dead, please let him not be dead, Chiara thought, and the refrain was as familiar to her as a lullaby. Let him have had a different life elsewhere.

'Sorry,' the woman said and blew her nose. 'I am trying to find out about him and I wondered if you could help.'

'Why?' Chiara said. It sounded brusque. And it wasn't the right question. But the woman's words weren't what she was expecting. Chiara wanted answers, not questions.

'Because, I have just recently discovered, just been told . . . ' The voice faded away again.

'Pardon? Can you speak more loudly?' Chiara said. She too sounded tremulous.

'Sorry, sorry,' the woman said. 'I didn't think I'd get through and I haven't thought properly about what to say.'

'Daniele Levi,' Chiara said, to help the woman focus.

She hadn't spoken that name out loud to another for a very long time. She suddenly grasped that this must be the woman in Cardiff. It gave her a shock. She hadn't allowed for there being consequences. When she had mailed her letter, it had been a private act, a kind of ritual, reminiscent of when she and Daniele used to climb up the Janiculum hill to their special place where they posted notes to his mother. Like the prayer of an unbeliever and like those long ago notes, the letter had not been sent with the expectation of a response.

'He was your lodger, I think?'

Chiara bridled at this description of the relationship, but her old instinct around Daniele – to dissemble, withhold, not give anything away – was strong.

'Yes,' she said. 'He lived here a while. A long time ago.'

'He was my father,' the woman said, 'apparently.'

Chiara put her hand to her chest. She was glad of the closed, solid door of the junk room at her back. Through the wall hanging that covered it, the doorknob was pressing into her spine.

'Signora Ravello. Are you there?' the woman said.

'What did you say?' Chiara asked.

She said it again.

The other person wasn't a woman with a young voice, but a girl, Chiara realised. As she struggled to grasp what she was being told, she allowed herself to slide down the wall so that she was sitting on the floor. The place at the end of the hall-way, where the lights danced when the afternoon sun shone and where she had thought she might display her red bowl, was dark.

It was impossible, what the girl was saying. It didn't make sense. Daniele couldn't have fathered a child in Wales.

And then she thought, with an implacable clarity, even if he had, what was it to her? Hadn't she done with all that? Hadn't she closed that door?

'I'm sorry,' she said. 'It must be a mistake.'

'Do you mean that you don't think it's true?'

An image of the briefcase she used to take to work came into her mind. Calfskin. The click of the catch shutting.

'I don't see how it could be,' she said, making her voice dis-missive and cold.

'But why would my mother lie?' the girl asked and started to cry.

Chiara had no answer to that. She listened to the unknown foreign child weeping. After a while she said, 'I'm afraid I can't help.'

'Sorry to have bothered you,' the girl said snuffily through her tears, and hung up.

Chiara stayed put. Asmaro emerged from the deep shadows at the end of the hallway and stepped delicately into the circle of her lap. Chiara stroked him absent-mindedly, staring at the photograph hanging on the wall opposite, of her mother and father on their wedding day, until her eyes glazed over.

A conversation with Daniele came into her mind. They had gone out on the hunt for supplies. Some soldiers had come past, and she had tugged him into the antiquarian bookshop in the street behind San Filippino, out of their path. They had gone right to the back of the long, narrow store where there was a fusty smell of old magazines. She had picked up a book of photographs of Rome taken in the first three and a half decades of the century and flicked through it, showing him pictures and naming the buildings. At one point he had put out his hand to stop her turning over the page and mumbled something.

'Pardon?' she said, but he hadn't repeated whatever he had said. He had only just started to speak again after three months of silence, but his words were still sparse.

She thought he had said, 'Mamma.'

The photograph was of an imposing statue of a woman on horseback. Chiara read the caption out loud, discovering that it was a monument to Anita Garibaldi, the wife of Italy's national hero, and that it had been erected on the Janiculum hill in 1932.

'Have you been there?' she said.

He nodded.

'Shall we go one day?' she said. 'You and me?'

But he had just blinked at her and she saw he had retreated into himself. Quickly, she had turned the page to distract him.

There was a photograph of the synagogue just after it had been completed in 1904 with great empty spaces around it where now there were buildings.

'Do you know where that is?' she had said.

He remained silent. She thought he hadn't recognised it as the place where he had grown up and lived all his life until very recently, but then he ran his finger across the picture, over the empty spaces.

'All the people have gone away,' he had said. 'Except for me.'

'No, no,' she had said and started to explain that this was a picture of how it had used to be, not a vision of now or the future.

He had turned to her, not meeting her eye, because he never did at that time, but talking to her solar plexus instead. 'Are there more people dead than alive?' he had asked, his tone conversational.

It wasn't something she had ever thought about. She did a sort of sum, or pretended to, adding in defunct civilisations, the Assyrians and the Etruscans, trying to make a joke of it and faltering when she realised she was referring to genocide and then rallying when she remembered he was only seven and wouldn't know. All the time she was conscious of the boots outside on the street.

'Yes, I should think there might be,' she said eventually. 'Because if you add together all the people who ever lived before now and who have died, there are probably more of them than there are of us who are still alive. But that won't always be true, even if it is now.'

He was just waiting for her to get to the answer and didn't care about her spurious calculations.

'So dead's the thing,' he said. There was nothing in his tone to warn her.

'What do you mean?'

He lifted his eyes momentarily to her face and then dropped them again. 'Dead is the way we are, and living is just for a bit. For now.'

54

'I suppose that's one way of looking at it,' she said cautiously. 'God might see it like that.'

'Can I go back soon?'

'Back where?'

'Back to dead again,' he said.

'Not bad news?' Simone said as they walked towards the Farnese cinema.

Something buzzed in Chiara's head as if Simone were pressing the bell again.

'Sort of,' she said. 'I thought it might be an offer of work, but unfortunately not.' She turned to Silvia. 'Anything going at the university?'

Silvia worked in the Economics and Commerce faculty at Sapienza.

'Don't you prefer literary translations?' Silvia said.

'I can turn my hand to most things, as long as it's not too scientific and as long as I grasp the concept. Last month I translated a pamphlet for Motorola on the hand–held portable telephone they've developed.'

'The what?' Nando scoffed, as if she were making it up.

Nando had done something important at the UN but was now retired. He didn't usually join them.

The conversation felt stilted. Chiara couldn't tell whether that was her fault, bringing a suppressed tension to the group, or because of Nando being there. His presence denied Silvia her usual ten minutes of complaining about him.

'I'll ask,' Silvia said. 'If I can even get in the building. The bloody students are occupying it again.'

A rich smell of ripe cheese and salami emanated from Ruggeri's as they passed the corner. The shop was just closing for the day.

'Are we eating afterwards?' Chiara said. She was ravenous.

'I don't think we'll hang around. We'll just have time for a quick drink and then be on our way,' Nando said.

Silvia smiled apologetically and shook her head as if to say, 'Men, what can you do with them?'

She was trying to exchange meaningful little glances with Chiara or Simone, an invitation to collude against Nando's imagined wrongdoings. Chiara didn't want to join in. If you're with him, be with him, she thought.

That's how she would have been with Carlo, if he hadn't gone and got himself killed. Even now, after all these years of living without him, she remembered the feel of his hand holding hers when they used to walk in the park at Villa Celimontana. There was a thrill in it, absent when she held her father's hand, but still, with both, the knowledge of being that other person's special girl.

Who will hold my hand now? she used to think, after they died in quick succession, and, How will I walk alone?

Unannounced, as she crossed Campo dei Fiori with her friends, all Chiara's dead came crowding in. She turned away from the others as if she were looking in a shop window. She saw Cecilia, face-down in a puddle on a hillside. There was a pain in Chiara's breastbone and she pressed her fingertips there to try to release the pressure.

Simone appeared at her side. 'You and I shall go for a bite, shall we?' she said, tucking Chiara's arm into hers. 'Just the two of us.'

They walked on behind Nando and Silvia. Leftovers from the morning market, discarded outer leaves of cabbages and lettuces, were strewn outside the shops like a rim of washed-up seaweed. A small boy, contorted at the drinking fountain, was spraying water over the feet of passers-by.

The film had a far-fetched plot involving extremists kidnapping the president. If it weren't for the laughter of the others, Chiara would not have known it was meant to be funny.

The question the girl had posed sprang repeatedly into her mind, despite her efforts to quash it. Why would the girl's mother lie? And then, she would think again, she didn't care whether it was true or not. She wouldn't be made to care. She tried to concentrate on the screen, but a hat one of the characters wore reminded her of Daniele's skullcap and there he was again, lying on his bed with that look on his face that Simone took for insolence. His voice was breaking and when he laughed he sounded like a donkey.

'I haven't been to the bloody synagogue,' he said. 'I found it in that cupboard where you keep stuff. Why would I go to the synagogue?'

She never found out where he had been that time, but it was the beginning of a spate of absences. He was forever running away and disappearing for days at a time. Later on, after he had gone for good, she discovered that he probably went to Nonna's abandoned farm, but that didn't occur to her back then, when he was only a teenager.

After the film, they went to the bar on the corner of Piazza Farnese, which took them past Chiara's usual haunt, Gianni's bar. The others were discussing why so many new films, even the comedies, *especially* the comedies, Nando said, harked back to the war and the years leading up to it. Chiara lagged behind. A kind of dread had come over her. They sat down at an outside table, but she remained standing.

'What do you think? Nando said, looking up at her. She hadn't caught the thread of the conversation, but a moment earlier he had said, 'We haven't got it out of our system.'

'I think you're probably right,' she said.

In the anonymous dark of the cinema, she had thought perhaps she would mention the telephone call, air it and see what her friends thought, but the idea now made her squirm. This wasn't the stuff of anecdotes. She had to leave.

'I'm sorry,' she said. 'I'd forgotten that my author was going to telephone tonight. I must go.'

'Oh, what a shame,' Nando said.

Simone was looking at her quizzically. She was going to mention dinner.

'Right now,' Chiara said with undue vehemence.

'If those Motorola telephones catch on,' Nando added, 'you won't have to go home to pick up a call.' He laughed, and Silvia belatedly joined in.

'Her secret lover,' she heard Simone confiding in a stage whisper to the others as she walked away, but for once Simone's fabrication didn't make her smile.

Simone was probably offended, but that couldn't be helped. Chiara thought she would buy herself pizza on the way back. She made a detour to a place where they sold it by the slice, but there was a short queue, and she couldn't stand still long enough.

When she got home she poured herself a medicinal glass of Fernet Branca and fetched a packet of cigarettes. She wished she still had the letter from the girl's mother. It would have provided the address and, perhaps, telephone number but she distinctly remembered putting it in the bin after she had typed her reply. She stood at the kitchen window, blowing smoke at the pale vests and bloomers hanging in the gloom on the neighbours' line. They often left their washing out overnight. They either didn't know or didn't care about the ghosts who would enter such abandoned clothes in the witching hour and

58

haunt their wearers by day. Or so Chiara's mother had always warned.

She sipped the syrupy liquid. The idea of a shape-changing ghost sliding between sleeve and flesh, snaking under her armpit, curling around her ribcage, tightening its grip, made her skin prickle.

The parcel she had put in the junk room jumped into her mind. Perhaps it was only the envelope she had thrown away and she had put the letter among his things. There was no bulb in the light fitting. She hooked the hanging that concealed the door over its pole and groped about in the half-light from the hall. She took the parcel back into the kitchen with her and spread the contents out on the table. The letter wasn't in the package. She had known it wasn't.

She buried her face in his leather jacket. The lining used to hold his scent, but she must have sniffed it all out long ago. She left the trivet there on the table and carried the jacket to the lobby where she hung it up, draping her own coats and jackets over the top. She took the photo to her bedroom and slid it back into position behind the one of her grandparents. The frame was starting to come loose. She pushed it back together, pressing her thumbs on the little pins that held the backing in place. She returned to the kitchen, folded up the brown paper and put it away. That was brief, she thought, that period of relative equanimity.

She sat at the table and tried to picture the letter from Cardiff. What came to mind, though, was the first of the letters that Daniele wrote to his mother. He had made five copies and they posted four of them in secret places around the ghetto. The fifth, the one Chiara had retrieved, he left at the Anita Garibaldi monument. She knew it off by heart.

Dear Mamma,
   The lady gave me a chicken. His name is Cluck.

She had them still, all those letters. She used to pore over them, thinking they would provide a clue. They were in a box somewhere, but she couldn't think where. Probably at the back of the junk room.

The phone rang, and Chiara leapt. It was only Simone.

'Are you all right, my dear?' she said.

Chiara assured her that she was.

'Something will turn up,' Simone said.

Chiara didn't know what she meant. 'What?' she said.

'And if it doesn't, you can always sell off another bit of your flat.' After a moment in which neither of them spoke, Simone added, 'That was meant to be a joke.'

Chiara realised that Simone really thought she was worried about money and work. Better that way, she thought. She tried to join in.

'Or I could take a lodger.' She winced.

'You haven't really got room for a lodger, have you? You'll have to find yourself a rich paramour instead.'

Chiara chuckled obligingly.

'I told Silvia and Nando you'd got a secret lover,' Simone said. 'And they believed me.'

An image of Daniele walking hand in hand with a blonde girl along a walled lane flashed into Chiara's mind. The girl swooned into him as they walked, and she knew they were lovers. She wondered whether she had seen them together one time from a bus.

'You haven't, have you?' Simone said.

'Haven't what?'

'Taken a lover.'

60

'You've found me out,' Chiara said, then lowered her voice. 'I'd better go now. He's waiting.'

She thought of Carlo again, the jut of his jaw, his high serious brow. Forever young. If he had lived, he would have been sixty-five years old by now. He might have had white nostril hair, dentures and a wrinkly bottom. They might still have loved each other dearly. She pushed the thought of him away.

She imagined this new lover in the bedroom. She made him younger. He might be in his mid-fifties perhaps – not too dauntingly young. She gave him a thick head of greying hair and a solid, warm body. She climbed into bed without switching on the light so that she couldn't see that he wasn't there, but it made no difference to the crushing absence.

After a while, she got up once more and padded down the hallway to the entrance hall without putting on the light. She located her new glass bowl on the shelf and carried it into the kitchen. She poured herself a glass of water, sat down again at the table and lit a cigarette, one of tomorrow's quota but needs must. The bowl would make a handsome ashtray.

She had had the kitchen modernised in the early sixties when the apartment had been divided in two. A refrigerator had replaced the zinc icebox, and an electric water-heater had been put in instead of the old charcoal burner. But the layout was unchanged, and the table was the same as in 1943. She pictured Daniele there, standing on the other side. Not Daniele the teenager who had been so much in her thoughts since the girl phoned, nor Daniele as he might be now, a man of nearly forty, but the little Daniele whom she had picked up that day and brought home.

FOUR

Chiara is making an early lunch to sustain them on their journey into the hills, to Nonna's house. She has thrown some pasta into a pan of boiling water and is examining the available ingredients – the end of a cooked ham, a couple of onions – working out what she can concoct. Cooking always provides respite, whatever else is going on. She can descend into the calm of food preparation and provision. It is the one thing that she owns to inheriting from her mother. She is looking at the pink pieces of ham. He doesn't eat meat from a pig, she thinks. But then, he has to eat. She glances at the windowsill where she grows herbs in pots. It is October, though, and the pickings are thin. The sage has wilted and is dry to the touch. All the juice is squeezed out of everything these days. They live in desiccated times. She feels the soil. It is like dust.

The child is staring at Cecilia who is circling the table, round and round in her stockinged feet, asking him questions, talking in a babyish voice as if they are both little kids getting to know each other in the playground.

'What's your name? My name's Cecilia,' Cecilia asks the boy as she swishes past and he watches her, goggle-eyed. 'Ce-ci-li-a,' she says again, stretching the syllables, opening out her arms and greeting an imaginary audience.

Chiara can detect the imprint of her own fingers, red and mottled, on Cecilia's cheek. She had to stop the screaming, she tells herself, but she can still feel the shockwaves from the blow. A stinging in her palm, a burning heat in her own cheeks as if she too has been struck.

'I don't want it. Take it back,' Cecilia had screamed on being told that the child was to stay with them and, before Chiara had known it, she had found herself on the other side of the room, her hand had flicked out and she had slapped her sister's pale cheek so hard that Cecilia's head had swung sideways and a loose hairpin, flying out, had pinged against the wall.

'Not an it. A he. A little boy,' Chiara had said.

Swivelling away, her fists bunching as if spoiling for more, she had hurried from the room, gathering up the child cowering in the doorway, pulling the door to behind them to dampen the gasping sounds Cecilia was now making, bustling the boy along with her here to the kitchen, as if by her haste in fetching him away from the scene, she could lessen its impact. She had pulled out a chair for him, told him to take off his coat and sit, but he remained standing, his arms at his sides, his fists curled as tightly as her own had been a moment earlier.

As she stepped away from him, fetched cutlery from the drawer, filled the pan with water, there stirred within her the near certainty that this child had witnessed and experienced more violence in this last two hours than ever in his life before. Despite the privations, despite the laws that had made him and his family into second-class citizens, he came from a home where kindness and respect prevailed, and hands were not raised in anger.

'I'm sorry,' she said when Cecilia came in a few minutes later. 'I'm sorry that I smacked you.'

But Cecilia, who had pulled out the remaining hairpins so that her hair hung loose and wild, took no notice and embarked on her ungainly sliding waltz instead.

There is a lightness to the onion in Chiara's hand that tells her it will be mushy inside. The magnitude of what she has done washes over her again, and she stands there, at a loss. The face of the boy's mother comes into her mind. She clutches for the name that was on the tag that she tore out with her teeth.

'Signora Levi,' she pronounces and nods at the boy who looks up at her with luminous eyes, 'your mother, Signora Levi, asked me to look after you while she is away. She said you were a good boy.'

Cecilia flows about the kitchen, opening out her arms and closing them as if she is swimming. Chiara keeps her focus on the boy as Cecilia brushes past.

'Take off your coat and sit at the table now, like a good boy,' she says.

And he does.

'Now,' she says, encouraged, 'we will pretend that your name is not Levi any more, because the bad soldiers are look-ing for all the people called Levi.'

She stares at him, wondering how much he understands. He stares back.

'Just for now, your name,' she casts about, 'is Gaspari.'

It was her fiancé Carlo's surname. As she articulates Carlo's name, she pictures him leaning out of the window of the bus that took him away into internal exile for anti-fascist activities. She sees him again, kissing his hand and blowing the kiss to her, and she has the fleeting sensation of that kiss finally reach-ing its destination.

'Oh,' she says and runs her onion-tasting fingers over her lips, trying to catch and hold the feeling.

'I'll be back before you have time to miss me,' he had said.

But he had been wrong. If they had married before he left instead of just getting engaged, if she had been with child, then their son would have been more or less the age of this little boy, who now turns from her and resumes his examination of Cecilia.

Usually, it gets on Chiara's nerves when Cecilia behaves in this baby-girl fashion, but now she's grateful, because it seems that Cecilia is making an effort, reaching out to the child. Perhaps, unlikely though it seems, Chiara was right to slap her. Perhaps she should have done it years ago.

She lowers her gaze to the chopping board, picks up her knife and slices sharply through the first onion. Inside, as she expected, it is soft and half rotten. Cecilia undulates by, holding a hand now to her scorched cheek, chanting her own name to the tune Chiara invented twenty years ago or more.

'Cecilia Teresa Ravello, tra-la-la-la-la,' she sings as if mocking, but her sister lacks that kind of guile.

Chiara chops the onions carefully, cutting out the soft brownish-green parts and throwing them away but not wasting even the tiniest sliver of what is usable. There is no oil. There will be oil up in the hills, she thinks, but stops her mind from floating off there. There is the journey to manage first. She throws the onion pieces in with the pasta, just for the last minute, to soften them. She drains the pasta and tosses it with the pieces of ham. She snaps off some sage leaves, crumbles them in to add flavour. There are plenty of dried chillies left, but do children eat chillies? She doesn't know. She won't risk it.

The boy is mesmerised by Cecilia. 'Daniele,' he whispers.

'How old are you?' she says.

'Nearly eight,' he says.

'One, two, three, four, five, six, seven. That is seven,' she says.

'Seven,' he repeats.

'Have you got any brothers or sisters?' Cecilia says.

She pauses beside Chiara, leans in and sniffs the cooking pot. Her thick, black hair hangs down, masking her face. Chiara can smell her sister's hair, perfumed and dark.

'Two little sisters,' the boy says. His voice is louder this time. 'Another one coming soon,' he adds as Cecilia curls away and swishes round the room again.

And it seems that perhaps, after all, it will work like this. That Cecilia and the boy, both mistreated and manhandled by Chiara, will become allies.

And Chiara, what will her role be? Of course, she will be the wicked stepmother, half-provider, half-tyrant, and they, her two misfit children, will gang up and comfort each other, whisper secrets and turn their stony faces towards her when addressed. And she will have to bear it and find her comfort elsewhere if she can. Or do without.

Cecilia pauses and takes hold of the chair-back opposite the boy. She does a clumsy plié and then lifts one foot, pointing it out to the side. She used to be a good dancer when she was little, before the fits.

'My mamma is dead,' she says sweetly. 'Dead, dead, dead.' She leans towards the boy, her face an inch from his, and says, 'What about yours?'

Chiara's heart seems to stop for a second. She stands holding the two-handled pot in front of her, the steam rising and with it the pungent scent of the sage, so that she is wreathed in a herb-infused mist. Through this she observes the other two.

67

The boy's mouth opens but no sound emerges. Chiara doesn't know what understanding shivers through him in that moment, but she sees it enter his jaw and stiffen it, clamping his teeth together. The silence inflates, occupies the corners of the room and travels up to the ceiling.

Then Cecilia punctures it. She starts to hum a tune. It's that song from the musical she likes, about the path through the wood.

They leave Rome the following day. On the first train Cecilia dozes and the boy stares out of the window with watchful, uncomprehending eyes. Chiara has given him his own bag to carry, her cloth one. The strap is too long for him and the bag, stuffed with an old blanket and a picture book dated 1921, hangs down almost to his knees when he walks. It lies on his lap now and on top of it is a hat with earmuffs that she found in a chest of drawers in her grandparents' room. An ancient hat that might have belonged to her own father when he was a child. She planted it on his head.

'To keep your ears warm,' she said. He snatched it off.

Cecilia too holds her hat on her lap, a felt hat with a brim that matches the grey tailored suit with navy piping that she is wearing and that she herself made.

Chiara looks at the face of her sleeping sister, so innocent and unblemished. The mark on Cecilia's cheek where Chiara slapped her is still faintly visible. It puts her in mind of the time Cecilia had a fit of such violence that it knocked a picture from the wall that struck Chiara as it fell. It was the picture of the Sacred Heart of Jesus that used to hang over their bed when they were children and lived with their mother and father in the apartment in San Lorenzo.

In the picture, Jesus wore a white robe with a red cloak

slung over one shoulder. His right hand, the wound from the nail clear to see, was held up in blessing; his left hand pulled back the folds of his cloak to reveal his radiant heart, surrounded by a crown of thorns, like a thicket, or a cage of barbed wire. Above his sacred heart was a golden cross, the same colour as the border of his white robe as well as that of the emanations, like rays of the sun, from the white glow of his halo. His brown and wavy hair came down to his shoulders. His brow was smooth and untroubled, and his cheeks were pink like a girl's or a very young man's, but he had a beard and a moustache. He wasn't in an actual physical place, merely floated in goldenness and light.

One night, a sharp blow to the face woke Chiara to tumult and chaos as if she were in the middle of an earthquake. She remembers screaming and people coming running. Their maid, Anna Lisa and Nonna, who must have been staying, and another figure she can't identify although she remembers grey hair – one of the great-aunts on the maternal side, was it, one of those old ladies that got left behind when the family emigrated. And these women were all making shushing noises, but doing nothing to rescue Chiara, marooned on the jangling island of their bed.

Then their father was there, the pipe smell of him, his voice cutting through the clamour, calling for calm, calm, for the love of God, leaning over the frothing, fitting creature that had taken Cecilia's place and plucking Chiara up to tuck her, still shrieking, against his shoulder.

Beyond him stood their mother who must surely have been the first to speed along the passage but who had frozen there on the threshold while the others had pushed past her into the room. Her long black hair in the lamplight, her white nightie bunched in one hand, her mouth open in a scream that echoed

69

and amplified Chiara's own, she slumped in the doorway like a stupid, useless girl and not like someone's mother at all.

And then Chiara was put in her *nonna*'s arms, while their father tended to Cecilia.

There was blood on the sheets, and her mother thought it was the blood of Jesus, his sacred heart bleeding.

'Antonella, look, look at Chiara's face,' Babbo said, 'the frame must have hit her as it fell. It has cut her cheek.'

But it made no difference. For their mother, Chiara's face might be bleeding, but Jesus had bled too.

'He turned His face away,' their mother whispered. 'It's the devil in her that hurts Him so.'

Chiara heard them in the kitchen while Anna Lisa was dressing her wound. Her *babbo* forbade Mamma from taking Cecilia to the priest, from having this thing done, whatever it was.

'I won't have it,' he said. 'Superstitious nonsense,' he said. 'The child has enough torment without that. Give the medicine a chance to work.'

Their father was going away on business. Anna Lisa had laid all his clean, pressed shirts on the bed, and he was choosing which ones to take. Chiara was helping. She was rolling his ties, furling them like snails, the dark-green one with the red diamonds, the grey one that she preferred.

'Remember, Cecilia must have a spoonful of her medicine every night,' he said to Anna Lisa.

'Yes, sir,' she said and left the room.

'Are you frightened,' her father said to Chiara, 'to be in the room when she has the fits?'

And Chiara said, no, she wasn't.

He told her she was a good, brave girl. He said if it happened when he was away, she was to fetch Anna Lisa rather

70

than Mamma, because Anna Lisa was more like a nurse. He hadn't seen, as Chiara had, Anna Lisa crossing herself when she passed Cecilia and muttering an invocation under her breath to keep the devil away. That was when Chiara knew. No one else was going to protect Cecilia. It was down to her.

The sky is darkening when they alight at Orte where they must change trains. They wait on the platform, along with about a dozen other passengers, and it starts to rain again, the same murky drizzle of the day before, as if some pot of waste-water is being tipped out. They step back under the overhang, but the wind still gusts the rain at them. Cecilia is humming under her breath. The boy stands next to Chiara on the other side from Cecilia, with them but not. He is silent, as he has been the whole journey.

'I'm going to tell Nonna,' Cecilia says.

She has removed her gloves and is tracing circles on the palm of one hand with the forefinger of the other. Her hair is pinned up under the felt hat. Her raincoat hangs over her arm. She is easily the best-looking, the most stylish woman around.

You wouldn't know from looking at her.

'What are you going to tell her?' Chiara says gently, placing her hand over Cecilia's.

Cecilia looks confused. 'Nothing,' she says.

A railway official appears, flanked by a soldier. In the half-light, Chiara cannot distinguish the soldier's uniform to discern whether he is Italian or German. Either way he is their enemy.

She drops to one knee and adjusts the boy's coat. 'Remember,' she says, 'your name is Daniele Gaspari.'

He gives no indication that he has heard, as if the silence in which he has encased himself works both ways. Fear presses on her heart. She stands.

71

There'll be no more trains tonight, the guard announces. The line has been commandeered because troop reinforcements are coming through.

The soldier walks past them up towards the end of the platform. It is the distinctive crunch of his heels, as if something is being ground to powder underfoot, that tells Chiara he is German.

They could have caught the regional train from Roma Tiburtina that follows a different route. She had been in two minds, but Tiburtina had been damaged in the San Lorenzo bombing back in July, and she had imagined the main line from Termini station would be more reliable. Termini, anyway, was easier to get to and meant they could avoid seeing again the rubble and ruin where their family home used to be.

Rubble, Chiara thinks, and the devastation of San Lorenzo fills her head. There is the mountain of debris, the dust rising up like smoke. The gaping hole where their old apartment building had been, the shock of its absence. The dreadful smell, people scrabbling through the rubble with handkerchiefs over their noses, and others just standing staring or with their heads bowed.

Chiara rubs her aching jaw. She reminds herself again that their mother refused to move with them when she and Cecilia took over their grandparents' apartment in Via dei Cappellari. That no one foresaw the bombardment. She must not let her mind stray there now.

She looks up and down the platform. If they had left yesterday, straight after lunch as she had intended, they would be safely at Nonna's by now. She should not have delayed. She had thought she might discover a safer place to take the child. If she hadn't spent yesterday afternoon cycling around in the drizzle, asking the wrong people the wrong questions, they would already be there. Coming this way has stranded them here, on what turns out to be the German army supply route.

A few of the passengers leave by a turnstile gate at the far end of the platform and disappear into the dusk. On her own, or in daylight, she might have taken her chances out on the road. Watching them leave, she feels the spirit within her reach out longingly in their direction with a yearning for that level of freedom, to be on her own in the dark, to hide in a ditch or a roadside barn, to hitch a ride with someone or beg a bed for the night, to rely on her wits and with only herself the loser if she took a wrong turn.

She snaps it back. They must stay here for the night and make the best of it.

'Come on. Let's get in out of the rain,' she says, as if this rather splendid idea had just then occurred to her.

Chiara, Cecilia and the boy follow the other remaining passengers across the track and into the waiting room, which smells of paraffin and warmed-up dust. People are claiming places on the benches and spreading themselves out, but Chiara leads her charges to the back of the room, to the space between the farthest bench and the wall, telling them quietly how she will make a nice bed for them on the floor, how this is a good place, out of the way, where they won't be disturbed by people moving about.

She keeps up a murmured, running commentary because she can feel that Cecilia is skittish at her side. She ushers them into the narrow area, first Cecilia, who puts her case down in the corner, then the boy. She lifts the cloth bag from his shoulders and tugs out the blanket. It is a patchwork of knitted squares that Nonna made a long time ago.

Daniele stands staring out at the room, his gaze unfocused, his fists clenched at his sides. From outside there comes the

73

rumble of another train slowing as it enters the station, and Chiara whips around to face the door. Perhaps the guard was wrong and there will be an onward connection. Or perhaps it is the troop train and they are going to disembark here. Hordes of them are going to march in, with their boots thumping and their round metal helmets glinting. She clutches the blanket to her chest.

Another batch of passengers, twenty or more, comes piling in, complaining and muttering. She lowers the blanket and shakes it out. Cecilia looks across at her, uncomprehending.

'Unpack your blanket,' Chiara says. 'We are staying here. Just for tonight. No more trains today, dearest. But it will be fine. We'll get an early one in the morning.'

The boy has shrunk back against the wall. Chiara reaches over him and pats her sister's shoulder.

They watch the newcomers, who did not want to come to Orte either, who were on the way to Rome or further south. Their train has been rerouted, and they have been dumped. They fill up the spaces on the benches and the floor. Those who had already stretched themselves out are obliged to sit up. The waiting room becomes noisy and animated as people negotiate for space. A man among the new arrivals, the only adult-but-not-elderly male, wants an explanation, information. Brandishing his ticket, he blusters out of the waiting room to demand answers. In his absence, its inhabitants adjust, accept and start to settle.

Cecilia doesn't want to sit. The floor is dirty, she says. It will stain her clothes. She wants to go home.

'Well, we're going to Nonna's,' Chiara points out, 'so it's like going home, isn't it?'

She fishes out her handkerchief and crouches down to wipe a space clean. She is flicking the handkerchief about when the boy, all of a sudden, sits down on the floor next to her, his back against the wall, his knees drawn up to his chest and his hands clasped around his shins, hugging them in. She sees he is utterly exhausted. The invisible wall he has tried to construct around himself is caving in.

'I'm going to make you a nice little bed here,' she says softly as she unrolls the colourful blanket onto the space she has swept, 'and tomorrow morning, early, we will catch the train that goes up into the hills, and after four stops we will get off.'

She glances up, aware of Cecilia looming. Her sister is glowering down, her face contorted, the way their mother used to hang over them when they were in bed, staring at them as if they were strangers, and they would pretend to be asleep until she went away.

'That's my blanket,' she says.

'Yours is in your case.' Chiara strives to retain the same even voice she is using with the boy. 'Remember, you packed it yourself. This is a spare one.'

She turns back to her bed-making and her tale.

'There will be a man with a horse and cart at the station,' she says, 'and he will give us a ride along the ridge to the higher village, and from there we will walk or, if we are tired, we will send a message to Gabriele to come and fetch us.'

An image of the shepherd Gabriele comes to her, emerging from among the trees, his face, which might have been hewn from one of them, the colour of the fallen leaves.

'Good old Gabriele,' she says, twisting to smile up at her sister, but Cecilia seems now to be absorbed in examining a poster on the wall.

'There,' Chiara says, smoothing out the blanket and turning to the boy, whose head has lolled forward. She lowers her voice. 'When we go down the track through the wood, we

75

come to a bend from where you can see into the next valley, and halfway down that slope is Nonna's farmhouse. You can't actually see it from there.' She shakes her head, even though he has obviously fallen asleep. 'Because there is a steep drop on the far side of the olive grove, and that hides the house, but sometimes you do see the smoke from its chimney.'

The last time she visited was in early springtime. She thinks of the mint-green of the new growth on the trees in the fore-ground and the pewter-blue of the farthest line of hills where they melt into the softer blue of sky, and all the shades of blue and green between, as if they were a wide silk ribbon with which to bind them together, she and Cecilia and the little boy.

She rocks back on her heels. 'Now, of course,' she says, 'it's autumn, and so the colours will be different. The hillside opposite is covered in trees, thick with all sorts of them, and it will be a mass of red and gold and orange.'

She swirls her hands in front of her face to demonstrate the flaming palette of the forested slope opposite her *nonna*'s house. It might be too early in the year for the leaves to have changed colour. But, autumn or not, there will be the blue and the green, the bright green of grass and the silver green of the olive leaves, and that faraway blue might be more muted, but it will be there, framing and holding the rim.

The boy's grip loosens, his legs tumble apart and his head sinks between them so that his knees, bony little buffers, cradle his head.

'What I wanted to tell you,' she says quietly, 'is that the view from that bend in the track is the loveliest in the world.'

She has been hesitant about touching him, conscious of her earlier roughness and instinctively respecting somehow the pathetic cloak of silence in which he has swathed himself, honouring the illusion of his impenetrability. But now, rising onto her knees, she inserts her hands into his armpits and, with a quick movement, hoists him sideways onto the blanket. He stirs but doesn't wake, and she remains crouched over him, inhaling the warmth of his breath. His eyes are not totally shut.

'Daniele,' she says to test the depth of his slumber, but sees he is utterly gone and cannot hear her.

She glances up. Cecilia seems to be spelling out the words on the poster. Her mouth is moving. Chiara cranes back to see better. It is an advertisement for the previous year's Exhibition of the Fascist Revolution. Cecilia had been taken to it by one of her clients, a woman whose husband had worked with Chiara at the ministry before their department was closed down. The wives of Chiara's colleagues are the main users of Cecilia's dressmaking skills.

This particular family had treated Cecilia as a sort of pet, taking her about with them in a condescending manner that set Chiara's teeth on edge, but which Cecilia didn't notice. Mussolini had actually been present at the exhibition the day they'd visited, and Cecilia had been personally introduced. For a while it was the Duce this and the Duce that, and when his hectoring voice came on the radio, she would simper as if he were speaking to her. And though that soon wore off, and Cecilia confessed to Chiara that he smelt of boiled beef and that spittle shot out from his mouth when he spoke, ever since, whenever she said, 'Duce,' she would briefly incline her head the way their mother used to do when mentioning Jesus.

Chiara turns back to the child, examining his sleeping face, his straight little nose with its faint scattering of freckles that continue onto his cheeks and then peter out, the eyelashes that are fairer at the tip than at the root, the downturned curve of his mouth and the pucker of his soft, pink upper lip. The way his thick hair – which when she first saw him on the lorry (was it only yesterday?) was parted on one side and decorously smoothed down – is now mussed and unruly. On the back of his right hand there is a brown stain. She touches it with her forefinger. It does not rub off. The skin there is not raised, only a different colour. A horseshoe-shaped birthmark. Gently, she lifts his hand and tucks it under the blanket.

So absorbed is Chiara in her contemplation of the child that she only half realises that something new is going on in the waiting room, that the door has opened and banged shut again, and the sleepy atmosphere has been banished. There is a bristling, a sighing and a muttering. As she becomes aware of the change and gets to her feet, a shiver goes down her spine, despite the fuggy warmth.

'Papers,' the guard says, 'show them your papers and state the purpose of your travel.'

There are three soldiers with him now, two German and one Italian. One of them grips the arm of the self-appointed spokesman, who has lost his swagger. The soldiers fan out, and there is a rustling and a shuffling. Some people are shaken awake.

Chiara glances at her sister, still strangely absorbed in the poster, then down at the sleeping boy. She has literally backed them into a corner. The soldiers are speaking to each other over the heads of the obedient people proffering their papers.

Did they say Jew? All day she has been hearing that word, or imagining she hears it, first in Italian and now in German, swinging her head towards the sound each time, not sure where it's coming from or what form the threat will take, but certain each time, for a foolish, lurching instant, that they have been found out.

With her toe she flips the blanket over the boy's face. She places herself in front of him. Just a bundle on the floor. Perhaps they won't notice him. She thinks she hears him cough. Suffocating him is not the answer. As she bends to uncover him, he coughs again and flings off the blanket. His eyes are wide open. He stares up at her and she has the sensation of falling. She grips the back of the bench and straightens as the boy scoops himself into a seated position.

The soldier on their side of the room is now working his way along the occupants of this last bench. It is routine, this checking of documents, but thorough. The soldiers have nothing better to do until the troop train arrives and they want to show who is boss. That is all. It cannot be a concerted search for stray Jewish children. But still.

'Cecilia,' she says in a loud, clear voice, 'you have Daniele's papers, don't you?'

It is farcical but it is all she can muster to imply somehow that each thought the other had the boy's papers and so they must have been left at home. How Chiara can carry it off without Cecilia's complicity or understanding, she does not know. Cecilia, oblivious, is still facing the poster on the wall in the corner, muttering. Chiara reaches over the boy and yanks at her sister's arm. Cecilia turns, her mouth working and indistinguishable sounds emerging.

'What is it?' Chiara says, but all of a sudden she knows what it is, and in her head there is a white storm.

The soldier is upon her, tapping her shoulder. She turns to face him and for a blinding moment she thinks it is the same soldier from the day before, but this one is younger, big-jawed, with blond stubble on his chin. Behind her, Cecilia's mutter becomes a snarl. It is the very noise that made their mother believe her elder child was possessed by the devil all those years before, a low and bestial sound that cannot possibly emanate from this delicate creature and yet does.

Chiara clutches at the soldier's arm.

'Help,' she says as Cecilia lets out a blood-curdling growl from behind.

The soldier pushes Chiara aside and raises his pistol, pointing it at Cecilia in the corner beyond.

'No, no,' Chiara shrieks, 'it's an epileptic fit,' and then, wildly, wailing, 'Help, help,' she moves to dive under the soldier's arm.

But someone is holding her back, and her arms are pinioned. The soldier barks an order, and Cecilia barks back, something guttural, vaguely Germanic. She advances towards the soldier, intoning her menacing, meaningless words.

'*Acker hoch*,' she says.

'It's a fit. A fit. An epileptic fit,' Chiara is shrieking over and over again, pulling uselessly against her captor.

Cecilia's hands flutter up, she clutches at her face, her eyes roll back in their sockets and she keels over backwards, falling onto the patchwork blanket.

There is a sudden hush in the room in which Chiara doesn't know, cannot tell, whether, in among the clamour and her own shouting, a shot has rung out, whether the trigger was indeed pulled. Her sister's prone body almost fills the length of the narrow space between the wall and the bench. Then Cecilia's feet start to drum at high speed on the floor, her back arches, her head twitches, thumps once, twice, and she lies still.

The soldier lowers his gun and turns round, and Chiara, released, catches a look of bafflement and scorn on his big face as she moves past him. She kneels at her sister's feet, tugs the navy skirt, which has ridden up, down over her knees. Cecilia's mouth is ajar, her breathing shallow but unobstructed. Chiara clasps Cecilia's slender ankles and continues to kneel there, as if praying. The German soldiers are having a discussion in the otherwise silent room, and another voice, speaking in German but with an Italian accent, joins in. If she hears the click of the pistol, she will fling her body over her sister's. One bullet will do for both of them.

And then she remembers the boy. She can see the cloth bag poking out from under Cecilia's head and the blanket he was wrapped in that has cushioned her fall, but the boy, impossibly, has vanished.

She is prodded in the back. She twists, sees a different soldier standing there, older, with crinkles around his eyes, round spectacles and a smooth pink face, an officer.

'Papers,' he says.

She gets to her feet, retrieving Cecilia's documents too. The big blond one stands in the aisle between the two rows of benches. He has put the pistol away but now has a machine gun in his hands. He bends his knees, swings the gun in an arc so that the people he pinpoints around the quiet room feint and cower.

'Tak tak tak,' he says.

Did that soldier yank the child away when her attention was elsewhere? Where then has he put him? The officer keeps hold of the papers and steps into the aisle, indicating with a curt nod that she should follow. She glances back at Cecilia who now has a familiar little smile playing on her lips. Her breathing has deepened. In a minute she will start to snore.

The Italian soldier acts as interpreter. He is a small man, not much taller than Chiara, but with a large bushy moustache. He stands very close and takes hold of her elbow in a familiar way. His breath is sulphurous.

Chiara states where they are going and that her sister's

condition is under control, that she is capable of caring for her, that the mountain air will revive her.

'Are you travelling unaccompanied?' the officer asks via the soldier.

She wonders whether this is a trick question, but she answers, 'Yes, just my sister and myself.'

Her inability to identify the moment of the boy's disappearance, to grasp the mechanics of the thing, makes her giddy. She is almost glad of the steadying grip of the vile, eggy-breathed little man. It is as if some alternative version of events might have been going on, outside of her ken and her vision.

The man whose blustering had brought the soldiers into the waiting room in the first place is standing across the aisle, hangdog, his cap in his hand.

The hush that began with Cecilia's first growl continues. No one gainsays Chiara's statement, and the child is not produced from a hidden location like a rabbit from a hat. It appears that the whole waiting room is in fact waiting, and as the attention still seems to be on her, Chiara launches into a story. An explanation of how and why they are alone in the world, she and her sister, a tale about how their mother died in the Allied bombing just three months ago.

'Everything was lost,' she hears herself saying in a faltering voice. 'All the precious things.'

Cecilia, lying in her blanketed corner, erupts into a great snorting snore, and the blond soldier, as if targeted, lunges forward and points the machine gun at her. Chiara's words dry up, and she just stands there in a daze. Cecilia snores again, settles into a proper rhythm, and the soldier speaks, asking his superior a question over his shoulder. Chiara doesn't follow the words, but from the stiffening of the little man at her side, from

82

the throwaway but malicious tone, she gets the meaning, something like, 'Shall I put her out of her misery?'

The older one smiles pleasantly. He says something that makes all three of them chuckle, reaches sideways and affably pushes the barrel of the gun. He hands Chiara her papers, and the three of them leave.

The blond one exits last. He turns at the door and waves his machine gun one last time. 'Tak tak tak,' he says.

Among the precious things on display in the entrance lobby of the San Lorenzo apartment there used to be a Libyan scimitar that their father had picked up on one of his business trips to North Africa. It had a curved blade with a double-edged point and was of a type carried by tribesmen in Cyrenaica. As a child, Chiara was not allowed to touch it.

She pictures it now. She can almost feel the weight of it, the balance of the pommel and the blade, the warmth of the brass hilt in her palm. She hears the whistling noise it makes when swished through the air. She imagines hurtling after the big blond soldier and, with one vast swipe, cleaving his head from his shoulders so that it rolls onto the railway tracks. She observes his flailing, headless dance before he crumples to the ground.

She wipes her hand on her dusty handkerchief, plants a foot either side of Cecilia and hefts her sister onto her side, tugs out the excess blanket bunched beneath her body and folds it over the top so that Cecilia is ensconced now in the bed Chiara had prepared for the child. The snoring abates. She has not had a fit of this magnitude for years.

Chiara sits on the bare floor at her sister's feet behind the bench. An elderly man gives her a paper cup filled with red wine. He tells her about someone he knew, a youth, who also had fits. It's a worry, he says.

They are brutes, his wife whispers without specifying whom.

There is a milling about in the waiting room, a restlessness, an unpacking of paper-wrapped food for a last bite before sleep. Some passengers mutter to each other, others come and go, making visits to the washroom out on the platform and then returning. Stuck in transit, with their onward journey out of their hands, they want at least to assure themselves they may go on exercising their paltry right to use the public conveniences. Eventually children are quieted and people start to settle down again. No one has mentioned the boy. It is as if he was never there.

Chiara sits drinking the wine, and the room darkens, the only light the yellow platform lamp hanging outside the door. The worst thing, as bad almost as the mystery of his disappearance, is that he has left no trace.

He is gone. Daniele Levi, so transiently there, is gone and only she to mourn his passing. Her mind bangs against the impossibility of his vanishing as if at a bricked-up doorway.

She drains the wine. Nothing presents itself as a way forward from here. And before she can stop it, the thought is there; it has slipped in.

She is better off without him.

FIVE

Flat, wet leaves brushed and branches slapped against the bus windows. The trees to either side of the road wanted to meet in an arch, and the bus was tunnelling through them. Sometimes, Maria would sit at the front and pretend she was driving a hovercraft or a space vehicle, gliding over the roofs of cars and the heads of pedestrians, dodging the flicking branches, but not today.

She was on her way to the first of her O-level exams, chemistry, and she was cutting it fine. She had period cramps, and the painkiller was only just beginning to have an effect. She had meant to catch an earlier bus but she had got caught up in a tussle with the neighbours' cat.

She placed both hands over the pleats of her school skirt, holding her stomach, and closed her eyes. The pains came in waves, ebbing and flowing. When one subsided, she glanced out of the window. There was the grey school building through the trees, and the bus was sailing past. She pressed the bell, but the bus sped on until it came to its next allotted stop, half a mile farther, on the edge of the village of Llandaff that the school was named after.

She would be late. Perhaps they wouldn't even let her in.

These thoughts induced a frisson of excitement, which stayed with her all the way back to the school and the examination hall, then left her as soon as she stepped inside.

The room was packed with girls in bottle-green uniforms bent over their papers, scribbling away. The only sounds were the scratching of pens on paper, the scrape of a shifted chair, the occasional cough, but these were all part of the whole atmosphere of concentrated studiousness and application. That morning, when Maria had been crouching in the neighbours' garden, these girls had been checking their understanding of the periodic table and sharpening their pencils.

The invigilator, Mrs Lloyd, the deputy head, signalled from the rostrum to the teacher patrolling the back of the room. Then she pressed the pencil to her lips, urging silence, as if she suspected Maria might be tempted to let out a scream. Maria waited at the door until the other teacher came and led her through the grid of tables, pressing a pathway through the thick, brainwave-filled air. Maria's designated place was right in the middle.

It was pointless her being there because she didn't know any chemistry at all. She had never listened in class, preferring to doodle and daydream, and had got away with it by always being partnered for experiments with a girl to whom chemistry made sense. There were mysteries into which you might want to be initiated, and then there was chemistry. Maria had given up on the subject long ago. Or it had given up on her. She wasn't even going to bother turning over the exam paper.

She had practised her Italian on that cat.

Ciao, bella. Come stai? Mi chiamo Maria.

And the cat had turned out to be a monster.

The neighbours' garden had been Maria's refuge. She would

sit there for hours at a time, her books propped on the bench, sometimes open, usually not. Honeysuckle grew up the wall.

Quite o'er canopied with luscious woodbine, she would think.

There was a drooping tree with hanging orange blossoms where spiders spun white webs like patches of fog between the leaves and the stems.

Season of mists, she thought.

Allowing phrases from her English literature books to dangle and sway in the fuzz and bramble of her brain was the nearest she got to revising, and Tabitha had been her companion throughout.

Then this morning, she, Tabitha, the monster, had come strolling with a swagger from behind the lilac bush with a shivering, quivering little creature in her mouth. Its mouth, Maria corrected. Tabitha didn't deserve her gender. Its jaw, its bestial fangs. It had dropped the creature — a mouse — and the mouse had fallen over, staggered to its feet and tottered about like a tiny drunkard. The cat had reached out its paw and batted the mouse to the ground. The mouse got back up. The cat batted it back down. The cat lunged forward and scooped the creature up again, shaking it so that its tail coiled and whipped back and forth.

The next time, Maria pounced, picked Tabitha up, ran, holding her at arm's length, threw her into the kitchen and banged the door shut.

The mouse lay half hidden in the grass with a quiver running through it. Maria crouched over it, breathing shallowly. She knew she had to leave for her exam but she couldn't bear to go. Something began rippling and pulsing in a horrible way, as if parts of the mouse were breaking off and moving independently. She leant in closer. Ants, big stinging ones, were crawling all over the mouse, eating it alive, piercing its minute body. Frantic, she ran to the shed, found some ant powder, hurtled back and sprinkled it liberally in a circle around and over the little beast.

She had sat next to the mouse and kept vigil. She would have flung the cat off a high building and trampled the ants into the ground to save that mouse.

From the rostrum, Mrs Lloyd was eyeing her.

Maria turned her exam paper over and scanned it. She filled in the answer to 'What is a catalyst?' She drew a picture of a Bunsen burner and a test tube and labelled all the parts. Then she sat back and looked at the clock. There was another hour and a half remaining. The period pain had abated. She would have liked to leave but to walk out was too grand a gesture.

She placed over the top of the answer sheet a piece of the scrap paper given them for notes and workings-out, and started to write.

'Catalyst,' she wrote. 'Flame.'

She pressed the pen hard into the paper, scratching in the words.

'*Dear Mum*,' she wrote. Then she crossed out '*dear*'.

What was our catalyst, do you think? I'll tell you what it wasn't. It wasn't the moment when you told me that Barry wasn't my biological father. It wasn't even you sleeping with some Italian boy when you were eighteen. (Was it only the one boy, Mum?) It was the fact that you waited until I was sixteen before you bothered to tell me, and that even then it was only because you had to because I found the letter. So it's the lying that's the catalyst, Mum. When you tell me that Barry isn't my real dad, what you're also telling me is that you're not my real mum. How can you be? A real mum wouldn't lie to her daughter every day of her life.

Once Maria got going, she found she had plenty to say. Or rather she had the same thing to say over and over again, with fierce jabbings of the pen. Liar, cow, bitch, she wrote.

A ten-minute warning was given, and then it was the end.

'Maria Kelly,' Mrs Lloyd called out, 'put down your pen.'

When the papers were collected, she handed in her drawing of the Bunsen burner and her definition of a catalyst. The teacher held out her hand for the other sheets.

'You're not allowed to take them out,' she said.

Maria tore her ravings into confetti and the teacher swept them like breadcrumbs off the table surface and into her hand.

It was only chemistry. It didn't really count because she hadn't been going to pass it anyway.

The second exam, on the following Monday, was history, one of her better subjects. As the bus shot past the school and she stayed on board, the excitement returned, stronger this time. It surged down her arms and made her fingers tingle. She got off in Llandaff and went to a café next to a hairdresser. She bought herself a cup of tea and a doughnut with money for the bus fare home. Ordinarily she might have been an object of note in her uniform, wandering about in the middle of a school day among the elderly residents, but in the exam period, when pupils came and went at odd times, it was different. She could pass unnoticed.

She wandered down to the Anglican cathedral. It was open and empty. She had never been inside before. It didn't smell of incense like the Catholic churches. She sat in a pew at the back. Nobody would know her or look for her or even realise she was there. She was incognito.

She walked slowly all the way home, keeping away from the main roads. She went through Sophia Gardens, on the overgrown path beside the river Taff, and then across Bute Park behind Cardiff Castle. It started to rain, and she shrugged up her blazer collar, tucked her hair inside her beret and pulled it forward. She kept her head down when she walked past the university buildings in case Brian emerged from one of them. She didn't know what she would say. She might pretend she was someone else.

'Oh, that girl I look like, yes, people are always mistaking me for her,' she would say. 'But I'm Maria Levi,' and she would roll the R in 'Maria' in an Italian way. She had been practising rolling her Rs. If she saw Brian, she might just run away very fast.

She got home at her usual time, and there was the smell of curry. Monday tea was always the leftovers from the Sunday roast. Cold cuts and pickled onions if they had had beef or pork. Curry if the roast had been chicken. Patrick and Nel were romping about in the front room.

'How was the exam?' her mum asked.

'Fine,' Maria said.

She felt a delicious thrill of power. She had hardly been able to be in the same room as her mother or Barry for the last fortnight, since the Daniele Levi revelation. When it was unavoidable, mostly at mealtimes, one or other of them would prattle on and Maria would remain silent, getting the meal over as quickly as possible. She always had the excuse of revision to do. Now, she stayed in the kitchen, watching.

'Good,' her mum said. 'Well done.'

The chicken carcass was in the pressure cooker – there would be a soup made later from the stock – and the room was hot and steamy with a pervasive boiled-bones smell that made Maria nauseous. Her mother scraped the chopped chicken she'd picked from the bones into the curry sauce bubbling on the hob and wiped her hands down the front of her overall, patting the pocket as her hand passed over it. There were smears where she had made this gesture a hundred times before. She fetched a bag of sultanas out of the pantry, shook a handful into the curry and stirred them in. She wiped her hands again.

Maria picked up the tub of curry powder and put it back where it belonged, at the centre of a circular yellow stain that wouldn't wash off.

'Are you sure Daniele Levi was my father?' she said, speaking into the open cupboard.

She heard her mother's intake of breath but she didn't turn round. Behind the curry powder was a jar of dried mint that would be mixed with vinegar to make mint sauce when they had lamb. They didn't often have lamb, though. Next to that was a bottle of salad cream.

'Yes,' her mother said. 'There wasn't anyone else.'

'Did you love him?' she asked.

'Yes,' her mother said, softly.

'So how come you left?' She turned round.

Her mother was standing in the middle of the kitchen, pressing her fingers into her cheekbones, holding them in place, as if her face might dissolve. The hollows under her eyes were bluish.

'My mother was ill. Your nan. I had to come home in a hurry.'

Her nan had died before Maria was even born.

'I couldn't find him to say goodbye. I thought I'd go back, but, um, I couldn't.'

'Oh,' Maria said.

'I left a note for him with Helen. I didn't know where he lived.' Her bottom lip was trembling. 'I didn't know I was pregnant when I left.'

91

Her mum took a step towards Maria. Perhaps she thought it was a truce. She delved into her overall pocket and held out her clasped fist. Maria automatically reached her own hand forward and a ring dropped into her open palm.

'He gave me this,' her mum said.

It was there in Maria's hand. She wanted to disparage it, but it was a real, solid, thing. Incontrovertible.

'Ta,' she said and spun out of the kitchen up to her room.

Edna stood in the middle of the kitchen, listening to her daughter thumping up the stairs and slamming into her bedroom. She heard the squawking noises coming from the front room where Pat and Nel were playing, unaware of the drama in the family home. Behind her, the pressure cooker hissed. She waited for the music that Maria would inevitably put on. She guessed it would be Billie Holiday, turned up loud. 'Gloomy Sunday' perhaps. Or it might be Miles Davis. She steeled herself in case it was Chet Baker. Her oblivious daughter, playing the soundtrack to Edna's snatched youth.

The ring had been the first thing Edna had noticed about Daniele. His hand on her arm, and the ring glinting on his little finger. She was at a jazz club with her friend Helen, and Helen had elbowed a passage for them through the crowd with Edna hanging on to the back of her cardigan. They broke through to a little space, right next to the rail at the front.

Helen leant in to whisper in Edna's ear.

'Cool West Coast jazz.'

They were two British girls out on the town. They were wearing their glad-rags, their frocks, nylon stockings and kitten heels. Their lips were daubed pearly pink. Edna's long blonde hair had been put up in a topknot, held in place with a tortoiseshell clip.

Chet Baker strolled onto the stage. Helen nudged her.

The music began. Edna could feel Helen swaying beside her and others too, around and about, moving to the beat, but she didn't know what to do with herself. She had never heard anything like it. It was as if the music were not an outside thing created and performed up there, but was inside her. She stood stock-still, rigid, as if to let the music move her would be her undoing.

She had been in Rome for two months. She had arrived in February, in the coldest winter it had ever known: the city white and frozen and almost at a standstill. The family she worked for lived to the south, in the suburb of EUR, which seemed the most un-Italian of names, difficult to pronounce and sounding like an expression of disgust. The letters stood for the Roman Universal Exhibition, an event that would have showcased fascism to the world, but it never took place because the war had come along to stop it. EUR in 1956 was like a giant building site with occasional, monumental white edifices of over-smooth arches and hard square edges, solemn and self-important.

The family were reluctant to allow her out in the evening unless in a group or with suitable, vetted escorts. Her charges were a fat baby who had to be wrapped up in woollens, mittens and hats before being tucked under blankets and wheeled out to the park; and a little boy, Paolo, who clung to her side, frightened of everything. She was sometimes surprised that anyone would entrust children to her, but she did her best.

It was not, after all, the children's fault that none of this was what she had imagined when she responded to the advertisement in the *Lady*. She was going to be Audrey Hepburn on her day out in *Roman Holiday*, free and lovely and fêted. She had not expected Rome to be chilly and restrictive and judgmental. Until she had met Helen, it had been bleak. Helen's family was more liberal, or lax, and she had a supply of escorts. They were out with two of them now, Renzo and Cristofero, the bespectacled, spotty, earnest sons of Helen's neighbours. The girls had given them the slip and snuck up to the front on their own.

The lights dimmed, and the spotlight was only on Chet, who held the microphone and sang into it tenderly. From his other hand hung his trumpet. It was the way he held that trumpet, the way it swung, the insouciance, that precious thing hooked lightly over his curled fingers. It was the tone of his voice, reaching through her. It spoke straight to her heart. It was the words.

She closed her eyes. Barry came into her mind. She and Barry weren't engaged, not formally, but they had a sort of understanding. He was being sent to Egypt for his national service. When he finished, in two years' time, or a bit longer because he hadn't even gone yet, they would get married. Barry hadn't been at all sure about her going off to Italy. Neither had her parents. But she had convinced them to let her. She had made it happen.

'You don't know what love is,' Chet Baker sang, and she opened her eyes, forgot herself, forgot Barry.

The tenor sax started up. It was as if she were being drenched in the music. She was standing underneath it, and it was cascading over her. It was everything. She started to move.

A hand clasped her forearm. A male hand, broad and strong; a gold ring glinted on the little finger. She looked down at the hand, surprised, then leant around Helen's back to see a young man. He wore a black jacket with a dark shirt underneath, the top button undone. No tie. His hair was slicked back.

He pulled her towards him and they danced, although it was

nothing like the dancing she was used to, the foxtrot and the waltz that she and Barry had been perfecting at the Saturday-night hop. It was more like sidling. They sidled around each other, ever closer, treading water in the music. She waited for his wave to engulf her.

He picked her up on her afternoon off on a borrowed motorbike. She hung on to him, clinging to his ribcage, his torso tightly encased in a white T-shirt, her hands inside his leather jacket, her face buried against the collar. They soared up into the Castelli hills, roaring around the bends. He was intoxicatingly beautiful.

James Dean was his hero.

'Too fast to live, too young to die,' he said in his funny accent. He had no family, he said. An orphan boy. She couldn't get enough of him.

They thundered along the Sea Highway and ate spaghetti with clams at a café on the beach at Ostia. They walked in the pine forest and lay down among the cones and needles. They knew only a few words of each other's languages. Mostly, they bypassed words.

She watched him parading in expensive winkle-pickers with silver buckles in a shoeshop on Via Veneto. The dangerous look in his eye made her breathless. When the assistant went to the storeroom, he took her hand and tugged her.

'*Corri*,' he said. Run.

He came or he didn't. It was all on his terms. Once they shot down the little street he lived in, right in the centre of Rome, on the motorbike. But he didn't take her to his home.

Helen didn't approve. She said he was no good, a waster. Helen was jealous, Edna thought, although she also knew that Helen was right. But she didn't care.

'Cover for me,' Edna pleaded, 'please.'

And Helen, reluctantly, did.

He arrived in a small white car, a brand-new Fiat Sei Cento. His, he said. He drove her to an abandoned crumbling farmhouse in the mountains, and they walked among the olive trees. They dropped stones into an ancient well and waited to hear the distant plosh. He was quiet, playing with his ring, twisting it around his little finger.

'That ring looks precious,' she said, for something to say.

'Precious' was one of those words that could be said in an Italian way with a roll of the R and an O on the end, and it was the same, more or less. *Prezioso*.

'Precious,' he repeated. 'It is.'

He slid it off and tossed it across the well to her. She reached out, caught it in the palm of her hand on the downward arc and closed her fist around it. If she'd missed, it would have gone down the well. He laughed at the look of shock on her face.

'For you,' he had said.

The golden dangle of Chet Baker's trumpet and the gold spin of the ring in the spring air were together in her memory, different facets of the same precious thing, catching the light on the way down.

Maria's next exam was a morning one. English language. Somehow, she and her mum were leaving the house at the exact same time – Barry had already left with the kids – and so they were obliged to walk down the road as far as the bus stop together, the way they always used to do when her mum was on the nine o'clock shift.

'Good luck, darling,' her mum said at the bus stop. She knew better than to try to kiss Maria now. 'Not that you need it,' she added and walked briskly away.

96

This was her daily exercise, the march to work and back. Sometimes the bus came before her mum had turned the corner, in which case Maria would wave from the upper deck as she went past. Other times, like today, her mum reached the corner first and would turn and wave one last time before heading up Wedal Road to the hospital. She did that now. Maria waved back with a minimal gesture, the merest flutter of the hand. Then her mum disappeared round the corner.

Maria was already halfway across the promenade by the time the bus came. She bought a packet of ten Number Six from the kiosk on the other side of the lake. Ten and a half pence well spent. She was going to take up smoking.

'You'll get fat,' her non-biological father had said when she refused to go with him on their customary runs around the lake.

He kept turning up at her bedroom door in his tracksuit, failing to get the message. Smoking was an alternative way of keeping thin. The first cigarette was disgusting but she knew it took practice. At home, she took off her uniform, put on her nightie and got back into bed. Missing English language meant that she was going to have to miss them all. English was her best subject. She could have walked it, even without doing any revision. She pulled her knees up and hugged her secrets to her chest.

That would show them.

SIX

The library windows had been thrown open to let in some fresh air. The sun pouring in was already hot, awakening the innate smells of the objects it alighted on – the old studded leather chairs, the panelled walls, the bound tomes on shelves or in glass-fronted cases – and drawing them out, evoking their origins: the animal skin, timber, glue and thread, the paper pulp. A bee buzzed somewhere up high, pinging itself frenziedly against the panes. Down in the courtyard garden, the wisteria was in full bloom. The heavy vines, supported on trellises, created private, flower-enclosed compartments in between the brick pathways, and in one of these scented arbours sat a priest. Only his legs, crossed at the shins, were visible.

In the library gallery, Chiara, sitting in the pod of warm light next to the open window, was trying to decide which priest it might be. It wasn't Father Pascale because he would be wearing sandals at this time of year, and it wasn't Father Pio who was corpulent and so couldn't have such slender ankles. She was wondering whether it might be her friend Father Antonio, by whose grace she was allowed to come and use this private library attached to the pontifical university.

The page proofs of the book about shipping in the Mediterranean in the Middle Ages lay open in front of her, an oblong of white light that was too bright to read even if she squinted.

She decamped to the street side of the building where the mullioned windows were set too high to see out. It was darker and stuffier here, more conducive to study perhaps. She laid out the pages again. She put her elbows on the table, her head in her hands and her thumbs in her ears, although there wasn't any noise to shut out, other than the bee. The other, very occasional, users of this library were young theologians, but today she was alone with the ancient volumes. It was a peaceful place to work and it carved a separation between her home life and her working life. The walk between her apartment and the ancient palazzo where the pontifical library was situated marked the transition between the two. And then there was Antonio to have a coffee with if she wanted a break. They used to work together in State Archives in the olden days, before he took holy orders. His was a late vocation.

She was reading through the chapter on the maritime republic of Genoa.

'Spices, incense and opium were hugely in demand,' she read for the fourth time.

Each translation posed its own challenges, some untranslatable core element. With this one, written by a British academic, it wasn't the subject matter, which would be, if anything, more familiar to an Italian reader. It was the register. The conversational style didn't befit an academic treatise in Italian and would undermine the seriousness of the research. She had opted for a halfway kind of language. Something in between the convoluted, multiple-claused sentence structure that an Italian academic might have used and the punchy, staccato style employed by the author. She had pulled it off. She had rendered the flavour, and the author, who knew some Italian, was pleased too.

A little wavering square of luminous colour, cast by the light beaming through the diamond shapes of green glass that patterned the windows, played on the page. She put her hand there and observed her green skin. She needed to press on. The publisher was waiting. She got up and moved everything back over to the courtyard side. Down in the gardens, the priest had changed position, and she saw now it was indeed Antonio, a bible and a notebook on his lap.

She went down to join him.

'Not coffee time already?' he said with a delighted smile.

He always looked as if she had made his day by turning up, even though she came regularly, and they went out for their morning cappuccino together at least once a week.

'Not yet,' she said. 'But I can't concentrate today.'

She looked at him, weighing the idea of telling him about the phone call. But that would mean bringing up Daniele's name, talking about Daniele, which was not something that she and Antonio did any more. She had stopped asking Antonio for news years ago.

'Haven't you heard anything? Hasn't he been in touch?' she used to say as if Antonio might just have forgotten to mention a letter or a telephone call or a visit.

'I will tell you,' Antonio would reply, 'if there is anything to tell.'

No, the subject of Daniele was closed.

All of a sudden, that silence between them seemed to her like a sheet, a shroud-like wrapping, and she was bound inside it, her mouth gagged. She took a deep breath, inhaling the scent of the wisteria, and sat down on a rock opposite

Antonio, under a roof of flowers. If they had been in the confessional, with the grille between them, it would have been
easier. Antonio would be God's mediator rather than Antonio,
the man. Not that she believed all that stuff, but he did, and
that might be enough for both of them.

Antonio patted his pockets and pulled out a packet of cigarettes. She accepted one though she had already used up three
of today's precious five during the long night.

'You look tired,' he said.

'I am,' she said. 'You go on with your work. Ignore me. I'm
in a funny mood.'

'I'm writing a sermon,' he said and bent to the task.

'Bless me, Father, for I have sinned,' she would say. 'It has
been . . .'

How long had it been? Years? Decades?

'A very long time since my last confession.'

She and Cecilia kneeling next to each other in the cavernous gloom of Sant'Eustachio, waiting their turn. The
pitter-patter of nuns' feet somewhere to the side of the altar.
The cold, holy-water smell. She was conscious of wrongdoing
now, and a need to expiate it, but shaky about the exact nature
of her new sin. Was it the way she had dismissed the girl out
of hand? As if Daniele himself had walked back into her life,
and she had looked the other way. *Help me*, he had said, but
she had no longer known how.

'Whatever is troubling you, it will pass,' Antonio said.

Platitudes. It hadn't passed in all these years, and just when
she thought she'd entered a new phase, along came this dreadful girl to stir it all up.

Antonio leant across the space between them, reached for
her hand, gathered it up from her lap and held it in his.

'I am your friend and I am here if you need me,' he said.

Looking up at him, seeing the way the sun glinted on his round glasses, she had a sudden image of him ten years before, when he had faced down Daniele's creditors. Her loyal friend Antonio, who had wanted to be more than a friend but had settled for that, who had stepped in when things had got desperate and she had needed help, and who had made it all go away. That calm certainty he exuded. Not only did he know what the right thing to do was, but he did it.

A flash of such resentment shot through her that she had to lower her eyes.

You sent my boy away. Why did you send my boy away? she wanted to scream at him. Sent him into exile, she sometimes thought, when she imagined Daniele wandering the world, a pack on his back, without a home.

'I've dealt with it,' Antonio used to assure her when she was at her lowest ebb, in the first few months after Daniele's departure. 'Don't worry yourself, we'll talk about it when you're stronger.'

And then, when she was stronger, it turned out that there was nothing to talk about. Daniele's banishment was total. How had she let that happen?

'I didn't banish him. He refused my help,' Antonio had told her when she had made him repeat all the things Daniele had said before he left.

'She is better off without me,' was one of them.

Then he had disappeared and, in all those years, there was only one time that she had had news of him. Not really news, but an inkling that he was still alive.

It was about eighteen months after his departure. She and Simone had gone up to Nonna's farm. Another earthquake had finished the place off, and the house itself was ruined and uninhabitable, but she was investigating whether she could sell off the land. There were still debts and she needed to raise more cash. It had always been there in the back of her mind as a final resort, but it turned out there wasn't much land attached to the property; all the pasture had been leased from the neighbouring farm. It was just a broken-down house; Nonna's vegetable patch had long become overgrown and the well was hidden under brambles.

People had said that a wild man had been living there for a while. He might have been sleeping in a cave up in the hills higher up but he had been seen in and around the farmhouse. He was long gone by the time they had arrived, though. Still, it had comforted her to think he had found a refuge for a while at Nonna's farm. And to realise that it was probably where he went the other, earlier times that he had disappeared.

They had sat a while in the neglected olive grove, she and Simone, and she nearly told Simone about the night that Daniele had climbed into the hollow of Nonna's most ancient tree under a full moon to make a wish. But Simone wanted to believe that Chiara didn't think of him all the time and so Chiara hadn't spoken. And anyway, she had learnt later what he had wished for that night and it didn't make for such a pretty story.

'Thank you,' she said to Antonio now and looked up at him again.

There he was, her kind and constant friend, gazing at her with concern. He had only been acting in her interest after all. His version of what her interest was.

'It's nothing,' she said now. 'I'm fine.'

She thought that having the desire to be fine and replete and happy was half the battle. There was pleasure to be found in little things. She remembered her red glass bowl. She would move it to the other end of the hallway and see how it looked.

She did have the aspiration to be fine, she reminded herself; she had been cultivating it for years. It all seemed very tragic to the little British girl at this moment, but she would get over it. That too would pass. And what could Chiara tell the child about Daniele that would bring her any comfort? Not a single thing.

She shifted her position on the hot, hard rock. 'So what's the gossip?' she said.

Antonio told her about a cardinal from Argentina who had come to visit and been lodged in the Franciscan monastery where he did nothing but complain about the standards of hygiene. He claimed there were dog hairs on the carpet in his room, which was 'a palatial suite', according to Antonio, 'worthy of the pope himself.'

'What would our patron say if he could see this?' the cardinal had asked the abbot, who had refrained from reminding the venerable man that St Francis had been rather fond of animals.

Chiara wondered briefly about monastic cells and whether they had gone out of fashion, about what Argentina – where she had never been but where she had distant relations – might be like. What if the girl telephoned again while she was sitting listening to Antonio's prattle? She held still, telling herself again it was for the best. She became so conscious of not moving, of clamping down on the previous night's conversation, that it was as if she were sitting on a volcano about to erupt. She could feel its heat beneath her buttocks.

She sprang to her feet and took a step forward. Daniele's daughter, she thought. He had a child. She suddenly remembered the name from the mother's letter. Kelly. Edna Kelly.

'Am I boring you?' Antonio said in his mild way.

'Sorry,' she said and bent to kiss him. 'I've got to go.'

At home, she telephoned the international enquiry service. There was a whole page of Kellys in Cardiff. She needed the first initial. No E. Kelly was listed.

'Can you read out all of the addresses?' Chiara asked.

She would recognise it if she heard it, she was sure. After all, she had written it on the envelope, and so there must be some trace somewhere in her memory.

'This is a service for telephone numbers, not for addresses,' the operator said.

She would wait in, she decided. She could work just as easily at home and she would be on hand to receive the girl's call, should she phone.

On the morning of the third housebound day, Assunta arrived to do the cleaning.

'Saints in heaven,' she exclaimed as she appeared at the kitchen entrance, buttoning up her housecoat.

Chiara twisted round from the window; she was hanging half out of it, smoking. 'Good morning, Assunta,' she said. 'I'll be working at home today.'

Assunta flapped her hand in front of her face and coughed ostentatiously. Chiara quickly stubbed out her cigarette in the tin she was using as an ashtray. It was full to overflowing, she noticed with dismay. She went over to the stove and lit the gas underneath the Moka pot.

Assunta had taken hold of the door and was pumping it back and forth to create a current of air. The hand-flapping was inadequate to disperse the fug, it seemed.

'Let's not exaggerate,' Chiara said.

'But, signora, what has been going on here?' Assunta said.

Over the previous days, Chiara had carted the book man-uscript about, laying it out in different sites, reading snatches but without taking in the words. She had made sporadic calls to International Enquiries in the hope of finding a more amenable operator, as well as occasional pointless and dispiriting forays into the junk room. Not only had she failed to find the letter, she hadn't even located the main bulk of Daniele's leftover belongings. The wooden crates packed with his clothes, books, records, his first trumpet, the paraphernalia that was left in his room when he fled. There was no trace of them at the back of the junk room where she had always confidently imagined they were stored.

She had taken up smoking again with a reckless and renewed fervour, even getting up in the early hours to pace the flat and puff furiously or lighting up while still in bed so that the bedclothes stank of smoke. In the mornings, when she woke contorted and bound up in sweaty sheets, she coughed as if her innards were going to come out. Still, none of this was any business of Assunta's.

'Nothing at all,' she said.

'But, signora, you never smoke in the house,' Assunta said.

Sometimes Chiara played with the notion that Assunta was not who she seemed but was really the novelist Elsa Morante. She imagined that Assunta, once around the corner away from the house, would slip off her crimplene jacket and put on a pair of horn-rimmed spectacles. Like Morante, Assunta had the same untamed bush of hair cut into a rough page-boy, the same wide cheekbones and the same knowing expression. Assunta's imperious air was at odds with her status.

Simone couldn't see it. She called Assunta 'Mamma Roma' and said she was a woman of the people. But because sometimes Chiara thought that Assunta might indeed really be Morante on an undercover assignment, researching her new book, or on her uppers and without other more marketable skills, she was particularly careful not to treat her with undue deference.

'I do sometimes,' she said. 'If I feel like it.'

She busied herself at the stove and started to cough. The raucous, phlegmy seizure took her by surprise. This time she couldn't stop. She stood hawking and croaking, grasping at the work surface for support. Tears streamed down her face as she retched and choked. Assunta started whacking her on the back, but it wasn't an obstruction that could be easily cleared. Then Assunta pushed a chair into the back of Chiara's knees and she flopped down onto it, bent double, made a last gravelly scraping noise and sat back up, tentatively.

'Signora Ravello,' Assunta said. 'This won't do.'

'I know,' Chiara said.

She took herself off to the doctor, leaving Assunta with a phonetic transcription of a message to enunciate if a non-Italian speaker should phone. 'Signora is out. Call after midday.'

Doctor Bruni had retired. His replacement was new, young and enthusiastic. He asked her about diet and sleeping patterns. He gave her some pills to help her relax but warned her they didn't mix with alcohol. He tapped her chest and lifted her shirt to thump her on the back and listen to her lungs. Then he said, with utter compelling gravity and in words she didn't like to contemplate fully, that she really must stop smoking, that the other things would pass, and that there was nothing else wrong with her. That it sounded as though the damage to her lungs was not irremediable. He could detect no signs of emphysema. She was a bit underweight, but that was probably to do with her metabolism and not a cause for worry.

No more half-measures, she decided on the way home. She would quit immediately. It would give her something to think about, other than the girl. She smoked her very last cigarette with her cappuccino at Gianni's bar, sitting outside in the sunshine. The chef from the restaurant on the corner was standing in the alley diagonally opposite her, smoking. He nodded across before grinding out the cigarette end beneath his heel and disappearing back inside. She was going to have to forgo more than the actual cigarettes, she saw. It was the whole community of smokers. Those companiable pauses between tasks.

Oh Antonio, she thought with a pang. Their mid-morning outings to the café near Ponte Sisto. How could those continue without the cigarettes? For a moment, the sensation of loss she felt was as intense as if giving up smoking meant giving up all savour and delight and friendship.

She hadn't smoked that cigarette with sufficient ceremony, she realised. She ordered an espresso and a vin santo, waiting until Gianni brought them out before lighting up once more.

'This is my last cigarette ever,' she told him.

'Then I will join you if I may,' he said.

He snapped his fingers, told the boy to bring him a coffee and settled into the chair beside Chiara. The waiter from the restaurant on the corner appeared with a watering can and doused the little bay trees that were lined up outside in pots. Their dark green leaves shone as if they had been polished.

Chiara was trying to endow the cigarette with significance, to smoke it in a weighty and contemplative way.

'Do you know what the doctor said to me?' she said.

'No, what?'

'Smoke or live, your choice.'

'Oh dear,' Gianni said. 'That is hard. They do say it's very bad for you, this smoking business.' He blew smoke out in rings that curled up between them. 'But I've always found it a great comfort.'

'Me too,' Chiara said.

109

Across the way, a tabby cat emerged from the alley and lapped at the pools of spilt water around the plant pots.

When Gianni's had reopened after the war, she used to bring Daniele for a *frullata* here. She recalled his legs dangling when he sat on the stool at the bar.

'Do you remember Daniele?' she said and turned to see Gianni's face change, his jaw set.

'I'd rather not,' he said.

What had she been thinking?

For your sake, signora, I won't prosecute, Gianni had said.

'Sorry,' she said.

She handed Gianni the half-full packet of cigarettes to distribute as he saw fit. 'Good luck,' he said.

On the way home Chiara made a deal. If I keep off the fags, then, on the third day from now, the girl will ring again. If she doesn't, then it wasn't meant to be, and I will resume my life.

If the girl rang, she would allow herself one conversation with Daniele's daughter. Just one.

Assunta had all the windows and doors propped open and was scrubbing the kitchen floor with some lemony-scented product. She had stripped and changed the bed. The washing machine was juddering away in the bathroom, and there was a soapy, sudsy smell. No one had rung.

Chiara told Simone she was sick, needed solitude and would telephone her when she was recovered. For the next three days, she wandered around her home as if she were a ghost haunting its corners. She worried and fretted over where Daniele's belongings might be, but this led to no useful or constructive form of action. The lack of cigarettes was a hole into which her life was falling. Everything was loss. There was a denuded feeling to the apartment, she noticed as she paced its confines, pushing her way to its very boundaries, plunging

110

into her dressing room and parting the clothes hanging there to stare at the blankness of the white wall beyond. She tunnelled right to the back of the junk room, clambering under and through the legs of a folded-down, gate-leg table and then scrambling back out, fearful that the phone would ring and she wouldn't get to it in time.

She had the sensation that the empty space where Daniele's possessions should have been was spreading outwards. It was a sort of existential emptiness and therefore unchecked by the abundance of solid things in the flat – the mass of both inherited and acquired furniture, the objets d'art, the glass collection, the paintings and the books, the draperies, wall hangings, shelves, mirrors, clothes and cloth, the knick-knacks. Concentrating on her work was unthinkable. She couldn't even read a book.

She patrolled the apartment or lay listlessly on the sofa, listening to the radio turned low. There had been an attack on the Rome office of the Italian Social Movement, the new fascist party. In Milan a grenade thrown at the police headquarters had killed four people and injured forty. There were suggestions of secret service involvement and complicated double bluffs.

She was lying there one time, staring vacantly at the piece of green chenille that covered the side-table the radio stood on, when she noticed, as if for the first time, that the little low table was in fact a box. The sight of it shook her. She didn't need to lift off the heavy radio and remove the chenille to know that this was her old strongbox, where she used to keep the jewellery she had inherited from Nonna. She didn't need to, but she did it anyway, whipping the cloth away as if to catch the box unawares the way it had caught her, squatting there for who knows how long, posing as something it wasn't.

111

'I'm in trouble, Ma,' Daniele had said.

Ma. He'd picked it up from some American film. He owed money. Such a lot of money. A mountain of promissory notes.

'If I don't pay today,' he said, 'the notes will be sold on and the next debtors won't be . . . ' He looked blankly at her, swallowed. 'So understanding.' He was quoting someone.

'I could sell the furniture,' she said, casting about.

'Nobody wants this kind of thing any more,' he said. 'All these knobbly, heavy wooden things. It's the 1960s. Haven't you noticed? People are ripping this stuff out and throwing it away. It's junk.'

He was right. Formica was all the rage.

'Wait a minute,' she said. 'I know what to do.'

She fetched the little key from the kitchen jar and ran to her bedroom where she kept the strongbox under her bed. It contained the string of pearls; the gold and pearl earrings like gold leaves that sat on the lobe with a pearl, like a dewdrop, in the centre; the diamond and sapphire brooch; the amethyst tiepin that must have been her *nonno*'s and probably wasn't worth anything much; Nonna's rings – her wedding ring (she must have donated some other less precious one when Mussolini called for Gold for the Fatherland in 1935); and her eternity ring set with tiny diamonds. The rings were too big for Chiara's fingers, but she had kept them because one day Daniele might marry, and she would pass these on to his wife, but that didn't matter now because the present need was greater.

He called 'Ma' after her, 'Wait, Ma,' but he didn't follow her.

She was thinking, this would have to be it, everyone was always telling her to stop bailing him out, and this would be the very last time, truly the last time, and he would have to

112

mend his ways. She had already given him her father's precious gold ring, but it had disappeared from his finger.

She dragged out the strongbox. It was empty except for a scrap of paper, saying, 'Ma, IOU.'

He was sitting with his head in his hands when she returned to the salon. For once, she could think of nothing to say. She did not fill the silence.

'Have you got anything else?' he said.

'You've had everything,' she said.

He told her he was done for.

And here was the strongbox under her nose all the time. Still empty.

At night she took the sleeping pills and dropped into black unconsciousness. It wasn't sleep as such, but sleep's deformed sibling.

By the third day Daniele's daughter and cigarette abstinence had become inextricably entwined. Chiara was gasping for a phone call.

'Signora Ravello,' the girl said in her tentative, weepy way. 'I hope you don't mind me calling you again.'

And Chiara, instead of delight or vindication, felt a sweeping irritation. A little voice like an insect near her ear pointed out that this might be to do with the nicotine craving, but she swatted it away.

'Yes?' she said as if she were a very busy person who could hardly spare a moment, instead of someone who had been waiting for this call for days and who had put the rest of her life entirely on hold.

'I'm sorry to bother you,' the girl said. 'I know you were only his landlady, but,' she dropped her voice, 'Daniele Levi really was my father.'

Chiara allowed herself again to be thus relegated. She had no intention of telling the girl the sad history. She wanted only to hear his name and to speak it again herself. To have news of Daniele, even if it was third-hand and superseded. But she needed a cigarette to accompany the conversation. She felt as though she couldn't do it alone.

She made an effort to concentrate on this unknown girl in faraway Wales, whispering stories of things that had happened before her own birth but under Chiara's nose, that she knew about and Chiara didn't. The girl was explaining how Daniele had come to meet her mother, and Chiara was thinking, I remember that dreadful winter, Rome covered in snow and ice. And then after the thaw, Daniele was always zooming off on that motorbike he used to borrow. She knew he went too fast on the bends.

'Drive carefully,' she used to say.

'Super careful,' he would say.

Sometimes before he left, he would pick her up and spin her round. Had she glimpsed him with the blonde girl, zooming down Via dei Cappellari on the bike? Oh, that was the summer he had been sweet again. Yes.

'Pardon?' she said, tuning back in to the girl.

Although it was daytime and light outside, the girl's subdued tone gave a nocturnal, furtive feeling to the conversation, so that Chiara pictured her huddled in a darkened room.

'Do you mind if I ask you a few questions?' the girl asked.

'Wait a tiny moment.' Chiara went and fetched herself a stool from the kitchen so that she could sit down to listen. 'Go ahead, Maria,' she said, thinking what a most Christian name for Daniele's child.

'Was he handsome? My mum said he was,' the girl said.

He was beautiful. He could be ugly.

114

'Yes, I suppose he was,' Chiara said, 'quite handsome. And fair-haired, which is much admired here.'

'I'm fair,' the girl said excitedly. 'What work did he do? How did he earn his living? Do you know?'

Chiara cast about. Theft. Extortion. Delivery boy for criminals. Dealing. Or worse. But that summer, the summer of 1956, he had acquired a little car and he had done some deliveries for contractors. That's what he said. She hadn't enquired too closely. It seemed at the time to be gainful employment and almost honest.

'He had a driving job,' she said carefully. 'And he was studying at the university.' He was enrolled at least. He might have gone to a lecture for all Chiara knew. 'Philosophy,' she added.

'Philosophy,' Maria breathed, as if entranced. 'Why did you,' she paused, audibly swallowed, 'why did you write that it wasn't known if he was dead or alive?'

'Because I hadn't heard from him.'

'But would you have expected to?' A pause. 'He wouldn't necessarily keep in touch with his ex-landlady, would he?'

Chiara tried to think. Caution was needed.

'He left some of his belongings here. He was going to come and collect them, but he didn't return,' she said.

'His things,' the girl exclaimed excitedly. 'What sort of things? Is there anything you could send me?'

'I am sorry,' Chiara said. 'This was many years ago. I couldn't keep them all.'

With that, a sudden vision of the loft space above the junk room opened as if it had been hammered shut in her own head. She saw the workmen fitting the boards across the struts and Simone supervising the lifting of the crates.

'No, no. Of course not,' the girl said. She was trying not to cry again. 'Oh God,' she said and the line went dead.

Chiara looked at the receiver and then replaced it. That was a strange and unsatisfactory conclusion. She had promised herself more. It was like the first of her ultimate cigarettes. It didn't count.

She stayed where she was, thinking the girl would phone back any minute.

She gazed at the photo of her parents. Antonella and Alfonso in 1907. Neither of them smiling. Antonella appeared childlike. Coils of thick black hair down to her waist. She was wearing a short lace headdress more like a mantilla than a bridal veil, pinned in place with flowers.

'I took her with nothing,' her father liked to joke. 'Just the clothes she stood up in, her blessed parasol, and a trunkful of prejudices.'

As Chiara stared at the photograph, she spotted something she had never noticed before. She lifted the picture off the wall to examine it more closely. Her mother held a posy of the same flowers as were in her hair, dark roses encircled by clouds of tiny white flowers, and the second finger of the hand that held the posy was unmistakably crossed on top of the forefinger. She pondered that. Her mother, on her wedding day, had her fingers crossed.

She rehung the photograph and sat back down on the stool. The telephone rang.

'I'm sorry to bother you again, Signora Ravello,' the girl said.

'It is not a problem,' Chiara said.

'I didn't mean to be rude but I heard my mum come in. I couldn't talk with *her* in the house.'

There was a sneer in the way the girl referred to her mother. 'Does your mother know that you telephone me in Italy?'

'No,' the girl said.

116

'You were born in 1957?' Chiara said.

'Yes,' the girl said, expectantly.

'I don't know how it was in those times in England, or in Wales. It might not have been as, how do you say, restrictive, no, more than that, suffocating, yes, as in Italy, because here, you know, we have the Catholic Church. But an unmarried girl who became pregnant. My God, you cannot imagine the shame. The terrible shame.'

The girl didn't say anything.

'The pressure,' Chiara said.

'Pressure?' Maria said.

'They would send you away. Hide you in a convent. They would make you have the baby adopted. You were not fit, you see. Not fit to raise a child.'

'Oh, I don't think it was like that here,' the girl said.

'Ask your mother,' Chiara said. 'Ask if she had to fight to keep you.'

Silence again.

'Danicle liked jazz music,' Chiara said. 'He used to listen to West Coast American jazz. The trumpet was his favourite instrument. Miles Davis, Chet Baker, Dizzy Gillespie. He had some records, and I used to allow him to play them on my gramophone player in the evening.'

He had taken her in his arms, high as a kite and stinking of whisky. 'Come on, Ma, come and dance with me,' and they had stumbled around the salon, banging into the furniture.

'I know those records,' the girl said. 'My mum has some of them.'

'I can't tell you anything else,' Chiara said. 'I didn't know him very well.'

She wondered whether that was true. It must be, or she would know where he was now, *if* he was now.

117

'If you were looking for him, what would you do? How would you go about it?'

'I would renounce.'

'Pardon?'

'Renounce.'

'Give up?'

'Yes.'

'Oh,' Maria said in a little defeated voice. 'You think he is dead, don't you?'

There was a silence in which Chiara listened to the girl breathing and resisted saying more. She was struck by her own hypocrisy. Renounce, indeed. She was good at handing out the advice but not so good at listening to it herself. She who had never given up.

'I'm so sorry,' she said. 'I have to go back to work now. So I will say goodbye.'

'Goodbye, signora,' Maria said.

As she walked to Gianni's, Chiara congratulated herself on having held the girl at arm's length. There was a sense of relief. She knew there would be a sort of grief later, but it would probably be an entirely manageable sadness like when your neighbour's dog went missing, or the government fell.

Something still nagged at her, though. It was to do with the name, Levi. That Daniele had told the girl's mother his birth name.

She sat at the window with her cappuccino and the paper.

'Still off the fags?' Gianni said.

'Yes,' Chiara replied and instantly wanted to run to the tobacconist and buy a packet. 'Three days,' she said.

'I am impressed,' Gianni said.

She could have drawn the child, who was at a very vulnerable moment, into a circle of pain, but she hadn't. She

118

would have liked a photograph, but it was better this way. Maria had an image to store away of Daniele, the music lover, the handsome one. Chiara herself had the knowledge that Daniele had fathered a child and that, out there, completely divorced from her and not in need of her contribution, he lived on, through Maria.

Chiara felt much better after a few days of not smoking. She was learning moderation at last, she reflected. Everything was slotting into place. She would be able now to resume her life and maybe even to add something new. Not tango. A socially useful voluntary activity. She would steer clear of politics, though. She could emulate Simone and teach adult literacy classes.

Of course Simone had the advantage of not having to earn a living any more and so had more time, and Simone, anyway, would say that every act was political. Whatever, the feeling of spaciousness was beginning to return in which she could make choices about how she spent her non-working time.

Gianni was wiping down the tables.

'Lovely day, isn't it?' Chiara said.

Gianni looked around. 'What's got into you?' he said.

'I don't know really,' she said. 'But everything feels rather hopeful again.'

'Does it?' he said, pointing to the paper where there was a picture of a barricade of burning cars on Via Merulana.

She went on to the pontifical library, worked with great efficiency and speed on the page proofs and completed them in three hours. The post office was closed because the postal workers were on strike in solidarity with the car manufacturer unions in Turin, and so she caught a bus out to the publishers and delivered the proofs by hand.

She was sitting in her editor's office when a colleague of his popped in and she was introduced. His translator had been taken ill, leaving him with an unfinished manuscript.

'I'm free,' she said, 'and available.'

The man looked at her dubiously. It was a new translation of Keats's letters.

'I'm a Keats specialist,' she said.

It was her dream job. One door closes and another one opens, she thought as she set off home with the parcel in her bag.

'You're back in the land of the living then?' Simone said when she called.

'Yes, I am,' Chiara said.

'Good, because it is so much duller when you're not around,' Simone said. 'Can you come for dinner on Saturday? Umberto the third is cooking.'

'Who is Umberto the third?'

'You have been out of action for so long. He is my new cleaner. He's from the Philippines and he's a wonderful cook. He can do all sorts, actually. He's going to do something with fish and spices.'

'Can I bring my nephew?' Chiara said.

He had come to Rome from Calabria to study architecture at the university. She was supposed to be casting an occasional eye on his activities.

'You know, my cousin's son, Beppe?'

'Not your fascist cousin?'

'Ex-fascist. He put away the riding crop and the fez a few years ago now.'

'Is he good company?'

'I don't know yet. I've only just made his acquaintance. But he's very decorative.'

'Bring him then. Of course. But what about your secret lover?'

'Oh, he left,' Chiara said. 'I sent him packing, I mean.'

'Did he get too uppity?'

'Something like that.'

'I often think,' Simone mused, 'that men are like spices. They need to be crushed to get the full flavour.'

'I haven't had a cigarette in a week,' Chiara said.

'That's what the purdah has been about!' Simone was unimpressed. 'I don't see how you can be so addicted when you didn't even take up smoking until you were about forty.'

'That's still over twenty years.'

'Goodness,' Simone said, 'and you but a slip of a girl. How can that be possible?'

Chiara laughed. 'I am rather proud of myself,' she said.

To have emerged from whatever this test had been, relatively unscathed, was nothing short of amazing. She, who never got away with anything. She felt her dissipated and squandered life forces coming back to her, reassembling in the home that was her self.

The girl was in a terrible state, crying and snuffling at the other end of the line. It was difficult to make out what she was saying.

'What's the matter?' Chiara said.

She should have said, Why on earth are you calling? This has nothing to do with me, whatever it is. Haven't I made that clear?

But the girl was so upset. An awful row, she was saying, with her mother and *him*, her so-called father.

As the girl wailed and sobbed down the phone, Chiara realised that any clarification there might have been had taken place only inside her own head. But it had never occurred to her that the girl might want to continue the connection with someone she thought of as Daniele's erstwhile landlady. The poor creature. She was so upset. Chiara would have to say something quite pointed and no-nonsense to make her understand that such calls were not welcome.

'They've found out,' the girl said.

The telephone bill had arrived, and her family had discovered she had been making these calls to Italy and at peak time, which made it worse. It was going to cost a fortune.

'Oh dear,' Chiara heard herself saying. She would hear out the girl's woes first and then she would tell her.

And Maria hadn't sat her exams, important, public exams. Her parents had discovered that too.

Chiara didn't need to ask why not. She knew all about the protests of the powerless, the slapping-yourself-in-the-face kind of protest. But that couldn't be helped. She must not get involved. She steeled herself.

'I'm sorry, Maria,' she began but faltered. She was going to have to find the right words to push this child away. Daniele's daughter.

'Can I come and stay with you?' the girl said.

'What?' Chiara said.

She felt the blood drain from her face. She reached for something, anything, to stop the girl right there, but no words suggested themselves. Nothing had prepared her for such a proposal. Her brain was clogged. The girl had lost all sense of proportion. She was ranting. Come all the way to Italy to stay with a virtual stranger! As if her parents would even let her.

'Of course you can't,' Chiara managed to say, eventually.

But the girl was telling her that her mother had agreed, if she worked hard and sat the rest of her exams, to pay her fare.

Her mother had even telephoned an old friend who lived in Rome, but she didn't have room to put Maria up, she had a houseful. And then Maria had thought of Signora Ravello and if her father had lodged there, then perhaps she could too.

Chiara shook her head to clear it and something whirred. She steadied herself against the door jamb. She was like a little planet spinning out of orbit, pulled by strong magnetic forces.

'We don't even know each other,' she said. 'Not really. We're strangers.'

Maria was undaunted. She had stopped crying and was pressing her case. It was as if she knew that, whatever Chiara might say, she did not feel entirely entitled to turn down her preposterous request.

'Please,' Maria said. 'Just for the summer. I wouldn't get in your way. I could learn Italian properly. I've been teaching myself. I could help you with your translations.'

Chiara's defences were imperfectly erected. There was a hidden tunnel that she had neglected to barricade because nobody ever used it any more and somehow Maria had known to come that way. The girl needed her. Daniele's child was asking for her help.

'We could have a trial period,' Maria said. 'Two weeks. And if it worked, I could stay for the summer, and if it didn't, you could send me back.'

Those were the words that clinched it. *Send me back.* Chiara thought of all the times she had wished she could send Daniele back.

'A fortnight's trial?' she said.

'Yes. Thank you. Thank you. Thank you. Will you speak to my mother?' the girl said.

Chiara found herself assuring Maria's mother that it would not be inconvenient at all, that she needed some help with her translation work and that she would set out terms and conditions in a formal letter. She wrote the letter quickly before she had time to reflect. It would be a month before the girl came because she had to sit the remaining exams first.

A month was a long time. The girl might change her mind. Or Chiara might find a way of calling off the whole venture. All sorts of things might happen. There were a hundred let-out clauses. Anyway it was only for a fortnight. She wasn't going to think about it. She was going to put it out of her mind. It was a whole month away.

SEVEN

The wine has gone to Chiara's head. She gets groggily to her feet and gazes over the slumped shapes of the dozing passengers through the window to the platform beyond. She strains to believe that the child is in a safe place. Knowing no different, she might as well believe it. By some mysterious process, he has been spirited away. And she was never in a position to take him on in the first place. Not really. Not with Cecilia.

A train thunders by at high speed, setting the lamp swinging, which makes the shadows in the room elongate and then ping back. She wraps herself in her blanket and lies down on her side, her legs bent and her feet resting against someone's suitcase in the aisle. She faces into the dim underworld beneath the bench where stockinged and trousered legs, a dangling shoeless foot, stacked cases, rolled-up coats and the occasional body, stretched out or curled up on the floor, form a composite pattern. There are puddles of relative light between larger blocks of dark.

She becomes aware of a faint rise and fall somewhere to the right, a subtle movement in her peripheral vision. The blanket is scratchy against her cheek as she tilts her head to peer at an area of particular density, there under the bench, a place

125

where the darkness itself is not static. She discerns a paler patch within, which slowly forms itself into a small face. She gasps, sucks in air through her mouth in little bursts like sobs and holds the breath in, her heart flapping like a landed fish. Once she recognises the face, she is able to configure the rest of the dark patch into the form of the child. Now that she can feel as much as see the gleam of his eyes and know they are wide open, she realises that he is lying as still as a small, restless boy can. He is less than a metre away, flat on his stomach, his hair grazing the underside of the bench.

She lets out her pent-up breath. 'Clever boy,' she whispers.

It must have been in the moment when Cecilia first started to moan, when Chiara turned away to face the soldier, that he scuttled or rolled under there. Cecilia's fit was timed perfectly to cover the boy's vanishing act.

'You can come out now,' she says.

He does not respond. She can hear his breathing. It is fast and shallow.

'They've gone,' she whispers, 'you can come out.'

He neither moves nor speaks.

It wasn't only the soldiers that he was trying to escape from.

With this realisation comes a profound sadness. It cuts a channel between all her previous pools of sadness so that they flow into each other and she is cast adrift in their chilly, swirling waters. Lying at the feet of her bovine, dependent sister, an arm's length from the child who has no friend in the world but her and yet rejects her, she feels again the chill in the middle of her spine and is certain that it is spreading outwards to claim her entirely. If she reached out a hand to the boy, he would not take it. If she woke her sister and asked for under-standing, she would not get it. Each of them will drown in their own separate pool, and there is nothing she can do.

126

She turns over to face the wall and pulls the blanket over her head. But instead of the cold comfort of hopelessness, what floats into her mind is a phrase from the book she has been reading, a tattered old copy of Keats's letters that she covered with brown paper in case reading in English were deemed subversive by the authorities in this part of Italy.

I am in that temper that if I were under water I would scarcely kick to come to the top.

The words so exactly express her sentiment that the feeling itself seems to her like a bubble in the water, and it immediately pops. Somehow, despite herself, she is already kicking back up.

He's only a little boy, she thinks. A lost little boy. There are people who are not at all fit or ready to be parents and yet they manage. She has to be more able than that. She thinks of her own useless mother and has a momentary vision of her leaning against a door jamb, wailing like a spoilt child. She has to be better than that. She thinks of all the children with deformities or maladies, and here he is, a child of staggering perfection, a boy healthy and, until now, cared for and loved. All she has to do is accommodate his grief. She's good at grief, surely. She has had enough practice.

As she wriggles round in the dark and struggles in the cramped space to get herself into a kneeling position, she pictures, as if above the surface of her pool of sadness, the lambent blue sky, bordered by the purple, wavering outline of the hills around her *nonna*'s house. She thinks again of their multi-coloured layers and of how she thought of them as a thing to bind them, she and the boy and Cecilia. On top of the vivid green of the grass in the fields are the dots of moving crimson that are the crests of the chickens as they roam and peck, and the shining scarlet berries in the rose bushes that Nonna makes into a kind of tisane. That is where they are going. To a place where the country air, the freedom from the city, from rubble and deprivation, will give them all a chance to wait out the war, to find their pocket of peace.

She fetches out the other cover from her sister's suitcase and shuffles backwards into the aisle. She tidies and arranges the sleeping area she has vacated. Then she presses out a space for herself, with her feet in among the bags and bundles in the aisle, and she backs into it, curling between them, wrapped in the last cover. She whispers to the boy under the bench, talking now to the top of his head. She tells him that if he wriggles his way out, he will find a little bed made for him at Cecilia's feet and that he will get cold if he stays where he is.

He doesn't move.

She says his mother would not want him to catch cold and then waits quietly for whatever the next thing is. Still nothing happens, and the whole room of people sigh and breathe and mumble around her. The face of the boy's mother standing on the back of the lorry comes to her. Instead of meeting Signora Levi's implacable gaze, Chiara imagines, quite simply, closing her own eyes and waiting for the moment to pass.

'Oh,' she says aloud as a torrent of possible other outcomes tumbles through her mind.

Then, as if the silent child could hear her treacherous thoughts, and because she will neither be party to his pact of silence, nor abashed by it, she starts to talk.

'Once, when I was little, probably about your age,' she whispers, 'I went with my father on the train. No, I must have been a bit older. I was nine, because Cecilia was eleven. She's two years older than me, but you wouldn't think so, because she is smaller and her face is so smooth, but that is how it is

128

with adults. Some of them stop growing before others, and some of them have sweeter faces.'

She shakes off a monstrous image of Cecilia with her eyes rolling back in her head.

'She kept having fits, like she did today, one after the other, and that summer she was in hospital.'

She pauses because she has never framed this memory before. It has always been a bright, stand-alone moment, and only now does she grasp that while she was revelling in the rare treat of their father's undivided attention, Cecilia was suffering. That was the price.

'So, it was just me and my *babbo,* and we had the whole carriage to ourselves. The sun was shining in, and the light through the train window was white like smoke.'

It doesn't seem like much of a story now she is telling it, but she has held it dear for so long. This image can appear as if a door slides open in her mind and there he is, her father, in a shaft of sunlight, dozing opposite her on the train. He is always there, behind that sliding door. Later on that same journey, when she can tell by a pink tower they pass that they are approaching their station, she will wake him by kissing his warm forehead, and he will open his eyes and say, 'Thank you,' and she will say, 'You are welcome,' and they will both laugh.

And at the station, instead of climbing straight onto the cart, they will go into the café where he will order a coffee, a double one to wake him up properly, and for her a strawberry ice cream, and she will say, 'What about Cecilia?' because she has never had an ice cream without Cecilia having one too.

And he will reply, 'I will buy her one when she's better.'

'And not me?' she will say.

And he will pat the end of her nose with his finger and say, 'Do you want one or not?'

And she will say, 'Yes, please.'

She doesn't know now, as she didn't know then, whether her father was thanking her for the kiss, or for waking him, or for watching over him while he slept, or perhaps for all three and something else beyond. But she knows she did watch over him. She stood in front of him, very close, and she picked up the hand that lay in his lap and stroked it. She straightened the ring on his little finger. She ran her fingers up and down the protruding veins on the back of his hand, pressing them softly, squashing them down and letting them plump out again. She examined the side of his face that was turned up to the sun. She looked at the creases around his mouth and the dark stubble just below his skin, waiting to spring forth like a miniature forest if not scythed back. It was as if she were a queen and he was in her power, belonging to her alone. She was regal and benevolent and inexpressibly tender.

'It was just me and my *babbo*,' she says, 'and we ate strawberry ice cream and we were happy.'

The child is wriggling his way out from under the bench. She can hear his panting breath. She heaves herself to her knees one more time, manoeuvres round and flips the blanket over his small, quivering form. At some point the lamp outside has been switched off, and it is too dark now to see him. Another phrase from her book comes to her, something about the comfort of allowing others to help you being 'like the albatross sleeping on its wings'. She hovers over him, picturing him not as an albatross but as a tiny bird, a linnet perhaps, a fledgling fallen from the nest.

Someone shakes her awake from a dream of underground caverns and unlit tunnels. She blinks at the weak morning light

130

as if it hurts her eyes. In her dream, she was a nocturnal creature. She could see in the dark. She sits up and immediately looks at the corner behind the bench. Neither Cecilia nor the boy is there. She puts a hand over her mouth as her flailing heart thumps.

'Don't worry,' a man's voice says, 'she is all right, your sister. She has gone with my wife to use the facilities.'

She recognises the gentleman who gave her the wine the night before. He looks crumpled and pale.

'There is quite a queue,' he says.

She pulls herself up. 'Where is the boy?' she asks.

'What boy?' the man says.

In her dream she was a bat, she remembers, and she slept hanging by her toes. She had a different perspective. She swings her head down now and peers under the bench, under all the benches, but the boy isn't there. When she swings her head back up, the man is still there, watching her.

'The train for Rome has come in,' he says, 'and it is leaving in ten minutes.'

She pulls herself to her feet. The population of the room has thinned. People are packing up and donning coats, coming in and going out again, and she sees that there is a train outside, waiting.

'Thank you,' she says, scanning the room one last time in case there's a cranny the boy has squeezed himself into, 'but we're not going to Rome.'

'Oh, we are and I thought you were too,' he says. 'I don't know why.' And then, watching her tug her boots on, 'That was a funny business last night, wasn't it?'

'I've got to . . . ' she says, picking up her small bag and slinging it over her shoulder.

'Don't worry, signorina. She will be fine with my wife. You

just take your time packing your things up and getting yourself ready. Your sister is in safe hands.'

'It's not that,' Chiara says. 'I, er, I need to go myself.'

'It was our son, you see,' he says, confiding.

'I'm sorry,' she says, clomping away from him without even lacing her boots.

She pushes the door open. Outside, the train's engine is hissing and chuffing. Smoke and steam puff out into the chilly air, and she can smell burning coal. The doors stand open, and a few people are already on board. She looks up the platform in one direction and eyes the noisy bundle of women and children queuing for the washroom. All the outlines are softened by the steam and the smoke, but she spies Cecilia and the old man's wife at the front of the queue. They disappear inside as she watches. She stares at each individual a micro-second, allows each face to imprint itself on her consciousness, and then moves on.

She looks in the other direction. At the water fountain, a youth is holding his finger over the tap to keep the water spurting, and another has his head beneath, getting thoroughly doused. He comes up for air and shakes his head, droplets of water flying off in all directions. Her gaze lingers on the two of them, although they are the wrong size.

At the far end of the platform, a man emerges from behind the furthermost building, doing up his belt and adjusting his coat as he walks. It's the man who made a fuss the previous night, and she feels a surge of ill-will towards him as if everything is his fault. She moves speedily towards and then past him, her boots flapping around her ankles, aware of him swinging up and into the train. A quick glance reveals that there is no one else in the area beyond the building from whence the man exited. The wet patches against the wall

132

between the bins, and the ammonia smell, show only that this has served as the men's urinal.

She hurries back down the platform. She has again the sensation of being watched, glances sideways, expecting to see the man again, looking out of the train, but there is no one at the window. She can hear her own breath labouring in and out of her body, as if the act of walking itself now requires a disproportionate expenditure of energy. Panic has her in its grip.

Two guards step out from an office door. They are different from the one the previous day. She can see behind them into the office. There is no sign of the soldiers. The troop train must have come and gone during the night. If she asks for assistance, will she raise the alarm? She dare not draw attention to herself.

The guards pause to confer, and Chiara drops to one knee behind them, using them as cover, as Cecilia and the lady come past on their return to the waiting room. She cannot afford to get held up with niceties now. She must find the child. Cecilia's arm is tucked into the other woman's, and her face is red as if her cheeks have been scrubbed. The other woman is trying to hurry Cecilia along. Cecilia doesn't like to be hurried.

Chiara quickly laces her boots and rises just as the guards set off in opposite directions, walking the length of the train and slamming the doors shut as they go. She stays where she is another second, the clanging of the doors, metal against metal, drumming through her body. She has to move now, act now, but do what, go where, she knows not. As she falters, door after door clangs shut.

She turns her head to the left and scans the people milling about on the platform again, to the right to do the same and then, suddenly, veers back to the left because there, at that empty window she passed earlier, didn't she see a little face disappear?

She starts to run down the platform, and at first it's like running in a dream, all effort and pumping of limbs but no forward propulsion, her feet sticky on the tarmac. Then she breaks through some invisible barrier and she is racing. Her body is in tune with itself, her strong, pliable, lightweight body that carries her about from dawn to dusk, day after day. She overtakes the guard, jumps on board at the next open door, thunders along the corridor and into the second carriage.

The boy is standing just within the door of the otherwise empty carriage. He flinches when she bursts in.

'This is the wrong train,' she shouts.

She takes in the dark hollows of his watchful eyes, a great smear of dirt down one side of his face, a matted clump of dusty cobwebs stuck to the sleeve of his coat, his hunched shoulders, his fists bunched and raised in front of him as if he is ready to land a punch. A feeble, little-boy punch. The ridiculous old-fashioned hat with the earmuffs is crammed on his head.

Don't rush him, she thinks. Don't shout.

She holds out her arms.

'Come with me,' she says.

From the front of the train, there is an unmistakable build-up of steam, the hiss–chug of the engine as if the train is clearing its throat, a sensation of gathering momentum.

'Please,' she says.

In a minute the whistle will blow. There is no time for reasoning and explanations. And, anyway, he is acting beyond the boundaries of reason. Stupefied, dumbstruck in his own no man's land.

She darts forward and grabs him. He squirms in her grasp, twists away so that his back is against her, and she holds him tightly as he silently wriggles and then, adjusting her clasp around his chest, she starts moving backwards. She tries to imagine herself as a fireman saving a small, mad person from a burning building.

'Sorry,' she says.

She is going to repeat her refrain about what his mother might have wanted him to do but as she drags him along the corridor, he starts banging his head against her chest, thumping his hard skull into her breastbone.

The carriage door is shut. She daren't let go of the child. Still he is straining to be free of her, although the head butting has stopped. She tries to push the handle down with her elbow but she doesn't have the strength, one-armed and battered and facing the wrong way. There is the clunk and chink of couplings moving apart and pulling out to capacity, and the train, with a lurch and a shriek, starts to move. She bellows for help.

'We're on the wrong train,' she shouts.

She cannot let this happen. She cannot be transported back to Rome and abandon Cecilia. Her breath is coming now in great gasping sobs, and boiling-hot tears spurt from her eyes, and she thinks, Let him go. Let him go before it's too late. Turn, open the door and leave now.

Then a man reaches past and over her and he's saying, 'Let me,' and 'Careful, signora, careful how you land,' and the door is flung wide open.

By the time it crashes against the side of the train, they are already airborne, she and the boy. Somehow he is with her still, his hand is in hers, and she clasps it. She has the impression of their unbuttoned coats streaming behind them like wings, of the ground falling away from them instead of rushing up to meet them, of their potential to soar upwards if they were so minded.

I will never let him go, she thinks.

They are inside a billowing, grey puff of smoke and they are flying. Then their feet hit the ground and they are forced to keep moving, in an ungainly canter. Somehow they manage not to fall. Their legs catch up with their bodies, until at last they slow down and then come to a halt. The train picks up speed and chugs out of the station, hooting and puffing as it goes.

They are cocooned still in the puffs of grey smoke. She drops to her knees, gathers the child's reluctant hands in hers. His face is glowing, and he is breathing hard. Now, quickly, while there is still the shine in his dark eyes from the flying leap and the running, she needs to say something clear and simple and true in words that a seven-year-old can understand.

'Listen,' she starts. 'I'm on your side.'

In the distance the train hoots twice.

'I'm only trying to look after you.'

These aren't the words that will do it. There is a thing he does with his eyes, a partial lowering of the lids, a hooding and dulling, and she wonders when he learnt it. Did he already have that trick in his repertoire or was it something he acquired yesterday, in her kitchen? Like a lizard. Does he even know that he is doing it?

'They are not in Rome,' she says, 'your family. The bad soldiers took them, didn't they? And your mamma gave you to me to look after, didn't she?'

She tugs at his hands.

'Did you hear me?' She yanks him, not harshly but so he will pay attention. 'Did you hear me?'

He nods.

'So for now, it's like I'm your mamma.'

As soon as they are said, she wishes the words unsaid. His head twitches. It's not what she meant to say at all.

136

'Not really,' she says, 'just pretend, so that the bad soldiers won't catch us.'

Words, she thinks, as a way of conveying meaning, are over-rated.

The smoke around them is dissipating. She drops one of his hands but keeps hold of the other, straightens, looks around and sees that they have hardly travelled at all. They are only a few metres beyond the last railway building, by the place where the men urinate.

She makes as if to walk down the platform, but he has planted his feet, his legs akimbo, refusing to budge. He is not looking at her but at their conjoined hands stretched between them. With his free hand he starts picking at her fingers, unfurling them one by one. She thinks of his mother, the day before, plucking his coiled fingers from her coat. Chiara stands there stupidly and watches him with the feeling that sense is slipping away. Each time he lifts a finger, she snaps it back, but he continues, dogged, starting over.

It is as if his hand were a small animal caught in a trap that he is trying to free.

Her hand springs open and she releases him. She turns away, her eyes momentarily blinded by tears. She tugs her coat sleeve down over her hand and uses it to wipe them away. Down the platform, she sees the elderly couple shuffle out of the waiting room carrying their suitcases, and Cecilia is between them.

'Oh, my Lord God,' she says.

She turns to the child again.

'I don't want to drag you and I don't want to carry you, but I will if I have to,' she says. 'You don't have to hold my hand but we have to run now. How about holding my scarf?' she says.

She whips it from around her neck and flicks the end towards him. He misses it but bends and picks it up.

'Come on,' she says and sets off charging down the platform again.

Perhaps it is the movement itself, something in physical exertion that activates him and overrides his stuck rootedness, because they are running along together once more and although she is half pulling him, his legs are going helter-skelter to keep up. Perhaps, like a puppy, he needs to be exercised daily. Both of them, she knows, would like to accelerate and hurtle away. They catch up with Cecilia and her companions just inside the door of the station entrance hall where the ticket office is.

'Here I am,' Chiara says, tapping the man on the shoulder.

He turns slowly and presents her with his long lugubrious face. His son, she thinks, suddenly grasping what he was wanting to tell her earlier. His son was an epileptic and he died.

Cecilia lets out a cry at the sight of Chiara, the lady starts making shushing 'There, there, dear' noises, and Chiara, without looking at the boy, tugs on the scarf and bundles him behind her.

'We were going to get them to make an announcement over the loudspeaker,' the man says. 'We didn't know where you'd got to.'

'I'm here now,' Chiara says. She can think of nothing to add. She has the child clutched behind her, and her mind is taut but empty.

'We've left your bags with a nice boy in the waiting room. We gave him a tip.'

'We couldn't leave her,' his wife says and she pats Cecilia's arm, still looped through hers. The high colour from earlier has drained from Cecilia's face.

Chiara knows she should apologise for causing the couple to miss their train, thank them for their kindness, but the man is now staring curiously at the child who, despite her one-armed effort to keep him tucked out of sight, is bobbing out from behind her. They seem to her more like busybodies than do-gooders. To be polite would invite further questions and intimacies. She doesn't know them. She can't trust them.

'You could have left her actually,' she says.

She is aware of talking over the top of the man. That he has asked, in a kindly manner, who this little chap might be. She summons a peremptory, dismissive tone.

'She would have been fine, just for a minute. She's not a child. She would have known I was coming back,' she says. 'Anyway, thank you. I'll take over now.'

'But she didn't know,' says the woman. 'She was crying for you.'

'You knew I was coming back, didn't you, darling?' Chiara says to her sister.

Cecilia blinks at her. She takes a moment.

'Yes,' she says at last, 'always and for ever,' quoting Chiara's own words, her eternal promise. She peels away from the woman and hooks her arm through Chiara's.

'Oh,' says the woman, suddenly bereft.

Her husband mutters something about checking the times of the next train. His wife seems to sag at his side. He clutches at her elbow and propels her towards the ticket office.

'Bye, then,' Chiara says.

They were just trying to be nice. They're not fascist spies. Just ordinary, beleaguered people, offering kindness and expecting a little in return.

'Thank you so much,' she calls after them, but it's too late.

'That horrible boy is following us,' Cecilia says as they collect their bags.

He is trailing behind them, holding the end of the scarf.

'He's not horrible. Why do you say that?'

'Tell him to go away.'

'No, dear. I will not.'

Cecilia turns to him. She flicks her hands at him as if he were a pigeon. 'Shoo,' she says. 'Go away. We don't want you.'

'We do!' Chiara says, looking around to see if anyone else has heard. 'Get it into your head, Cecilia. He's coming with us.'

'Dirty boy,' Cecilia says. 'Smelly.'

EIGHT

A double bass twanged a deep and reverberating note. The heroine's voice could be heard in the semi-darkness while the spotlight tried to locate her. It illuminated a pile of stones, a signpost warning of excavation work, a clump of pink-flowered weeds, their leaves laden with brick dust, before finding Clytemnestra, bare-armed, clad in purple. She finished her speech, gathered up her robes and scuttled behind a pillar.

Simone and Chiara were attending a spectacle among the ruins of the Theatre of Marcellus. The play was ostensibly an updating of the myth that, according to the leaflet, 'provided a provocative commentary on contemporary power games'.

Simone's enthusiasm for avant-garde happenings was boundless. Recently it had taken the two of them to Villa Celimontana on the night of a full moon for a masked ball, to Cinecittà to audition for parts in an epic about the twentieth century (Simone regularly worked as an extra in films and had had bigger roles in low-budget art-house pictures), and to a sit-in in Piazza Cavour to protest moves to change the labour laws. Their presence there had raised the average age considerably.

'Age doesn't matter,' Simone had proclaimed.

However, Chiara took the view that when you were obliged to sit on a camping stool in the gloaming on a coolish spring evening for nearly two hours, while urgent young people appeared from behind pillars or stumps of pillars to harangue you, it did.

Chiara thought they might slip away during the interval but before she could make the suggestion, Simone said, 'Brilliant, isn't it?' and then, 'Will you go and fetch our complimentary cups of wine? With your young legs?'

On the way to the wine table Chiara had to stop, put her hand to a pillar to feel its solidity, and take a moment. She was light-headed. The ground seemed to be sliding sideways as if presaging an earthquake, but no one else seemed to notice. She took a few deep breaths and carried on. When she returned, Simone was holding forth to the people next to her about the power of myth and declaring that the play offered a redefinition of democracy in the post-Vietnam era. Chiara pretended to read the programme.

She wanted to talk to Simone. To claim Simone's attention so that she could tell her about the girl coming. She didn't understand how she had let nearly three weeks go by without mentioning it.

A letter had arrived that morning. It was in her handbag. It confirmed the day and time of the girl's arrival and contained a photograph so that Chiara would recognise her. They had given her a shock: both the image – a blonde girl laughing in a garden, noticeably like him but much fairer and with blue eyes – and the imminence of her incursion into Chiara's life. She was coming in five days' time. It was too late to write, telling her not to come, that some urgent business was calling Chiara away from Rome. She would have to telephone instead to make an excuse. But she hadn't.

She got to her feet, casting about for something to distract her. Down that unlit path, strewn with tumbled sections of ancient Rome, lay the ghetto. Out of sight, around the corner but within a hundred metres of where they were gathered, was the very place where the Jews had been rounded up thirty years before. Daniele Levi, she thought.

Her head was a jangle. She made herself sit down again and sipped her vinegary wine.

The arches of the Theatre of Marcellus were softly lit from beneath, giving them the appearance of hollow eye sockets.

She pushed her mind backwards in time to before the war, before the massive excavation work that began in 1926 (to reunite fascist Rome with its imperial past in a direct glorious line; she could remember the martial music they played on the radio to accompany the announcement of a new piece of Rome being liberated). Back then she had been a child. The ground used to be much higher – the area where the performance took place would have been underground – and there were little shops and businesses in those arches. Behind the place where they were sitting, where the road now was, there used to be cramped tenements and narrow alleys, with a square that opened out in the middle. Piazza Montanara, it was called. That was where the peasants and small farmers brought their produce to sell from the back of carts.

She used to come with her *nonna*, who brought her own empty tubs and jars in her green cloth bag, getting them filled at a stall that sold walnut sauce and pickled walnuts, as well as a creamy, oozing cheese that smelt of wet grass. She might try making that walnut sauce. And then, as if it had been nestling inside, there came another memory: her father lifting her onto his shoulders and the feel of his dark coat that she held

143

bunched in her fists like rudimentary reins, and he her high horse.

The second half of the performance was even worse than the first. Chiara kept trying not to listen, to hang on to the remembered sensation of her chin resting in the felt crown of her father's hat. There was a nihilism at the core of the play that frightened her, as if these young people – who didn't remember the war, who weren't even born then, but who were fired up with the idea of overturning everything – might take them all back to that terrible time.

Afterwards they repaired to a trattoria up the road for a bowl of spaghetti carbonara. Their audience neighbours, a bunch of loud young people, came too, and there was no opportunity for a private word. Chiara sat miserably, not joining in with the conversation that got more lively and political the more red wine they imbibed. Her head ached. She hadn't slept properly for an age. Sleep occupied a room to which she was denied full access. All she could do was curl up in its antechamber like an old dog or a dutiful retainer, half in and half out. She had given up on the sleeping pills, blaming them for the sick, dizzy feeling that kept accosting her at unpredictable moments.

'Oh no,' Simone said, when Chiara whispered that she had a headache and was leaving. 'Don't go, my dear. We haven't had a chance to properly chat.'

Simone's eyelids were pink. She was quite tipsy. The wine had arrived a long time before the pasta.

'Sit back down, have a coffee – that's good for headaches. Let's order you one,' she said, waving her hand in the direction of the strings of multi-coloured chilli peppers dangling above the aperture to the kitchen.

The young man beside her was holding forth about the

post-war betrayal of the people's aspirations. 'The Red Brigade is a direct descendant of the partisan resistance,' he announced.

'Order a coffee, go on,' Simone said, followed by, 'No,' directed to the table at large. She couldn't resist rejoining the fray. 'It's completely different because the circumstances are not the same. The one cannot be used to justify the other. Of course I understand the pernicious role of the Catholic Church,' she was saying as Chiara slipped out of the door.

She was already in bed when the telephone rang. She swung her legs to the mat, felt with her toes under the bed for her slippers, shuffled her feet into them, padded down the hall to the phone.

'You left!' Simone said.

Chiara wearily agreed that she had.

'What a shame. I won't see you now for ages because I'm off to France to see my cousins.'

Chiara was silent, taking this in. Simone was going to be away.

'The Algerian clan are coming over, and the *grande dame sans merci* is hosting a gathering. I have been summoned,' Simone said. She was referring to her ancient, imperious and wealthy godmother.

'Oh,' was all Chiara managed. And then, 'How long for?'

'A week or so.'

'Oh,' Chiara said again.

There was a pause. 'Very interesting play, wasn't it? And what fascinating young people they were. So *engagés*.'

'*Mmh*,' Chiara said.

'Are you all right, my dear?'

'Just very tired.'

'You're not cross with me, are you?' Simone said.

And Chiara, who realised that she was, but unjustifiably so, said, 'No, I'm cross with myself.'

'Tell me.'

Chiara sighed. 'In a rash moment I agreed to put up this British girl for the summer.'

'What girl?'

'She's someone's daughter.'

'Well, we all are,' Simone pointed out.

'Someone I used to know.'

'At the institute?' Simone said.

Chiara made an assenting noise. It wasn't a downright lie, because Daniele did occasionally come into the institute. She remembered that, once, when he was sick and couldn't go to school, she had taken him into work with her, and he had lain under her desk on a cushion, sleeping. He was quite a big boy then. Eleven perhaps, but no one had even known he was there. His hot-looking face as he slept. The way his eyes were always open a slit, as if he could never completely relax.

'Yes, it was a chap at the institute. He wasn't there long. His daughter is in the UK now and wants to learn Italian, so they asked me whether I'd put her up.'

'But you don't want her to come.'

She could say it now. This girl is Daniele's daughter, she could say, and Simone would understand. 'Not really,' she said. 'That's the thing.'

'Why did you say yes?'

'I don't know,' she said. But, suddenly, she did.

'You're too accommodating. That's your problem,' Simone said. 'It's also what makes you so wonderful of course. Telephone these people and say you made a mistake and you don't have room. Which is pretty much true. You do live in a

146

one-bedroom flat, although I suppose you could use the salon, but you don't want her. And that's that. Just tell them. You don't owe them anything.'

She did owe them, Edna and Maria Kelly, she thought as she replaced the receiver. She remembered now exactly when it was that someone referred to him as Daniele Levi: 1960, the middle of Italy's economic miracle. March 1960, to be precise.

She is sitting in the salon, smoking, pretending to read the paper. The Christian Democrats have done a deal with the right wing. That is the front-page news. She reads the head-line repeatedly, but she doesn't care about the outside world. It can go hang, the outside world. Because in her own little world, she has struck a different deal and she is bereft. She has sent her boy away to a clinic. And he was incapable of under-standing that she did it for his own good and that he was going to die if he didn't stop and that it broke her heart. But he was right, she was a liar, and so, for perhaps the first time in their shared life, she had said nothing. Explained nothing.

'Don't come back until you are clean,' she told him, and he gave her such a look.

Oh, how will she ever recover from that look? As if he hated her. Simone says she has done the right thing. A brave and wonderful thing. That he will come back freed of his addic-tion and he will thank her.

But in this moment, sitting alone in her vast, empty apart-ment, she thinks she knows better. That he doesn't want to be saved. He never really did.

He has gone and he hates her.

The doorbell rings. She doesn't answer it. She cannot bear to speak to anyone.

It rings again and again. And in between the rings, she can hear, more faintly, the buzz and ping and bleep of other doorbells, like an echo. Someone is pressing the bell buttons of all the flats in the building.

She goes to the intercom. She needs to make this person go away.

'Yes,' she says.

'Is Daniele Levi there?' a woman's voice says.

Nobody calls him Levi.

She answers without thinking. 'No,' she says, 'no one of that name here.' And she sits down again, sinking into her torpor once more.

Days later, when she bumps into the upstairs neighbour, Signora Persighetti, on the stairs, she hears that she went down to talk to the distraught young woman at the door. There was a child with her, a small girl with blonde curly hair. Signora Persighetti said she looked like a little angel.

She was up ridiculously early. She would go to Gianni's for breakfast and then for a walk to clear her head. And then she would telephone the girl to explain that it would be better if she did not come. She would say she was sick. Again, it was not a downright lie. These dizzy incidents were increasing. Something was awry. She was at odds with herself.

In the square they were still setting up the market. Stalls were being erected, frames slotted and snapped into place. Vanloads of produce were being unloaded and people were shouting at and to each other. The flower seller that she always frequented, who had only a trestle table and not a complicated structure to assemble, was arranging her blooms. She had bucketloads of sweet peas, and to Chiara, who hadn't even had a coffee, their scent was sickly sweet.

She turned down Vicolo del Gallo and went into Gianni's bar. It was more than an hour before her usual time, and the clientele was different. Her table at the window was occupied. The only space to sit was in the internal room, where market traders were smoking and chatting. An open packet of Marlboro lay on the nearest table, a cigarette smouldering in the glass ashtray. The desire to snatch it up and suck the smoke into her lungs was strong. She spun on her heel and pushed her way back through the bustle of people. Gianni was caught up with the cluster around the bar, people drinking their coffees, calling for water, a biscuit, a *cornetto*, and did not notice her. Two old men drooping over the central table had grappa chasers. Chiara stepped out onto the street again with the sensation of not having left a trace.

Invisibility creeps up on you. It is impossible to pinpoint the moment of its onset. Older than you might imagine when you're young. A forty-year-old woman, for example, has a pull. Perhaps around the age of fifty, it begins. Chiara had thought herself immune. But recently there had been a fading. A feeling of being used up, a sort of creeping pointlessness indefinably entwined with giving up smoking and with the dilemma of the girl. There was a time when she had practised passing unnoticed. Now she didn't even have to try.

She crossed Piazza Farnese, where the street cleaners had just finished, and the cobbles gleamed silver grey. A few young and not-so-young people leant or sat around the fountain. She scanned their faces, as she always did, even now, but she didn't recognise any of them.

She wandered down Via dei Giubbonari where the shops weren't yet open. She bought a newspaper from the kiosk at the corner of the main road and walked in the direction of the river. The bar near the Gramsci Institute was just opening. A young man had unfastened the metal shutters and was ratcheting them up with a sort of bent pole that he twisted and turned. It seemed a complicated and challenging task.

'Go on in, signora,' he panted, 'I will be with you shortly.'

Chiara ducked under the half-open shutter into the semi-darkness. She didn't usually frequent this bar but it had a quiet feel, and a kind of pleasant stuffiness, a closed-in, coffee-scented warmth that took in the tables and chairs, the glass-topped bar, the glasses hanging from racks above it, the bottles behind it, the curved till at its own wooden counter at the far end, and the shelves of cigarettes. Not the sharp, wake-up smell of fresh coffee but something more comfortable and homely. For the briefest of moments she was back in the downstairs room of the house in the mountains, Nonna laying out the cups on the table.

The boy outside, still wrestling with the shutters, made a sound. It was only a little grunt, but Chiara detected a different note. She hurried outside. He was leaning back at a difficult angle and seemed to be holding the whole weight of the shutter with the bent pole as if it were a fishing rod and his catch an impossibly heavy, giant fish.

'I've done it wrong,' he said.

She saw he really was only a boy. A plume of black hair, crisp white shirt with an apron over, dark fluff on his upper lip. He looked at her in desperation. He seemed too young to be working.

'What happens if you release it?' she said.

'It will smash,' he said in a strained voice, his eyes rolling at her in desperation.

She was examining the workings, something she'd never done before.

'It will crash and break and Signor Bellucci . . .' His voice

150

rose to a squeak. 'Bellucci will sack me,' he said. He made the sound again.

'Let it go,' Chiara said authoritatively.

He did so, leaping backwards out of harm's way for the catastrophe that would ensue, but the shutter rolled back on its runnels fairly quietly to the correct place and stopped.

'I think you have done it,' she said.

They went inside, and the boy took up position behind the bar.

'What can I get you, signora?' he asked.

As he switched on the espresso machine, wiped down the steam wands, slid the steel portafilter baskets out to check and then slotted them back in, he settled into himself, taking on a more confident air.

He was called Luca and he was fourteen years old. He was training to be a barman and he had worked there for two weeks. It was an exceptional thing to open up by himself – the boss had telephoned him at home very late the night before to say it was an emergency. Everyone was sick. They were depending on Luca. He had been early that morning to the boss's house where he had collected the key and been instructed in how to do the shutter, but he hadn't really understood. He couldn't connect what the boss had told him with the mechanics of the thing.

'You needed to be shown how to do it properly,' Chiara said. 'I think you've done very well.' She had the sudden sensation of being rather good at talking to young people.

'If signora would like to sit at a table.' He indicated the tables. 'At no extra charge.'

'I should think not,' she said, smiling to soften it.

She scanned the headlines. In America the committee investigating the Watergate scandal was continuing with its hearings, and they were being shown on television. Andreotti had been there, having dinner at the White House with Nixon and Frank Sinatra, a couple of months before. She had seen the photograph on the front page.

'Crooks and villains,' she said, as the boy placed a steaming cup on the table.

'Excuse me, signora?' he said.

'Politicians,' she said, 'and mafiosi.'

So much that was hidden. So many broken promises. The government had resigned now, and the Christian Democrats were trying to form a new coalition. Always cobbling deals together, they were. No one seemed to have a vision.

The cake delivery was at the door. 'Excuse me, signora,' the boy said again.

He and the delivery man unloaded trays of brioches, bread rolls, *medaglioni* and the thin sliced bread for making sandwiches. She thought about the strange unfathomable winds that blow people one way rather than the other and wondered whether or not it was a good thing for Luca to be training as a barman and what future there was in it.

'Would you like to have your own bar one day?' she asked after the cake man had left, as Luca was arranging the confectionery behind the glass counter.

He shook his head wonderingly. She saw that his imagination had not reached that far, and she had disconcerted him.

He got on with preparing the sandwiches. He said that soon there would be an influx of people on the way to work, and he needed to get them ready now because after that he would be too busy.

'There used to be a bar over there, on the other side of the road and down the street,' she said.

'In the ghetto,' the boy said without looking up from his work.

'Yes,' she said and lapsed into silence.

The face of a man came into her mind. In fact there were two men, but she only remembered one of them clearly. They had been leaning against the wall. Rather than seeming poised to spring, they looked more ready to saunter away or perhaps casually light a cigarette and smoke it languidly. The one she remembered had dark hair, was close shaven. Nowadays they depicted all German soldiers as blond and Aryan, but it wasn't so. He was lean and dark with an aquiline nose. It was true that they were mostly meatier than the Italians, but this one, you could have swapped him for one of the people being rounded up, and no one would have questioned it.

For a moment she allowed herself to imagine it. The tables turned. The persecutors stripped of their uniforms and weapons, and clothed instead in the patched-together out-fits of the ghetto inhabitants. The rabbi nudging them forward with the tip of his machine-gun onto the trucks. She had watched a woman with a bundle being stopped. They had bayoneted the bundle and its pathetic contents had spilt out onto the cobbles: her clothes, a Torah wrapped in a pinny.

'Was it that little one with the postbox outside?' He was mashing tuna with the back of a fork in a glass bowl.

'No. I'm talking about thirty years ago,' she said.

'But the bar with the postbox is very old,' Luca said. 'It must have been there for centuries. On one side it has a real post-box and on the other there is a slot in the wall where you can put money for the orphans.'

'Yes, Bar Toto.'

Daniele flashed into her mind. She saw his look of

153

concentration as he folded the note he had written to his mother into a tiny square and forced it through that slot.

'The one I'm talking about, it's not a bar any more,' she said. 'It's a sort of shop. A wholesaler selling electrical goods or something like that.'

She didn't know why she had mentioned Gennaro's bar. Poor, brave Gennaro. One bullet to the back of the head in March 1944.

Luca was waiting for her to say more. She made a show of looking at her watch. 'I must be off,' she said.

'Thank you for your help, signora,' he said.

'You're welcome,' she said.

She paused at the threshold and turned to look back at Luca. A faint undercurrent of the dizziness stirred in her head, and she kept one hand on the door handle. Luca was rinsing glasses now and setting them out upside down to drain on a white cloth he had draped over the counter. She was thinking again about how they used to post those notes to Daniele's mother, and at the same time about the letter she had sent to Maria's mother. She seemed to be waiting for a link between the two, a sort of bridge, to manifest itself.

Luca, aware that she hadn't quite left, looked up. 'Make sure you come back another time, signora,' he said.

'I have a girl from Wales coming to stay with me,' she announced.

'Wales?' he said.

'Yes, it's in Great Britain, next to England and Scotland and Ireland. And she's coming here to learn Italian. She's not much older than you.'

'You should bring her here,' he said. 'If you come between six and seven in the evening, we do snacks with the aperitifs. We have soft drinks too.'

'I will,' she promised. 'I'll bring her on Tuesday evening if she's not too tired.'

'I'll be here.' He grinned.

'It's a date,' she said.

The street was busy with traffic as commuters, buses and cars rumbled past. In between them she could see the entrance that led to Via del Portico d'Ottavia and the ghetto, but she turned her steps towards the river instead.

First, she would go to the Basilica of St Cecilia in Trastevere. On a clear-skied day like this one, the light flowing down through the high arched windows made the painted ceiling glow. The effect was uplifting. However, she didn't go only for that. Under the altar, there was a marble sculpture of the saint, said to be a true likeness done when the tomb was opened a thousand years after her martyrdom and she was found to be intact, the wounds on her neck still fresh. This statue of St Cecilia lying on her side – face turned down towards the earth, her feet bare, her arms in front, her dimpled hands with their ringless fingers softly curled – never failed to touch Chiara. She would go there and light a candle for her sister, and she would make make her peace with the decision to let Daniele's daughter come. Let it settle within her so there would be no more prevarications.

Then she would climb up the Janiculum hill, past the botanical gardens, all the way up to the top, to the monument to Anita Garibaldi. Of all the places that Daniele chose to leave notes for his mother, this was the one that they fixed on. Long ago and for many years, she and Daniele used to visit it religiously mid-afternoon on the first Friday of each month. Now, Chiara was going to go there and she was going to leave her lost boy a note. She would tell him that he had a daughter. It

155

was a ridiculous, pointless thing to do, but she didn't care. She was going to do it anyway. She checked in her handbag that she had a pen and her notepad.

Afterwards, after she had folded up her note and inserted it, the way they used to, in the hollow on the frieze at the back of the monument, she would catch a bus back home and prepare the apartment for the girl's arrival.

She quickened her pace. There was a lot to do.

NINE

Assunta laid her basket on the floor at the top of the stairs, put one hand out flat on the wall and the other on the small of her back. She paused long enough to catch her breath, examining the middle door of the three on the landing as if she hadn't seen it many times before.

The stone stairs always shocked her with their steepness. The smell of cooking wafted up the stairwell, a slowly simmering meat sauce. It was early in the day to be cooking meat sauce. The two doors to either side were identical, fine-grained, ancient wood panels with brass knobs and ornate lock fittings, while the one in the middle, although it filled the same-sized aperture and had a similar sort of handle, was made of a different wood. The patterns in the grain went in swirls, and in their contours, as Assunta had discovered on a previous occasion, it was possible to discern the backside of an elephant.

At some point in its history, Assunta was vague as to when – anyway, after the war, for sure, but before Assunta had begun working here seven years ago – Signora Ravello's apartment, the one Assunta was about to enter, had been divided in two, and the other part sold off. The elephant door was the entrance to the apartment made from the hived-off section and was of a more modern construction. Assunta liked to imagine, although she knew it was fanciful, that the wood came from Africa and that was why an elephant had left its imprint in the grain.

Abyssinia, perhaps, in that brief time when Italy had its empire. She almost seemed to recall an image of natives, tall and impossibly thin, armed with spears, guarding their forests against the Italian invaders. She might have seen it on a news-reel at the picture house. Maybe even Libya, because Signora Ravello's father had done business there and might possibly have imported timber. Or was Libya a desert?

Assunta's secret elephant reminded her every time she came to this stairwell that we are all God's creatures, and the world is a weird and wonderful creation of His devising. So she would take a moment here as she caught her breath to reflect on this truth.

Assunta's duties were normally confined to ironing blouses and bedlinen, sweeping and washing the tiled floors, and cleaning the bathroom (Tuesdays) and the kitchen (Thursdays). She had come in today on a Saturday, at Signora Ravello's special and urgent request, to make the apartment ready for the arrival of the foreign girl who was coming to stay.

She imagined Signora Ravello would have left a note for her as to what she wanted doing. If not, she intended to wipe down all the skirting boards; brush the cat hairs off the uphol-stery; pull out the lighter pieces of furniture in the living room, or the salon as the signora liked to call it, and sweep behind; polish all of the furniture; and hang the rugs over the line and give them a good beating. There wasn't much more that could be done, given that the apartment contained twice the amount of furniture that it could comfortably fit, crammed to the rafters with all the old pieces inherited from its former, grander self.

At the end of the hallway that led nowhere there was even one piece of furniture piled on top of another, a foolishness that meant both items were effectively useless. The cabinet pinned the chest shut and the chest elevated the cabinet out of reach. Assunta shuddered to think what might be concealed therein. But it was no use pointing these things out to the signora. She would talk about heirlooms, and usefulness not being the only measure, whatever that meant. No, the only cleaning to be done in this apartment was very superficial. The mere idea of a spring-clean was preposterous.

She put her key in the lock but before she could turn it, the door was flung open and there was Signora Ravello, wearing old paint-spattered clothes and a plastic rain-hood. The moulting cat slid between her legs and out onto the landing where it hissed at Assunta's back.

'I thought we'd get more done if I pitched in,' she said in a bright, forceful way.

Assunta was of a mind to turn right round and go home. All of her other clients either kept out of her way or, at the very least, ignored her when she was working, treating her as if she were invisible. That was as it should be. Them getting on with their business, she getting on with hers. She had no idea why Signora Ravello thought herself the exception to this unspoken rule. She suspected that the signora's propensity to follow her round the apartment, giving advice or getting in the way, was something to do with her being a leftie, possibly even a communist. Certainly she left copies of the *Manifesto* newspaper lying around the house for Assunta to tidy away.

159

She wasn't having it. People trying to tell her how to do her job. It was probably her own fault for letting the signora get too familiar. She had even stayed for lunch with the signora on more than one occasion, but not any more. They weren't her sort, the signora and her funny old friend Madame Simone, who had introduced them in the first place. They were a couple of old biddies and it was about time they admitted it instead of racketing around the town at all hours.

Assunta remembered the words the signora had said as if they'd been branded with the hot iron on her own forehead.

'You have to dampen linen like that to get the creases out.'

That was it. Assunta had laundered and was ironing a mass of stiff cloth that the signora had found in the junk room. The signora had the notion that she was clearing things out and was going to sell them at the flea market. But, often enough, when Assunta came in on a Tuesday, another 'objet' – an ornate vase, a little painted cabinet, a glass paperweight – would have appeared, and Assunta would know that the signora had indeed been to the market at Porta Portese on Sunday but had bought rather than sold.

The cloth in question wasn't linen at all but ordinary calico cotton, which Signora Ravello's sister, who had been a dress-maker back in the day, probably intended to use for cutting out patterns or for children's school aprons, but which was not worth anyone's time or money to wash, peg out, bring in, press. The cloth, though, still smelt of naphthalene, which gave Assunta a sense of comfort and hope, as if her own old mother were somewhere near by, packing away the winter blankets in the box that went under the bed. The stains were ingrained, and the creases more so; it was all a waste of time, but hers was not to reason why.

She hadn't minded the signora's presence at all, because she was telling a tale about dresses her sister had made for the fat twin daughters of someone important, and Assunta had been thinking what an entertaining little personage the signora was, despite her heathen, socialist and bossy ways, and what a lively manner she had when telling a story, and how that was a sort of gift, a talent not to be buried.

She had been thinking too that there were women who did, and there were women who had things done, and that the signora, in some ways and in common with Assunta, fitted better into the former category – when, all of a sudden, the signora had come out with the comment about dampening the linen.

And then, before either of them had perhaps noticed this might be dangerous ground, the signora had tripped across to the sink, fetched some water in a tumbler and, dipping in her fingertips, started flicking it over the cloth on the board. And Assunta had felt her face redden and not, as the signora seemed at first to think (but was quickly put right), out of shame at not having adopted this method without prompting. There had been sharp words and harsh looks, and since then the signora had made herself scarce when Assunta came. She wouldn't call it a rift between them exactly, but it was a cold feeling that hadn't been there before. She didn't like it, but there it was.

Now here was the signora, in her bewildering headgear, twittering around Assunta as she hung up her coat, telling her how she'd been trying to clear some space for the girl, but that she seemed to have made more mess. Assunta didn't need telling; she could see piles of rubbish outside the doorways the length of the wide hallway. The cabinet on top of the trunk at the far end listed as if the signora had tried and failed to heave it from its perch.

Assunta took her rosary and her book of saints out of her bag and transferred them to her apron pocket.

'Let's see what's what,' she said.

'Oh, can I smell the coffee burning?' the signora said and clattered into the kitchen, leaving Assunta to carry out her tour of inspection alone.

'Holy Mary, Mother of God, pray for us sinners,' Assunta said when she saw the living room.

She fingered the rosary in her pocket and leant heavily against the door frame. She was reminded of the devastation her littlest grandsons caused when she allowed them to make dens at home. Assunta remembered hearing that there had been something not right in the signora's sister's head and wondered whether it was hereditary, whether the signora was now displaying the signs.

The pianola had been pulled out into the centre of the room, gathering and bunching the rug between its castors on its journey so that the rug welled up behind in a frozen, unwieldy wave. Behind it the pull-out bed that Assunta had only ever seen closed was a mass of springs in its crooked iron frame. On top and around the pianola, even wedged into the carpet's stiff folds, was debris from all corners of the room. Two semi-dismantled sewing machines; a dozen or so picture frames with woodworm, containing hideous old paintings in various stages of dilapidation; a variety of tin and wood trunks and chests filled with pieces of wire, electrical leads and bits of other electrical items; the brass ends of a single bed; a giant pouffe of rich green velvet that had lost most of its stuffing. Splinters of wood were heaped to one side, like kindling. It looked like a funeral pyre.

She stepped forward and leant over the pianola, which she had never seen out of its corner. The yellowing paper cartridge inside the apparatus emitted a chemical aroma of decay, like blackened bananas. She stepped quickly back to the doorway. Her impulse was to gather her belongings and leave. She wanted nothing to do with this, even if the signora was paying her double for coming in on a Saturday.

But something nagged at her and she was moved to pull out her book of saints and open it. She read slowly but she persevered. She read about St Nereus and St Achilleus, whose feast day it was, throwing away their shields, their armour and their blood-stained javelins. She didn't know how that helped, but it slowed her thoughts.

She looked again at the chaos. The signora must have attempted to wheel the pianola out from its awkward position behind the sofa in order to make room for the pull-down bed to be extended. In shifting the sofa, she had uncovered the stack of mouldering paintings and fat old books with smelly covers that had lain there undisturbed for who knows how long, presumably long forgotten by the signora, but which Assunta swept around on a weekly basis.

That much Assunta deduced and could understand. But then, something else had happened, a wild and wanton kicking and savaging; the side table had been reduced to splinters as if an axe had been taken to it; cushions had been ripped open and their feathers strewn, as if a fox had got into a hen-house. She surveyed it all and then, quite suddenly, she understood.

Assunta, who would not normally sit down while working, took the chair opposite the signora when she returned to the kitchen. This room at least was still intact.

The signora poured them both a small coffee and pushed a cup across the table to Assunta.

'What do you think?' she said.

Assunta stirred three spoons of sugar into her coffee. What she thought was that all of this should have been done weeks ago, that what was needed was a specialised removal firm to come and take away some of these ancient, cumbersome and broken pieces of furniture, that two women of a certain age could not possibly sort this out in a morning. She thought that the signora, who was younger than Assunta, was not young enough by a good fifty years to excuse this foolishness.

But because she had seen and had understood that the signora had come up in a violent and unpleasant way against her own declining physical powers, she didn't say these things. She knew that, until that moment of horrible realisation in the living room, the signora had somehow hung on to a notion that it was all a question of will and determination, of which she had bucketloads, and that when she had been proved wrong, the illusion had shattered.

So Assunta said, carefully, 'Where is the girl going to sleep?'

'I was going to put her on the fold-down bed in the salon, but then when I folded it down, it fell apart.'

'I saw,' Assunta said.

The signora, hunched over her coffee cup, looked up at her from under the rain-hood. It was one of those plastic transparent hoods with ties under the chin, that came folded up in a tiny purse, perfect should it start to rain, but entirely wrong in a domestic setting. It was tied loosely so as not to disarrange the upward, gravity-defying sweep of the signora's hair. What Assunta saw on the sharp little face protruding beneath was trust.

She took out the book of saints and placed it on the table, glancing at the signora again. The look was still there,

164

unwavering. She ran her finger down the list and read out the words bequeathed them by Julian of Norwich.

'He said not "Thou shalt not be tempested, thou shalt not be travailed, thou shalt not be diseased"; but He said, "Thou shalt not be overcome,"' she pronounced. She got to her feet. 'I've got three hours. Let's see what can be done.'

They washed up their coffee cups, put them on the draining rack and went together into the living room.

Assunta surveyed the devastation for the second time with the signora standing quiveringly at her side. She had wondered why the signora hadn't telephoned one of her friends to come and help because it wasn't cleaning as such that needed doing here, but as they stood there she realised why. She, Assunta, was privy to something. It could have meant she didn't matter, but she knew otherwise.

'I thought I could make it all lovely and spacious,' the signora said.

'Enough of that,' said Assunta. 'What we have to do is make the best of it. I'll see if my big grandson can come and cart the rubbish away, create some space, clear the junk room if you like, but that won't be for a while yet because he's on a course.'

The girl was due to arrive on Tuesday.

'I could give her my bedroom, and I could sleep on the sofa,' the signora said.

'But, signora,' Assunta said, 'no.'

She gave the signora a look to make sure she had understood the suggestion was ridiculous.

By dint of the signora crawling around and tugging at the carpet, and Assunta lifting corners and shifting, they freed the pianola, wheeled it along to the junk room and wedged it in. The rusted, fold-down mechanism on the bed had snapped through, and the remaining screws holding the bed part together had either buckled or popped free. The signora was dispatched to the hardware store two streets away for replacement screws, a screwdriver and sturdy refuse bags. Assunta straightened the carpet, swept up the feathers and then, when the signora returned, she got on with filling the bags, while the signora set to on the fold-down bed.

Assunta thought it best not to enquire what could be thrown away and what kept, but to make her own decisions. She stuffed the leads back into the boxes and stacked them one on top of another behind the door. Other unwieldy objects – the broken sewing machines and larger paintings – she placed at the door of the junk room. There was no room just inside the door because of the pianola, and no way of passing farther inside where there might be the odd space. Instead, she arranged them in an orderly row. They would have to wait. The little piles she had spotted when she first entered the apartment – musty coats and scarves, newspapers and sewing patterns, mush, broken lamp parts – she bagged and put out on the landing.

In the living room, the signora was squatting on the floor with her knees up beside her ears, screwing in the last screw. Assunta thought the posture unladylike but impressive for a woman in her sixties. As far as she could recall her own body had never folded into that position.

'There,' the signora said, creakily standing up.

They both looked at the cobbled-together, precarious contraption. It would never fold away again but, as a bed, might serve.

'Let's hope she's not a fatty,' Assunta said, realising she had no idea who this girl was or why she was coming. That, she supposed, was because of the weeks of their hardly speaking after the ironing incident.

'She isn't,' said the signora.

The signora made five trips, carrying the rubbish down to the big bin on the street corner, up and down those two flights, while Assunta made up the bed. It didn't look so bad with sheets and a pillow. Then the signora was back, looking done in.

'You'd better put your feet up this afternoon,' Assunta said.

'Can we just, before you go, can we just, between us, take these things down to the rubbish?' the signora said.

She meant the sewing machines and the big pictures.

'I can't,' Assunta said.

The signora put her hands together. She was going to plead, and Assunta forestalled her.

'I'm not up to it,' she said. 'I know my limits.'

It wasn't meant to be a reproach. Not really.

'You need to get rid of some of this stuff,' Assunta said.

And the signora, instead of defending it or talking about heirlooms or odd ideas of beauty that she had transiently seen in these objects, said meekly, 'I know.'

Her rain-hood had come awry. Her hand swept up to tug it off her head, her hair popping back up into its bristly shape, and Assunta nodded, agreeing with something unsaid.

At one of the other apartments where Assunta cleaned, the man of the house had his own dressing room. On a walnut chest of drawers there were laid out enamel-handled paraphernalia: an instrument of unknown function like a pair of miniature fire tongs, three brushes of varying sizes (the smallest would have been for grooming his moustache if he weren't clean-shaven), a comb, a cut-throat razor and a shaving brush. Only the comb ever seemed to have been used. Assunta had a fondness for the shaving brush, however, because it was a miniature replica of Signora Ravello's hair,

167

and every time she lifted it to dust beneath, she was reminded of the signora.

At the sight of the shaving-brush hair now, she felt her heart soften.

'Shall I get Marco to come and see what can be done?' she asked.

'Yes, please,' the signora said.

'Your apartment is good enough for you and so it's good enough for a little foreign girl. She's not a princess,' Assunta said.

She buttoned up her coat, picked up her basket and let herself out.

Chiara went to the window and waited there until Assunta emerged. She watched her load her basket full of cleaning products onto her scooter and *put-put* away down the street. Then she returned to the pile of rubbish in the hall.

She bent to the first picture, braced herself, lifted it with both hands, raised it above her head and threw it with all her might over the pianola into the far reaches of the junk room where it made a thunderous noise as it landed in among the stacked furniture. She fetched the stepladder, heaved the other items one by one onto the top of the pianola and pushed them off. They clattered and banged until they found their places. The second sewing machine wedged itself at an angle between the pianola and an old screen propped behind. When she jammed the door shut, she could hear noises from within, objects adjusting to their new space, slowly subsiding and settling, and then a horrible sliding, crackling noise as if an avalanche were coming. She stood with her back against the door. When it had all quietened down, she reattached the wall hanging.

She wondered whether perhaps, after all, everything could be kept in its separate compartment. Like on one of those trains where there is no connecting corridor between carriages.

The thought of this train made her shiver.

TEN

Trains from the north come and go, one of them no doubt carrying away the elderly couple, whom they do not see again. Chiara buys apples and hard bread rolls at inflated prices from a vendor with a pushcart. They drink the water from the faucet on the platform. The guard announces an unspecified hold-up farther down the track and that no trains are getting through at present from the south. They retreat to the waiting room.

Cecilia sits on the bench, wrapped in a blanket. She is always exhausted the day after a fit. She ignores the boy, who opts for a position on the floor behind, where he huddles with his knees drawn up to his chin. Sometimes his head falls forward and he nods in sleep but then, inevitably, he jerks back up and stares around as if he can't believe what he sees, where he is. As if this is the dream, or the nightmare, and he would like to wake up. The irises of his eyes are so dark they are almost black, so that pupil and iris seem to merge. Liquid eyes, Chiara thinks. If he catches her looking at him, he adopts his lizard face. It might be funny if it weren't so sad. She might laugh, if she weren't in a state of such acute tension that the inside of her head pulsates like the beam in a lighthouse, and

171

her thighbones ache with a suppressed desire to run. And if it weren't so sad.

In the moments when the other two are both asleep, Chiara paces the platform, underneath the colonnade, pausing each time she passes the waiting-room door to peer in and check they are both still there. Another troop train comes rumbling through without stopping. The noise it makes is deafening but moves slowly. It must be an entire German division, a series of flat cars loaded with immense tanks, anti-aircraft guns and other armaments she cannot name, and, at either end of each car, steel-helmeted soldiers with rifles pointing. The guard waves his flag and blows his whistle.

'We don't have a hope in hell, do we?' he remarks as he walks past.

A train going in the right direction finally arrives in the late afternoon. It is a local one with only three carriages that will stop at every village on the line and is already full. They clamber aboard and find a pull-down seat in the corridor for Cecilia.

'Sit on my case,' she tells the boy, and she stands in the space between the two. Both of them, Cecilia and Daniele, despite all their napping, are pale and drooping.

'I'm so tired,' Cecilia says.

'You had a fit last night, darling. Do you remember?'

'No,' she says in a mournful voice.

Chiara stands at the window, looking blankly out across the tracks. Her mind jumps forward to the next leg of the journey and the one after, because there's a weary way to go yet, lifts to be negotiated and walking to be managed, in the dark at this rate. She's wondering how she will keep the boy and Cecilia going, where she will find the resources and the stamina.

And she is willing the train to depart. *Get us out of this place,*

172

she is thinking over and over again until at last the hiss of steam heralds departure. *Let's go. Let's go. Let's be on our way,* she chants in her mind.

Then, she will sit herself down on Cecilia's case and she will try to have a little nap, for half an hour or so, recoup some energy. And the door in her mind slides open, she sees her sleeping father and the corners of her mouth twitch up. It is going to be all right.

She still has this sort of smile on her face, she can feel it stuck there, as another train, a great long one, a locomotive pulling dozens of wagons, draws up against the platform opposite. Some of the wagons are high-sided and open, but most are sealed cars with metal grilles. A cattle train, she registers without thinking about it. Afterwards, she tells herself that the boy didn't see, can't have known what he was seeing even if he did. That she hardly knew herself. That anyway she blocked his view. When she remembers it, she thinks that she was half smiling because she was happy that they were finally leaving Orte and happy to be visited by her softly sleeping father, bathed in the strong sunshine of her memory.

She is not curious about the train opposite. Because it just happens to be in her line of sight, she becomes aware of a movement at the grille on the car directly facing her, a pale thing, flapping. She squints at it and sees that it is an arm, a slender human arm squeezing out from between the metal bars. Behind the grille is the face of a young woman. Her mouth is open as if she is calling or singing a sustained note, but any sound she might be making is drowned out by the cacophonous clanking, hissing and rumbling of the trains.

Chiara glances to the side. There are other people standing on this stretch of corridor but only one is, like her, facing outwards – a middle-aged woman with a muffler and a grey coat.

173

She turns and looks at Chiara, wide-eyed, open-mouthed and horrified, and it is this other woman's expression that confirms Chiara is not hallucinating.

They both look out of the window once more. The engine noise of the other locomotive abates and, in the second-long interval before their own train noisily cranks into gear, an eerie wailing can be heard. If you weren't staring straight at the gaping mouth of a young woman, you might take it for the screech of an unoiled brake or an off-key whistle or the sighing of the rails as the metal contracts. But if you are looking, if you have half seen the other faces pressing against the grilles, bearded men, women old and young, you can identify it as the sound of many human voices, male and female. And although you catch only a half-choked syllable before your own train hoots and lets off a loud spurt of steam, drowning out all other sounds, you can recognise a word.

Two words.

Help.

Water.

The boy is beside her. She does not know how long he has been standing there. She puts her hand on his head, on the cloth of the funny hat, and presses him back into his seat.

'Bad soldiers,' she hisses. 'Keep down.'

She maintains the pressure on the child's head. She keeps looking as their train chugs away. They form the corners of a triangle, she and the grey-coated woman along the corridor and the woman in the cattle truck across the track, until the angle becomes too acute, the hypotenuse impossibly over-stretched, and the line breaks.

Now there are only ordinary houses and trees spinning past.

She and the woman along the corridor stare at each other, and then both glance away. Chiara bends to talk to Daniele and looks into his stricken eyes. Did he see? She feels as if her own face mirrors the half-glimpsed woman's, her mouth open, her throat parched. She swallows.

'At Nonna's farm where we are going now,' she says, in a kind of croak. She swallows again. 'There is an olive grove. Some of the trees are very, very old. So old no one knows how long ago they were planted. Four or five hundred years. Yes,' she says and taps the top of his head, his hat, for emphasis because although his gaze is in her direction, he appears to be looking through her into a dark place. She drops her voice, dramatically.

'And in this grove, there is one tree that is magic. We call it the Mago.'

She can't be sure whether he is listening or not.

'Shall I tell you why it is called the Mago?'

She doesn't wait for a reply. She is gabbling.

'There are three reasons. You know in magic stories, there are always three. One.'

She takes her hand from his head and counts with the fingers of one hand on the other. The boy follows this with his eyes.

'It is so old you would think it was nearly dead and could no longer bear juicy, fat olives, that it is dried up and finished, and the bark is so flaky and wrinkly you can snap off twigs easily, like that,' she snaps her fingers and he starts. 'But still every three years, it produces the most marvellous, abundant crop of olives, and they make them into the most delicious olive oil.

'Two, inside the trunk there is a hollow, and you can climb all the way inside. Can't you, Cecilia?' she says and looks up at her sister for corroboration, only to be confronted instead with a glare of such outrage, as if Chiara is betraying some trust,

175

some confidence, their sisterly bond, that Chiara loses her thread.

'Three,' she says. She doesn't have a number three. She casts about.

'That boy pinched me,' Cecilia says in a sudden loud voice. 'When I was asleep, he pinched me.'

It is the longest sentence she has spoken all day. She proffers her hand with a red mark on the back of it.

'I don't think he did, darling. Perhaps you caught it on something,' Chiara says.

She turns back to the boy. She has lost him. He is staring into the black hole again.

'Number three,' she says in a fierce whisper, 'is that when it is a full moon, when the moon is big and silver, you can climb inside the Mago and you can make a wish. Only one wish,' she says, holding up her forefinger, 'not three. So think about what you will wish for.'

She adds a proviso.

'We don't know if the wishes come true or not, because no one ever tells what their wish is. Except for Gabriele, who always wishes for olives.'

She imagines smiling reassuringly at the child, but her facial muscles won't oblige.

Cecilia is twisting her hands together and writhing in her seat.

'Show me your hand, Cecilia,' Chiara commands.

She holds her sister's hand and rests her other hand on the boy's head once more. She steadies herself between them as the train rattles along the track.

ELEVEN

'Are you all right, signora?' a man said.

He was youngish, with dark ringlets trailing down his back, dressed in a navy pinstriped suit. He had been there all the time on the periphery of her vision, checking items off on a clipboard as two other men in overalls carted huge cardboard boxes on trolleys from the back of a lorry parked on the cobbles to one side of Chiara.

Chiara blinked at the man, whose expression indicated irritation rather than concern. She wanted to say she was fine. That was what decorum dictated. To protest that there was nothing the matter, to smile apologetically and move out of his way. Not that she was physically in his way, but her presence, her weeping presence she now realised with horror, was disturbing the flow of his morning transactions. But she found she couldn't summon the words from anywhere. Even a little white lie to a stranger was beyond her. She felt as if she had been undressed and made to stand there, naked and dumb, in this street in the ghetto, in front of the building where Gennaro's bar used to be.

She turned away in a sudden sharp shift, and the world spun. A car came trundling over the cobbles, moving quite hesitantly as if the driver might not have intended to drive into this labyrinth of narrow streets at all and was seeking a way out or a place to turn. Chiara saw the car approaching, but something snagged in her processing of the information. She couldn't configure events into their chronology.

She stepped out. The car caught the edge of her foot, and she abruptly sat down on the roadside, the base of her spine cracking against the kerb-stone as she landed.

A little crowd quickly gathered, and a clamour set up.

Chiara allowed her eyes to close, to contemplate her injuries, such as they were, from the inside, rather than seeing them reflected in the reactions of the audience. A juddering was travelling up her backbone. Her foot throbbed faintly like a weak pulse but hardly hurt, not yet.

She opened her eyes. A woman showed the flat of her palm in a no-nonsense gesture that said 'Halt' when she tried to get up.

'No, no, signora,' the woman said, 'don't even think of it. Call an ambulance,' she said to someone else. 'The signora mustn't be moved.'

A discussion started up about the driver's responsibility and what should be done if the foot turned out to be broken or if the accident had caused some other loss or damage. A man in dark glasses with onion breath and yellowish skin knelt and tentatively examined her foot.

'I've had training,' he said to no one in particular.

There was another man, older, standing just behind, as if waiting for an audience with Chiara. 'I'm so sorry,' he mouthed.

She gave him a careful nod to indicate that it was fine, he needn't worry. The fingernails of the fellow poking at her foot were black and bitten.

'I don't think it's broken,' he mumbled, but no one was listening to him. They were all engaged in the burgeoning row. The man who had apologised was caught in the middle of it. He was the driver.

Bearing witness on the one side were two elderly ladies from the dry cleaner's. They had been sitting on their bench outside the shop and had seen the whole event, they claimed.

On the other side of the argument was the ringletted man in the pinstripe suit, who had become the driver's unofficial spokesman. The apportioning of blame teetered first one way, then another. It took in Chiara's injuries, real or potential. Contusions and swellings were mentioned, fractures and shock. People going about their business when other people didn't have the wit to look before crossing the road also came into it. There was talk of ambulances and medics, of reckless drivers and dangerous pedestrians.

Chiara was watching a hand like a creeping rat inching towards her handbag, which had fallen open at her side. The hand reached the brim, and exploratory fingers dipped inside. She looked up. The sickly man at her feet appeared to be staring straight at her as if he didn't know what the little animal on the end of his scarred arm was doing, as if it had its own independent life. There was something she recognised.

'Do you know Daniele?' she said in a very low voice. 'Daniele Levi.' She couldn't see his eyes, because of the dark glasses. 'Or Daniele Ravello?'

She had been mistaken. It wasn't the man she recognised. It was the gesture.

'Best just sit there,' the man said, withdrawing his hand and standing up.

His trousers were candy-striped. She followed his progress

179

as he meandered through the small throng, standing close first to one person and then another, finally sauntering away.

Chiara's foot started to pulsate in the offbeats of her spine's throb. She had nothing to do but sit in the road. *Boom* went her spine, *pa-pa-te-pa* went her foot, *whoosh whoosh* went her head, like drums played with brushes rather than sticks. A coffee stiff with sugar was put in her hands, 'For the shock, signora,' and she sipped it pleasantly.

The row was hotting up. It seemed to go beyond the particular case in question and to relate to something farther back, more deeply rooted and visceral, not so much to do with rights and responsibilities, but with blame. For Chiara, still mute, still mainly tuned in to the syncopated rhythms of her body, notions such as that of fates being decided on a whim or a whisper at street corners, the elusive quality of fairness and even the nature of persecution, fluttered past in a loosely connected and abstract way, like paper dancers unfolding in the breeze.

A pen and notepad were brought out so that details could be written down. It made Chiara think of the note she had left up at the Anita Garibaldi monument for Daniele, and an image appeared of him climbing up and retrieving it. She pictured him lean and healthy and with a spring in his movements. She thought of all the times they had visited the monument together and he had posted the notes to his mother, and how, afterwards, she would go back and collect them.

Something had been said, something irrefutable and strong, while Chiara's attention was wandering. The man in the pin-striped suit had lapsed into silence because now, it seemed, he was on his own in championing the hapless driver, and the dry-cleaning ladies were winning the day. The driver himself was still apologising.

'Signora,' one of the dry-cleaning ladies said to Chiara, 'don't worry. We will testify when you denounce this man.'

Chiara, with a sudden rush of clarity and responsibility, wondered what she was doing, sitting dreaming in the sunshine, listening to her own internal jazz while entertaining fanciful notions that her letter to Daniele had been received. It was up to her to put an end to this tomfoolery.

She looked at the driver properly for the first time: a man in his middle years, pleasant tanned face, big nose, grey wavy hair pushed back, touching his collar. A blue shirt in soft cotton, gold-rimmed spectacles. He seemed more of an observer than a participant. As if he couldn't quite take seriously all this baying for his blood and was just waiting for it to run its course.

He was looking at her. 'So sorry,' he mouthed again.

She held out her hand to him. He stepped forward and took hold, not of her proffered hand, but of each of her wrists, encircling them with his big hands. She was pulled lightly to her feet, taking most of her weight on the uninjured foot, the driver supporting her the whole time. He muttered something in her ear and Chiara quietly assented. He spoke out for both of them, taking command.

'I am taking the signora to the hospital,' he announced in loud, authoritative tones with traces of a Milanese accent.

'This gentleman is taking me to the hospital,' Chiara said, feeling called on to demonstrate to the crowd that she wasn't being kidnapped. She cleared her throat, tried again with more gusto. 'Please cancel the ambulance if you have called one,' she said.

Leaning heavily on her rescuer, she allowed herself to be led towards the car, still in the middle of the road, the driver's door agape where he must have leapt out. He could have just kept driving, she thought. Some people would have done.

181

A shriek came from one of the dry-cleaning ladies.

Chiara faltered, but the driver propelled her forward. 'Keep going,' he said in an undertone. 'It's some new drama. Nothing to do with us.'

Us, she thought as he handed her into the comfort of the car and closed the passenger door. A phrase from long ago came into her mind – 'There is no us' – but she didn't like to recall who had said it and to whom.

The driver was at his side of the car, one foot braced on the running board, leaning on the roof, listening to whatever the new drama entailed. Chiara wasn't an expert on cars and didn't herself drive but she paid attention to the smart and extraordinarily long vehicle in which she sat. She had seen an advertisement for it in a magazine with a miniskirted girl lying on the bonnet. The latest Lamborghini. In reality, she noted, there was room for several girls to lie on the extended bonnet if they had a mind. You didn't get many big cars like this in Rome.

Then the driver swung in, switched on the engine and a disembodied male voice said, '*Skylab* is now in orbit.'

'Here we are,' the driver said, as he reached forward and turned the voice off. He drove to the end of the road and said it again, 'Here we are,' raising his eyebrows at her in a twinkling way.

It was as if they had pulled off a heist, she and the man, and were now making off in the getaway car. Chiara had never before been in a car with a built-in radio. The seat squeaked with newness as she shifted her weight. There was a smell of caramel.

They turned into the dense traffic heaving along Lungotevere.

'You will have to direct me,' the man said. 'I don't know my way around. I'm down from Milan, to talk about a film we might make. I was on my way to a meeting and I took a wrong turn.'

'Just drop me anywhere along here,' Chiara said.

'No, no,' he said. 'We need to get you checked out,' he said, 'to make sure.'

'Honestly,' she said. 'It hardly even hurt.'

The traffic lights at the crossroads with Via Arenula were red. He looked sideways at her. 'You must be tougher than you look,' he said, shaking his head as if in wonder at her prowess.

She resisted the desire to say something self-deprecating about tough old meat.

'Oh, I am,' she said. 'This is a good place to let me out.'

They were coming up to the Mazzini bridge. She could dive off to the right and be home in ten minutes.

'Here?' he said.

He was jammed in the middle lane. He braked, wound down his window, stuck out his whole left arm and made circular motions with it. Perhaps it was a gesture that had a different meaning in Milan. Here it set klaxons howling and horns hooting. Someone bellowed at him that he was a parrot.

'I can't stop here,' he said, not looking at her, 'these bloody Roman drivers won't let me.'

They drove along in silence for a while. He kept craning round to see if he could shift to the nearside lane as they traversed the whole length of Lungotevere, following all the loops and turns of the river. She would have to get a bus back at this rate. To Chiara it felt as if the city were whizzing past at dizzying speed.

'I'll stop when I can,' he said.

Eventually, he jostled his way into the nearside lane,

manoeuvred the big car over to the right and drew up half on the kerb.

He turned to face her. 'Listen,' he said. 'I can't in all conscience actually just drive off without knowing that there are no bones broken, no lasting damage.'

The phrase 'lasting damage' rang in her head.

'I'm fine,' she said. 'Really.' She opened her door and swung her legs out.

'Let me see,' he said. He jumped out, came round to her side and knelt at her feet. 'Show me,' he said.

Chiara was wearing what Simone called her 'nun shoes', low-heeled lace-ups that were good for marching about and even, she fondly thought, laid claim to a certain downbeat elegance. She saw now the falsity of this notion. But she stuck her legs out, and they both looked at her slender ankles. That would never go out of fashion, she thought, a nicely turned ankle.

'It doesn't look swollen,' he said. 'Let me see you walk.'

The man stood to one side, with the walls of a building behind him and pedestrians bustling past, squeezing through the gap. To the other side was the kerb, a green iron lamppost, a stone bollard. All this was usual. What was different was her feeling of tentativeness about the enterprise. She wanted handholds.

She took two steps and suddenly lurched sideways. It wasn't her foot giving way so much as the ground dipping and buckling, the lamppost at the corner of her left-hand vision sliding forwards. It was as if, for an instant, she could feel the earth's rotation and her stumble, rather than a loss of balance, was her attempt to keep on her feet in an unsteady world.

*

184

In the casualty department, a nurse bandaged Chiara's ankle and gave her a typewritten sheet with some exercises to do.

'Keep it moving,' the nurse said.

Chiara found she wanted to go the long way round to get to the consulting room door, her fingers touching the walls at all times. But the nurse was watching her, and so she launched herself out into the space, shuffling rather than stepping so that a greater portion of foot remained in contact with the ground.

'Don't limp,' the nurse said. 'Put weight on it.'

Chiara concentrated on reaching the door frame. The spin had abated but, nevertheless, she held the door to anchor herself before slowly swivelling around. No sudden movements: that seemed key. She was surprised to find the nurse was right behind her, close enough for Chiara to see that what looked like a growth on the nurse's nose was actually a blob of terracotta-coloured make-up. She must have dabbed it on but forgotten to rub it in. It occurred to Chiara that perhaps she ought to mention the dizziness. That the foot injury was merely a symptom of the actual problem.

The nurse picked up the watch pinned to her pocket, consulted it and then let it fall back. She was waiting for Chiara to leave so she could follow.

'Do you think I could have crutches?' Chiara said.

'It's not broken,' the nurse said.

'Or a stick? A walking stick?' Chiara clarified.

Perhaps the nurse was short-sighted. Perhaps she had removed her glasses to apply the make-up and then couldn't see what she was doing. She was squinting at Chiara now.

'We don't do sticks,' she said and squeezed past Chiara to speed off down the corridor in her soundless shoes.

Chiara continued leaning there for a moment. A silver-haired porter holding an empty wheelchair winked at Chiara.

'I'll see what I can do,' he said mysteriously and propelled the wheelchair through some double doors.

The film-maker from Milan was no longer in the waiting room, but then the porter reappeared. 'Your husband has gone to make a telephone call. He'll be back soon,' he said and then, 'Have this. It's been lying in lost property for a year,' and he gave her a walking stick. It was just the right height for her.

Cheered beyond measure by the porter's assumption, Chiara took a moment to go to the ladies', put on some lipstick and comb her hair. In the mirror she had a ravaged but jaunty look. The stick had a lovely carved handle that fitted snugly into the palm of her hand. If she had to make her way about in this tilting world, then a stick like this was just the ticket. She was in a state of buzzing excitement. Jittery.

'All OK?' the man said when he returned. 'No plaster, no crutches?'

She waved her stick.

'The meeting's rearranged. We're doing lunch, which is better. Would you join me?'

She couldn't see why not. Everything was ready back at the apartment for the girl's arrival, the bed made up, the kitchen cupboards packed with special provisions.

'Go on, you'll be doing me a favour. And you have to eat. I'll drop you off afterwards,' the man said.

And there she was again, rumbling through the streets of Rome in this stranger's car. She directed him now to Via Ostiense and to a restaurant there that she had never been to but whose address he read out. Al Biondo Tevere, it was called. The physical whirling had abated, but she felt she had entered another sort of whirl altogether.

His name was Dario Fulminante and he was a documentary film-maker, but hoping now to break into fiction.

'Do you know that other Dario?' she asked. 'The one who makes horror films?'

But he didn't.

'I think he's very well regarded here in Rome,' Chiara said. 'Innovative montage techniques. Use of music.' She waved her hand airily.

It was Simone who had told her these things.

Dario Fulminante said Italian cinema was going in a different direction now, a post-Fellini direction.

'But Fellini is still going strong, isn't he?' Chiara said.

Dario wagged his head from side to side as if to say, depends what you mean by strong. Chiara felt vaguely offended on Fellini's behalf.

He found a place beyond the restaurant to park his big car, and they walked back along Via Ostiense, buses and cars and great lorries hooting by in the other direction, a torrent of traffic heading out of town. He took her arm and led her through black iron gates into a quarry-tiled courtyard where large succulent plants in red pots were set between round tables covered with red-and-white checked gingham cloths.

It seemed clear to her now that in this hiatus before the arrival of Daniele's daughter, she had been given an opportunity to celebrate, to find whatever peace and joy and acceptance she could, to raise a glass to her departed loved ones, as well as to prepare herself mentally for the arrival of Maria and whatever that might entail.

The tree that pushed its way out of a hole in the red tiles and grew all the way up and through the trellis that formed the roof was set there for her delight, and she bestowed a quiet smile upon it. The vine leaves that canopied the trellis, their fresh, dark, early-summer green, and the sun that shot down in between them like so many little spotlights, singling out the odd pink flower or shiny leaf, were an invitation. There was a grapey wine smell and the aroma of cooking.

Delicious, she thought. It was like when you're ill, definitely unwell but not life-threateningly so, and you let all your worries and duties slide away from you and allow yourself just to be. That was what she was doing. Just being. Thoroughly occupying this limbo place, this in-between moment, and this man, Dario – with his wet brown eyes, like the dog she had loved but had never been allowed to own – had turned up right on time to be her companion.

The men he was meeting wore suits and sunglasses. Not at all the bohemian types she had imagined. Financiers, she thought. He introduced her as his new, but dear, friend. A glass of straw-coloured wine was put in her hands, and the party made their way up a short flight of steps that led to the terrace overlooking the river.

They stood in a sort of huddle while the waiter prepared their table; the men exchanging hearty pleasantries before they got down to business, Chiara among them but hardly listening. She was leaning on her lovely stick, dreamily drinking the yellow wine, watching the waiter. He shook out the white linen cloth so that it caught the light and was momentarily transformed into an icebound tundra with bluish slopes and dark shadows before it cascaded like snow over the table.

'You don't mind, do you?' Dario said to her in a low voice, meaning, she supposed, if they talked shop.

She said, no, not at all, and the huddle tightened with Chiara on the periphery. She looked out at the river, leaning on her stick, a delightful affectation.

It wasn't like the rivers flowing through other capital cities – such as the Seine, the Danube or the Thames. It was like a country river. As she watched, a family of ducks floated past.

It flowed faster here than downtown, the waters funnelling along a narrower channel. The banks were a confusion of bushes, bulrushes, trails of convolvulus, clumps of bracken and ferns, the odd fig tree. It was a slender stretch of bucolic wilderness within the confines of the city.

A barefoot man wearing earth-brown clothes came running through the long grass. She reflected that until two days earlier, Friday, when she had left the note for Daniele, the sight of this man would have set up an internal commotion, a raggedy choking pain, and she would have scrutinised him with a kind of dread, tormenting herself with the idea that he belonged to some rag-tag community that knew, or knew of, Daniele, that she must learn where he had gone, investigate. That it might even be Daniele himself, because he was good at hiding right under your nose, at camouflage. She would have made enquiries. She would have tramped pointlessly through the undergrowth.

But no longer. She had let all that wash away. She was emptied out. She was like a transparent vessel, a glass jar snagged momentarily in the river's stream, the sparkling waters swirling past and through it.

Over to the right, towards the city centre, etched against an azure sky, was the black, cylindrical outline of the gasometer. She put her wineglass on the table and picked up the water instead, aware both of a deep thirst and a desire for sobriety. To imprint on her consciousness this rich, layered now; this new newness in which, by way of golden light and emptied-out emotion, Daniele's absence and Daniele's daughter's imminent presence flowed.

In the morning, on the day of the girl's arrival, she went to Gianni's for her cappuccino and *cornetto*.

189

'It's nothing,' she said when he enquired about her bandaged ankle. 'A foolish accident but not serious.'

That wasn't why she was there.

'I have a young British girl coming to stay with me for a week or two,' she announced. 'Welsh, actually. The daughter of an old friend.'

Gianni stroked his moustache and eyed her. 'Welsh?' he said.

'Yes. You know, from Wales, next to England.'

'Ah. England,' he said. 'You'll be making her a pot of tea.'

'Oh, good idea,' she said. 'I'll buy some tea.' Chiara herself didn't drink tea, a tisane now and then, but not tea as such. 'They take it with milk, don't they?'

'In the North of England they do, but not in Wales. They take it with lemon in Wales and they like to have a saucer,' Gianni said with authority. 'Bring her in for an aperitif,' he said.

Chiara remembered the appointment with Luca in the bar near the Gramsci Institute.

'I will,' she promised, 'but not this evening, because she will probably be tired after the journey.'

She went to Ruggeri's and bought a small yellow packet of Lipton's tea.

'I have a young girl from the UK coming to stay with me,' she confided to the shop assistant. 'They drink a lot of tea over there.'

'Yes, I know,' the assistant said. 'My brother works in London in a restaurant. You have to make sure you boil it for a long time.'

'I will,' Chiara said, storing the information.

She stuck her head into the foyer of the Farnese cinema. 'Do you ever show foreign films in the original language?' she asked the receptionist, who was painting her nails a luscious red. 'Or are they always dubbed?'

The receptionist frowned and blew on her fingernails.

'Only I have a young Welsh girl coming to stay with me, and her Italian's not very good and I wondered . . .'

The receptionist shook her head. 'We never have films in Welsh,' she said. 'Not that I know of.'

'Ha ha, no. I was thinking English. Films in English. They might be American or British or even Australian films, I suppose.'

'Your best bet is the Pasquino in Trastevere,' the woman said.

'You're right,' Chiara said. She knew this already. She was a regular at the Pasquino. 'I'll get a newspaper and find out what they're showing.'

She meandered back across the middle of Campo dei Fiori market. She bought some figs at one stall, some flowers from another and a melon from a third. She made sure they all knew about the girl coming. When she popped into the shop on the corner to buy some bread, she told the chief baker and the lady at the till.

She took the supplies home. She arranged the flowers in a vase and stood at the window, looking down into the street, at the people milling about and at the way the light glinted off the handlebars of the scooters close-parked against the wall of the building opposite.

She had made a start. But now she needed to tell someone who really mattered. And in the absence of Simone, that was Antonio.

All the people wandering about down below, looking in the shop windows, seemed to be smoking. She hadn't had a cigarette for over a month but suddenly, urgently, she wanted one. It would be just the thing to give her – not courage exactly, because why would she need courage to talk to her dear friend, but it would help her gather herself together, consolidate her sense of this being the right thing to do. And perhaps, yes, a little bit of courage because she was going to have to break through the thick barrier of silence that had built up between her and Antonio on the subject of Daniele.

She looked up. Across the way, diagonally above her, a man in a vest stood at an open window, smoking and observing the activity in the street below. She didn't know him but she had seen him sometimes, setting off in the morning, carrying a bag of tools. She had a feeling he was from the South. A labourer. A masonry worker. Something like that. The building he lived in was two storeys higher than her own with an ever-changing itinerant population. There were at least ten names next to the numbers beside the front door.

She leant against the window rail, observing the smoke plume out from his mouth and then disappear against the blue of the sky. He was fascinated by something going on down in the street, but Chiara realised she couldn't follow his gaze to find out what it was. The tilt of her head brought her to the borderline of dizziness. She could sense its proximity, like a shadow in her brain, an ink blot. To extricate herself safely, she would need to dip her head leftwards and down. She brought her hand to the side of her face to guide it but, fearful of the spin, not quite ready, she continued to gaze up at the man as if she were utterly captivated, as if she were looking at a painting, taking in all its details.

The man's glance fell on Chiara, and he pulled his head back in surprise. Chiara became aware that with her other hand, the one not holding her head in place, she had two fingers raised to her lips and was miming smoking a cigarette. Before she could melt back into the room, he repeated the mime back to her. She gave a tiny nod and wagged the middle finger of her right hand, hoping he would take this for assent. He bent out of sight and reappeared, holding a cigarette, which he hurled with gusto down and across the street towards her. It fell short, tumbling down to the cobbles below to be trampled. He put up a finger to indicate he'd be a minute and disappeared again. He was soon back, making a flicking motion with the back of his hand, banishing her. She stood back, braced herself against the bookcase and took the opportunity to right the angle of her head. Nothing happened. Nothing spun. Things remained in place.

A projectile came hurtling through the window and landed on the sofa. It was a biro and attached to it with tape was a cigarette. She waved her thanks up at the man and he mimed writing. He wanted the pen back. She made as if to throw it back up but he indicated no. He was right. She would undoubtedly have missed. He spiralled his hand. Another time, he was saying. Then he gave her a wave and went away. What a delightful transaction, Chiara thought. Not a word had been exchanged. Perhaps the man thought she was mute.

Daniele and his three-month silence came to her mind. Elective muteness, it was called, she had found out later. Brought on by trauma.

She settled herself in the chair nearest the window and lit the cigarette. This would be her very last cigarette, ever. She meant it.

How strange it was that Daniele had never enquired about the fate of the letters he left for his mother. It was understandable that he wouldn't have asked when he was little, when everything was an unexplained mystery. He would post his note in the crook of Anita Garibaldi's arm on the bas-relief at the back of the monument. When they returned a month later, the note would have gone. She still had them all somewhere, in a box that was probably in the sealed loft above the junk room.

The cigarette was foul. It wasn't worth it and there was no comfort to be had there any more. She was finished with cigarettes.

She found Antonio in church, officiating at mass. It must be a holy day of obligation because the congregation was quite big. Assunta would know. When people started filing out, she went up the side aisle to the altar. He was snuffing out the high candles, and there was a strong scent of burning wax.

'Chiara,' he said, turning to her with a smile, holding the brass candle-extinguisher aloft, 'what a nice surprise. Oh, but you've been in the wars. Poor thing, what happened?'

'It's not serious. It's fine. I need to talk to you,' she said, 'about something else.'

'I'm hearing confessions now,' he said, nodding back down the church to where a few congregants were kneeling in the rows next to the confessional. 'But I'll be free in about an hour.'

'I haven't got an hour,' she said. 'I've got to be at the station at two.'

'Come into the confessional then,' he said. 'Don't look so horrified. I just mean we could have a quiet and private little talk straight away. Walk with me so I can explain to the ladies who are waiting that you have special dispensation to jump the queue.'

There was someone already ensconced inside the confessional who wouldn't be budged.

'Ten minutes,' Antonio whispered to Chiara. 'As soon as this one leaves, just come on in.'

He still had the candle extinguisher in his hand. Propping it against the church wall, he ducked into his part of the confessional box, leaving Chiara standing in the aisle, staring at the carved door, where cherubs with fat little stomachs blew bugles among oaken leaves. She didn't want to wait. She wanted to get this conversation over and done with.

She took a seat and allowed thoughts to come of that last time.

They had been in the office at the pontifical library. There was a penholder on the desk, a bird made of alabaster with a hole in its back where the pen rested, and one of its fluted wings was broken, snapped clean off. The curtains were drawn, and it was stuffy. She remembered the penholder and the curtains and a desk lamp and a sort of tray-cum-basket containing envelopes and paper and paperclips. Daniele was next to her, both of them facing Antonio. If she had known she would never see Daniele again, then she might have found the strength to turn and behold him, and she would have that picture of him in her head to keep. But she hadn't.

In among the stationery in the basket-tray thing was the shorn-off wing, lying there, carefully kept, as if one day someone might glue it back on.

She did not have a clear memory of that meeting. What was said. How things were decided. At some point Daniele had left with Antonio to go and collect some of his things from the apartment, and then Antonio had returned on his own and given her back Daniele's keys. Daniele had gone and wouldn't be bothering her again, and she wasn't to worry, she was just to look after herself now and get better.

She remembered the sensation, as she was walking home, of

utter desolation, and then the chaos of the flat awaiting her. By then part of it was being sold off to settle the debts, and everything was just stuffed into her side, piled up. There was no room anywhere, no space, no air, and all the paraphernalia of Daniele's existence that he hadn't deemed essential in that twenty minutes he had been given to pack were scattered about. She had lain down in her bed and pulled the covers up over her head.

And of course Simone had come round. She had tidied the flat, arranged things into some sort of order, engaged a workman to build the loft above the junk room to store Daniele's things when Chiara wouldn't let her throw them away.

Chiara lived among the muddle, muddling along, thinking sooner or later he would be back. Later on, when she realised no one at all, including Antonio, knew where he was, she took to frequenting Porta Portese flea market, ostensibly to get an idea of how much all the antique furniture riddled with woodworm might be worth, but really to look for Daniele; she thought that was the sort of place he might turn up, trading in something.

She always came home from the market with a treasure, an object that justified her regular trips. Eventually her interest got caught up with the acquisition and search for these little somethings, until it became as if they were really what she was going for, to look out for whatever her current collectible thing was, and the apartment got more and more crammed. Still she added to the hoard of useless, pointless objects. As if an accumulation of things could hide the emptiness.

There was linen for a while, lovely old linen with embroidery and lace, and she would wash it and starch it or, later on, when she was earning again and had taken on Assunta, she would get Assunta to do it, squeezing it into already-full drawers.

Then there were the clothes. She loved the clothes, and one of the effects of the apartment division had been to create a funny little space, not a room, but a small chamber off her bedroom; this she filled with rails of glorious clothes that didn't even fit her, and this was also the place where she kept the bolts of cloth that were Cecilia's legacy.

For a while she had been keen on little keys. Then things made of blue porcelain. Sewing machines with wrought-iron treadles, even though she didn't sew. And now Murano glassware.

For such an age she hadn't got it. That, in a litany of last times, that one, in the office of the pontifical library, really had been the last one.

She turned to look at the confessional door, which remained stubbornly shut. Surely this was longer than ten minutes. She transferred her gaze to the candle extinguisher. It was a miniature version of the implement carried by the lamplighter of her childhood to douse the gas lamps when the sun rose. She looked again towards the altar, where a solitary candle that Antonio must have missed still burnt. He hasn't managed to douse all the lights, she thought, despite his efforts.

The occupant of the confessional emerged.

Chiara knelt inside the wooden box, separated from Antonio by a patterned grille. She remembered the lines from long ago – Bless me, Father, for I have sinned – and she felt their pull, the power and the comfort of ritual, of formula, of things laid down before, of rules. She would have to speak over the top of them, but to start at all was hard. A thought had come to her, a horrible equivalence that held her silent. If she opened her mouth, the wrong words were going to come flying out.

197

'I'm listening,' Antonio said.

She was thinking about how when the SS rounded up the Jews in October 1943, they gave them twenty minutes to pack their belongings. There was a list of the things they should take and the things they should leave behind. She knew that many of them had not even had the presence of mind to get dressed. She wanted to ask Antonio whether, when he had given Daniele twenty minutes to gather his possessions, he had supplied him with a list. She wanted to say that if Daniele had been thinking straight, he would not have left his trumpet and his leather jacket.

On the other side of the grille, Antonio sighed.

Poor, long-suffering Antonio, she thought. But he wouldn't thank her if she let these words loose. She cleared her throat.

'Daniele,' she said now. 'Daniele has a daughter.'

She was glad she couldn't see Antonio's face. It meant she didn't have to take his reactions into consideration and, once she got going, the anonymity of the confessional was very liberating. She was off, recounting the story of the letter and the phone calls from Cardiff.

Suddenly the grille slid open and there was Antonio's face, looking red and strained, and so disconcertingly close she could smell his peppermint-and-tobacco breath.

'I didn't know that opened,' she said, taken aback.

'She's coming?' he said. 'This girl is coming?'

'Yes,' she said. 'I'm meeting her at two.'

He pressed the palms of his hands together and touched his fingertips to his mouth, tilting his head back and forth slowly, pulling his lower lip open and closed. She looked at the embroidered sleeve of his cassock, a pattern of white on white, only visible this close up. Cecilia could have sewn that, she thought irrelevantly.

After a while, Antonio shook his head and lifted his chin to rest it on his hands. 'What possessed you to say yes, Chiara?'

'She's Daniele's daughter,' she said. 'My boy. His daughter.'

And suddenly it did seem quite blindingly obvious.

'Your boy,' he said. 'Right.'

He lifted his hands in front of his mouth again and stared down as if he were looking off the edge of a high building.

'What?' she said. 'It'll be fine.'

'What are you going to tell this girl about *your boy*?'

She didn't like his tone. 'Maria,' she said. 'She's called Maria. And I'm going to tell her the truth.'

'What truth? That he was a junkie, that he stole from you, bankrupted you, that he was a criminal? Are you going to tell her about the time he and his cronies broke into the pharmacy?'

She was taken aback. Antonio was always so kind to her. She could not remember him uttering a sharp word to her before.

'Not straight away,' she said, 'and not like that.'

'The protection racket? The night he got stabbed? When he stole Gianni's keys and emptied the safe and tried to make it look like a burglary? The times in hospital? The overdoses?'

'Those won't be the first things,' she said.

Why was he being so cruel? Nothing had prepared her for this cruelty.

'Oh, I know,' he said. 'You're going to tell her that you said you wished you hadn't saved him. That he had ruined your life.'

She didn't speak. This was Antonio, her friend.

'Well, that's the truth,' he said, pursing his lips.

'Never mind, Antonio,' she said, standing up rather shakily.

'I don't need your approval. I did not come here to ask you for advice about the wisdom of allowing Maria to come. I was merely informing you that she is coming and, really, I can't see why I bothered.'

She could say a lot more, but she didn't feel up to it.

'Wait a minute, Chiara,' he said. 'Don't rush off. Hang on. *Pax*,' he said, wafting his hands up and down soothingly. '*Pax*.'

She waited.

Antonio didn't seem to know what to say. 'The thing is that he *was* ruining your life. And his own. And what he did, how he treated you, was unforgivable,' he said eventually. He fluttered his hands again.

She knew better than to plead mitigating circumstances for Daniele. Antonio was, after all, the man who had taken it upon himself to send him away without establishing a line of communication.

'Nothing's unforgivable,' she said. She hoped very much this was true.

'Isn't it?' he asked.

For a moment she seemed to catch a desperate look on his usually calm face and she wondered what he could possibly have done that might require such a level of forgiveness.

'Look how well you've done without him,' he said, rallying and pushing his own troubles, whatever they were, to one side. 'How you've rebuilt things. What a rich, full life you have.'

Dario Fulminante, golden wine by the glittering river, all her friends, Assunta and her holy pictures, her funny nephew Beppe from the South and his queer friend, her beloved work, her lovely cluttered home, the glorious depth of colour in her red glass bowl, a hundred happy occasions with Simone. Asmaro, a prince among cats, came slinking into her mind, bringing up the rear.

'Don't let this girl spoil that. As soon as you tell her more than she already knows, the floodgates will open. She will start digging things up, asking questions.'

'She will anyway, I should think, whatever I do or don't tell her. I am not going to be frightened of that. I am sick of lies and half-truths.'

Antonio didn't speak. He just stared at her glumly, biting his lower lip.

She didn't know why he couldn't see it.

'Listen. This is a chance for me to move on and make a fresh start. To clear things up. To greet and welcome Daniele's daughter – who is not Daniele . . .' She waved an admonishing finger at Antonio. 'Yes, I have constructed a life for myself, it's true, and I don't want to jeopardise that, but I want it not to be one where his name is never spoken. I want to enter the next phase, and this girl will be the key. Why would you want to deny me, and her, that?'

'I fear for you,' he said. 'That is all. With Daniele, you were too fond.'

'There is no such thing as too fond,' she said.

'There is, Chiara. There is. And that is why telling this girl everything is a mistake. Stirring up all these old passions.'

'Oh, Antonio,' she said, 'do you really still not understand that those feelings have never gone away?'

The look on his face seemed more anguished than her statement warranted.

'You never stop loving your child, whatever he has done,' she said.

Whatever you have done to him, she added in her head.

Antonio was looking down now, shaking his head, his hands clasped in front of him.

'I have not heard a single thing from Daniele in a decade,'

she said, 'and I don't expect to now.' A little noise escaped from her mouth. 'I wish I knew what had happened to him. I pray that he is safe. Sometimes, I imagine him in a sort of isolated community in the mountains somewhere. In clean air. Living close to the earth. I can't imagine how else he would ever have got off the drugs and stayed off.'

She paused again and took a deep breath.

'But in my heart I think he must be dead.'

There. She had never said that out loud before. She wished there was a seat in the confessional and not just a kneeler. She leant heavily on her stick.

'I have been mourning him, grieving for him, for ten years. Now it is time to bury him.' She felt suddenly very old and frail.

Antonio raised a hand to his brow and sank his head into it.

She waited for him to say something, but he didn't. 'What is it?' she said. 'Tell me.'

She had a strange sense of role reversal, as if she were the priest and he the sinner, burdened with unspoken transgressions.

He raised his head, rubbing his hands across his face as if he were wiping away tears. 'OK,' he said. 'The girl is coming.'

She nodded at him.

'So, can I ask you to wait before you tell her? I would like to be there when you do because . . . ' His head twitched as if the reason escaped him. 'Because I had a part in this story too.' He put his hands together again. 'But I'm away for a few days now.'

'OK,' she said. She hadn't planned on blurting out the story at the train station anyhow. She opened the confessional door and stepped into the aisle.

'I am only thinking of you, Chiara,' he called after her.

She was glad of the walking stick as she walked to the main road to get a cab. The encounter with Antonio had left her feeling drained.

Antonio slid the grille shut.

'*Mea culpa, mea culpa, mea maxima culpa*,' he muttered and he tapped his breast softly with his closed fist.

The action shifted some phlegm, and he cleared his throat. He had done it for the best, he reminded himself. Acted in everyone's higher interests. He had been saving them from themselves. They were on a highway to destruction, the pair of them. Chiara had been too fond. Never drawing a line for the boy, apart from that one disastrous time that she sent him to the clinic and he came back worse; always giving in, indulging him, making excuses, claiming that no one but she knew what he had suffered. Going back for more. Love thy neighbour as thyself, the Lord had said, and where was Chiara's self-love in that abasement? And the boy, biting the hand that fed him? Someone had to do it.

'Lord,' he said, 'help me.'

He stepped out into the aisle. 'I've been called away,' he announced to the waiting parishioners. 'An emergency. Confessions are cancelled. Say an Act of Contrition and five Hail Marys each.'

He made the sign of the cross and intoned a general bless-ing, then hurried out of the church.

Antonio had not been pleased when Daniele had got in touch after four years' absence. Chiara was doing well. She seemed happy. She didn't talk about Daniele any more. He had gone to meet Daniele, who claimed to have been in Israel, working on a kibbutz for some of the time, but from the look of him he had definitely been living rough. He was in a bad way. Antonio had seen straightaway that the man was still an addict, not that he denied it, to give him his due. He wanted to get off the drugs and come home, he said.

Antonio did a deal. He would help Daniele get back on his feet but he must stay out of Chiara's life. If and when Daniele had managed to stay clean for a whole year, he, Antonio, would broker a meeting.

'If she needed me, I would come running. She knows that, doesn't she?' Daniele had said one time.

They had been standing on the beach in Ostia, on the edge of the anarchic shanty village where Daniele was living. Why would she ever need a junkie Jew boy? Antonio had thought at the time, but had confined his response to a nod.

Back at the rectory he had to hunt for the number of the boarding house where he used to leave messages for Daniele and where they had their final meeting three years ago. He knew it was on the inside cover of his address book, identified only with a D. But he had a new address book now. Chiara had given it him for Christmas.

He knelt beside his bed and pulled out the suitcase that he used as an extra drawer.

As he was on his knees anyway he offered up a little prayer for Daniele as he did periodically.

'Lord, let him not have fallen back into bad ways,' he said.

Then, as if in a vision, he saw Daniele as he had been when they had their last conversation, and he sat back on his heels, feeling himself go hot.

'I've done it,' Daniele had said. 'A whole year.'

He was standing in the middle of the front room at the boarding house, his sleeves rolled up, holding out his sinewy arms, his palms turned up, as if offering himself for inspection.

Antonio saw that it was true. Daniele was like a man who had climbed a mountain with no equipment and was clinging to the rocky pinnacle. He could see how close to the precipice Daniele was, that dangerous black glow he had, that notion that if he had managed a year, perhaps he should celebrate by shooting up or whatever they called it. But also: that he would not.

Antonio observed Daniele in his bizarrely biblical pose, and a voice in his head, which he did not recognise as his own, said, 'No.'

Daniele took two paces backwards. His arms fell to his sides, and his fists bunched. He stood with his back to the window, the sea framing him in blue, and stared across the room at Antonio. The light was behind him, and Antonio couldn't see his face, but he could feel the piercing gaze.

In Antonio's memory, there followed a long, uncomfortable silence in which he felt the other man's eyes boring into him, while he looked beyond to the glitter of the ocean. A man on a fishing boat cast his line, and the black swoop of it sliced momentarily across the skyline.

'I wouldn't want to see me again either,' Daniele said eventually.

Antonio became aware that he had been shaking his head. He stopped. He made his voice gentle. 'I'm sorry,' he said.

Daniele had thanked him for all that he had done but told him there was no need for him to come again.

Antonio had the sensation of something slipping from his grasp, as if he were trying, with clammy hands, to keep hold of a delicate crystal glass. 'Lord help me,' he said, rocking on his heels.

Here was the book, and here was the number.

He had to hold on to the bedside cabinet as pins and needles shot up his legs. He had been sitting on his feet too long. When he had recovered, he hurried downstairs on trembly legs to the telephone in the hall.

Let him be there. Let Daniele Levi still be somewhere in that squalid quarter of Ostia, and he, Antonio, would eat humble pie.

The landlady of the boarding house answered. Daniele hadn't been seen for three years. She didn't know what had happened to him. Gone, vanished. Antonio swallowed. Something hard and prickly was stuck in the back of his throat.

'Was he using again?' he made himself ask.

She didn't know. She couldn't remember. Probably. 'They all do,' she said. 'They climb out of their hole, but something always pulls them back in.'

Daniele hadn't been pulled. He had been pushed.

As Antonio replaced the receiver, an image came to him of Daniele toppling backwards into the abyss from the mountain top, in his own guilty hand the blade that had cut the lifeline. He stood in the rectory hallway, staring at the pattern in the floor tiles as if it might be a code that he could decipher and that would tell him what to do.

'*Mea culpa*,' he mumbled under his breath.

He left messages for his fellow priests, telling them that he had been called away, that there was a person in great need, and could they cover his duties for the next few days. He would go to Ostia and he would search for Daniele or news of him, in among the flotsam and jetsam, the human detritus that littered the shoreline there. He would go to the village built on the old seaplane base at the mouth of the Tiber. He would wander among those precarious dwellings that were always at risk of flooding and collapse, should a storm cause the river to surge.

He would ask questions. If Daniele were anywhere to be found, he would find him, or discover his fate.

TWELVE

Squinting against the light of the low November sun, Chiara tries to make out the figure of Daniele moving in the boughs. He is helping old Gabriele by shaking the ripe fruit down. A shower of purple, green and yellow olives plop onto a blanket spread out beneath the tree. The boy and the tree are the same colours, shades of greenish-brown, brownish-green, muted greys. He is standing on a thick branch, his arms above his head to hold a higher one, using his whole body to make the tree rock and sway. She sees that his absorption is so total that he has forgotten all the rest. He is pure physical self. She would not call it happiness, no, but still, he is just a little boy, bouncing in a tree. Being bounced.

She is on the alert for these moments. She notices them. She stores them, and when she can she stokes their faint flames.

'We went on a slug hunt last night,' she says to Gabriele as she helps him lift the blanket by its corners and funnel the fruit into the last sack. 'Didn't we, Daniele?' she calls up into the branches. She doesn't expect an answer. He has not uttered a word since he fell silent on the first day.

'Bad this year, the slugs,' Gabriele says. 'They like the wet.'

The different-sized olives tumble over each other into the sack. She savours the intense quality of green that the green ones hold. She can detect their faint scent.

'He wasn't going to come. He preferred to stay cosy by the fire with Nonna and let me go out on my own,' she says, loud enough for the camouflaged boy, still swinging in the tree, to hear.

Halfway to the vegetable patch, he had caught up with her. Sure-footed in the dark. He followed her along the rows of cabbages, broccoli, late salad leaves, chicory, spinach, and past the white domes of the fennel poking out of the ground. The fronds, dark green and feathery in the light of the torch. She shone it on the small, mud-coloured slugs, showing him what to look out for, the ragged holes in the leaves where they had been having a feast.

'It's us or them,' she told him.

Each slug she found, she squeezed between thumb and fore-finger and dropped into a jar of vinegar she carried. She pointed the torch down into the jar so he could examine the noxious, lumpy, slug liquid. On the second row, he tugged at her sleeve and pointed back to a slug she'd missed.

'You spot them, I'll catch them,' she said.

They moved slowly together along the rows of torch-lit veg-etables.

'We're going to make slug pickle, aren't we?' she calls as she and Gabriele heave another sack onto the two-wheeled cart.

Daniele drops down from the branches. Out of the corner of her eye, she thinks she sees his head jerk as he lands, as it would if he had cracked his chin against his knees. She remem-bers doing the same thing more than once as a child, recalling the judder as the impact reverberated up through her skull, the blood filling her mouth the time she had bitten her tongue, the rust taste of it. Daniele makes no sound. He has twigs in his hair and a sprinkling of greenish powder, lichen dust perhaps, over the skin of his forearms and on his nose. He remains in a crouch, his head hanging down. He seems to be examining something on the ground.

She sees that his brief interlude is over and he is plunged back into the full weight of his situation. She looks away. She has enough to contend with. The farm is a mess, the chickens have been requisitioned by the military, half the sheep have vanished, strangers occupy the barns and outhouses; Nonna, a depleted shell of her former self, has let it all go. Cecilia is fey as the wind.

With Gabriele she lifts the final sack onto the back of the cart.

'You coming?' Gabriele says with a nod in the boy's direction.

Daniele is still in the crouch. For an instant, she sees him like a diminutive boxer, stunned in the ring. He stands up, wiping the back of his hand across his mouth. On it there is a smear of blood. Bloody child, she thinks, locked in the remote tower of his silence. Shutting them all out. Shutting her out. There is a new rip in his trousers. He has been wearing the same clothes, day in, day out, for a month now.

'He can't go,' she says quietly to Gabriele, 'he has no papers.'

'I'll look after him, signorina,' Gabriele says. 'Not on the cart. It'll topple,' he says to the child as he makes to clamber aboard. 'Come here at the front, the other side from me. Keep her steady.'

The boy takes up his position as directed. The donkey lifts her head and pricks up her ears. Chiara runs her hand along the animal's flank and holds it there, feeling her warmblooded, solid presence, the life running through her. She rubs her thumb in a circle in the soft place behind the donkey's ear while Gabriele tightens the halter. She wants to say something. She doesn't know what it is. To tell them to take care. To come back safely. To hurry home before it is dark. To leave the olives there at the press to be collected another day if there's a queue. When she lifts her hand from the donkey, it brushes against the dry, hard skin of the old man's elbow and it feels like bark. Safe as a tree, Gabriele is. No need to say a word.

She likes the way Gabriele is with Daniele. Not offhand exactly, certainly not unkind, but with a take-it-or-leave-it attitude that allows the child to join in and feel useful without pressure or forced jollity.

Nonna too, when she is sufficiently alert to pay the boy attention, has an easy way with him. Little man, she calls him.

'Go to sleep, little man,' she said, the first night they were there, after Cecilia had been tucked away upstairs, and they had made a bed for him beside the hearth and put in a hot brick to warm his feet, 'nothing will hurt you here.'

And then she had gone back to sitting in her faded floral chair with her crochet in her lap, just as she had when they had first come tottering in, all bedraggled and wispy-wet, like soggy leaves blown in by a harsh wind, and she had said, 'You're late,' as if she had been expecting them.

Every time the boy looked up, he saw Nonna still there with her crochet hook going in and out of the wool, in and out, and it allowed him finally to let go of his tight and terrified hold on wakefulness.

Chiara would like to be more like Gabriele or Nonna, calming and steady and measured in her speech, but ever since the night on the train she can't seem to let up when she is in

212

Daniele's presence. She is a babbling brook, a stream of words, pouring over and around him, as if his silence is an umbrella he holds up and she the rain pitter-pattering against it, dripping off its rim. Telling him stories, drenching him in them, calling him back into this world, the one they are in.

'Bring us some beautiful oil,' she calls out now as they set off up the track. 'I'll bake bread and we'll eat it as soon as you're home.'

The cart trundles along behind them, and the donkey's hooves send loose stones clattering. Daniele has slipped his hand under the halter and into the fur of the creature's neck. She is glad for him of the animal's warmth. She watches them as far as the crest of the first mound. They are outlined there, etched against the sky, the old man, the boy and the donkey. Then they drop out of sight.

In the yard, a young man dressed in army trousers and boots but with only a vest covering his upper body, his bare arms gleaming pale and streaked with mud, is sweeping up fallen leaves. At the sound of the latch on the gate lifting, he brushes with extra vigour, beating a last recalcitrant leaf out from under the stone doorstep and brushing it towards the pile in the centre of the yard. Among the motley community that has taken refuge in and around Nonna's house, there is a permanent element and a transient one, of runaways, like this man. They sleep in the barn, stay a few days to get fed, rested, have their uniforms made to look more like civilian clothes and then, like it or not, they move on.

'Any other jobs for me, signora?' the man calls out.

He pitched up two days before and has been making himself useful about the place. Sometimes they come alone, more often in pairs. A few of them are possessed with a fervour and a clear goal; they're going to join the partisans or the co-belligerent army. Many of them, especially the ones from the South, are aiming to skirt the enemy lines and find their way home. Those ones reckon their war is over. All of them are keen to avoid being press-ganged by one of the fascist militia or captured and interned by the German forces.

'No, I don't think so,' she says. 'But you can come and wait inside if you are cold.'

'I prefer to keep busy,' he says. 'I'm good at . . . '

He casts about, looking round the yard at the leaves piled for mulch, the basket of chestnuts by the door, the logs stacked under a tarpaulin, the wheelbarrow leaning up against the wall, the terracotta tiles on the outhouse roof, the gate to the kitchen garden hanging from one hinge.

'At fixing gates,' he says. 'Where do you keep the tools? I can do that.'

She can't afford to become beholden to him. There isn't enough food to keep them all.

'The thing is,' she says, 'all the jobs, we've pretty much got them covered.'

He looks her up and down. His gaze is lascivious, and she feels something stir within her in response. She thinks he's going to make a suggestive remark and braces herself.

'It must be lonely here without your husband,' is one of the favourite approaches.

'My regiment,' he says, taking an unexpected tack. 'We were stationed near Venice. A few of us were out on patrol on the morning of 8 September.'

He's talking about what happened after the government signed the surrender in Cassibile; 8 September was the day it was made public. She knows what he's going to say because she's heard these stories from others but she has to let him say it. It is his story. Not all of them want to tell their tales. They are still in the middle of them, and it isn't yet time for the telling. It's the ones who think that time may never come who tell them anyway.

'Yes,' she says.

'When we got back our base was surrounded by Wehrmacht. We didn't know what was going on. No one had told us. We had no orders. We were on the same side, but they were killing us.'

Whatever the goal that has spurred him on and kept him running, it is failing him now. He is thinking he might have arrived. Some of them, they are not running *to* anything, they are only running *from*. They offer her money sometimes, but there is nothing to buy up here in the hills. Probably not down in the towns either. Food is the currency now.

'We might all be dead tomorrow,' he says. He takes a step towards her, pulling the broom over the paving stones.

She licks her dry lips, holds her ground. She remembers his name and summons up her landlady tone.

'But Goffredo,' she says, 'you managed to get away. You're a survivor. That's what matters.'

He doesn't respond. He leans on the broom, biting his lip. At the doorway, she turns to say something else. He has propped the broom against the wall and stands there, facing the stones, in his vest and trousers, his arms hanging uselessly at his sides. She is going to tell him she is sorry but she thinks better of it. What use is her sorrow?

The air inside the long, low-ceilinged downstairs room of the farmhouse seems colder than it is outside. Cecilia is sewing at a small table set under the side window at the far end. Opposite, on the other side of the heavy, old-fashioned bed that has usurped the kitchen table, Nonna is sitting beside the cold grate. Wrapped in shawls, her crochet hook and ball of wool on her lap, she is in conversation with the empty armchair on the other side of the hearth.

'Not so much as a bleat,' she says, in the high, soft voice she uses nowadays. She is recounting for the umpteenth time the story of the night when half the flock went missing.

The room has the disconsolate smell of yesterday's ashes. The stove at the kitchen end is kept burning, but the main fire is lit only in the evening.

'Not even Gabriele knows,' Nonna says, shaking her head, because her greatest source of wonderment is that Gabriele, the fount of all rural lore and knowledge, is as mystified as she by the sheep's disappearance.

'Perhaps they'll come back, Nonna,' Chiara says, making her way around the great, cumbersome bed and plumping down momentarily on the edge of its mattress, which lets out a horsey whiff. 'Like the one lost lamb.'

'The good shepherd went and looked for that one,' Nonna says, 'he didn't just wait for it to reappear.'

'Gabriele's got a lot to cope with,' Chiara says.

'I know,' Nonna says. 'I'm not gaga. I know there's a war on. I was just telling your *nonno*,' she says, waving her hand at the empty chair, 'about the sheep.'

Chiara gets up again and goes over to her sister's corner. Bending to kiss the top of Cecilia's head, she notices that her sister's hair is not just unbrushed, but matted at the back. Everyone is a bit grubby, bundled in together as they are and with inadequate and overstretched washing facilities, but in Cecilia, normally so groomed and fragrant, it is more noticeable. After that first mammoth seizure in the railway waiting room, she has had a series of minor attacks, small spasms that might almost pass unnoticed. Sometimes they are no more than an extended shudder as if a spider has scuttled across the back of her neck.

'Shall I wash your hair for you before dinner?' Chiara asks.

Cecilia's eyes flick up and then back down to her work. She shakes her head, not so much in refusal as a shaking-off of the suggestion, as if it is rather foolish. Her glasses are smeary.

'Let me clean those,' Chiara says, lifting the spectacles from her sister's nose.

She wipes them on her pinny, one lens at a time, and Cecilia gazes at her blearily as if her vision has blurred, even though the glasses are only for close work, and she can see perfectly well without them.

'I can ask that man in the yard to draw some water.' She places the glasses back on Cecilia's nose. 'That would be a good idea, wouldn't it, Nonna?' she says, wanting an ally, but Nonna has dropped off.

'What are you sewing?' Chiara says, although she can see quite plainly that it is Goffredo's jacket and that Cecilia has clipped off the insignia of the Royal Italian Army and has been pulling out the loose threads. She wants to get Cecilia to talk, to coax words out, because Cecilia seems to be giving up on speech, or it is giving up on her. It is as if she is following Daniele's lead, although where his descent into silence was sudden and total, Cecilia's is a more meandering decline. Now, rather than answer, she holds up the jacket she is working on for Chiara to examine.

Cecilia has become adept at transforming uniforms into new, civilian-style outfits, removing the insignia and exchanging the military buttons, unstitching the side seams and cutting away an arc of cloth from each side to reshape them, then employing the surplus strips to make lapels. The resulting garments would not bear close examination. It would be better if

217

they could dye them too. Nonno's plundered wardrobe has provided some of the raw material. The work is not dissimilar to what Cecilia had been doing before, in Rome. She was known for it there. Women brought their old-fashioned dresses and suits, their mothers' or their grandmothers' gowns, and Cecilia refashioned them into something more modern. It is just that she is working with coarser material now, and her clients are men.

Chiara sits down opposite and watches as Cecilia feeds the fabric into Nonna's old sewing machine. Cecilia's foot starts to work the treadle, and she begins to hum. It isn't a recognisable tune so much as an echo of the treadle's sound.

'How are you getting on with the outfit for the little boy?'

Cecilia has reached the end of the seam. She clips the thread, ties a neat knot, turns the jacket over and smoothes out the other side.

'The little boy I told you about who has no clothes.'

Cecilia pauses, glances up. 'Where's the dirty boy?' she says. She has a greedy look on her face.

'He doesn't stink like you do,' Chiara says in English. 'I'm going to make the bread,' she says, getting up.

At the kitchen end of the room, she ties the apron around her waist, takes the dough from where it has been left to rise above the stove and slaps it onto the wooden counter. She presses it down with the fingertips of one hand, pushes the heel of the other into its centre and stretches it away from her. She scoops it back on itself and repeats the process. She picks up the dough, slaps it down, stretches it out, over and over again.

She lifts a thin membrane of dough between her hands to check its consistency. It is wrinkly and semi-transparent like the skin on Nonna's cheeks. She bundles it into a ball and sets it to prove again.

Mario and Furio, two brothers from Lombardy who are lodged in the lean-to shed with the donkey, are the household's hunters. By day they melt away into the woods with their slingshots and their traps, and at night they reappear to share the hearth. They bring rabbits mostly, once a hare, wood pigeons or small, scanty-fleshed birds that in fatter times would hardly be worth plucking.

'Here we are, signora,' Mario will say with a facial contortion that might be a wink or a tic or, as she fears, some kind of comment on the fact that she has everyone call her signora, when she is not a signora at all, and that he knows this. She has taken to wearing her father's gold signet ring with the face turned in towards her palm as if it were a wedding band. If people assume Daniele is her son, she does not have to explain him. But Mario and Furio were here before she put the ring on.

The latest haul is a brace of rabbits, which Chiara paunched, skinned and boned straightaway. Now she dices the meat into smaller pieces, calculating how many it will have to feed, what she will add to give it bulk. Potatoes would be good, but they don't have any. She surveys her collection of condiments. Rosemary and garlic, salt, bay leaves and juniper berries. She crushes some juniper and instantly the forest scent perfumes and freshens the air. She takes a deep breath of it and is suddenly aware of her own relative youth and strength.

The Allies are coming, the war will end, prisoners will be freed and there will be dancing. She turns to smile the length of the room at Cecilia.

The completed jacket lies on the table next to the sewing machine. Cecilia has removed her glasses. One elbow is on the table and her chin is resting in her hand, fingers over her mouth. She might be looking out of the window. She is facing

219

in that direction. She might be lost in thought. She might just be lost.

We might all be dead tomorrow.

The words reverberate in her head like an invitation. She sets the pot on the stove and then lights the lamps around the room. She scoops up Nonna's ball of wool from where it has fallen and drops it into her lap. Nonna awakens and unhurriedly resumes crocheting as if she doesn't know she's been asleep.

'Do you want to come with me to get some vegetables?' Chiara asks Cecilia. She brushes her floury hands on her apron and rests them lightly on Cecilia's shoulders. She bends forward to press her cheek to her sister's.

'Mm,' Cecilia says.

'Come on then. Quick, before it's too dark to see them.'

But Cecilia doesn't stir. It wasn't assent. It is just the noise Cecilia makes that signals a slight awareness of another person's presence and no more.

Chiara goes quickly and alone to the kitchen garden. Goffredo is gone from the yard. She picks two big cabbages and stares up the hill. The sun is setting. She feels a stab of alarm in her breastbone, a cold piercing. Gabriele and the boy should be back. She wishes she had not let him go.

Cecilia, on her return, hasn't moved.

'Why don't you go and have a lie-down?' Chiara says. 'You're tired. I'll call you when it's dinner time.'

Cecilia allows herself to be led up the narrow staircase to the room they share under the sloping ceiling where the two beds, the bigger one and the truckle bed, stand side by side, separated by a low chest. Chiara lights the candle and puts it on the chest inside its glass frame.

'So you'll know where you are if you wake up before I come back and it's dark,' she says.

Cecilia sits on the side of the big bed. 'I don't know,' she says.

Her face is pale and shadowed, lit from below by the flickering flame, with deep hollows under her eyes. She doesn't know what it is she doesn't know. She knows only that she doesn't know it.

Chiara kneels and unbuckles Cecilia's shoes. 'You'll feel better if you have a snooze,' she says.

'Don't leave me,' Cecilia says.

And so Chiara sits on the lower bed, holding Cecilia's hand. She stares at the crucifix hanging on the wall but she thinks instead about the picture of Jesus that used to hang over their bed in the apartment in San Lorenzo. How, after the time that it fell from the wall, when their mother came to light the red lamp with the taper, a new supplication was added to their prayers: 'Do not turn Thy face from us, Jesus.'

She remembers that she became attuned to any change in Cecilia's breathing pattern. The first bleating sounds would insinuate themselves into Chiara's own sleep, into her dream, so that she would think she was here, up at Nonna and Nonno's farm, and that a sheep had strayed. That would be her signal. She would snap awake, slide out of bed and grip the bed-end, ready. When the seizure began, she would press her whole weight against the bed, bracing it against the wall so that it didn't bang and shake Jesus loose, and no one would know. After the fit had passed and Cecilia slept, Chiara would check that her sister's tongue was not going to choke her, then she would lie down again, holding Cecilia's hand to keep her from straying. In the morning it would be hard to wake Cecilia, and she would be drowsy and uncommunicative over breakfast.

'Was she all right in the night?' Mamma would ask, and Chiara would nod.

'Yes, but it was noisy, and we couldn't sleep.'

It was true. In the street outside, men were drilling into the pavement and turning it all over. As if they were ploughing the cobbles. Not to plant, though, but to uncover what was hidden beneath. The rich treasure of ancient Rome. Rome reunited with itself, with its own past in a seamless line, the wireless said. Glory days.

Mamma would narrow her eyes at bleary Cecilia and then at Chiara, who would yawn too to demonstrate their tiredness more convincingly.

'Cover your mouth with your hand,' her mother sometimes said. 'We don't all want to see your tonsils.'

Chiara looks at her sleeping sister. How tired I am, she thinks.

She goes across the landing to Nonno and Nonna's room. It is cold and smells of mould. Some tiles have come off the roof on this side of the chimney, and the heavy rains they had back in October have found their way in. A greenish stain like seaweed on the chimney breast is spreading outwards. Things these days are either too dry or too wet. The balance is missing. Nonna can't get up the stairs any more, so the bed has been taken downstairs and reassembled there. The boy sleeps at her side on a nest of blankets on the floor.

'We don't bolt the door,' Nonna said, the first night they were here.

'We do now,' Chiara replied, sliding it across and turning the key in the lock.

'What if we need to go in the night?'

'You can use the commode.'

When she comes down in the morning these days, she finds Nonna already up and the little boy asleep in the bed.

The floorboards sigh and bow as Chiara crosses the room.

She peers out of the window, hoping to see Gabriele and the boy appearing over the brow of the hill. The wind has got up, and the pomegranate trees bow their heads. She shivers, feeling a soft crumbling at her core. Bleak outside and in.

She turns away and picks up a book from the bedside table. *A Guide to Italian Mountain Birds.* The pages are stuck together. She prises them apart and there, out of a page depicting a bluethroat perching on a twig, comes a faint whiff of her grandfather's cigar. She aches for him as he was when she was a child, when he would stride off up the track in his hobnailed boots with Gabriele and the men from the village, his rifle over his shoulder, his hessian bag to carry the catch strapped to his belt, his trousers tucked into the thick woollen socks that Nonna knitted on five needles.

The picture that comes to her, though, is of the old, old man, the sad old man who outlived his only son.

She turns away and fumbles her way down the dark staircase.

'I need to go,' Nonna says. 'Help me up.'

Nonna has two sticks that Gabriele fashioned for her. She uses only one when she's in the house but both when she ventures out unassisted. Chiara gives Nonna her arm, and they walk slowly across the yard to the outhouse. She waits at the door for Nonna to finish her business. The sun has not entirely disappeared, and the sky to the east is a radiant lilac. She can see the first shimmer of the moon. Somewhere, a long way off, she can hear explosions. It can't be thunder because the sky is clear.

'I'm glad you're here, Chiarina,' Nonna says on the way back to the house. 'I can't be here on my own. It's not right. I'm eighty-seven and I can't hear very well and my legs don't work. Eighty-seven. Those men, they said, we are your friends. We will get you a good price for your sheep. But I don't know them.'

'What men?' Chiara says.

'Those ones that like killing things,' Nonna says. 'Alfonso is very quiet these days. I worry.'

'Who?' Chiara says.

She leads Nonna over the threshold to her place in front of the hearth. Alfonso was her father's name.

'But where is he now?' Nonna says as she settles into her chair. 'My little man.'

'He's gone with Gabriele to the olive press. I told you. They'll be home soon.'

They should be back by now.

Chiara goes to the kitchen, stares at the stew bubbling in the pot and gives it a stir. She steps down into the cold pantry, lifts her pinny and holds it against her eyes. After a minute she returns to the kitchen. She moves the stew to the oven. She divides the bread dough into two loaves, pummels them one last time and sets them on a tray to bake in the other, hotter side of the oven.

At Cecilia's table, she snaps the cover back over the sewing machine and picks up Goffredo's jacket.

'Won't be a minute,' she says to Nonna and hurries out the door.

She crosses the yard and goes out onto the track. The man from Viterbo, who sleeps with his wife in the grain store, is having a coughing spasm. When the hacking sound finishes, he spits. Chiara slips past, down the track to the barn. She opens the door quietly and stands just within, one hand behind her on the latch, the other holding the jacket. Goffredo has not lit the lamp, but she can see him in the slatted half-light, the glow of his cigarette. He is lying in the hay, smoking, his arms behind his head, gazing up at the rafters. His vest moulds to his ribcage, hugs the hollow of his abdomen.

'I brought your jacket,' she says.

He starts and turns his face towards her. He extricates one of his arms from behind his head, takes the cigarette from between his lips and pushes himself up on one elbow.

'Thanks,' he says.

She pulls the door shut and lets the latch down.

'Do you want to try it on?' she says, taking a step closer and holding it out.

'It'll fit,' he says, 'it's my jacket.'

'But still,' she says and she walks towards him, kneels down in the hay at his side. She sees how young he is. She would put him at nineteen or twenty. Black hair sprouts from his armpits.

He examines her face. 'Your husband on the Russian front, was he?' he says.

She doesn't know where he got this idea, but why not, she thinks. 'Yes,' she says and she shivers at the cold there, out on the icy steppes.

'You've not had news of him?'

'No,' she says.

She lifts his hand with the cigarette in it and holds it to her own mouth, takes a puff, tastes on her lips the smoke and his salty fingers. He removes the cigarette, pinches its lit end between his finger and thumb and puts the stub in a tin by his side. He puts his hand up towards her but it stops midway, hovering in the air. She reaches out, takes hold of his wrist and guides his hand to her breast, to the place in the middle near where her heart wildly beats.

'It doesn't mean you can stay,' she says, her voice muffled by the press of his flesh. 'That's not what it means.'

But she knows he's not listening, and he doesn't care what it does or doesn't mean.

It's the donkey that alerts them to the return of Gabriele and the boy, her hooves clattering and then her bray, the 'I'm home, fetch out the oats' call that she always makes at the bottom of the track where it turns towards the house.

Chiara draws blood when he presses the palm of his hand against her mouth to muffle her cries.

Blood for blood, she thinks.

When she steps outside into the yard, smoothing down her apron, Gabriele, with the help of two men she has not seen before, is hauling the first barrel of oil in through the door.

'Two more for dinner tonight,' Gabriele says, introducing them: Manfredo and another one whose name she doesn't catch because she has caught sight of the child behind them, his eyes burning bright like hot coals. It is one of those moments again, when he is back in this world, truly present. They are coming thick and fast these moments, she thinks, for both of them.

She grins at him. He doesn't smile back. He never smiles, never speaks. But one day, she thinks, he will, and she'll be there.

Her hands smell of the man now, stronger than the juniper and the dough, the meat, blood and earth, overlaying every-thing, even the decay. They might all be dead tomorrow, but they're alive today.

'Never says a word. He just pulls at my sleeve, and I look down, thinking he wants to stop for a piss, excuse my way of speaking, signori, and he's got his finger on his lips, shushing me. I look up where he's looking and I see them, two of them, standing on the higher path.'

Gabriele's voice rises, creaking like the wind in the trees, and he coughs to adjust it.

'I had my head down. I didn't see them, didn't hear them,' he says, his pitch lower, heartier.

He looks around the circle of faces as they sit in the firelight, their plates on their laps. Gravy drips from the piece of bread in his hand.

'Two of them,' he repeats, 'and one switches on a torch and he starts shining it around and about. Me and him,' he jabs his thumb towards Daniele, 'we creep behind a bush, me and the little man, eagle eyes.'

She can smell Goffredo on her fingers although she rinsed her hands before dinner, and she can feel his eyes on her, but she is watching Daniele, on the opposite side of the hearth. He shrinks further into the shadowy space he has chosen between the side of Nonna's armchair and the hearth.

'We can't move the donkey without making a noise so we leave her there, out on the track, by herself. Any minute, it could have . . .'

Gabriele shakes his head at the impossibility of explaining all the things that could have happened: that the donkey, left alone, might bray or move a hoof or snuffle or snort or rumble forward with the cart; that the torchlight might find her; that they might be discovered out after curfew, and seized, arrested or worse. That the oil, God forbid, that the oil might be taken.

'But it didn't,' he says.

They are so many tonight the room is crowded. It is good they have the oil and the bread to fill them up and make the dollop of unexpectedly tasty stew – which might have burnt, neglected as it was, but instead is cooked just right – go further.

All these years, she thinks, all her life in fact, she has known Gabriele, the shepherd. He has come and gone according to his own law and sometimes he has eaten bread and cheese at their table. But never, until this war, has she sat down and supped with him, night after night, as an equal.

'He doesn't say much but he's a clever little bugger, excuse my way of speaking, signori,' Gabriele says. 'Signorino,' he adds with a kind of bow to Daniele.

He mops up the last of his gravy, solemnly chews the crust of bread and gazes into the flames, his moment of unaccustomed animation at an end.

They have blown out the lamps and are eating by the light of the fire because they don't want the house shining out like a beacon if the German patrol should come in this direction.

Everything already tasted better in the orange glow and heat, with everyone crowded round in a circle, sitting where they can, on benches and on the floor and two to a wooden chair, and with the thick, peppery-sweet oil to help the food slide down. But now, hearing how hard-won the oil was, how nearly lost, the flavours are enhanced. They tear off pieces of the fresh bread and dip them in the green-gold liquor. It flows down the inside of their throats, coats their tongues and loosens them.

The woman from Viterbo, Signora Morelli, who now announces that her name is Beatrice, is coquettish in the firelight on the end of the bench where Goffredo and the newcomers also sit. She starts on a story about her own encounter with an advance guard of German soldiers, the day of the battle for Rome. Chiara, only half paying attention, replete in new and unfathomable ways, hears the phrase 'holding the line' and is left with the impression that if there had been more like Beatrice, Rome might not have fallen.

She gazes around at the faces in the firelight, lingering a moment on Goffredo who is leaning in, talking in a low voice to Manfredo and his friend. Perhaps he will team up with them. No one, after all, wants to be alone. He raises his eyes to her, and she switches her gaze away. One of the brothers

228

from Lombardy pipes up, something about the chickens he and his brother have spotted in the valley at the German encampment and a daring plan to steal them back one at a time.

She's thinking, Don't do that, it would be foolish. Don't draw attention.

People have found new versions of their tales, reached them down from a sagging shelf and given them a polish, buffed them and turned them so that the side that shows is the best side. The hopeful one.

She seeks out Cecilia in the flickering glow and then she realises that Cecilia is not there. She has forgotten to wake her.

THIRTEEN

On the train to Italy, Maria had the space under the window where she slept fitfully, wrapped in her purple crushed-velvet coat, the last in a close-packed line of six recumbent bodies.

Her mum had bought a couchette ticket.

'I need to know that you're safe,' she had said, as if a tightly tucked-in bunk bed in a single-sex carriage was the answer.

Maria hadn't objected because she was speaking to her mother only when it was strictly necessary but she had returned to the travel agent the following day and changed it for a cheaper place in something called a recliner carriage. She had imagined languid ladies in silk gowns reclining on chaise longues, but in reality it just meant that the seats slid forward and the armrests retracted, so that the whole thing transformed into one uncomfortable and incomplete giant bed.

Until Paris, there had been five of them, which was bad enough, but then another person had come aboard, clambering over the others and squeezing in beside her. His stockinged feet brushed against her cheek.

Sleeping with other people wasn't something Maria was much used to. She had always had her own room. The strain of holding herself apart from the newcomer reminded her of the time she had shared a bed with her granny, long before her brother and sister were born. She had awoken, sticky with heat, her Bri-Nylon nightie clinging to her skin as if she were ill. Granny had left the electric blanket switched on. It was cooking them both, releasing their juices as they baked. Granny's smell was pink and musty, dried roses with an underlying crumbling damp, like the section of the pantry wall where the rain came in. Her own perfume was subtler. She had recognised it without quite being able to smell it. A sense of herself as other and separate and on her own had come to her then, and whenever the vision of this moment presented itself, that was the feeling that accompanied it. The clock tick-tocking out on the landing, and she alone and apart and delineated, on the high, hot bed. She must have been three years old. She had always thought this was her earliest memory but now, revisiting it, she sensed something older, more wordless, hidden lower down, as if tucked beneath. It was bright red, flapping in sunlight, a kite or a banner. As she reached, it flicked away.

Granny. Why had they left her with that woman who wasn't, as it turned out, even her grandmother? I don't like Granny, she used to think. Now she understood that it was Granny who didn't like her.

Erstwhile granny, former granny, ex-granny. Ha! She would never again have to eat mutton and barley stew for tea on Thursdays.

Ex-Granny, of course, must have been in on the deception. The smugness of it. The perfidy. Maria had made her non-biological father, Barry, list them, all the people who knew. No one's treachery was on a par with her mother's.

'I forgave her. Can't you?' Barry had said on one of his

peace missions to her room, where she kept him on the threshold, barring his way.

'What did you have to forgive her for?' she had asked him and then she realised before he had thought of an answer. 'For me,' she had said. 'You forgave her for having me, didn't you?'

The train was rattling through a tunnel. She lifted the crook of her elbow to her nose, pressing flesh against skin, but she couldn't seem to detect her own unique scent, whatever made her *her*.

She awoke to pressure. She was on her back. The boy next to her must have inadvertently flung out his arm in his sleep. It lay across her thighs and had found its way underneath her coat, like a mole looking for its burrow. She picked the arm up gingerly by the sleeve as if it did indeed contain a small wild animal. The boy snored. She pushed the arm into the crack between them. The boy sighed a quivering sigh as if he were having a sad dream of loss.

She fell so profoundly asleep again that when someone shook her awake, she struggled to grasp where she was. Two men in uniform were at the door of the carriage, and the other passengers were already sitting up, answering questions. The light had been switched on, and people looked ghastly in its glow. The men had a dog. They were looking at her, expecting an explanation.

'I gave my passport to the guard,' she said.

Perhaps he hadn't been a guard; perhaps he was an imposter who stole British passports to sell on to forgers and criminals. The foremost of the uniformed men already had a bunch of passports in his gloved hand, among them two navy-blue embossed ones. She didn't understand what he was saying. A kind of deafness descended on her when she was nervous, an inability to make sense of language, even her own, especially when it was transmitted over tannoys, radios or loudspeaker systems, especially if it was important.

Then she understood that they were saying her name, and she nodded.

'That's me,' she said. 'Maria Kelly.'

She might change her name by deed poll. She knew a boy who had changed his surname from Jones to Gilmour so he could seem to be related to the Pink Floyd guitarist. The uniformed men slid the door shut and left.

'They do spot checks at the border sometimes,' the boy next to Maria said in a faintly posh kind of voice.

He must be the other British citizen. A strawberry birthmark crept up from inside his shirt, staining his collarbone and the underside of his chin. His hair was lank. The exoticness of his not being French but boarding in Paris was undone by his appearance. She gave him a half-smile, sorry for his sad dreams and his disfigurement. He smiled back as if he knew her, and she swerved her eyes away.

Everyone shuffled back into position.

Maria sat scrunched at the window with her coat over her knees. She tried to feel the marvel of being in Italy where she had never been before, of being in her third country in less than twenty-four hours and far from home. She watched the sparse lights of an anonymous town flash by. She was gazing through her own reflection. She drew her gaze back to her hollow-eyed image and then looked through herself again. She was a ghostly apparition in the Italian night. 'Me and My Shadow' played plaintively round and round in her head.

She took out from her pocket the signet ring that had belonged to Daniele Levi. The ring was heavy, solid gold with a pattern like a sunburst engraved on the flat oval front, seven bevelled lines radiating out from a central point. On the inside, the letters AFR could still be read, but only just, their edges softened by time and wear. To see them, the ring had to be held at a certain angle. She put the ring on her forefinger, twisted it so that the round, flat part was on the inside. She closed her fist around it, tight against her palm, feeling its weight.

She lay down again, pulled the coat over her head and stuck her thumb in her mouth for comfort.

There had been another realignment of bodies by the next time she awoke. The strawberry-faced boy was now the same way up as her and they were lying face to face. There was a yellowy half-light in the carriage. He was staring at her. His breath smelt of toothpaste. Maria closed her eyes against him and manoeuvred herself round to face the window. He was too close and she didn't like it. She fished about down the gap between the seats for her handbag, hooked it out and climbed across the bodies to the doorway. Strawberry Boy had pulled his sleeping bag over his face.

The corridor was striped with blinding bands of early-morning light. Maria propped herself against the wall in one of the darker patches and pulled out her packet of No. 6. There were only two left. She had meant to invest in a carton of two hundred duty-free on the ferry from Dover, but it seemed a lot of money to part with in one go. She blew smoke out and watched it plume in the strip of sunshine streaming in through the dirty window. She wished she hadn't given a cigarette away to some unknown boy on the ferry. She took a step sideways so she was in sunlight, shut her eyes and let it bathe her. There was an orange glow behind her closed lids.

She hadn't slept at all on the ferry. She had sat in the garishly lit café on F deck with her stomach churning, surrounded by

235

people, hordes of them, drinking tea and beer and showing the insides of their mouths. A child at the next table was being sick.

She had climbed the internal stairs as high as she could get, wrenched a heavy door open and stepped out onto a narrow walkway where a powerful rush of wind had nearly blown her over. It was so harsh and cold that it had scraped the hair back on her head and made her eyes water, but it had also carried away the clogging stench of fuel and cold greasy fittings. She had battled her way against it to the far end. There the torrent of air became a virtual wall, an invisible force field, so that when she pushed her way through it to the other side, it was as if she had passed through a portal into a different dimension from which the wind had been banished. She had hunkered down next to a lifeboat. With her hands cupped over her shocked and frozen ears, in a haven of her own discovery amid the thrill of the dark waters thundering by, she had smoked a cigarette in her own little private space.

But when she had stood up to go she had seen that farther along the walkway, back the way she had come and would have to return, a hooded man was leaning over the rail. She had squatted down again, thinking to wait until he left. Then he was standing in front of her, his face hidden inside the hood of his duffel coat.

'Excuse me,' he had said, 'I couldn't bum a fag off you, could I?'

He was talking about feeling sick and coming outside for fresh air, asking her where she was headed. Gate-crashing.

She had given him a cigarette.

'I owe you one,' he had called after her.

She opened her eyes. She stubbed the cigarette out in the metal ashtray screwed into the wall. The guard was approaching. He stopped at each carriage, sliding the doors open and announcing something to the occupants, handing back passports. The corridor filled up in his wake as people spilt out.

'I owe you one,' a voice said. The stained boy was at her side.

She looked at the proffered cigarette and then at him. He must be the boy on the boat. It would be nice to have a back-up cigarette.

'I'll save it for later,' she said.

'Sorry if I was squashing you,' he said. 'I turned the other way up because I thought my feet were smelly. You wouldn't want my smelly feet in your face.'

The guard approached. Unlike the earlier one, he was young and handsome with a confident swagger about him. He pushed his cap back on his head and said her name, 'Maria Kel-ly,' rolling the R in Maria reverberatingly and lingering over the double L as if her name were a musical instrument and he was plucking the notes.

She smiled at him. '*Si*,' she said.

He flicked open the passport, looked at the photo, then at her and held the open passport to his chest, pressed against his heart. He said some words to her that seemed like the words of a poem. He held the passport out, but when she went to take hold he snatched it playfully away. He spoke again.

'He asked what you would give him in exchange,' the strawberry boy said.

Maria shook her head, out of her depth.

The guard laughed, handed her the passport and moved on.

'Nice alveolar trill he's got,' the boy said.

Maria didn't ask what he meant. 'What did he say before?'

'I think he might have been quoting Petrarch,' the boy said.

Maria watched the guard make his way down the carriage, swaying to the movement of the train, perfectly balanced.

237

'Fourteenth-century poet,' he added. 'He wrote love poems to a woman he knew could never be his.'

The guard disappeared from view.

'Didn't you get on at Paris?' she said.

'No,' he said, shaking his head in an innocent way. 'I just switched carriage there. The one I was in was full.' He looked away from her, out of the window where electricity pylons sped past.

She understood that he had been following her.

'We'll be in Milan soon,' he said. 'We could go for a coffee.'

She wondered at his boldness, with him being so marred. 'I'm going to Rome,' she said.

'Oh, shame,' he said. A silence fell between them.

'How come you speak Italian?' she said eventually.

'My dad lives in Milan. I've just been back in London visiting Mamma, who is Italian, but my *babbo*, who's English, works in Italy.' He made a snorting noise as if mocking the topsy-turvy world that was his family.

'*Babbo?*' she said. She liked the word.

'It means dad. Or you can say *papà*.'

'So you're half Italian?' she said carefully, feeling the tremor in her spine, the wobble of a diving board beneath her feet, conscious of holding herself back from its edge.

'Yes, I am, officially, yes, but I don't feel Italian. I was brought up in England. So I've come to live with my dad to discover my *Italiano* side.'

In profile he looked better. His nose was very straight. Now that he was getting off soon, Maria found she didn't mind him so much.

'They never spoke Italian to me when I was little.'

Mine never even told me, she thought. The words were

238

fizzing on her tongue like hundreds and thousands. She would never see him again. She could say it.

'I could have been brought up bilingual. What a leg-up that would have been. To have your feet firmly in two cultures,' he said.

Maria imagined the Thames lapping grubbily around one foot, sewage and old, oily things streaming between the toes, and the other foot in the Tiber. She didn't know what things might float in the Tiber or be hidden beneath its surface but in her guidebook it referred to it as 'Tiber the Blond', so the water must be golden and limpid and restorative, light made liquid. She imagined floating in those waters and this heaviness being lifted from her.

'Apparently a child can learn up to five languages in their early years,' he was saying. 'They get them mixed up at the beginning, and it delays speech by six months or even a year, so a polylingual child might not actually make an utterance until he's two or even three, but it's just because the brain is internalising and making sense of all the data. And then when they're off, they're off, switching from one to another without a problem. Imagine how that must expand your mind. Like being able to play five different instruments. But each one like a soloist.'

Maria added musical instruments to her translucent vision. A harp.

'What's your mission in Rome?' he asked.

She liked that notion, that she had a mission. But the moment when she might blurt something out to a strawberry stranger had passed.

'I have a job for the summer with an Italian lady. I'm going to be her companion and correct her English pronunciation which is' – she sought the word Signora Ravello had used in her letter – 'execrable.'

Maria had had to look it up in the dictionary but she didn't think this boy would need it explaining. Signora Ravello was going to be waiting for Maria at Roma Termini station in front of the newspaper stand. She would have a copy of *Il Messaggero* under her arm and would be wearing a mushroom-shaped hat. How strange it was that this unknown lady had agreed to have her to stay.

'Sounds interesting,' the boy said. 'I have to get my stuff together. I'm Tom. Tommaso.'

He smiled apologetically, perhaps to indicate that he knew how ill-fitting the Italian name was, with his skin a patchwork of red and white, and his hair the colour of the dust that collects under the bed.

The seats in the carriage had been pushed back into their daytime version, and people were gathering their things. It seemed that everyone but Maria was getting off at Milan.

As the train pulled into the station, Tommaso presented her with a piece of paper folded many times and then tucked into itself.

'If you ever come to Milan,' he said, then added, 'I might come to Rome sometime,' just as she said, 'I would like to see *The Last Supper*.'

It was the only thing she knew about Milan. That Leonardo's painting was there, hanging in a refectory. She had a brief vision of a school canteen, knives and forks clattering, children stuffing themselves with sausages and gravy, oblivious to the benediction of the famous painting glowing on the wall above them.

'It's terribly faded,' he said. 'Bits have disappeared entirely. It's covered in white spots.'

He bent to do up his shoelaces, talking now about the different binding agents Leonardo had experimented with, while

Maria's eyes filled with tears, as if the notion that the painting might vanish entirely before she had seen it was more than she could bear.

Everyone is leaving me, she thought, resenting Tommaso now for still pontificating about tempera and gesso, when he too was leaving her.

She put her face to the carriage window to watch as Tommaso disappeared among the crowds in the domed vastness of Milan station. Sunshine streamed down between high iron arches onto the heads and faces of the noisy people thronging the platform.

After Milan, the family Maria shared the carriage with — three teenagers and a stout lady with a moustache who seemed too old to be their mother, too young to be their grandmother — tried to engage her in conversation.

Maria had been teaching herself Italian. She had bought an old grammar book from the second-hand bookshop in the arcade in town and had borrowed a series of records from the library, sitting for hours in her bedroom, ostensibly revising for her exams but actually listening over and over again, repeating the phrases, memorising whole dialogues. Those words had accompanied her in her daily life, so that when she was walking home from the bus stop, or eating her dinner against the backdrop of her parents' strained conversation, they played like songs in her head. She had felt that somewhere within her was a well of this language that would rise up once she was in Italy. But now, surrounded by the sheer concentrated Italianness of it all, she couldn't understand a single word.

'Do you have that handbag in another colour?' was the only phrase that came to her.

They gave her a sandwich. The unbuttered bread was dry, chewy and dense. Inside there was a piece of something quite horrible. Flabby ribbons of it got instantly stuck between her teeth. The family made sucking noises at her in an exaggerated pantomime of people enjoying their food. It required a lot of chomping, an unaccustomed sideways movement of the jaw to mush it down into a form that could be swallowed. They watched her with interest, as if they were leaning against a farmyard fence and she in the field beyond, chewing the cud. The slimy thing was pasted to the back of her teeth.

The woman spoke.

'I don't understand,' Maria said in English. 'I don't understand,' she repeated, in Italian this time.

The phrases from the record were back. She trawled through them, joining the beginning of one to the end of another.

'Can you repeat?' she said, or might have said. 'I speak bad?' That was a rhetorical question, she wanted to add, but all subtlety was lost. 'What is this?' she asked, indicating the contents of the sandwich.

The woman said the word for ham.

Maria took out her Collins pocket dictionary and checked. Yes, that word definitely meant ham. She showed the younger son who was sitting next to her. He looked and nodded, added another word, found it in the dictionary and showed her.

Crudo. Raw.

She stared out of the window. She had been eating raw meat. She thought she might be sick. She put the napkin to her mouth, spat out the piece of slime curled inside her cheek, wiped her lips, crumpled it further and stuffed it into her bag.

The boy moved back to the other side, the better to ogle her, it seemed. In between poking through the contents of the basket on the old lady's knee, or whispering in her ear, or leaning over to read the older one's papers on his lap, he would revert to staring at Maria, goggle-eyed. She started to wonder whether he was a bit simple. It's rude to stare, she wanted to say. His mother or gran or whatever she was should tell him off. But then this was the woman who was sitting with her legs akimbo in a way that revealed the veins right at the top of her stockings and who fed her family on raw meat.

Once the food was put away, they had a sort of limited conversation, using the dictionary, sign language, the mongrel phrases Maria managed to splice together. They wanted to know where she was going, where her family was, who was meeting her, why she was so far from home. They discussed her answers to these questions among themselves. It seemed to be a source of strangeness and mystery to them that a girl so young should be allowed to travel by herself, and they couldn't get over it, exclaiming in various ways that she didn't understand but shaking their heads and tutting in a way that she did.

She heard the word 'mamma' repeated often. It started to get on her nerves. My mamma, not that it's any business of yours, she would have said, agrees with you that I am too young.

Maria bit her lip in order not to cry.

'I can see why you want to punish us, your father and me,' her mum had said when the school had told them about Maria missing her exams, 'but this is about you and your future.'

She had been sitting at the desk in the back room with the letter from the headmistress in front of her. She had been trying to persuade Maria to sit the remaining exams. She must have forgotten to put on her overall when she had made dinner because there was gravy down her front.

Maria could actually feel it. A hardening of her heart, as if that organ were turning into a very hard nut, a brazil.

'He's not my father,' she said.

Her mother had put her head in her hands. 'I don't know what to do with you,' she had said, and started to cry.

The sharp upper edge of Maria's brazil-nut heart had been digging into the bottom of her throat from the inside. She swallowed, but it kept pricking.

'I don't know either,' she had managed to say. Then she had discovered that she did. 'Let me go to Italy,' she had said.

She sank back into herself. She had fought so hard. She had threatened to sabotage the rest of her exams, to run away. She had bargained and shouted. She had made them let her come. To be sitting here on a foreign train by herself. Alone.

She looked out of the window. Yellow and green fields dotted with farmhouses the colour of peaches. Blossom-laden trees. An old tractor, and a dog with a squashed black face, wearing a red collar, tied to a gatepost. She thought of her mother running along beside the train at Victoria, her stricken white face bobbing.

Good, she had thought. Now you know how it feels.

She clutched for that sensation of triumph but it eluded her. I wish, she thought, but couldn't finish. There was nothing to wish for. It couldn't be undone. Once something was known, it couldn't then be made unknown.

FOURTEEN

The bedroom is bright with moonlight, and something is awry. Chiara's first thought is for Cecilia, because Cecilia has taken to wandering in the night. Twice Chiara has fetched her back from Nonno and Nonna's old room across the landing where she stood, swaying in the middle of the sagging floor, her arms held out, as if on a tightrope in the wind. Chiara wonders whether it is her medication, if it needs adjusting. Another time it was Nonna's cries that had alerted Chiara. She ran downstairs and was less astonished somehow to find Cecilia uselessly rattling the doorknob, her eyes open but unseeing, than Nonna and Daniele sitting up in bed next to each other, wide-eyed and vaguely guilty, like an illicit couple caught in flagrante. Now, though, her sister is fast asleep beside her, just a lump under the bedclothes.

She gets up and goes to the window, lifts the curtain. The moon is full, making the steep field and hillside look like slopes of ice. The olive trees scattered about the grove are etched black against the silver. It is an other-worldly scene, but nothing seems out of place. There is no disturbance.

She turns back into the room, holding the curtain up to let in the silver light, and looks at her sister, her face soft and

245

peaceful. She listens to the movements of the house, the faint creaks and stirrings. The hiss and puff of air down the chimney, the sighing of old soot, the faint coo of a night-time bird, the scurrying of little clawed feet up in the roof. Nothing untoward.

She returns to the window. Her eyes are drawn to the edge of the grove, where the olive trees are replaced by oak, sycamore and ash, and the tree-line thickens. There stands the most ancient tree of all, the Mago, that she had described to Daniele on their train journey. Near the bottom of its gnarled and twisted trunk there is a hollow big enough to fit a person, or two small ones at a squeeze.

She pulls on her shoes, wraps a blanket around herself like a cloak. It is the coldest night yet. She carries the lantern out onto the landing and lights it there so as not to awaken her sister. She swings the lantern ahead of her down the stairs, casting strange shadows on the lumpy white walls. She steps close to the bed and holds the lamp aloft. Daniele's nest of blankets is piled up next to Nonna, who breathes soft and low, with a faint whistle on the out-breath. Chiara does not need to poke the blanket pile to know it is empty.

The front door is still locked and bolted. In any case the bolt is too heavy for Daniele to open unaided. And she has the key upstairs with her. Without moving, she sends her mind around the whole of the downstairs, testing the windows. She lights her way the length of the room to the kitchen, pushes the pantry door open and peers in. The high little window is swinging open, and a stool has been pulled underneath. She climbs onto the stool and sticks her head out into the courtyard. She can see how the woodpile stacked against the wall below the window might provide a sort of landing point halfway to the ground.

Gently, she slides open the bolt of the front door and steps out into the courtyard. The air is sharp, and a night wind rustles through the few remaining leaves on the fig tree, rattling the fruit that still hang like spent lanterns on the leafless persimmon tree, stirring up a crackle among the new fallen leaves. She tucks herself against the stone wall in behind one of the buttresses. They were added after an earthquake shook the house loose, stone props to nail the building into the hillside. She feels the weight of the house at her back, sensing the temptation lurking within its ancient stone and crumbling mortar to call it a day now, to collapse back into rock and rubble, to slide down the hill in its own miniature avalanche, taking with it the woodpile and the outhouse, the lower vegetable patch and the barn, rolling and tumbling, snagging on trees and tussocks and old stone walls, gathering pace before it crashes into the stream at the bottom of the hill.

She shakes her head to dispel the image, and her breath plumes ghostly white in front of her face. She looks towards the gate from where she would be able to see up into the olive grove but stays where she is. The gate is spotlit by shafts of silvery moonlight pouring down over the tops of the trees. To stand there would be to reveal herself to the child and deny him his secret. She imagines him crouched in the hollow, bathed in moonbeams.

Let him be, she thinks.

Her bare feet on the cold stone are freezing. Her urge to spy on him dissipates. She needs only to know that he is safe. She hurries back inside and bolts the door. By the light of the lamp, she takes a look at her sleeping *nonna*. She is the real buttress, and while she is there, quietly breathing, the lungs of the house, it will hold. She blows out the lamp and retreats up and around the bend of the stairs. She waits.

247

Eventually she hears him scrabbling at the wall outside and his panting breath as he tugs himself through the window, then a clatter as if he has knocked the stool over and fallen. She holds her breath. She thinks she can hear stifled gasps, but he does not cry out.

This child will break my heart, she thinks.

She waits, straining to hear. She is about to go down again to investigate when she hears the pantry door shutting and, a few seconds later, the thud of his shoes being kicked off, his snuffly breaths, the creak of the bedsprings.

She creeps back up the stairs and slips under the covers. She is moved to formulate some sort of prayer and knows it will not be valid from the comfort of her bed. She needs to suffer in some way.

She climbs out and lowers herself, lifting her nightdress away so that her bare knees meet the hard cold floor.

'Let him, dear Lord, please,' she mumbles. Whatever he has wished for, she wishes it for him too.

On winter mornings scents are fewer but more pungent and they seem to carry a greater distance. Chiara wakes to the aroma of coffee wafting up the stairs and the noises of Nonna moving slowly about below. She can lie in her bed and identify Nonna's different activities from the sounds. The rattle and scrape as she adds some logs to the stove and gives the fire a poke, the clank of the oven door, the chink of china as she sets out two cups on the table, the gurgle of the coffee rising.

Sometimes Chiara opens her eyes and looks at the yellow curtains at the steamy window, smells the coffee and experiences a moment of pure joy. Cecilia is there beside her, safe if not sound. She has even, finally, started to make new clothes for the child. Or, at least, she has taken him into their bedroom for fittings more than once, although there is as yet no sign of any actual clothes. He doesn't like the fittings. He likes being out roaming the land.

The child and Nonna are downstairs. Gabriele is out there somewhere, sniffing the air to find which way the wind is blowing, mending the fences, tending the animals. She has to be careful with their supplies, but they are not going hungry, not yet. Goffredo has been replaced by a succession of different men on the run – Paolo, Luigi, Sergio, two Marios, Filippo and a stream of others. They come and go, blur into each other. One way or another, before she sends them onwards, she gives them each some love.

Today she is brimming with joy as she lies for a moment, listening to her grandmother clattering about below. She doesn't know why, and then all of a sudden she remembers the child's night-time escapade. To make a wish, she reflects, there needs to be hope. The child is hopeful.

Soon, with Gabriele and perhaps with Daniele too, they will sow seeds for spring.

In a way, life has never been so simple. It is a question of surviving, doing the best she can in the circumstances, looking after her charges. In the mornings, when she has the most work to do with baking and cooking, washing and cultivating the vegetable garden, Daniele runs free or accompanies Gabriele. In the afternoons they sit at the kitchen table and she reads out loud to him from the only three books in the house (apart from the copy of Keats's letters in English and the old picture book they brought with them): the *Children's Poetry Compendium* from 1913 that had been used to prop up the rickety table and has to be returned to its place after each session: Nonno's bird manual; and the bible. She gets him to copy out sentences and is surprised by how quickly he acquires the skill. He is only seven and he can't ever have gone to school, because the race laws were introduced in 1938.

That first slice of morning, when she and her grandmother are drinking their coffee, and the boy is asleep still in the big bed, is when Nonna is at her liveliest.

'I told the little man to hop in and keep warm when I got up,' she always says, maintaining the pretence of separate beds.

They will both look at the child, ensconced in blankets, tumbled into a heap on the edge of the bed as if he has been dropped there from a height, and Nonna will reminisce about Chiara's father when he was a little boy, Alfonso and Daniele sometimes merging.

'Do you remember?' she will ask about events that happened thirty years before Chiara's birth. Time has concertinaed so that yesterday for Nonna might be a yesterday of fifty years ago but it shines more brightly than more recent days.

Afterwards, Chiara helps her grandmother wash and dress. She brings her a bowl of warm water, and Nonna dabs at herself under her woollen petticoat, which she refuses to remove.

'I don't want to take things off. I want to be putting them on,' is her refrain as Chiara wraps and bundles her into her layers as if she were swaddling a baby.

This morning, when Chiara comes softly down the stairs, she catches Nonna peering at the sleeping child.

'He has bad dreams,' is all she says.

They take their coffee beside the stove, standing up.

'Putting off the moment,' Nonna says. Once she sits down in the armchair, as a rule she doesn't get back up, except for visits to the outhouse.

'Are the buds late this year?' she asks.

'No, Nonna, it's only December.'

'Is it? I thought it was later.' And then, 'If I'm still here in the spring, I'll take my petticoat off then.'

Chiara looks at her and smiles, assailed by a brief image of a bizarre celebration where old ladies dance naked among the green shoots.

'Where else would you be but here?' she asks.

Her *nonna* takes one clawed old hand from the coffee cup, and points down at the flagstone floor. 'Under there,' she says.

'Oh, Nonna,' Chiara says. 'Don't.'

'Look after the little man for me, won't you. I do worry what he'll do without me.'

'He doesn't have to do without you,' Chiara says.

'I'm not long for this world,' Nonna says. 'It's all in the cabinet in my bedroom.'

'What is?'

'All the papers, documents of ownership, my will. I've left it all to Alfonso, but he'll see you right. You and Ceci. Why doesn't she like him? Keep an eye on her. Don't let her stray into sin.'

'Who, Nonna? What sin? I'm not following you.'

'In the cabinet. Go and check.'

'I will, but what sin?' Chiara says.

'Ooh.' Nonna shakes her head, turns it to look towards the far end of the room, twists her furrowed lips into a deeper furrow. 'One of the deadly ones, I expect.'

And then, before Chiara can get to the bottom of any of it, can unpick what is sense and what is nonsense, what was then and what might be now, Nonna calls out, 'Good morning, little man,' and there he is, sitting up in bed with the blanket pulled up to his chin like a bib, fixing them with his dark, unfathomable eyes.

And Chiara wonders, as she often does, how long he has been there, silently watching and listening.

Chiara drains the big pan of chickpeas that have been soaking overnight, picks out the brown and grey ones from among the mound, adds fresh water and puts it on the stove to come to a boil. A dark shadow, two shadows, pass the window, and she glances up, misses seeing whoever it is, but something – the clack of the boots on the cobbles, the shape of the helmeted heads, or perhaps a belated awareness of having heard a distant engine sound not long before – kicks her into motion, and she is hurtling the length of the room, a bulb of garlic clutched in her hand, knowing only that she has to get to the door before them.

Silently, agonisingly, trying to avoid the screech it can make, she pushes the bolt home. They bang at the door. Daniele – sitting at the table, copying a picture from the bird book, his feet dangling, his left big toe like a wrinkled yellow chickpea poking out of a hole in his sock – looks up.

'Hide,' she says.

He slides down, stands bewildered, casting about.

'Not in the house,' she says. She makes a motion towards the pantry and, soundlessly on stockinged feet, skidding across the flagstones, he is gone.

'Open up,' the German voice outside bellows. Another rap.

'I'm coming, I'm coming,' she shouts, 'the bolt is stiff.'

She rattles the door once to show willing and then surges back through the room like a tidal wave, snatching up Daniele's shoes from under the table and pushing them up the chimney onto the little ledge around the bend, sweeping his drawing, book and pencil into the table drawer, yanking out a uniform jacket from Cecilia's sewing machine, tearing at the coarse fabric, breaking the needle. The timbre of the rapping at the door sharpens, made not by a fist but a weapon.

'Coming,' she shrieks to be heard above the noise and Cecilia's frightened yelps.

She runs to the pantry, whips away the stool, pushes the window shut, runs back to the door and starts to slide the bolt, panting.

'Coming, just a moment, hold your horses,' she shouts and sees she has the uniform still bunched in her hands.

And she spins, literally spins, then runs to Nonna, who says weakly, 'But what's happening?'

Chiara thrusts the jacket at her and is back at the door, wrenching it open. There are three of them and they step immediately inside, pressing her along with them. 'The bolt gets stuck,' she says. 'I have to keep it bolted because we are just three women on our own here.'

'Just three women,' Nonna pipes up in a shrill little voice. 'It's a scandal,' she says, tugging at her outermost shawl, pulling it more tightly around herself, tucking it into an in-between layer. She has secreted the jacket somewhere about her person.

The foremost soldier surveys the room, stares at Cecilia sitting at her broken sewing machine, whimpering, at Nonna all bundled up in front of the cold grate.

'Who else is here?' he says.

'No one,' Chiara says.

He turns to look at her. His eyes are a soft blue. 'No one?' he says.

'No one but us in the house,' she says. She thinks quickly. 'There are people staying in one of our outbuildings, a sick man and a woman who have lost their home.'

The Lombardy brothers will be out hunting and by day they

leave no trace of their occupation of the donkey's stall. For the men in the barn, she can do nothing. Only hope that they are out.

The soldier nods at the other two men. One thunders upstairs, the other begins poking round the room, in and out of the pantry, behind the curtains; he opens and shuts cupboards, lifts the lid of the pot of chickpeas on the stove and recoils. They show the officer their identity documents. Through the open door, Chiara sees two more soldiers coming up the lower path. They have between them the man who is staying in the barn.

She is escorted outside by all three of the soldiers.

'Who is this man?' they ask.

She looks at him. He arrived two days before, the youngest son of a farmer from Tuscany. Last night he told her that until he tasted their olive oil, he had thought his father produced the best oil in the land. He has a mole on his left shoulder. His big toe and the one next to it are joined, up to the first knuckle. Duck feet, he says they are. His jacket is stuffed inside Nonna's shawl. He is Filippo Pistelli from Panzano.

'I don't know,' she says.

'He was in your barn.'

'In the barn,' she gasps, and clutches her hands to her chest. 'Thank you for finding him. There are so many vagabonds in the hills. That is why we keep the door bolted.'

'Vagabonds,' Nonna says. She has made her way to the doorstep, creaking on her stick. 'They stole my sheep.'

'It is an offence to harbour fugitives,' the leader tells her.

'I didn't know anyone was in the barn. We don't use it any more.' She knows that there are cigarette ends, bedclothes, a lamp in there. 'I will be more vigilant,' she says and now she does it, for the first time in her life: she makes the fascist salute.

He salutes her in return, seems to click his heels. 'Do you have a telephone here?'

'No,' Chiara says.

'Do you have any way of notifying us if more *vagabonds* arrive? A *child* you can send to the village with a message?'

Is it his accent that makes him put the stress on odd words? She wants to protest that there is no child here. But she refrains. Only shakes her head.

'Do you keep chickens?' he says.

She blinks.

It was that damn chicken, she thinks. The Lombardy brothers said they found it by the side of the track. They claimed that it must have escaped from somewhere and been mown down by a passing truck. Road-kill, they said. Chiara didn't believe them. No one, not even a German patrol, would pass up a free dinner. But the deed was done, a whole fat chicken, and she made a sort of *cacciatore* with it. That damn chicken had alerted them.

'Not any more,' she says.

'But you would like to make a contribution to the war effort?' the man says.

'Excuse me?' she says.

She follows his gaze out of the side gate to the meadow where one of the remaining sheep can be seen munching grass. Gabriele took the rest of the flock with him earlier to higher pastures, but this one is lame.

'Of course,' she says.

Two of the soldiers march Filippo up the track, dragging the ewe. The others head out through the gate in the opposite direction, across the olive grove. They fan out into the woods.

Chiara stands very still at the gate. She fixes the hollow of the Mago with her gaze.

Don't come out, she wills him.

From behind her, she can hear the solitary bleat of the sheep as it is manhandled into the Germans' vehicle, up beyond the ridge. Then the sound dies away, and silence falls on the hillside. It feels to her like the silence of an unrung bell; her clapper heart suspended and a deafening absence of noise.

Then comes the shuffle and clack of Nonna's sticks on the cobbles, and Chiara breathes again. Her grandmother parks one of her sticks against the fence and takes hold of Chiara's arm.

'He has been baptised,' she says.

Chiara wrenches her eyes briefly from the Mago. 'What?' she says.

'The little man.' Nonna gives Chiara's arm a bony squeeze and nods knowingly.

'What do you mean?' Chiara says. 'What are you telling me, Nonna?'

She can't look at Nonna because she has to keep her attention focused on the Mago, in case it is her fixed gaze that keeps him there.

'Tell me,' she says.

She can hear the shouts of the soldiers in the woods now. They must be down by the stream, thrashing through the undergrowth, beating at it with their weapons, leaving the deep footprints of their heavy boots in the muddy banks.

'They can't take him away. He's a Christian now,' Nonna says.

'But the priest hasn't been for weeks,' Chiara says, eyes fixed, steadfast, on the hole set among the wrinkles of bark, the smooth lid of curled wood around its upper rim, the paler whorl that encircles the dark hollow at its centre.

An eye for an eye, she thinks.

'Not the priest. Me. I did it. I poured water over his forehead and I baptised him in the name of the Father and of the Son and of the Holy Ghost.' Nonna lifts her hand from Chiara's arm and makes the sign of the cross.

A fleeting image comes to Chiara, of Nonna clutching the child in her fierce and feeble grip, dousing him with water from a silver bowl.

'But what does that even mean?' she says. She cannot fathom how or what Nonna knows about Daniele.

'Lay people can perform the sacraments in an emergency,' Nonna whispers, 'and I did it.' She reaches for her stick. 'He told me to.'

'Who?'

The soldiers are coming back out of the woods now. They are empty handed. They pass the Mago without a second glance and gather in the middle of the grove where their leader addresses them, pointing up the hill. Are they leaving? Is that it?

Chiara steals a glance at Nonna who is manoeuvring her sticks into position to set off back across the yard.

'Who told you to, Nonna?'

Nonna gives a little shake of her head and sets off. 'Here we go,' she says.

'Didn't he make a fuss?' Chiara asks.

Nonna stops in her tracks. 'Make a fuss? God? I wonder what that would look like.'

Chiara is surprised by her own sudden snort of laughter. 'I meant the boy,' she says.

'Alfonso,' Nonna says over her shoulder, 'is not a fussy child.'

The leading soldier is at the gate. The others have formed themselves into a phalanx and are marching up through the olive grove, a quicker, steeper way of getting to the ridge above. She steps back to allow the man through.

'We will return,' he says and he too departs, taking the slower but more dignified route up the track.

While Chiara is still in the yard, waiting and listening for the engine noises to die away, the Viterbo woman appears and starts jabbering at her, telling her that they can't do it any more, sheltering deserters, it's too dangerous, they put themselves at risk. Chiara strains to hear beyond the woman's hectoring voice. If it wasn't for the obvious poor state of health of her Ettore, Beatrice says, they would probably have carted him off too. Chiara can't listen to her.

'Excuse me,' she says, 'can we talk about this later?'

But the woman won't be shushed, and Chiara turns away, pushes open the gate and runs into the grove, up the slope, scrambling up the grassy banks between the olive trees.

She arrives up on the ridge, panting. She wants to make sure that the men have really gone and that they haven't left a spy behind. She examines the tyre marks and the footprints in the dirt all around. She plants her feet there and stares up the track to where it bends sharply to the right and disappears around the curve of the hillside. The image of the sheep and the man being led away comes to her, and in its wake the phrase 'like a lamb to the slaughter'. She shakes her head to shift the notion that she has been party to – has brokered, even – some kind of unholy deal.

She turns back towards the farm and sets off, running back down the slope. She needs to see Daniele's face. She is picturing it in such detail, his dark eyes staring up at her, the freckles across his nose, the jut of his chin, and is so certain that she will find him crouching inside the Mago that when she grasps its rim and tips her head into the woody hollow, she cannot at first take in that it is empty. She thrusts her head further inside and peers down at the muddy pool at its base where a twig and two soggy brown leaves float.

She pulls out again and looks around. 'Daniele,' she calls.

And then she is running down into the woods, looking about her as she sprints, stopping to bellow his name and then careering on again, all the way down to the stream.

She stands in the dell, where the leaves on the trees drip like slow rain all around, and the water of the stream comes gurgling and whispering over the stones. She shouts his name over and over until her throat is raw.

Eventually Gabriele, back from the high pasture, comes and finds her and leads her back to the house.

'He wasn't wearing any shoes,' she says.

Gabriele tells her about two places he can think of where Daniele might hide: an oak tree that the boy likes to climb, and a little grotto in the hillside that they discovered the night of the olive-oil escapade.

'That's good,' she says, 'two,' but thinking three would be better. And anyway, despite herself, she sees the child running, endlessly running, like a wind-up toy with a broken mechanism. He will not stop running until he drops and then he will be lost.

Gabriele escorts her back to the farmhouse and heads out to search.

Cecilia has pushed the broken machine to one side and is sewing something by hand on her lap. Nonna sags lumpily in her chair at the unlit hearth.

Chiara looks at the mess of the half-prepared meal. She fetches the bulb of garlic out of her pocket and places it beside the lump of unkneaded dough, the onions, the carrots and the bunch of rosemary.

She lowers herself into the chair opposite Nonna.

'It wasn't enough, was it?' she says after a while.

Nonna looks like an old rag doll on a string, her head

shaking tremulously. The slight movement probably doesn't indicate a considered response but if it does, it's a 'no'.

Chiara returns to her calculation. Filippo and the sheep, they weren't a high enough price to pay. She is trying to think what might have shifted the balance in Daniele's favour, but it is not clear to her. If Mario and Furio have been taken too – their source of meat – might that provide a sufficiently heavy counterweight? But what if Mario and Furio were indeed the ones who, either knowingly or not, alerted the Germans to the presence of their little community here high in the hills? Would that negate their value in the equation or even, God forbid, count against him?

Beatrice and Ettore appear at the door.

'Can we come in?' Beatrice asks and then does so before anyone has replied. She surveys the quiet, cold room. 'Fetch some wood,' she says to Ettore. 'I'll take over the cooking, shall I?' she says, rolling up her sleeves. She busies herself at the kitchen end, muttering to Ettore when he comes in and out with logs and kindling.

'What will they do to Filippo?' Chiara says.

Ettore, who is kneeling at her feet to lay the fire, looks sideways at her and shrugs.

'Transported to Germany, most likely,' Beatrice says. 'To a labour camp.'

'They might make him fight,' Ettore says.

Chiara has not been this close to Ettore before. He has pale pitted skin on his cadaverous cheeks and a sweaty brow. When he inhales, something rattles in his chest.

'You don't think . . .' Chiara says and then she stops, feels herself redden, realising the bargain she is again making in her mind.

If Filippo dies, will that be a high enough toll to bring the boy back? She is offering a life for a life as if any of it were hers to give. She stands up, horrified, her hand over her mouth.

'No,' Beatrice says, reassuring. She must think that Chiara's horror is at Filippo's possible fate, not at the perfidy of her own heart. 'They'll make him work one way or another. He's more use to them alive.'

'It won't catch,' Ettore says, looking at the dead fire.

'Let me,' Beatrice says. She helps Ettore to his feet, and he shuffles out of the way over to Cecilia's corner. 'Let's hope Gabriele finds the boy before it's dark,' Beatrice says, unpacking the kindling and the logs. 'Because if he's fallen and hurt himself, he can't cry for help, can he?'

Nonna lets out a whimper, a forlorn out-breath.

Beatrice restacks the logs with more space in between them.

The possibility of the sure-footed child falling and hurting himself had not occurred to Chiara. She imagines him plummeting from the crown of the oak tree that Gabriele described, then tumbling into a deep hole at the back of the cave, falling down and down through coldness into the earth's fiery core.

'He can speak, you know,' she says. Her tone is sharp.

Beatrice raises her eyebrows. 'Oh really?' she says. 'Silly me.'

Chiara watches Beatrice as she gets up, walks to the oven with the fire tongs in hand, brings back a burning log and inserts it into a space she has left in the middle of the pyramid of logs in the hearth. 'That should catch now. Come on, Ettore,' she says. 'Let's leave the ladies to it until dinner time.'

'Your sister is sewing an outfit for the child,' Ettore says in a placatory manner, joining his wife at the door. He attempts a smile.

'He used to speak,' Chiara explains, just as Cecilia bellows something unintelligible from her corner.

Beatrice is not mollified. 'Can't speak, won't speak,' she says.

'He keeps his own counsel,' Ettore says, soothingly.

Beatrice tuts. 'Oh, we know you love him and you're worried. We'll pray for you,' Beatrice says.

Love him, she thinks, closing the door after them.

'I said no,' Cecilia shouts as they leave.

'No, what?' Chiara says, swinging round to confront her sister who, in answer, raises the little shirt she is hemming and flaps it. 'What do you mean?' Chiara says.

Out of the corner of her eye she becomes aware of Nonna, sunk even further into her chair, holding her hands to her temples and rocking. Nonna is speaking in a tiny little voice out of one side of her mouth. She might have been speaking for some time.

Chiara leans down to hear. 'What is it, Nonna?' she says.

Nonna's face close up is like an empty paper bag, more crumpled on one side than the other. 'Bed,' she seems to be saying and then something else.

Chiara helps her *nonna* remove the outer layers of wadding, including Filippo's jacket, half carries her to the outhouse and finds, for the first time ever, she has to go in with her, hitch up the skirts and petticoats, haul down the drawers and hold her steady.

Nonna repeats the phrase from earlier, but her voice slurs. It sounds like, 'I have lived too long.'

'You're just exhausted, Nonna,' Chiara says.

She tucks her *nonna* into the big bed in the middle of the room.

'Come and sing Nonna a lullaby,' she tells Cecilia.

Cecilia lays down her work and sits on the other side of the bed. She hums a tune, but the words elude her. Nonna lies unmoving on her side, staring at the fire for a long time until, eventually, her eyes close. Chiara and Cecilia stay sitting on the bed, looking at the flames. Occasionally Chiara gets up and adds another log.

At dusk, Beatrice and Ettore come in and light the lanterns. Gabriele returns soon afterwards as they are serving up the *minestra*.

'No sign,' he says and sits down heavily by the fire.

They eat their supper perched here and there about the room with Nonna asleep in the middle of them all. The Viterbo couple eat quickly, clear away their bowls and say their goodnights. After they have gone, the others sit in silence, Chiara on the corner of Nonna's bed, facing Gabriele in the chair opposite Nonna's at the fireside, Cecilia over at her sewing table by the window. The only sounds are the crackle of the fire and Nonna's creaky snuffle. Outside it is dark.

Chiara is waiting for the moment when Gabriele will stand up and take his leave. She is dreading it because it will be their white flag. Their signal of surrender. It will mean the boy is not coming back.

Please, no, she prays.

She is watching him for signs that he is about to get to his feet, but it is Cecilia instead who leaps up, screaming. She shrieks and gesticulates towards the window. 'No!' she shouts.

Gabriele is on his feet, but Chiara is faster. She is already out the door, scooping up the child from where he stands pressed against the tree, carrying him back inside and planting him on the mat in front of the fire, where he drips a black slime onto the floor.

Daniele is filthy. Covered from head to toe in mud, splattered and plastered in it.

'I thought you would be inside the Mago,' she says.

He shakes his head. He has another place.

'You are such a clever boy,' she says. 'So good at hiding.'

She wants to clasp him in her arms, filthy as he is. She puts her hand on his shoulder instead, grips it.

'Hiding in the mud, were you?' she says. 'Mud boy?'

It's hard to tell in the gloom, with the mud caked on his face, but she thinks she catches a flash of teeth. She looks again. No, his face is as grim and blank as ever. She must have imagined it.

The screaming has woken Nonna. She gazes in wonder at the muddy child and mumbles something.

'She's tired beyond words. But she is so happy you are back,' says Chiara, translating. 'We all are,' she adds.

She glances across at Cecilia, who has laid her head on the sewing table and is making a droning noise, something between a hum and a moan. Gabriele, standing beside the fire, his bowl still in his hand, sits down again.

'Little man,' he says. He nods at the boy and resumes eating.

'Time for bed, Cecilia,' Chiara says.

'After you've eaten, I'm going to give you a proper bath,' Chiara tells the boy. 'And then tomorrow you can wear your new clothes that Cecilia has made you.'

She has her hand on his shoulder still and the shiver that goes through him transmits itself to her. Tomorrow, she thinks, some decisions will have to be made. But not tonight.

'I'll put the water on to heat right now,' she says, 'or you'll catch a chill.'

She lays a piece of paper on Nonna's armchair so he won't dirty it, sits him down opposite Gabriele, wipes his hands clean with a squeezed-out flannel and brings him his food.

She is glad to be doing again after hours of inaction. She fills pans with water and sets them to heat, while Gabriele and the boy sit companiably opposite each other, eating. She fetches the tin tub from where it hangs on the wall of the outhouse, swills it out with a bucket of water and drags it into the kitchen in front of the range.

When they were children, she and Cecilia, and they were staying with Nonno and Nonna, bathtime was a once-a-week ritual. Nonna would draw water from the well and put the big copper pan over the fire to boil. There wasn't the tap out in the yard at that time. They would take it in turns. She and Cecilia went first, because theirs was 'innocent dirt, not dirty dirt', Nonna used to say. Nonno went last because his was the dirtiest dirt.

There was a game they played, sitting opposite each other in the deep tub, the warm water up to their chests, their legs entwined. Gripping each other's wrists, they would move back and forth, the tin bath rubbing against and scratching their bottoms despite the velvety water. They were two halves of the same aquatic creature, stirring up the water and creating waves that moved in counterpoint to their own motion. While they slipped and slid they sang the 'Slippery Slide' song. Or Chiara would sing it, and Cecilia, who always forgot the words, tra-la-la-ed the tune. Their stomachs would ache from repeating the movement over and over again and from laughing and singing so loud. When the waves were lapping the rim of the tub, they would pause, hold their position, and then change their rhythm. The trick was to create a watery turbulence, their own maelstrom, without sloshing water over onto the flagstones, which put Nonna in a rage and which they would be made to mop up afterwards.

They were the fore and aft of a small human boat, sailing in choppy seas.

'Go to bed, Cecilia,' she says on her way out for the last bucket of water. 'You can't see to sew now,' because Cecilia has her scissors out and is snipping at something.

On her return, Cecilia is gone and Gabriele has dozed off. She shakes him awake.

'I'll be round in the morning for you, little man,' he says and leaves.

'Take everything off,' she orders Daniele. 'Hop into the tub. I need to wash your clothes and you need to scrub yourself and then I have to do your hair. You were starting to smell like an old sheep's cheese even before you coated yourself in mud. Pecorino, I'm going to call you.'

She puts the stool he used for climbing out of the window next to the tub.

'Use that as a step,' she says. 'I will look the other way and I will count to twenty. When I turn round you'd better be in the water.'

She turns away and starts counting.

There is a strange smell in the room. She thought earlier that it was some odd ingredient Beatrice had added to the soup. Now it is stronger, and smoke from the fire is backing up, acrid fumes. She suddenly remembers Daniele's shoes in the chimney. She fetches the tongs, hooks them out, charred, crisped and smoking but not yet actually on fire. He has nothing else to put on his feet, but for some reason it seems hilariously funny to her. She puts the shoes outside the door to cool down and, wheezing with suppressed laughter, beholds them smouldering on the doorstep, burnt offerings.

Back inside, she hears him climb in with a kind of sharp inhalation through the mouth, as if of pain, followed by a long sigh that denotes, she can tell, a sort of relief.

The water comes up above his shoulders. He is still at that age where his head looks too big for his body. His little neck poking up out of the water is like a twig, snappable. She dips in a jug for hair rinsing.

266

'Do you want to duck under and get your hair wet?' she says.

He slides beneath. He's gone longer than she thinks he should be. She counts to twenty again and resists the desire to hook him out. Then he bobs back, his face as blank as usual.

'Been for a swim, have you?' she says, rubbing the soap into his thick hair. 'Catch any fish down there? You could have brought us up a nice little fishy for our tea,' prattling nonsense, thinking sound and chat and normality might soothe. His hair is a golden-brown colour, much lighter than her family's.

He is hunched in the water, his shoulders lifting to his ears. She would kiss his bony shoulder if only they were on those terms.

'Don't worry, I can't see it, the water's so dirty now from your ragamuffin body, my Pecorino, that you don't need to hide anything,' she says.

She has the sense, ridiculous though it is, that he has exercised a choice in coming back. She imagines him burrowing into whatever muddy hole he had squeezed himself, down into the soil like a worm, and staying there, tight-packed in the earth. Or coming out, in his new brown guise, his apparel of mud that makes him invisible to the ordinary human world, and roaming the hills bare and light-footed like a little wolf.

Thank you for coming back, she thinks, but says, 'Help me rub the soap in.'

He lifts his arms and she gasps. She catches at one of his hands. He squirms away. She catches it again and holds his arm aloft.

'What's this?' she says.

Like buttons on the inside of his upper arm, half-moon-shaped indentations, some already with scabs, others pink and raw, purple bruises beneath. With her other hand she picks up the lamp and holds it to cast a better light.

'Who did this to you?' she says, although she already knows.

She sets down the lamp, lets go of his arm, rinses his hair, reaches around his slippery wet body and lifts him out into a towel. She stands him on the stool and pats him dry. He lets her. The scars and wounds cover all the parts of his body that would normally be concealed by his clothes. On his buttocks there are longer cuts, slash wounds, as if made with a knife. Or scissors.

Cecilia would have used the nail on the forefinger of her right hand to make the crescent-shaped incisions – the fingernail on her left was trimmed short because it was her thimble finger. She must have dug in until she had pierced the tender skin and then squeezed and twisted a pinch of flesh beneath.

Chiara binds him tight in the towel and sits with him on her lap, holding his tense body in her arms and rocking him. He smells clean and sweet, the scent of childhood.

'When your mother gave you to me,' she says, 'I promised I would look after you. And I will.'

She slips the nightgown over his head and tucks him into bed next to Nonna.

'Sleep,' she says. 'Safe and sound next to Nonna. Tomorrow is a new day.'

She holds the lamp over the two of them, Nonna and Daniele. She will talk to Nonna in the morning, first thing, over their early coffee, when Nonna is at her most lucid. She will ask, What does that mean, now, in these circumstances, what does it mean to look after this child? Because she can't see a way clear.

The boy is staring up at her. He won't close his eyes while she is watching him.

'Sleep now,' she says and moves away.

At the bottom of the stairs, the lamplight catches the mess of cloth on Cecilia's sewing table. Cecilia is usually so neat.

Chiara pauses, puts the lamp down on the side, picks up the first piece of cloth and then the second. The outfits Cecilia had made for the child, cut to ribbons. Chiara lets them run through her fingers and fall back to the table.

A great hammering at the front door intrudes on her sleep and she leaps up before she is even properly awake, thinking they are back, they have come back already, she thought there would be more of a breather, how will she hide him, where will he go? I should have left, she thinks. Last night, I should have dressed him in his old clothes and burnt shoes and fled. I've left it too late.

She pulls on her cardigan over her nightdress as she flies down the stairs. It is almost light outside. The boy lies next to the still, small lump that is Nonna, awake but unmoving. His dark eyes follow Chiara as she crosses the room. Someone shouts from outside. She recognises Gabriele's voice and starts breathing again.

'I was wanting the boy to come and collect chestnuts,' Gabriele says when she opens the door. 'I thought I'd keep him close today.'

'What time is it?' she says. 'Come in. We're late. We all slept in.'

Nonna never sleeps in.

'Daniele,' she calls, 'jump up. Here's Gabriele for you.'

They are going to look for chestnuts, she remembers, so she can make chestnut flour and turn it into bread and pasta. The wheat flour is almost finished.

'You'll have coffee, will you?' she says.

The stove is nearly out, and the room has a bitter chill.

'Oh,' she hears Gabriele say behind her. 'Oh, it's like that is it? Up you come, little man.'

She turns to face them, looks along the length of the room as if it is a theatre and she the audience. She raises her hand to her throat and feels the tears start to well, her stomach start to cramp, her body grasping that Nonna has gone before her mind has processed the scene.

Gabriele stoops and gathers the boy out of the bed. The boy twists in Gabriele's hold and they both look down at Nonna, still there, curled on her side, like a dead leaf.

FIFTEEN

'Welcome,' the little lady said. Then she offered her face. Maria understood that she was expected to kiss the proffered cheek and be kissed in return and then, unexpectedly, do the same on the other side.

'Come, Maria, come,' the signora said. It sounded like 'comma', as if she were pointing out the need for Maria to punctuate her sentences.

On their way out of the station, the signora kept one hand on Maria's forearm to steady herself, and they moved forward slowly, Maria dragging her case, the signora's ornate cane hooked over her wrist, dangling between them, knocking occasionally against Maria's shins and threatening to trip her up. Maria had known it was the signora as soon as she'd seen her, even though she wasn't wearing a mushroom hat.

Outside in the dazzle, a yellow taxi was being kept waiting. The cab was there and didn't need hailing, but the signora stepped forward and waved her stick at it in a commanding way. The driver got out and handed Maria's case into the boot. She was dimly aware of hundreds of yellow buses and a mass of people, but she kept her eyes down, letting it all remain an undigested blur on the edge of her vision.

The car set off into the hooting golden haze.

'I ask your pardon,' the signora said. 'I have a – how do you say it' – she made a whirling gesture with her finger – 'in my head and I have experienced an incident.' She twisted her mouth to one side and looked at Maria hopefully.

'Oh dear,' Maria said.

'Not a grave incident,' the signora said. 'Accident,' she corrected herself. 'I want to say accident.' She gestured towards her bandaged ankle.

They both looked at it. 'Oh dear,' Maria said again.

'Maria,' the signora said, starting over.

'Yes,' Maria said. She was glad to own up to that trilling Italian rendition of her name.

'I am not myself today. Because of the incident. My English on this day is' – the signora paused, searching for the word. She scrunched her face up, puffed out her cheeks. She made a flapping gesture with one hand and drummed on the taxi window with a manicured fingernail – 'is very little,' she said, eventually. She held her finger and thumb close together to indicate how reduced it was. 'Talk to me. Tell me about your journey,' she said.

Maria shuffled through the journey in her mind. She settled on Tommaso.

'There was a boy who got off in Milan,' she said.

'Be careful of these Italian boys,' the signora said. She had sunk back into the upholstery but she wagged a warning finger. 'They will want to eat you.'

'He was only half Italian,' Maria said.

'But which half?' the signora said and laughed a surprisingly dirty laugh.

Maria, remembering Tommaso squashed against her in the night, found herself joining in. She told the signora about the raw meat.

'Raw meat?' the signora said. '*Prosciutto crudo?*' she said.

'Yes, that's it,' Maria said.

'It is a delicacy,' the signora said. 'It's a – how do you say?' She held out her hands as if waiting for the answer to be dropped into them from above. 'An acquired taste,' she said.

Maria wrinkled her nose.

'I tell you another thing,' the signora said and started to laugh again. 'It's what we got for dinner.' She clasped her hand to her head and sank back. 'Look out the window,' she commanded.

The hot afternoon sun was beating on the side of Maria's face. She turned to look out just as the taxi emerged from an enclosed shopping street into a large open space. It was a place of such startling golden-and-white, shining magnificence and grandeur that Maria forgot everything else. She pressed her hands flat together as if in prayer and made a little whimpering noise. They were only in the place for a fraction. A great expanse full of cars and coaches, traffic police, buses and darting people, and beyond them a huge white staircase leading up to a palace set on high, the ruins of more ancient buildings off to the side, other splendid domed buildings dotted about, an impossible-to-absorb extravagance of the ancient and the beautiful and the stuff of now, all thrown in together.

'Wow,' she said and in her mind's eye she was doing a gallop. 'Where was that?' she said.

'I take you tomorrow,' the signora said. 'After school.'

School. Had the signora said school?

The cab plunged back into a darker street where the buildings loomed tall on either side and then emerged into a lighter space. Great pillars and trees sprang up from a hollow in the middle of the square.

They drove down cobbled streets that were hardly wide

enough for a car to pass through and pulled up in one of these, underneath an archway.

The street at ground level was in shadow but higher up, nearer the roofs, the amber buildings were still bathed in sunshine. A delicious aroma of hot dough floated in the air.

Are we really going in here? Is this ancient doorway the front door? Maria thought, standing behind the signora who was fiddling in her bag for her keys.

The baking aroma was making her mouth water. She took in a deep breath and detected another smell that made her heart miss a beat. She sniffed again. Something dank, cool, faintly salty.

'What is that smell?' she said. 'It reminds me of something.'

Just then the signora said, 'Here we are,' and the door swung open.

Maria stared past the signora into the dark vestibule of the building. In her mind's eye she saw a rectangular shape, a wavering oblong like a window onto nothing. She sniffed again, but she could no longer detect the strangely familiar scent. Instead, an odour of vegetable peelings and soup drifted down from above.

She stepped inside, and the door closed behind them. She blinked. Stone stairs rose up straight ahead of them. The steps dipped in the middle, worn down by the tread of countless feet over the centuries. They were ancient. They were venerable. If she hadn't had a bag to drag, and the signora in front, Maria would have bounded up them.

The signora was telling Maria things, but her words were trailing off into the stairwell, and Maria was deaf to them, bursting with the newness and the strangeness of it all. Buoyed by a breathless excitement, she imagined she could have flown up if she'd put her mind to it.

Then she was following the signora into the apartment, the entrance lobby all stained glass and flashes of colour, a coat-stand laden with more coats than one little woman could ever possibly wear, cool tiled floors, old-fashioned, dark wood furniture, musty and overcrowded, but clean and smelling of beeswax and lemons. The kitchen rather bare in cream and chrome, like something out of an antiquated advertisement, the big refrigerator with a curved front. A square table with a yellow cloth over it and three wooden chairs set around.

She was given a guided tour of the whole flat: a bathroom jammed with the equipment you would expect to find in a kitchen: washing machine, ironing board but also – how delighted her little brother Pat would be if he could see it – a real-life bum-washer; the signora's bedroom, which she had only a glimpse of but enough to get an impression of draperies and hangings; a dead-end hallway stuffed with furniture; and, at the other end, round a corner, a huge living room, which Signora Ravello called the salon. Maria didn't like to ask where her room was. She thought she must have misunderstood or missed something. That there must be another door.

'Where did Daniele Levi use to sleep?' she said.

The signora, who was standing in the middle of the salon, adjusting a painted screen and explaining how it unfolded, stopped what she was doing and stood very still. She straightened up and looked at Maria as if she had said something extraordinary.

'Excuse me?' she said.

'Daniele Levi,' Maria said. 'Your former lodger, you know.'

The signora blinked at her as if she could not imagine how to respond. 'Oh,' she said at last, 'the apartment was bigger in those days.'

She gave a tight little smile and folded back the screen to

275

reveal a strange piece of furniture that included within it a sort of bed.

'And here is Asmaro to greet you,' she said as a lean black cat emerged from behind it. 'He is a prince among cats.'

She crouched to stroke the animal, still holding her cane but out at an angle as if she were about to use it as a prop in a dance routine. She spoke in Italian to the cat. '*Amore*,' she said, '*Amore*,' burying her face in its fur. She lingered over the word *amore* in a way that made Maria rather embarrassed for them all.

'I will leave you to unpack while I make you a cup of tea,' the signora said. 'Do you like tea?'

Maria nodded.

The signora tappety-tapped with her cane out of the room. The cat lingered a moment longer, examining Maria, and then followed.

Maria pushed the door closed after them. A tower of different-shaped boxes and crates behind the door wobbled.

In all her imaginings of being in Rome – which were sparse because it had been easier to launch herself without forethought – Maria had never, in a million years, thought that she wouldn't have her own room. But not only was she to sleep, it seemed, in a corner of the communal living space, but on a bed contraption that protruded from the jaw of a heavy dark piece of furniture that might snap shut at any time. And how was it possible for an apartment to have shrunk?

Maria's bedroom back home was a small and contained place at the front of the house where even her own brother and sister would know that if the door was shut they would need to knock. The only person who ever transgressed was her erstwhile father, Barry, who, in his cups of an evening, would open the door a slit, slip his hand in and turn off the light.

'Lights out, Maria,' he'd sometimes say but as often as not he'd say nothing and just stumble along the landing to the bathroom or wherever he was going.

Her own mother, at the height of all the turmoil, had only slapped at the door with the flat of her palms and pleaded, and when Maria hadn't answered she had gone away.

Her gaze darted round the room, bouncing off the ornate gilt-framed mirror, to the leopard-skin armchair, the baggy green sofa, the velvet footstool, the thick, greenish-gold rug, the dark-wood bookcase crammed with paperbacks, the painted tallboy in which she was to stow her clothes. It was like being in a museum. Nothing matched anything else, but there was an overall loveliness. There were ashtrays on the various little rickety tables set here and there, of coloured glass, various shades of green, one with tiny bubbles within the glass. There was more of this bubbly coloured glass on a shelf below the mirror. Bowls of varying sizes and extravagant, lipped shapes.

On a small round table inlaid with embossed leather stood a hinged box made of pale wood. Maria flipped it open. It was packed with cigarettes; long, slender ones. They looked posh. There was even a pack with a picture of the Colosseum on the front, containing tiny wax-coated matches.

She put a cigarette tentatively between her lips and hesitated. Was she allowed to take one? But then, she reasoned, these must be to offer to guests, and she was a guest. Wasn't she? Should she ask? The matches were so short that she burnt her fingers. The cigarette had a perfumy taste. She sat down on the sofa, tapping her ash into the green ashtray.

The signora rapped with her cane on the door and then burst in. 'No smoking,' she cried. 'No, no, please. Extinguish it immediately.'

Maria dumbly did as she was told.

The signora picked up the cigarette box. 'Come and have tea,' she said.

Maria lingered a moment before following.

I can't bear it, she thought, and then she went along to the kitchen where a large pan of water was boiling on the hob.

The signora tipped some into a small cup, set on the saucer a tea bag with a piece of trailing string attached, and placed cup and saucer in front of Maria. 'Tea, English style,' she said. 'I know you like it boiling,' she added.

How did she know this, Maria wondered.

She watched in horror as the signora opened the cigarette box and tipped the contents into a bag of rubbish, which she sealed with a tight knot. 'There,' she said and gave Maria a triumphant smile. 'You,' she pointed her finger at Maria, 'are too young to smoke. And I,' she pointed the finger at her own nose, 'have stopped.'

She looked intently at Maria as if expecting congratulations. Maria managed not to say, 'Bully for you.'

'Does your mother know you smoke?' the signora said.

Maria didn't answer. Mind your own business, she thought. She should ask whether it would be all right to phone her mother from the signora's telephone. She didn't want to phone her mother.

'You are thinking, why does she not mind her own affairs. You are right.' The signora held her hands up, palms outwards, in a gesture of surrender. 'And I am sorry. I know I am – how do we say it?' She lifted her hand into a sort of salute. 'Autocratic. It's true. But Maria,' she said and paused.

'Yes?' Maria said.

'No smoking in the apartment, eh?' She leant her chin in her hand and smiled.

'All right,' Maria said with relief.

That was manageable. She smiled back.

'Of course not. Did Daniele Levi smoke?' she asked, dunking her tea bag in the hot water and swirling it about.

The signora let out a little sigh. She pushed her hand up over her face, pressing her fingertips into her cheekbones to form a sort of muzzle over her mouth as if this might be something she was not allowed to divulge. Then, reconsidering, she slid her fingers down again.

'Yes,' she said. 'He used to smoke.'

'Which brand?'

Maria thought she would buy the same brand when she bought herself an Italian packet of cigarettes, when she had changed some money.

'I need to explain to you about Asmaro,' the signora said.

Asmaro, it seemed, had many places within the apartment where he might lay his head, but behind the sofa in the salon was one of his favourites. And so Maria understood that not only did she not have her own separate room but that she was, in effect, sleeping in the cat's bedroom, and the cat took precedence. She tried to look nonchalant. The signora handed over a set of keys and explained about the lock and how the street door needed the key pushing in and then pulling out a fraction for it to work.

'I will go and lie down for half an hour while you unpack,' the signora said, 'and then we will go for an aperitif, isn't it?'

As soon as she had gone, Maria unpicked the knot in the top of the rubbish bag and rescued the cigarettes.

She went out as she was. She didn't even look for her jacket. It was still boiling hot anyway. She lit the first cigarette on the landing, then ran straight down the stairs and out onto the narrow, ancient street, walking quickly along it. At home the shops would be closing now, but here they were all open. She walked up and then back down the little street, her heart beating wildly. She didn't want to go too far in case she got lost. Someone shouted down to her from an open window in the bridged section but she didn't dare look up.

She went along to the far end where the delicious smell of baking was strong and the street opened onto a wider space. She veered back, passing the entrance to a bar. She came across a dark arched opening, a tunnel-like, in-between place that connected her street with another similar one. Electric cables and exposed junction boxes hung like decorations on the walls. A handcart was parked in a murky recess.

She loitered on the edge of this shadowed space, smoking another of the signora's squashed cigarettes.

The tree-lined avenue where Maria lived with her family in the suburbs of Cardiff was very quiet at night. Nothing disturbed it. No one walked by. If she pushed up her bedroom window in the early hours as sometimes, restlessly, she did, a car might very occasionally be heard passing along the main road down the hill, but otherwise, nothing.

In the dark winter mornings, the first sound to break the silence would be the rattle of the milkman's van on his rounds, and the *plink plink* as he placed the glass bottles on the doorstep. In the spring and summer, when the sun would sometimes rise before the milkman arrived, he would be preceded by the chatter and chirrup of birds, fluttering between the branches of trees, alighting and taking off again.

If she stuck her head out of her window, she would be looking down onto the tiled front path, the bush in the middle of the small front lawn, the brick wall that edged their garden and those of the houses either side, and, if she craned her head, she would be able to catch a glimmer of the lake on the other side of the main road. Whether she saw the lake or not, her view was coloured by a sensation of its presence, its watery expanse.

But here in Via dei Cappellari, some form of activity seemed to go on all night long. First of all, human sounds, people calling and shouting in the lane below, and then later a hissing and a rumbling of wheels over stone. And later still, when she could see from a slit along the bottom of the shutters that night was giving way to dawn, came a watery whooshing, endlessly repeated, accompanied by scraping. Unfathomable and insistent noises that put her in mind of dwarf-like creatures rolling wine-filled barrels along the cobbles.

She lay on the provisional bed like a stunned starfish, her limbs flung out in all directions, a salty film of sweat covering her skin, awash with new experience. The unbelievably delicious and exotic flavours of the meal she had eaten with the signora the previous evening; the method for dry-curing Parma ham that the signora had painstakingly explained; the gurgle of the pale wine as it was poured into blue glass flutes; the faint throb now behind her eyeballs as a result.

'Do you drink wine?' the signora had said, standing framed in the yellow oblong of light from the open door of the fridge, holding a green bottle.

And Maria – who had only really drunk bitter in the one pub where she and her friends could get served, or cider sometimes for a special occasion with Sunday roast at home, and whose sole experience of wine was the stolen dregs in the bottom of glasses left after one of her parents' parties – nodded. Of course she drank wine. She glugged it down, rather too fast, it seemed.

Then the signora relenting on the cigarette-in-the-house

281

ban because, she claimed, nothing would ever tempt her to smoke again. How the signora was curious about Maria's mum – who had phoned and been reassured while Maria was down in the street – but Maria didn't want to talk about her. Their great, wide-ranging, digressive conversation where she seemed to remember telling the signora her life history as the signora washed the dishes and Maria leant out of the window into a mysterious dark shaft, puffing away. And before all that, the bar where they had gone for an aperitif, her first-ever olives and her determination to like them, and a boy who worked there, just a kid really, who greeted her as if she were famous.

The signora's speedy movements like a darting bird; her explanations of the strange malady that had befallen her; the way she would occasionally clasp her hands to her head and hold it as if it were about to fall off, claiming she could feel the imminence of the spinning sensation; her bewildering explanation of Maria's 'programme' for the next two weeks. And how occasionally she would pause in whatever she was doing to exclaim, 'Maria,' and twice she had flown across the room to bestow a kiss on Maria's forehead, and the way, stranger than strange, that Maria really hadn't minded.

She lay on her rickety bed, too hot even to pull a sheet over herself, and floated in and out of consciousness, in and out of dreams. It was as if she were on a raft, floating over the deep, dark waters of a different sort of lake from the one at home, where sinuous shapes swam beneath, entwined in weed. Every time she awoke, it was to the hubbub outside.

She woke once and for all to the cat breathing purrily in her ear and the signora tapping at the door.

'Maria. I go out one minute. I buy *cornetti* for breakfast,' the signora called.

'OK,' Maria said.

Cornetti. A sort of cake.

She thought of Tommaso, the boy on the train. She listened to the click of the signora's heels on the tiles, the thud of the door. She fished out his note from the side pocket of her bag. He had not written her the soppy love letter she had imagined. Instead he had drawn a comic strip, featuring scenes of Milan: a many-spired cathedral, a theatre, a park with a sort of castle, a pathway beside a canal. In each of them a boy with a striped face was waving.

'Give me a ring sometime,' the boy said in a speech bubble. His address and telephone number were written below.

She walked over to the window. The very action of flinging shutters open onto the day instead of drawing curtains subtly altered her so that, as she stood there in her nightie, she was different, rounder, sexier, on the verge somehow of being, for the first time in two months, *more* rather than *less.*

The little shops were already open for business, the picture framer smoking his pipe, stroking his moustache and admiring his display; the round metal tables and spindly chairs set outside the bar; two impossibly good-looking boys in tight jeans and open-necked shirts slouching under the archway; the whiff of pipe tobacco mingling with fresh baking. Even an underlying waft of drains seemed exotic. Different drains, foreign drains, *her* drains. She looked up to see the sky already blue and welcoming above the roofs, its warmth already playing around her. She closed her eyes an instant and was giddy with it. She opened them and it was all still there. There was a window directly opposite hers, as close as the other side of the room, where ivory-coloured lace curtains hung.

When she fastened back the shutter on the right-hand side, she saw a diminutive painted Madonna in an alcove, gathering grime and pigeon droppings, plastic flowers strewn around her feet. Snatches of language floated up to her, indecipherable and alluring. Someone walked past, singing in an operatic way, unapologetically noisy. Maria dismissed the lake back home and its quiet with a wave of her hand.

'Let me in,' she whispered to the street.

She rifled through the clothes she had brought – ragged-bottomed flared jeans, blouses with leg-of-mutton sleeves and long buttoned cuffs, a terylene midiskirt her mother had bought in the sales, a flowery maxiskirt she'd made for herself, her dungarees. Everything looked too hot and too British. None of it expressed how she was now, her burgeoning Italianness. She chose the pink hot pants and her white smock top.

'No,' the signora said with a shake of her head that made her earrings swing when she saw Maria's attire. 'Come with me.'

And Maria dumbly followed down the hallway, through the signora's own bedroom, into another tiny room that opened off it (she had *two* rooms, and Maria was stuffed into a corner of the living room!), which was filled with rails of clothes, shelves stacked with shoes and hatboxes, scarves trailing from hangers.

'Wow,' Maria said, 'what a lot of stuff.'

'Borrow what you like,' the signora said. 'They are old things, second-hand for the major part, but good quality and well laundered.'

'But they won't fit me,' Maria said.

'Yes, yes,' the signora said, 'the dresses here.' She swept her hand along a row of frocks. 'They will fit you in a different way. I leave you, Maria. I make coffee. This one, Maria. Hurry, eh?'

It was a dress from the olden days. Cornflower blue with a

black-and-white pattern of lines and swirls, fitted at the bust and waist, with a full skirt, short sleeves and a pointed collar. It fastened at the front with five black buttons, and at the side with poppers.

'*Bella, bellissima,*' the signora exclaimed when Maria made her entrance into the kitchen. She clapped her hands. 'Take what you want from my dressing room,' she said. 'I never put those things. I always wear like this.'

She gestured with both hands, outlining herself, her pencil skirt and silk shirt, her boxy jacket.

'It is my commody style,' she said.

'Comedy style?' Maria said.

'No. I want to say commodious style,' the signora said and, seeing Maria's face, she leant towards her and patted her arm, laughing in a husky way. 'I want to say comfortable. There we are. A comfortable style for me.'

And Maria, one minute outraged and dumbfounded by the little lady and the next enchanted, laughed uncertainly too. She sipped her delicious coffee.

'You said on the phone that Daniele Levi left some stuff here when he went and that you couldn't keep all of it, but I was wondering if you'd found anything since.'

She looked across the room at the signora's austere little face.

The signora was standing with her back to the cooker, holding a cup of milky coffee. She raised it to her lips and drank, then turned and placed the cup next to the sink.

'We have to hurry now or you will be late. Later we will discuss.'

And she made a strange gesture with both hands, holding them up near her forehead and fluttering her fingers around like a storm of startled birds.

They walked quickly, the signora tapping with her cane and

Maria rustling along at her side in the voluminous and un-familiar dress, conscious of having an effect, if the fake swoon of the old man in the shop opposite was anything to go by, but unsure whether it was an effect she wanted.

The signora paused on the corner of the piazza and peered down a side street. 'Shall we pop to Gianni's to salute him?' she said. 'Do we have time?'

She looked at Maria questioningly, as if she might have an opinion on the matter. The smell of savoury baking was strongest at that spot. Maria took a step forward into the square where crowds of people thronged the vegetable market. Customers were coming out of the baker's, clutching pieces of something hot wrapped in waxed paper, biting into it before they even got out of the door, so irresistibly delicious was it.

'What's that?' she said.

'Red pizza and white pizza. Let's go and see him but only for a little moment. You agree?' the signora said. 'You must be punctual on your first day.

'This bar is one of the oldest in the quarter,' the signora told her as they pushed their way into a smoke-filled room. 'Gianni, Gianni,' she shouted.

Out from behind a crowd of people standing at the counter appeared an oldish man wearing a white overall. He had a thatch of grey hair that resembled a Russian hat, and a cigarette hanging out of the corner of his mouth.

The signora had moved to one side, creating a space as if to spotlight Maria. At the sight of her, the man said something Maria didn't catch. He shook her hand vigorously.

'Pleased to meet you, signorina.'

She told him that she was very pleased to meet him too.

'She speaks Italian!' he exclaimed to the signora who had a

rapt look on her face that prompted Maria to try to say something else.

'I don't speak well but I intend to learn while I am here,' she said. It was her longest sentence yet.

'Not only beautiful but clever too,' he said, addressing both her and the signora but speaking slowly for her benefit.

Maria felt a blush coming on. She looked down at her toes and her Ocean Pearl toenails poking out the ends of her espadrilles. When the moment had passed, the focus had shifted, and Gianni and the signora were talking to each other. Maria raised her gaze, gazing vaguely across at the row of people standing at the bar.

A man with hair tied back in a ponytail was watching her. He looked her up and down as if she were an item in an auction and he was considering putting in a bid. She raised one eyebrow at him in her most supercilious way, but he wasn't at that moment looking at her face. She felt her body growing hot, the blush spreading down to her neck and chest and then lower, until at last he raised his eyes, looked at her full on.

'Come, Maria,' the signora said. 'We will be late.'

And they were off again, charging across the top of the market square, dashing over a main road before the lights changed, plunging down a narrow, shaded street and then out again into the vast open space of a huge piazza. As they sped past fountains and high façades and monumental white statuary, the signora flicked her walking stick about to point out sights of interest, while Maria swished along next to her in a hot vacancy. She could stop and look or she could listen to the signora or she could pay attention to her own thoughts, but she couldn't manage it all, so she did nothing other than keep up.

They went down more little streets between tall old buildings and across another square where a great domed building squatted, ending up, finally, in the reception area of the language school, where the signora kissed her quickly on both cheeks and handed her over to a surly receptionist.

Maria, it seemed, was late. Morning class had already begun.

The receptionist took her to an airless room the size of a broom cupboard and smelling of disinfectant, gave her a written test to do, instructed her that she had half an hour to complete it and then shut her in.

And Maria – despite not having truly grasped until that moment that this was where they had been heading, that her mornings were going to be spent in this establishment, and not out and about, wandering the streets of Rome at will; despite too the backlog of confused impressions jamming her brain, the sensation of being able to use only quite a small part of it, the discomfort of the tight dress and the poppers digging into her side – mustered what intellectual forces she could and applied herself to the test paper. If she had to do this, she absolutely and categorically did not want to be put in the bottom class.

Afterwards, when she was sitting in a classroom full of Swedish au pair girls conjugating verbs out loud in unison, the notion came to her that to acquire the language required a combination of external and internal forces: an alertness to the actualities of vocabulary, grammar and idiom, and then, through study and practice and repetition, an allowing of these to percolate through and awaken an inner core of knowledge that she was sure she must possess. Just as she had always been half Italian, whether she had been aware of it or not, so the language might also be inside as well as out, secreted in nerve clusters, in her cells, or in some previously unaccessed part of her brain. Now that she was here, there was a familiarity about it, something that couldn't be explained just by her study of the record from the library.

School finished at noon. The Swedish girls immediately filed across the road, under a stripy awning and into the ice-cream parlour opposite.

Maria lit a cigarette, the last of the signora's. She was on another narrow cobbled street, this one curved. She wandered round the bend. A man in uniform with a gun stood on guard outside a bank. She loitered in a doorway opposite, waiting for someone to go in so she could learn the protocol. Bank of the Holy Spirit was its unlikely name. No one went in or came out. She wondered whether perhaps it was not a real bank but something religious, to do with storing up virtue.

She put out her cigarette and boldly approached, pushing through the street side of the complicated door arrangement. She found herself in an in-between place that resembled an airlock. The door behind slid shut and clicked into place of its own accord. There followed a bleep. She took shallow breaths to preserve the oxygen, waiting for something to happen.

Nothing did.

She reached forward to the inner door, ready to throw her weight against it if need be. It swung open and she shot through, performing a little gallop to stay upright. She recovered, handed over her two ten-pound notes, was given quite a large stack of lire in return and emerged ready for the next mission.

She spotted a sign hanging above a shop farther up the street, a white T on a black background. She rehearsed her words before entering.

'I would like typical Italian cigarettes,' she said.

'What?' the tiny old man behind the counter replied.

She repeated herself.

The old man, surely too ancient to be working still, said something she couldn't catch.

'Can you repeat?' she said.

He spoke again.

He seemed to be saying they didn't sell that brand. She pointed at a pack at random. 'That one,' she said.

She wanted change for the telephone.

'Telephone,' she said helplessly, showing him the grubby notes he had given her as change. He exchanged them for some unlikely looking coins with a groove in the middle.

'What are these?' she asked, but he ignored her as if she hadn't spoken at all.

She went to a telephone booth and dialled her mum's friend, Helen. There was no answer.

She wandered back past the school entrance, trying to remember which way she had come that morning. The road curved round and there in front of her, on the other side of an open urban space, was the domed building again. Now she recognised it. The Pantheon. She looked at it in wonder and then at the people milling about in the square.

She walked back to the telephone box and dialled Tommaso's number. 'It's me,' she said, 'the girl from the train.'

'Maria,' he sang.

It sounded as though he was planning to go for a full-blown rendition of the song from *West Side Story* but then thought better of it.

'My language school is right next to the Pantheon,' she said.

'How chic,' he said.

'Isn't it?' she said.

She didn't want him to get the wrong impression so she told him about the ponytail man. 'Have you actually spoken to this dude?' he asked.

'No.'

'OK, I'm not going to worry about him. He'll open his mouth and he'll be a dickhead. He'll say something stupid and chauvinistic.'

'Unlike you.'

'Unlike me. Exactly.'

'He wouldn't be a feminist, like you.'

'Nope.'

'I'm half Italian too,' she said and found herself telling him about Daniele Levi.

'Welcome to the identity-crisis club,' he said.

He said he would telephone her one evening at the signora's flat if she didn't mind.

Snippets of the signora's earlier commentary flipped to the surface of her mind as she retraced their steps and came across the street full of basketwork shops and workshops.

'In case you should ever need anything made of raffia,' the signora had said, in a way that indicated she herself never would.

There was the church containing a famous painting, not to be missed. And here was the elongated square, Piazza Navona, with the three fountains, the water bouncing off the great white statues now and sparkling in the bright midday sunshine. It was a pedestrian zone, but this was the place, according to the signora, that the Rolling Stones had driven slowly around in a white Rolls-Royce. Back in 1967.

She wondered whether Daniele Levi had liked the Rolling Stones. Or whether he had been more of a Beatles man. Barry, who was a Beatles man, said you couldn't be both. You had to choose. Or perhaps jazz was always Daniele Levi's thing.

She passed the museum all about Rome and its history, which the signora, who had never been, had recommended.

Here was the shop that sold good-quality umbrellas, and the artisan bread shop, and here she was back in Campo dei Fiori where the market was still going on.

There was the stall where they short-changed you, and here the signora's favourite flower stand, and beyond was the statue of Giordano Bruno who had done something heroic and been burnt at the stake hundreds of years before, and here was the delicious bakers – *FORNO*, it said in big brown letters above the door – and here round the corner was their own darling street where she and the signora lived and there, at the bottom of the stairs, was that smell.

It stopped her in her tracks. She hovered there, breathed it in, as the door closed behind her. She shut her eyes. What was it? It conjured something inexpressible.

She opened her eyes. There on the wall, where it twisted around the stairwell, was a slanted rectangle of light. She looked behind her to see the source. Sunshine streamed in through a small barred and glassless window above the door. She stared. She had the strange sensation of standing beside herself, as if she might be able to hold her own hand. She saw the window in real life and at the same time she saw it as a picture in her head. As if she had already known it was there.

SIXTEEN

A squat big-bellied man, with mottled red cheeks that puff out and fold over the ends of his moustache, squeezes past the queue and out of the doorway, clutching his precious blood-ied package to his chest. There is some muttering as the queue shuffles forward. Did he get more than his fair share?

Chiara, queuing outside in the street on a cold, bright January morning, watches him waddle away at high speed. She would like to ask him a question. Every whisper on the street of food supplies – beans, dried vegetables, twists of salt, sar-dines in oil at Piazza Vittorio, sometimes coffee in an underpass near there, flour and sugar at Tor di Nona, canned goods and rice laid out on provisional stalls, no more than bits of cloth on the pavement, in the streets behind Termini – sends her hurtling from one part of Rome to another. She spends half her life queuing. She joins queues even if she doesn't know what the goods on offer might be. Often there is nothing at all, or it is gone.

She would like to say to this scurrying man, 'How come you are so fat? What's the secret?'

She glances down at Daniele – he is wearing an old pair of Nonna's chamois leather gloves, several sizes too big, giving his hands a crinkly, ancient-looking appearance. He resembles a ragamuffin but so many people do that it doesn't matter. Hardly anyone lives in their own homes here in Rome any more. He is holding onto the edge of her coat pocket, clutching the cloth. Not flesh on flesh, never that.

She follows his gaze across the road to a poster pasted on the window of the cobbler's opposite. It depicts a red-lipped black man, head thrown back and mouth open, laughing maniacally as he crushes a captive maiden in his massive, muscular arms. The maiden is draped in classical robes, with a smooth, alabaster breast, chaste thighs pressed together, an image of pale purity.

'The liberties . . . of the liberator!' reads the caption. A Stars-and-Stripes banner protrudes from the man's rifle. Rome is full of this lurid propaganda.

The queue moves forward. They are under the crimson oval sign with the protruding horse's head now. She can see through the window. Nothing hangs from the hooks above the butcher's head, and the metal trays she can glimpse between the waiting people are empty, scrubbed clean, but there is definitely meat left on the block, and perhaps the butcher has something else hidden down behind the counter. Afterwards, if they get some meat, she will call in at the cobbler's and see whether anything can be done about Daniele's burnt shoes. The toes curl up at the end, like a clown's. If she gets meat, if she cooks something tasty and nutritious for them today, other things can perhaps be mended too.

She thinks of the chickens she has acquired from Gennaro, flapping and scratching around the dining room, shitting on Nonna's oak sideboard. She thinks of how she has plundered Nonno's wine store, trading his Treviso and his precious Barolo for pasta, Parmesan, scraps. She thinks of the salon,

294

where bolts of Cecilia's cloth are strewn just as she left them, when she heaved them up and spilt them out on that last day; where she and Daniele sleep in among them, as if there were no bedrooms and they had nowhere else to go. They are like refugees inhabiting the apartment in a temporary kind of way, as if always on the verge of leaving. It is all a muddle.

The apartment misses Cecilia, tidying, keeping it in order, being there as a living presence to come home to, sewing things together so they seem to make sense. Making it into a home.

Chiara presses her fingers against her eyelids. Let her not start weeping in the street, in front of the child.

The word 'unremarkable' surfaces in her mind. The nun who handed her the fake identity documents said it.

'If you are out alone, you take your proper documents. But when the boy is with you, take these other ones that make you into a family, and that way you arouse less suspicion. You are unremarkable.'

Those words have stayed with her. There is a truth in them and a bleak kind of comfort. Because these times are so extraordinary that their story is just that. They are bereaved, orphaned, hungry, haunted, fearful. They are unremarkable.

Another customer leaves. The line moves forward. She and Daniele are through the door, past the threshold, properly inside. She gives her pocket a tug to catch his attention.

'I think we might be lucky today,' she says.

The cold blood smell is in their nostrils. There seems to be just one piece of meat on the slab, but it's a good size. Chiara prays it won't run out before they get to the counter, that none of the customers in front has any kind of special deal. The cleaver falls through the air, slicing through the slab of dark-red flesh. She watches the arc of its movement to see where it falls. They all do. They are worshippers at the altar of the chopping block, the butcher their high priest.

She feels a hand on her shoulder and a surge of adrenalin shoots up her spine. She makes a shrugging movement as if to slide the hand off.

'Chiara?' a woman's voice says.

She half turns to look up into the face of a tired-looking, middle-aged woman.

'Chiara Ravello?'

The woman grasps both of Chiara's shoulders, swivelling her so that they face each other square on, and Chiara, instinctively, unthinkingly, without even glancing at him, ushers Daniele behind her back and out of sight. She cannot yet place this tall person, who is gazing at her in disbelief and wonder and something else, some other emotion. She finds herself being drawn into the other's arms. She breathes in the other's scent, that unmistakable blend of roses and vanilla, together with something else she could never name when she was a child or an adolescent – something that she used to smell in her father's hair and in the crease of his pocket-handkerchief – but that now she recognises. Musk.

She tries to pull away, but her knees are trembling, and the other woman is holding her firmly. Simone Gauchet, her father's mistress.

'Call me Simone,' she remembers her saying the last time they met. 'Come and see me whenever you want.'

But Chiara hadn't ever wanted.

Any port in a storm, she thinks now, and allows herself to be held a bit longer. It is so long since she has been embraced by someone bigger and sturdier than herself. She has been the hugger, not the hugged, the comforter and not the comforted.

She struggles not to weep. She can feel the other's bosom heaving.

The woman lets her go and as she takes a step back, tucking Daniele more tightly behind her, Chiara notices that the years since she last saw Simone Gauchet soon after her father's funeral in 1938 have not been kind. She has lines around her mouth, her skin is pale and blotchy. She looks haggard. She is a big-framed woman, built to carry some flesh.

'I am so glad to see you,' Simone says. 'I feared for you in the San Lorenzo bombing.'

Her voice, unlike her face, seems immune to the ravages of time, husky, musical and low. A man might call it seductive.

It would be rude beyond measure to turn away. Chiara has to say something. 'We weren't living there. Cecilia and I moved out of the San Lorenzo apartment a few years ago,' she says. 'After my father died.'

'I was worried,' Simone says. 'When I saw those pictures on the newsreel with the pope there praying in the rubble, I thought, Oh no. Not Alfonso's girls. My darling Alfonso. His lovely girls.'

With the tip of her middle finger she smoothes tears away from her powdered cheeks.

'But you are fine. You are here. Oh,' she sighs a great sigh. 'You cannot imagine the relief.'

Chiara stares at Simone Gauchet saying his name, her father's name, out loud in the middle of the butcher's shop, as if he were hers, as if the wound of his loss were hers. Claiming some kinship with Cecilia and Chiara when she didn't even know them. Smiling at her now as if all is right with the world.

'You'll be sorry then to hear that my mother *was* there,' she says.

'Oh,' Simone says, as if winded. Her smile disappears and her tired face sags again. She looks sadly at Chiara. 'I *am* sorry to hear that,' she says.

Chiara can detect no evidence of sarcasm in the other woman's tone, no sign of ill-will or latent satisfaction that her rival is dead.

She hates me, Chiara's mother used to say, that trollop, she can't bear the fact that I'm prettier than she is.

'Your poor mother,' Simone says. 'Poor you.'

Chiara, abashed, stares down at the floor.

'And your sister?'

'She's fine,' Chiara says quickly, but not quickly enough to prevent an image of Cecilia, her pale sleeping face, like a child's in its unknowingness, from surging up in her mind. She does not want to be reminded of her sister. 'She's in the country-side, at our grandparents' farm,' she says firmly.

She is not going to tell this woman that Nonna is dead, that she has left Cecilia in the care of virtual strangers. That she said she would return within two weeks and circled the day on the calendar with a red pen. That the circled day is long past.

'It's safer for her there,' Simone remarks.

'Oh, much,' Chiara agrees.

And the thought that perhaps, just perhaps, this is actually true, enters her mind for the first time. Perhaps her guilt at leaving Cecilia is a self-indulgence, and her sister is thriving in her absence. Beatrice and Ettore, who were to move into the farmhouse for the duration, had promised to care for her as if she were their own. Perhaps she, Chiara, held Cecilia back.

Another customer leaves. Chiara moves a step closer to the butcher's counter and, in the movement, Daniele is revealed.

'You have a child,' Simone exclaims in a loud, astonished voice.

Daniele has the hat with earmuffs pulled down so far that it covers his forehead entirely. His dark eyes peer out and up at Simone as if from the shadowy space under a low bridge.

Chiara resists shushing her. She reminds herself that the false identity documents are in Daniele's inside jacket pocket. She is Signora Chiara Ravello Gaspari, as if she were Carlo's widow, and he is Daniele Gaspari.

Family, she thinks, clutching at the nun's words. Unremarkable. Even so, an urge to fill a silence, to pre-empt comments and questions, sets her talking.

'It's the chickens,' she hears herself saying. 'We were going to go back to the countryside but we were given these chickens and so, we, um . . .'

'Excuse me?' Simone says, but she is not really paying attention. She is smiling down at Daniele. 'I knew you were engaged. Carlo, wasn't it?' she says. 'But I didn't know you had got married!'

The realisation that Simone does not even know that Carlo is dead, that he died a month after her father, helps her control the urge to babble.

'This is Daniele,' she says.

She does not have to explain herself to this woman. It is no business of Simone Gauchet's that she has broken the eternal promise she made her sister that she would return. Always and forever. Neither does she have to tell Simone Gauchet why she might be exposing a child to the dangers and privations of the occupied city when she had a choice.

But in a way it *was* the chickens, she thinks. The chickens showed her that it was here in Rome that she could keep the boy safer. That here among the ruins was their best chance.

She had gone to see Gennaro for advice on procuring false identity documents. Not at the bar, which was all closed up in the ghost town of the ghetto, but at his house off the Janiculum where he grew vegetables and kept poultry. People had chickens on roofs and in their backyards. They grew vegetables on tiny plots of terrace and on the verges.

Gennaro told her about the nuns at Santi Quattro Coronati who provided fake documents. As she was leaving, he also told her that he had joined a different resistance group now, one that was planning an attack on an SS regiment.

'I can't,' she said. 'Not any more. I have to put the child first.'

She thought he might reproach her. Other people with children still took such risks, but instead he nodded and said, 'Do you want a hen? Then you will have eggs for the boy.'

'But where would I put a hen?' she asked. 'And how would I feed it?'

'They eat anything,' he said. 'Scraps. Give it scraps.'

'That's what we eat,' she said.

'You'll think of a way,' he said, 'and if you don't, you can kill it and eat the meat. You know how to kill a chicken, don't you?' He tied its legs together and packed it in her basket. 'Take another one,' he said, putting a second in beside it, 'to keep the brown one company. For the boy,' he added.

So she cycled home, hurtling at high speed down the Janiculum hill, with the two hens tied up in her basket, so quiet and still she thought they had died of shock and she mightn't even have to bother wringing their necks. She unloaded them onto the kitchen floor and, after a trance-like second or two, they started rocketing round the room, in and out of the table legs.

'Look what I've brought,' she said when Daniele came into the room.

At the sight of the squawking birds he clapped his hands

together. It seemed to be a gesture of delight. She thought he might be afraid of the flapping, but he wasn't at all, and she remembered how he had been with the donkey up on the farm, an easiness in his relationship with animals. He looked up at her, and she nodded, although she was not sure what the unspoken question was. He pointed to the smaller one, with creamy tail feathers and a speckled back.

'You like that one, do you?' she said.

He nodded again. She bent and caught it, pinned its wings to its sides to stop the flapping, held it to show him how and then decanted it into his out-held arms. Hugging it to him, nestled under one arm, he stroked its downy back with his other hand.

They were rapt. Boy and chicken.

'We need to give them names,' she said, scooping up the brown one. 'I am going to call mine Winston. What about you?'

Daniele tipped his head to one side.

'Cluck,' he said.

He spoke as if speaking were quite normal. As if he had not been utterly silent for three months. He rested his cheek on the chicken's back.

'You're called Cluck, aren't you?' he said.

She thought of it as the miracle of the chickens. In the midst of their makeshift, hand-to-mouth existence, a miracle.

'Pleased to meet you, Cluck,' she said and pretended to shake its claw.

'Pleased to meet you, Daniele,' Simone says.

'She's not my mummy,' Daniele whispers.

Chiara shoots him a warning look. Inside she cringes. He speaks only rarely, even now, but this is his refrain: *You're not my mummy.*

Simone has crouched down in front of Daniele and envelops the boy in her arms. 'Little darling,' she says.

Chiara watches the other woman bypass all the taboos, squeezing the child against her body, the foxtail around her neck swinging down and dipping into the sawdust on the floor, Daniele's feet in the ruined, misshapen shoes lifting momentarily off the ground.

'Signora?' the butcher says.

Chiara swivels towards him, shutting her mouth. It is her turn. There is one piece of meat remaining. The butcher wraps it for her.

'Finished,' he calls out, clanging his cleaver onto the block, and the message goes down the line, which quickly disperses. There is a rumour of tripe in Testaccio.

'Sorry,' Chiara says to Simone as they cross the road.

'Don't be,' Simone says. 'I don't have a child to feed.'

The cobbler's is shut. *Closed for holidays* a sign on the doorway reads. Perhaps the owner has fled. Or been taken. Perhaps he was a Jew and is in hiding.

The occupied city, she has discovered, hosts a network of convents, churches and safe houses that conceal Jews who escaped the round-up on 16 October and the subsequent sweeps. And not just Jews. Resistance fighters too. The news now, though, is that some of them got too bold after the Allied landing at Anzio a few days ago; they thought that the liberation of Rome was imminent, and many of the leaders have been arrested. Not Gennaro, though. His group is still in operation.

Chiara turns her back to the shop and gazes down the street at a bare wintry tree and the eruption of cobbles at its base. The only thing to do is to say goodbye to Simone and go their separate ways, and she can't think why they're standing here, pointlessly postponing that moment, as if they have anything more to say to each other.

Simone nudges her. She has her shopping bag open and is displaying its contents.

'I have rice and two tins of tomatoes,' she says. Her hair, streaked with grey at the front, shines like honey where the sun hits it.

This is the woman, Chiara thinks, who stole away my father from the family home with her honeyed ways, her mellifluous voice, her charming French lilt. The shameless hussy, trollop, husband-snatcher. The Algerian whore.

Chiara remembers her mother screaming at her father, 'Go to her then, your Algerian whore.' Chiara knew Simone by repute long before they came face to face.

She shakes her head.

'And a small sack of charcoal,' Simone says. 'I've got charcoal.'

Daniele has drifted over to stand next to Simone, where he is fluffing the fox fur. He might think that it's a toy.

The first time she saw Simone, at her father's funeral, she was wearing fur. A different sort. Swathed in it, muffled by it. Something dark. Mink, perhaps. Simone was on the outer edge of the mourners, a black veil over her face. She had not been invited, of course, even though Chiara's father had died of a heart attack in her arms. Still, she had come to the church and stood at the back and then gone on to the cemetery. As they were leaving the graveyard, she had stepped out from under the trees and called out Chiara's name. Under the veil, Chiara had caught a glimpse of heavy swollen eyes, the face of someone who has cried non-stop for days. She asked Chiara whether she would like to come and pick something of her father's to have as a keepsake, and some days later Chiara had gone.

Simone's eyes are puffy now too. She has disguised it with make-up, but the skin beneath them is purplish and bruised-looking.

'I'm glad you still wear Alfonso's beautiful ring,' she says. 'I think of him every day. I miss him every night. He was my beloved.'

Chiara takes a step back. She does not want this woman appropriating the memory of her father. 'Come on, Daniele,' she says.

'I know that it's dreadful. I am ashamed of myself. I am.' Simone starts speaking fast in her low, accented voice. 'But I just can't be bothered. I think, what's the point? And it is very cold in my apartment. The wind seems to rattle through it. It is like being up the mast of a ship. I think the building is swaying in the wind. It never used to sway, but now it does.

'And downstairs has been taken over by the SS. The second floor. And bad things, unspeakable things are happening there. I know they are. And so every day, every night, I imagine breaking in and rescuing whoever is there. But I can't and I don't, and every day that I allow it, pass that door, lie in the same building with whatever it is going on, I think what's the point of me, then?'

This is the woman who loved her father unstintingly for more than twenty years.

'Take the charcoal anyway,' Simone says, thrusting the bag at Chiara. She has a weary, desperate air as if, once relieved of the burden of charcoal and the necessity it implies of keeping herself warm, she might go and throw herself in the river.

This is the woman whom her father loved.

Chiara sighs. 'You'd better come to our house,' she says. 'It's not far.'

*

'Divine,' Simone comments, as she lifts another forkful of stew to her lips. 'I don't know how you do it.' She shakes her head in wonder across the table at Chiara. 'To the cook,' she says, raising her glass.

And Chiara, raising her own glass in response and unable to help smiling back, asks herself, How did this happen? That her dead father's mistress is not just sharing a meal, but is staying the night with them. And that she is glad.

She wonders whether it is to do with the way Simone exclaims in amazement and delight at everything. How she adores the great echoey apartment with its old-fashioned furnishings and is so pleased finally to see the place where her beloved grew up. How when they stood in the hen-pecked wasteland that used to be the dining room, in among the pushed-back furniture, with the netting over the balcony rail to stop the chickens escaping, Simone actually laughed out loud at the arrangement, pronouncing it 'genius'. Or how Chiara's grandfather's depleted wine store is 'an absolute marvel', but the use Chiara has made of it as a trading commodity, exchanging the odd bottle with the sommelier at a restaurant off Piazza Navona for Parmesan, pasta and leftovers (scraps for the chickens), is 'so resourceful'. Even the makeshift bedroom is 'extremely sensible.' It is, Simone pronounces, 'very practical to heat only one room', and they can 'expand outwards again when better times come'. It is as if Simone has flicked open the book that is Chiara, and it has fallen open to some brightly illustrated pages in the middle that Chiara herself didn't know were there.

Or perhaps it is something to do with the assumption of being utterly welcome that seems to govern Simone's behaviour, a kind of ease and confidence that calls up a corresponding feeling of generosity in Chiara's suspicious heart.

305

Or perhaps it is the way Simone lifts Daniele onto her knee to read a story and nestles her head into his neck, then picks him up and puts him down again, sending him off to play with the chickens as if it were the most normal thing in the world, and then says, 'What a sad little boy. Where did you get him from?' and how, when Chiara tells her, she weeps.

Spezzatino di cavallo is not a dish that can be rushed, and the meal has been a long time coming with an extended gap between the first course – a simple risotto bianco knocked up within fifteen minutes of their arrival – and this one. Over the course of the afternoon, while the *spezzatino* has been slow-cooking and the apartment filling with its nourishing aroma, the two women have discussed the state of Italy, the climate of suspicion in Rome, and the best place to get stockings on the black market. They have listened to the news and heard that an 'unbreakable German line' is preventing the Allied forces from progressing and is even pushing them back, agreed that this is Nazi propaganda and that the Allies will arrive before the end of February and, to celebrate, have drunk most of a bottle of Frascati from the precious wine store.

While Chiara has been busy in the kitchen, Simone and Daniele have spent time in the chicken run where they have witnessed the laying of Cluck's first ever real and proper egg (the previous one came out without a shell), which Simone has beaten into a sort of zabaglione for Daniele, who has eaten it with the smallest spoon that could be found.

Daniele has done a whole page of drawings of Cluck. Chiara has told the tale of Cluck's first attempt at an egg, imitated the strange constipated noises and movements the hen made while she was attempting to get it out, clucked around the kitchen table and made herself laugh out loud, actually snort with laughter. Daniele has looked at her aghast, and she wonders whether he has ever heard her laugh before.

'It was funny, wasn't it, Daniele?' she says, but he shakes his solemn head.

She has been amazed to discover that she is enjoying herself. Not in an edge-of-the-abyss-tomorrow-we-die sort of way, but genuinely. So that when Simone all of a sudden looked up at the clock and announced that she would have to leave to get home before the curfew, Chiara rushed to put some of the stew in a bowl and cover it with a cloth for Simone to take home, explaining how long it would need to cook, with Simone smiling and nodding and pulling on her gloves. And only when she was at the door did Chiara suddenly remember that Simone had no fuel.

'Come back in,' she said, almost tugging her. 'You can't cook it, can you? Stay the night.'

The meal has taken so long that Daniele has fallen asleep with his head on the table.

'And to the cook's father,' Simone adds, 'Alfonso Ferdinando Ravello. The love of my life.'

She looks steadily at Chiara as if daring her to contradict, but then she smiles. The wine and food have revived her. The colour has returned to her cheeks, and her hair is honey-hued. The grey streaks don't show in the dim kitchen light.

'Babbo,' Chiara says, raising her glass.

And then they both speak at once.

'Excuse me?' Chiara says.

'I am so glad to be here,' Simone says, 'that's all. I can honestly say that you have brought me back to life.'

She looks around the kitchen, at the leftover stew in its dish (Enough for tomorrow, Chiara thinks), at Daniele's hand lying on the table with the horseshoe birthmark, his grubby fingernails, his hair flopping forward, and then back at Chiara.

'You have saved my life,' she says, 'and I thank you from the bottom of my heart.'

Chiara feels herself blush under the other's ardent gaze.

'I'd better put the little man to bed,' she says. She shakes Daniele sufficiently awake to stand and bustles him, eyes half closed, out of the room.

Simone sleeps in Cecilia's room. She says she doesn't mind the cold because she is hot-blooded and produces a lot of excess heat.

'Your father used to say he didn't need a hot-water bottle when he was sharing a bed with me,' she says when Chiara leaves. 'Sorry,' she says when she sees Chiara's face. 'I overstep the line sometimes, I know.'

'I don't really mind,' Chiara says, surprised to discover that this is true. 'It's nice to hear his name, you know.'

'He was more of my life than I was of his,' Simone says. 'He had you and Cecilia and your mother. He even had his own mother and father still. I just had him.'

Chiara steps back into the room, tugging at the ring on her finger. 'I'm sorry I made you give me his ring,' she says. 'It should be yours, really.' She slides it off and holds it out.

'You didn't make me. You asked me for it, and I gave it to you.' Simone closes her own, much bigger hand around Chiara's. 'Willingly,' she says.

In the morning, with hardly any discussion, Simone goes across Rome to her own apartment, gathers a few belongings, comes back and moves in. Until the situation improves, they agree.

Simone has a gift for scrounging and wheedling, and Chiara

for making something out of almost nothing. Life with Simone moves up a notch from mere survival.

'We are more than the sum of our parts,' she likes to comment when yet another ingenious meal is put on the table, or another bag of charcoal somehow procured.

Sometimes they laugh, and it's as if Daniele is the adult, an old man bowed by the cares of the world, and they the children. He looks at them reprovingly, as if they are being disrespectful of the solemnity of the times. Our little memento mori, Simone calls him.

'I do admire you,' she says to Chiara one day.

Chiara eyes her warily. Admiration is not how she would describe the look on Simone's face.

'It must be difficult to live your life with Daniele, knowing that it could end at any moment.'

'It's the same for everybody,' Chiara says. She wants to say 'for every mother', but she stops herself.

'I didn't mean bombing and raids and all the . . .' Simone waves her arm towards the horizon.

'Rubble,' Chiara suggests.

'Yes. You have to be careful with him, but also with yourself. You have to live with him as if you will have to give him back.'

'What do you mean?'

Chiara hears a dangerous rise in her own voice. She feels something slide within her.

'Just a minute,' she says.

She gets quickly up and goes out of the room, stands just the other side of the door and takes a breath. Not now. She will think about this later. When she is alone, she will ponder when it was that she started to love him more than anything else in the world. Not now.

She returns to the room but she doesn't sit down again.

'I can't talk about this,' she says. 'You mean well, I'm sure, but I do not want to discuss this. I cannot see what good it would do.'

Simone ignores her. She lowers her head and holds her hand up, palm towards Chiara, like a traffic policeman holding back a lorry at a busy crossroad. She speaks fast and low. She brooks no interruption.

She says that she understands that Chiara has made it her life's work to keep this child safe, that she has risen to this task that was thrust upon her. That it is admirable, noble even. That she can see it is Chiara's contribution to the better world they hope will come afterwards. And that she knows it is difficult to live beyond the day, in these hard times, but that is exactly what needs to be done. When this war is over, they will come for him, not his family perhaps, but his community, when whatever is left of it returns and there is some kind of judgment, some elders perhaps, gentlemen with beards and little hats on the backs of their heads, women wearing scarves, they will come and they will claim him and they will thank her for keeping him safe, but they will take him back. And unless Chiara prepares herself, it will rip the heart out of her.

Chiara hears the words as if from under a waterfall.

'I can't love him only halfway,' she says. She is shouting to be heard above the thunderous noise. 'And what do you know about it? You gave all of your love to a married man. You didn't keep anything back, did you?' Chiara's fists are clenched, and tears are streaming down her face.

Simone's head moves again. It is more like a tremor than a shake.

She didn't like that, Chiara thinks.

'We're not talking about me,' Simone says. She lifts her head, looks up now at Chiara and raises her eyebrows.

Chiara is vaguely aware that Simone has said something else, something mild and deflating. Let's have a row, she thinks. Let's splatter the room with the mess of all these unsaid things.

But while she is calculating how best to goad Simone, another part of her mind is chasing another strand of thought, something she knows that Simone doesn't, something she has been holding in reserve that will clinch the argument. She clutches it and says it aloud.

'Nonna baptised him,' she says.

Simone wrinkles her nose. 'So?' she says.

'It means he is a Christian. He has to be brought up a Christian.'

Simone bites her lower lip. Chiara has seen that look before.

Chiara was there when the doctor came to see Nonno and listened to his wheezing old chest. She saw Nonna's face as she took in what he was saying. The realisation that the prognosis was worse than she had thought. That is how Simone is looking at her now.

Neither of them speaks for a minute.

Simone takes a breath and opens her mouth. She has the air of one about to impart bad news. 'If you are saying—'

Chiara lifts her hands as if in surrender. 'Don't,' she says.

But Simone is relentless. '—that because your *nonna* splashed water over the boy's head and muttered some arcane words, you won't have to give him back?'

Chiara lifts her hands to her face and presses her cold fingers into her cheeks, staring at Simone over her fingertips.

'I'm not saying half love him,' Simone goes on. 'Love him with all your heart. What other way is there to love? And let's face it, the poor little bugger needs it. But just, somehow, hold the idea too that it probably isn't for ever. That when this is all over and better times come, you can get on with your life, marry perhaps, have children of your own.'

'What if I don't want that?'

'Of course you want that. We all do. We don't all get it.' She gazes intently at Chiara. 'I am not just thinking of you. I am thinking of the boy. He doesn't need to be in a ghetto, that one; he carries it about with him.'

Chiara stops protesting. She lets what Simone is saying sink in. 'What can I do?' she says.

The answer comes so promptly it is obvious Simone has been thinking about it.

'I wondered,' she says, 'about getting him to write letters to his mother?' She holds her hand up again as if Chiara is about to interrupt, which she isn't. 'You could supervise him and you – we – can ask him where his mother used to take him, if she had a favourite place, and then you could go with him and hide the note and, I don't know,' she shakes her head, 'I don't know if it will do any good or if it will help that sad little boy or you, but ...'

SEVENTEEN

The signora was scrubbing a coarse stalk of celery under a running tap, rubbing the grime off with her thumbnail. Maria watched with fascination.

In Maria's opinion, there was no excuse for celery. At best, it was pointless, a quasi non-vegetable, a texture rather than a taste. Her mother usually served it unadorned in a glass tumbler, trying, perhaps, to pass it off as a table decoration. At worst, as part of a school dinner, stewed as an accompaniment to gristly mince with all the crunch – which was the only thing in its favour – lost, it was an insult to the name of vegetables. Sometimes, when guests were coming and she was preparing a buffet, her mum would smear its hollow with cream cheese, sprinkle it with chives and chop it into segments, and it would take its place alongside the cocktail sausages, the tinned asparagus rolls and the vol-au-vents, made with puff pastry and filled with a grey mushroom goo, which was actually, Maria remembered, slimy but tasty. Her mum was good at mushroom goo.

'Tell me all that you have learnt today,' the signora said.

Maria reeled off a list of seven irregular verbs. 'Shall I conjugate them for you?' she said.

She repeated them in the present tense and then with their past participles while the signora brought the celery to the chopping board and, using a sharp little knife, sliced the stalk almost through, then stripped away the threads running down its spine.

'I wanted to ask you. What happened to the mushroom hat?' Maria said.

'Eh?' the signora said, tossing the diced celery into a pan over a low flame.

'The mushroom hat you were going to wear,' Maria said, 'when you met me at the station?'

'It's not the season for mushrooms,' the signora said. She peeled an onion and popped two garlic cloves out of their skins. 'If you're still here, I'll take you.'

She looked up at Maria and gave a little nod, the promise of treats to come.

'Take me where?' Maria said, wondering at the turn the conversation had taken.

'The best place I know, here in Rome, is up in the gardens above Trastevere. There was a, ah, the word escapes me, a bunch, is it? A gathering? There is a very good word in English. I know it. Anyway, I found the spot two years ago. Huge *porcini*. Amazing.'

Porcini. Little porky things? Maria had asked about a hat and now they were talking about what might be piglets.

The signora made a curved shape with her hands, holding an imaginary ball, adjusted it to about the size of a football, nodded and resumed her chopping. 'Big as plates,' she said. 'The weather was perfect for them that year.'

'*Porcini?*' Maria said.

'Yes, you know, what do you call them in English?'

'I don't know.'

314

'Neither do I,' the signora said. 'Look in the dictionary.'

There was a whole row of dictionaries on the bookshelf in the salon. One of them was only in Italian but had illustrations. Maria brought that and an English–Italian one.

'Clump,' the signora said. 'I remembered. Clump. Good word, isn't it?'

Porcini were a kind of mushroom. 'There doesn't seem to be a proper word in English,' Maria said, doubtfully. 'We can say *cèpes*, which is the French, or *boletus*, which is Latin.'

'Perhaps they do not grow in Wales.' The signora added the garlic and onion to the pan, and the celery odour was subsumed.

Maria examined the pictures. They were like big brown buttons. 'Is your mushroom hat like a *boletus* mushroom then?' Maria asked.

'My hat! You mean my hat. I lost that hat, I forgot about it,' the signora said. She came and looked over Maria's shoulder. 'Perhaps it wasn't very much like a mushroom. Not really,' she said. 'I think I lost it when I fell down on Sunday.'

'Oh, what did the doctor say?' Maria asked.

The signora went to the store cupboard and took out a small screw-top jar, packed with curled and shrivelled slivers. 'It is a thing to do with my inner ear. And it will pass.' She unscrewed the top and held it under Maria's nose. 'Sooner or later.'

Maria breathed in a deep, earthy aroma of mushrooms that was on the edge of being rather unpleasant.

'*Porcini*,' the signora said. 'I dried them myself.'

She returned to the pan, gave it a stir and tipped in some white wine from the previous night's leftover bottle.

'That smell is fab,' Maria said. 'Fabulous. I can't even smell the celery now. I'd like to learn to cook.'

315

'I make you green vegetable risotto. Like Nonna used to make.'

Maria's own gran – her former grandmother rather, Barry's mum – made risotto too. Vesta beef risotto, it was called, and it came in a cardboard packet with a picture on the front of the Leaning Tower of Pisa. You had to add boiling water to the contents to make the rice, dried veg and little cubes of meaty stuff swell up. It was one of her gran's better meals. It was nothing like the small bowl of gooey rice with broad beans and peas (in which the taste of celery was now undetectable) that the signora presented her with. They sprinkled over the top a heavenly and pungent cheese. It was *parmigiano*, the signora said. Maria looked in the dictionary to check this meant Parmesan. That was what they called the cheese powder they had at home that came in a small plastic tub and smelt like sick.

By the end of the meal, Maria knew that this apartment had belonged to the signora's grandparents, her *nonna* and *nonno*, and that the signora had taken it on when they moved permanently to the countryside where they had a farm. The Italian word for 'farm' sounded as if it meant 'factory'. It was one of those false friends, like the word for 'bored' being more like 'annoyed' and *caldo*, which should mean 'cold', meaning 'hot' instead.

'I have just one picture of them,' the signora said. 'I will show you.'

She left the room, returned a moment later and placed in Maria's hands a faded sepia photograph in an ornate gilt frame. It showed a middle-aged couple, the woman with her dark hair looped up into a bun, a full-length dress and white gloves, the man in a dark suit with a waistcoat and what might have been a chain across his middle, hair smoothed to one side, mustachioed, smart and serious. They stood in front of a painted background of trees.

The signora, preparing the coffee at the stove, was prattling on about her *nonno* but she was speaking too fast. Maria, sitting at the table in a kind of post-prandial stupor, pleasantly replete, understood only the odd word. 'Bird' was one; 'hills' another. She moved her thumb idly up and down the side of the picture frame, where the photograph slotted in between glass and backing. She was very sleepy. Something, an older photo perhaps or a piece of card, protruded along the edge of the picture and she patted it back into place. She wished she had a bedroom of her own and she could go into it now and lie down, just for five minutes.

All of a sudden the photograph was snatched from her hands. The signora stood with it tight against her body with one hand and the other held to her head, as if in pain.

'Oh,' Maria said, taken aback. 'Sorry,' she said.

The signora spun as if on a pivot and shot out the door, clutching her head. Perhaps she had thought Maria was going to drop it.

'Here is one of my mother and father,' she said on her return, as if that were the explanation, as if Maria had said, I'm bored with this one, show me another. 'It's their wedding picture.'

The coffee was bubbling up and the signora went and switched off the gas. Maria gazed dutifully at the print on the table. She didn't pick it up in case there was some etiquette to holding family photographs that she had unwittingly breached once already.

'Look at the hands,' the signora said, going back to speaking in English.

Perhaps Maria had done nothing wrong after all, had simply misread the signora. She looked at the picture.

'Do you see her fingers are crossed? I noticed just the other day. Wishing for good luck, I suppose.'

317

'If you cross your fingers when you make a promise, you don't have to keep it,' Maria said, not thinking at all about what that might signify in the context of a marriage, taken up instead by her study of the man's hands. She was trying to discern whether the ring on the little finger of his right hand was the same one she had in the side pocket of her shoulder bag.

'Really?' the signora said. 'I never heard that before.'

'She looks very young,' Maria said.

'She was sixteen.'

Maria's head snapped up. 'No way,' she said. 'My age?' She gazed back at the girl. 'How come she got married when she was only sixteen?'

'I recount you the story,' the signora said. 'I tell you in Italian, yes, and you ask me demands if I go too fast or if you don't understand.'

And she told the tale of her father Alfonso's wooing of her mother Antonella when her mother's family was about to emigrate to Argentina.

It was so cosy and delicious, sitting in the relative cool of the signora's old-fashioned kitchen.

'And Daniele Levi,' Maria said. 'My *babbo*.' She smacked her lips over all the Bs, still gazing at the photograph of the signora's parents. 'When he lived here, did he use to eat in the kitchen with you? Or did he sort out his own meals?'

No reply came, and when Maria raised her head she saw the signora across the table, her eyes unfocused, as if she were looking through a rent in the fabric of the room, this solid kitchen with its old square table and its yellow cupboards, upon a scene of sorrow.

'Are you all right?' she said.

The signora blinked and recovered. 'Yes,' she said. 'This dizzy thing. It comes and goes.' She swirled her forefinger

318

around the crown of her head. She jumped up and clapped her hands. 'Come on,' she said, 'let's get this show on the road. That's how you say, isn't it? The Colosseum won't wait for ever.'

'Am I all right to go like this?' Maria asked.

She was wearing one of the dresses from the signora's collection: a red and white spotted one with a sweetheart neckline. The full skirt shimmied and bounced around her legs as she walked.

The signora looked her up and down. 'Perhaps a little jacket, for the evening chill later?' she said. 'In case we delay.'

Maria selected a linen bolero from the rack in the dressing room.

'Perfect,' the signora said and they spilt out into the melting golden afternoon.

They went by bus. They didn't need to book a professional guide, the signora said, because she had a book.

They started with the Forum, which was opposite the Colosseum. Maria trailed behind the signora, who read aloud from an out-of-date Michelin guide, enlivening dry facts and dates with a spirited delivery. They stood on a grassy mound with the sun beating down on the backs of their heads in front of a row of three columns.

'The Temple of Dionysius,' the signora read. She opened wide her hand introducing the columns to Maria, Maria to the columns.

'Yes,' Maria said.

The signora threw back her head as if to lead by example in admiring the intricacy of the capitals. Then she cried out and she was falling, the book flying from her flailing fingers.

It was as if a hockey ball had slammed into the side of her head. Maria lunged forward to catch her before she hit the

319

ground. She flung her arms under the signora's, encircling her torso, feeling the wildly beating heart within, and they both subsided backwards to the ground, Maria's wide skirt ballooning out around them on the grass.

The signora's yelps died away.

How extraordinary to hold a grown-up in her lap, to feel that this small person with her bony little ribcage was somehow in her care. Maria's thoughts flew to her little brother and sister.

'Don't worry,' she said. 'I'm here, I've got you.'

'I'm sorry, Maria,' the signora whispered.

Maria saw the word as if it were handwritten there in the air between them, the curly-topped Rs. *So sorry.*

She put the signora in a cab.

'The doctor told me not to do that thing with my head, but I forgot,' the signora said. 'I will lie in bed, have a little sleep. I will be fine later. You can find your way home from here, isn't it?'

'Can't you,' Maria said, automatically.

'Eh?'

'You need to say, "can't you", not "isn't it".'

'Ah yes,' the signora said. 'Haven't I? Don't we? Shouldn't they? Thank you, Maria. Again I say you sorry.'

She gave a woebegone smile from the back of the cab.

Maria flicked her hand in the air as if she were banishing whatever it was and smiled at the signora. 'You're forgiven,' she said.

Oh dear, she thought as the cab pulled away and she saw the signora's face crumple.

'The Colosseum is also known as the amphitheatre of Flavio, and is the largest such in the world,' she read.

A guide leading a bunch of Americans walked by, and she

tagged along, putting the book away. The group descended a ruined staircase and looked through a railing at a place where the gladiators used to prepare before going into battle, but Maria couldn't see it properly because she was at the back. The guide was speaking English with a strong accent.

'They used to do their toilet here,' she said.

Maria left the group and climbed back up into the sunshine. She spread out her skirt and sat on the stump of a pillar, gazing at the rows of colonnades and arches. It was nice to be alone. She leant back against the cornerstone and felt its warmth against the curve of her back, seeping through her dress to the damp skin. She loosened the tight belt around her waist one notch to let some air circulate. She loved being this hot. Never before had she walked about being hot all the time. All over her skin and in the folds of her skin, the backs of her knees, under and between her breasts, her eyelids. It was new to her but also familiar and almost comfortable as if she had known it before, in an unremembered time.

She took Daniele Levi's ring out of her handbag and held it in her palm. If it really was the same ring that the signora's father was wearing in the photograph, what would that mean? Had Daniele Levi stolen it? Ought she then to return it to the signora? But then the signora would know that he was a thief. Perhaps there was a different explanation.

On the other side of the walkway from where she sat, a child clambered onto another pillar stump, unsheathing a plastic sword from a plastic scabbard. He reminded her of her little brother.

She put the ring away. When she was alone in the apartment, she would have a closer look and compare it with the photograph. She might take another look at the other picture too, the one the signora had snatched out of her hands.

The child's parents approached, pushing a younger sibling. They were having a row. The child stood still as a statue, his sword brandished high above his head, and they walked past, engrossed in each other, not even registering his marvellous pose. He stayed a few moments, unmoving, and then he leapt down and ran after them, thwacking at the sides of the stone tiers, his red face scrunched up. He swiped low, slicing into the wheels of the pushchair. The mighty sword caught and was mangled in the spokes. The mother smacked the boy's legs, and he started to wail.

'At least you're not being fed to the lions,' Barry would probably have told that boy if he were here. Then he'd make him forget the raging injustice of his treatment by telling stories of bloodthirsty crowds, roaring beasts, bold warriors and hapless Christians.

She leant back and let the sun bathe her face. Barry, her erstwhile father.

She blinked, stood up, brushed from her exquisite dress some bits of twig and grass that she must have picked up when she caught the signora, and set off in the other direction.

On the way back home, Chiara had to ask the taxi driver to stop. She clawed at the door, stuck out her head and was sick on the pavement, emptying the carefully prepared lunch into the gutter, with people stepping out of the way and making disgusted noises. Back in her own building, she hauled herself up the stairs, clutching the banister. The nauseating whirl had abated but it hadn't gone away, and something was dislodged in her head, as if a stone that used to cover the hidden entrance to a cave had been kicked aside.

This girl. This alien being she'd allowed into her life, this girl with all her questions. When she realised she had actually placed the hidden photograph of Daniele in Maria's hands, she had nearly passed out.

She had imagined a child, a wispy sort of a creature. She had been fooled by the quiet little voice on the telephone, the tears and the hesitancy. Someone manageable, biddable, tidy-awayable was what she had had in mind. Not this large-breasted, tousle-haired, almost fully formed, *blatant* sort of creature – and yet, and yet, alongside the nausea and the dizziness and the what was it, she sought the word. Terror seemed too strong, but it would do, it was close enough. Terror, yes. And alongside that, another feeling, a kind of soaring, a thing she hadn't felt for such a long time she hardly recognised it. And the name of that thing was elation.

Daniele's daughter.

She needed to contact Antonio and tell him they were doing it now. The big revelation. She could not put off telling the girl any longer.

Father Pio answered the telephone. Antonio was away. He would be back after the weekend.

'Tell him to telephone me the moment he returns,' she said.

She wondered whether she could wait until the following week. Yes, if she planned things carefully, outings and excursions. The language school had a trip to the catacombs at the weekend. She would book the girl on that. And she would enlist the help of her cousin's son, Beppe.

She would keep the girl so busy that her feet would not touch the ground.

EIGHTEEN

One of Daniele's hands is hooked into Chiara's pocket and the other is stuffed into his own pocket, where he clutches the notes he has written to his mother. A surge of pride – that he can write so well and that she was the one to teach him – momentarily overrides her anxiety.

'Are you ready?' she says.

He nods.

'You know where we're going and what we're doing?'

They are going first to the ghetto and then to the Janiculum hill above Trastevere, the sites he has chosen.

'You have the documents?'

Their false identity documents are in his inside pocket in case they should be stopped. He nods again.

They set off and the anxiety returns. She is a tangle of fears. She is fearful of the effect on him, on them, of returning to the scene of his family's abduction. She is fearful that some military presence remains in the ghetto. She pictures a lone sniper, biding his time, crouched at the window of a high room, adjusting the angle of his rifle. She is fearful that Daniele might run away when they are on his home ground, might make a dash for it, disappear into one of the ghetto's narrow alleyways and hide. It is so strong in him, the impulse to run. And how will she ever find him again?

Chiara wanted to postpone this expedition. Two weeks earlier there was a partisan bomb attack on an SS police regiment and dozens were killed. Tension is high, rumours are rife. Nothing on this scale in the heart of the city has happened before. She had cycled up to Gennaro's place, but he wasn't there. She doesn't know whether he is in hiding, if he has been caught, or even if his group was definitely responsible, but she is full of dread. She has heard stories that the bomber was among the victims and that an SS soldier shot someone dead on the street just because his hands twitched when he had been told to hold still. There is talk of reprisals, of random people being plucked from the streets, children even, and old men who had nothing to do with it taken who knows where. People have disappeared.

Simone said that the time will never be right and they should go ahead.

Chiara and Daniele walk quickly and purposefully. Simone follows at a distance. She is their back-up, ready to set up a commotion to divert attention if necessary. The streets and squares of the ghetto are deserted. Even so, with each step, Chiara is conscious of resisting the urge to pick up Daniele and run. Just to be here with him seems a provocation, a wilful tempting of fate.

They cross Piazza Costaguti and walk through the dark passageway next to the little temple at the far end of the square. Daniele lifts a loose stone next to the doorway in the corner of the yard, the entrance to his family home. He places his first note beneath, where the spare key used to be kept. The thick walls of the buildings around, the eerie silence, the lack of an exit route other than the alleyway through which they entered, make the courtyard oppressive.

Daniele stands staring at the doorway. She can hardly bear to think how the emptiness and the quiet must strike him, what thoughts might be going through his mind.

'Come on,' she says. 'Let's go.'

The face he turns to her is expressionless. She sees that her fears that he might run away were unfounded. He appears to be in a sort of trance. He is a mystery to her. *I will never know,* she thinks. They walk on.

The second note slides easily into place behind the street sign.

They turn into Via del Portico d'Ottavia. He has chosen an ancient charity box embedded in the street wall for his third note. Chiara has passed it many times without ever noticing it. Beneath the slot there is an inscription, in Hebrew, she imagines, and beneath that its translation into Italian. *For the orphans.* The slot is for coins and the folded note will not fit through.

'Can I help?' she says.

He ignores her, opens the note out and refolds it. His movements are unhurried. He is taking an age. Her heart will burst forth from her chest and her legs collapse beneath her while his stubby child fingers fumble with the piece of paper. She notices a little keyhole in the metal box. She wonders who was the custodian of that key and where it might now be. She has a sudden vision of a great pile of unclaimed keys that would unlock the doors to the ghetto buildings. She looks away. The streets are still empty.

Finally, he is done and they move on, posting the last of the ghetto notes through the door of Gennaro's boarded-up bar. They continue along Via del Portico d'Ottavia, past the Theatre of Marcellus and out onto Lungotevere.

They cross over the little bridge onto the island in the middle of the river to St Bartholomew's church where they are to meet up with Simone. There is a service in full swing even though it is the middle of the afternoon. They stand at the back, just inside the door.

The priest is reading the gospel. 'Jesus went forth with his disciples across the Kidron valley, where there was a garden,' he says.

It must be Good Friday, she realises. The vegetable garden above Nonna's house appears in her mind and the valley on the other side of the hill.

'Now Judas, who betrayed him, also knew the place,' the priest continues.

Something long held down erupts and a wail bursts from Chiara's lips. She claps her hand over her mouth to stifle the sound but, behind her hand, her mouth is open in horror. There is a well of unshed tears in her and it is bottomless.

Then Simone appears and leads them back out into the porch where she takes Chiara in her arms.

'What is it?' she is saying. 'You did so well. You both did so well.'

Chiara cannot compose herself sufficiently to answer, but clutches at Simone's sleeve and sobs inconsolably into her bosom. 'Cecilia,' she manages at last.

Simone holds her and pats her and makes soothing noises. She reminds Chiara that she has left Cecilia in the care of the Morelli couple and that Beatrice sounds like a very competent woman. She mentions too the sturdy and loyal Gabriele. Eventually Chiara calms down.

Simone doesn't accompany them on the final stage of the expedition. She leaves them there. She is going to see whether she can find anything for them to eat that evening. Bread rations have been cut again. They have already consumed today's meagre quota and there is nothing in the shops.

The fifth note is to be left at the Anita Garibaldi monument, which Daniele picked out from a photo in the bookstore. Chiara feels weak and light-headed with tiredness and hunger and emotion. She imagines Daniele too must be weary and so, in the hope that a bus will come along and they will not have to walk the whole way, they follow the bus route.

Via Garibaldi zigzags up the Janiculum hill. As they climb higher and leave the city behind, Chiara starts to feel less tired. She breathes more easily and strength returns to her legs. It is a beautiful day and the oak trees are in bud. No bus comes by. They pause a moment in the vast square where the monument to Giuseppe Garibaldi stands. From here the privations and damage the city has suffered are not visible. Rome appears undiminished, intact. It shimmers in the soft spring air.

'How lovely,' Chiara says.

They walk farther and then there she is, Anita Garibaldi on her stallion. And Daniele, detaching himself from Chiara's side, gallops ahead to meet her. He gallops up to the monument and then twice around its base, holding imaginary reins. He rears up, whinnies and comes to a halt, pawing the ground.

He looks just like a child, playing.

Chiara stares at him, amazed. She feels she could even break into a gallop herself, but refrains.

'This is the right place, isn't it?' she says when she catches up. She means this is the place where the hope and possibility of a message getting through does not seem so far-fetched.

He nods.

The bronze statue depicting Anita Garibaldi, a gun in one hand and a baby in the other, is mounted on a plinth decorated with dramatic scenes in bas-relief. They climb the plinth steps and walk slowly around, examining the scenes. The parts that most protrude, banners held aloft by riders, flying manes, fetlocks and muzzles, are lighter in colour, with a greenish tinge. The frieze on the back of the plinth shows a scene of devastation, the aftermath of a battle, bodies piled on top of each other. Here that greenish sheen appears on an outflung hand, a sagging shirt-cuff, the heel of a boot pushing into someone else's face.

Chiara and Daniele are drawn to the figure of Anita herself, kneeling among the bodies; the curve of her back, the waves of her hair, the folds of her dress, alert and full of life in among the dead. In the crook of her right elbow there is a hollow. Chiara hoists Daniele up and he inserts his note, folded into little squares, into it.

Then she lifts him down and smiles at him.

'I can climb that tree,' he says, indicating a nearby oak.

'Show me,' she says and she sits on the plinth steps to watch him climb.

When they get home, they find Simone has managed to procure a bag of chestnut flour and Winston has laid two eggs. Chiara makes them a sort of sweet loaf and they eat it hot, straight from the oven.

NINETEEN

Maria knelt in front of the Pietà, contemplating its marble folds. Here was a cool and peaceful place to be. Although there was a steady stream of tourists coming and going in the huge church behind, muttering and possibly complaining about the indignity of being made to cover their arms and their heads (if they were female), or remove their hats (if male) before entering, they didn't impinge on her. Maria herself had a thin cotton scarf, borrowed from the supply at the church doorway, about her shoulders.

After days of frenetic activity – mornings at school; afternoons hurtling around Rome for sightseeing with the signora's nephew Beppe and his friend Carmelo, or some other friends of the signora who wanted to show her round the university; the whole of Saturday being taken up by an excursion with the language school, which the signora had booked her on, to Hadrian's villa – now, finally, before this most famous of statues, she had come, quite simply, to a halt.

She had seen the Forum, the Palatine hill and the Campidoglio, the nearest of the Catacombs and a bewildering number of churches, including one made of bones. She had worn a variety of exquisite outfits from the signora's collection and been much admired. Today she was wearing a knee-length, sleeveless tunic dating from the sixties. It was made of shot silk with a blue warp and a pink weft and oversized pink buttons down the back.

'Just begging someone to unbutton them,' according to Carmelo.

Not him, though, because he was not that way inclined.

She had visited Keats's grave in the Protestant cemetery behind the Pyramid and sat at the desk in the salon, puzzling over Keats's theories about life and love and consciousness, mansions of many apartments and dwelling in uncertainty. She had drunk chilled white wine, downed an espresso every day after her lunch and hardly missed proper cups of tea at all. She had learnt to twirl her spaghetti around her fork and not to slurp it, how to tell whether a melon was ripe, the names of seven different sorts of pasta and the difference between Parmesan and pecorino. She had eaten artichokes, aubergines, peppers and garlic, and her insides were lubricated with olive oil.

She knew to buy tickets at the tobacconist before boarding the bus, to ask for the till receipt in a bar in advance of ordering, and not to sit down in a café without checking the prices. But still, however much she learnt, she had the sense that something vital was eluding her.

She was thinking about something she had read in a novel about Michelangelo. How he would go up to Pietrasanta to choose the marble for his sculptures, and how it seemed more as if the piece of marble was calling out and choosing him. And then, as he chipped and chiselled, he felt that he was uncovering and revealing the figure within. She wondered whether, as a piece of marble was to Michelangelo, so Italian was to her, and whether her British crust was being chipped away and, if so, why it was taking such a long time.

She had been running to inhabit the Rome version of herself so that she could leave behind the other one, the sad, pale, listless British one. And sometimes the gap between the two closed, becoming infinitesimally small, but at other times the bright, bold, Roman Maria would skip out of her range, pulling away. She was as ignorant about Daniele Levi now as when she had arrived and, she acknowledged now, in this moment of stillness, despite being almost all of the time in company, despite the stream of admirers that Rome provided, the constant offers from men, the pinching and the groping to be fended off, despite or perhaps because of all that, some of the time she was gripped by loneliness.

She thought of her brother and sister, and of Barry who wasn't her father, and of her treacherous mother, then pulled the scarf up over her head and, hidden inside its folds, allowed herself a little weep. She wiped her nose with the scarf and rolled it into a bundle to drop in the box by the door.

There, outside, was Rome laid out for her in all its glory. She could always count on that. An endless, unfolding delight of winding streets and squares, fountains and stairways, hills and parks, statues, pillars and arches that drew her out of herself from hour to hour. And always on offer when it threatened to overwhelm her was the quiet, cool refuge of churches. The city tugged her from her confusion and sadness and then plunged her back into it, but before she had a chance properly to dwell there, she would be distracted again by this enchanted world. Despite what she sometimes thought about having been damaged and lost beyond remedy, Rome crept in. She inhaled it.

She stepped down into the huge square, her dress gleaming in the sunshine like a dragonfly's wings, iridescent. On the other side, she hopped on a bus to the railway station where she caught a metro out to the area of EUR, to the south of the city. Finally she was going to visit her mother's old friend Helen.

'You never told me, why did you never tell me, that I have been here before?' Maria's voice was shrill.

'Pardon?' Her mum sounded careworn, distracted and then, rallying, 'Maria, is that you?'

'Of course it's me. I've been to see Helen.'

'Oh, right.' There came a deep, tremulous sigh. 'Wait a minute.'

There was the clatter of the receiver being put down, background shouts and shushings. You could stretch the phone cord across the hall and into the living room. It only just reached. Then you could have a more private conversation, standing bang up against the closed door on the other side. Perhaps her mum didn't know this or perhaps she didn't want Pat or Nel to trip over the taut cord when they ran through the hall.

'Here I am,' her mum said when she'd done whatever she needed to do not to be disturbed.

'You brought me here when I was little,' Maria said.

'Helen told you.'

'No, I remembered.'

'You couldn't have.'

'But I did. We went up onto the roof of her building, where they hang all the washing. She wanted to show me the view. She said you and she used to go up there.'

'We did. It was our place. I can't believe you remembered. You weren't even three.'

'We came out onto the roof, through a metal door, and we walked to the edge of the roof, and it was, whoosh, I've been here before. Such a strange feeling.'

334

It wasn't the view itself, modern high-rise buildings, a park, a geometric lake. She didn't recognise that at all. Rather, it was the flap of the sheets, the way they flicked in and out of the edge of her vision, and the snapping sound they made as they unfurled and billowed in the breeze. More, it was the smell of them, of linen speed-drying in the hot afternoon sun, and the aroma of the coffee and an under-layer of something else, a faintly industrial odour, that seemed to be the smell of the building itself, its workings.

'It's come back to me before, that place, but I thought it was a dream. I remembered a red flying thing.'

'It was a tablecloth,' her mum said. 'You were charging around the roof, diving in and out of the washing on the lines.'

'Was I?' She felt a pang of tenderness for her early self. She wrapped the arm that wasn't holding the phone across her chest and tucked it into her armpit.

'Fancy you remembering!'

Her mum, she could tell, was delighted to hear from her.

'And why did we, Mum, why did you bring me here?'

Her mum made a little noise, almost a moan. 'To have one last look' – she paused, exhaled noisily – 'to see if I couldn't find him, Daniele, before . . . '

'Before what?'

'Before I, um,' her mum cleared her throat. 'Before I settled down.'

Maria was silent, taking in what this meant.

'Say something,' her mum said.

'So Dad, I mean Barry, doesn't know,' Maria said.

Her mum's voice was so soft Maria had to strain to hear her. 'No. I never told him,' she said.

The signora's apartment building came into Maria's mind,

the salt-and-stone smell just within the doorway, the rectangular image of wavering light on the stairwell wall.

'Oh,' she said.

A tremor ran up through her from her feet to her head, and she swayed, her spine arching forwards as if something had shunted into her from behind, things all of a sudden starting to connect.

'We went to Signora Ravello's street, didn't we?' she said. Her own voice too was a whisper.

Her mother's breathing was juddery. Maria could hear little slapping noises. She imagined her mother was patting her own chest to calm herself down. Something clicked into place.

'Oh, Mum,' Maria said. 'Oh, Mum.'

Her mother was speaking but she was crying at the same time, and it came out all a jumble.

She knew, she was sure, it was the right house, but there was no Levi listed on any of the name plates. She rang all the bells and asked for him, and someone, some sharp-voiced woman, said through the intercom, 'There is no such person here.'

And then someone else, one of the other residents, came down as they were standing there in the street. And there was nothing else to be done.

The man behind the counter, visible through a small window in the phone-booth door, held up his hand. She had had four minutes.

'Mum, I'm going to have to go in one minute's time. I'm so sorry. Ring me at the flat, yeah?'

Her mum's breathing quietened. She got hold of herself. 'How was Helen?' she said.

'OK, I suppose. She didn't have anything useful to say about Daniele Levi. I haven't got anything to go on. I haven't even got a photo. Didn't people take photos in the 1950s?'

'They cost a lot, cameras. Most people didn't have one.'

'Most people still don't!'

'Barry did say you could borrow his.'

She thought of Barry, jogging on his own around the lake. Second best.

'Is she the same age as you, that Helen?'

'Yes, pretty much.'

'You look much younger.'

Her mum made a noise that was nearly a laugh. 'I'll phone you at the signora's flat,' she said. 'At the weekend, when it's cheaper.'

'Are you going to be all right, Mum?' she said.

But her five minutes were up, and the phone had gone dead.

She got off the bus a stop early so she could have a think before she went back to the apartment.

They had been here before, she and her mother, and they had come to the signora's apartment building and someone, a peremptory someone, had turned them away.

She lit a cigarette and smoked it furiously as she walked along. A wave of sadness rose up in her. She wanted her mum. She didn't want her mum. Her poor mum. She was utterly alone. She wanted to throw herself to the pavement and howl. Words from Keats's 'Ode to a Nightingale' sprang up:

> *when, sick for home,*
> *She stood in tears amid the alien corn.*

She looked wildly at all the unknown Italians walking past, the alien corn.

Seeing that she was outside a church, she stubbed out her

cigarette and went in, blessing herself with the holy water as she entered. She was collecting holy pictures for the signora's cleaner, Assunta, and so could never walk past a church's open door. This, a vast one with geometric tiled floors, rust- and amber-coloured marble pillars, was dedicated to someone called St Crisogono. She picked up a picture of the saint, riding a white horse, bearing a lance and a red shield, and sat down in a row at the back.

Crisogono. That was a good one. Perhaps even Assunta wouldn't know about him.

Gasparo, she had said the other day, unloading the pile of pictures from her handbag.

Gasparo of Buffalo, do you mean? Assunta had replied, and Maria had admitted that was indeed the one.

Quirico, Maria had said, flipping over the next card.

Which one? Assunta had rejoined.

Quirico and Julietta? Maria had ventured tentatively.

Oh, little Quirico, Assunta had said, as if she were fondly remembering the lad, who was just a baby when he was martyred.

Assunta was an expert on the gruesome deaths of martyrs. Little Quirico had been flung down some stone steps. His mother had her sides torn off with hooks.

Maria became aware of the other occupants of the church. On her own row sat a woman with white hair scrunched up in a bun from which electrified tendrils radiated. She was bent double, as if with stomach cramps, her head down below her knees. Occasionally she rocked. Spread among the front two pews were five beige-clad nuns with white headdresses, kneeling. On the right-hand side of the central aisle, in a middle row, knelt a woman with ginger and brown curls – hair that matched and mirrored the colours and swirls of the marble.

338

She emitted a sudden noise. She might have been clearing her throat or it might have been an involuntary expression of anguish. She did it again, a sort of bark. The heads of the five nuns swung sideways to look and then swung back again.

Fortified by the strange delights of the church and its inmates, Maria wandered back out and along the road. It was a comfort to think you could just duck into a church and express your feelings by making ghastly noises or contorting your body, and nobody would interfere.

She crossed the Ponte Sisto. The river had turned out not to be blond at all, more a murky greenish-grey. Still, the gleam of it at this time of day, and the way the buildings on the other side put on the glamour as the sun was going down, glowing orange and red and yellow and amber, dazzled her out of her reverie and into a different one, just as it always did. It was like magic. She forgot about the alien corn because it was happening again, the way it kept happening every day, something she could never have imagined in a million years. The beauty got inside her and she felt herself more lovely, gilded by it. It was fanciful but she felt that in Rome sometimes, off and on like a defective light bulb, she shone.

The signora was not home when Maria got back to the apartment. She called out to make sure but then remembered that the signora was at the doctor's again, had been summoned back for some treatment. She walked the length of the hallway to the signora's room. Speedily, unthinkingly, she picked up the photograph of the signora's grandparents that stood on the bedside table, ran her fingers along the side, tapped it and out slid another, as she had known it would.

She looked at the young man in the picture, his leather jacket and his slicked-back hair. She thought, Cool dude. Was this Daniele Levi? She went and stared in the mirror, holding the picture up next to her face to observe them side by side. Did she look like him? She didn't know what to think. The only thing that was certain was that the signora was deliberately hiding things from her.

She put the picture back where it belonged and went into the salon where she stood, blankly, amid the clutter of furniture and draperies and books.

A vision came to her of tall trees in full leaf, carved angels with folded or outstretched wings, ornate and plain crosses, white and grey tombstones, box hedges and fragrant shrubs. She remembered a particular carving she had seen in the cemetery where Keats was buried.

She draped herself over the sofa back, angled one bare foot out behind her, allowed the sofa to take her weight, her arms and head to fall forward. She hung there, inhabiting the stance, feeling the blood going to her head, the tiled floor beneath the ball and heel of the one firmly planted foot, her own skin where the fingers of one hand rested on the other arm. She allowed herself to drop into the pose, replicating the posture of the Angel of Grief.

TWENTY

They throw petals at the feet of the American soldiers when they march into Rome in June 1944. Oleander flowers in all shades of pink, from pearly pale to deep cerise. The Germans haven't gone, they aren't defeated yet, but they have withdrawn from the city.

The people of Rome, thronging the streets, have never seen anything like these Americans. Whole battalions of black men, laughing and calling out to the girls, handing out sweets and chewing gum to the kids. Some of them are like giants. They are standing at the bottom of the Campidoglio stairs, she and Daniele, right at the front of the crowd, and an American soldier takes her in his arms and waltzes her around on the spot. He lets go only to scoop Daniele up, throw him into the sky and catch him with a guffaw, until Daniele's eyes are bright and his face scarlet.

The soldier dives back into the army of liberators sweeping on to Piazza Venezia, and the watching people surge into the space the soldiers have vacated. As Chiara grips Daniele's hand, telling him to hold tight and not get separated, she spots the face of a woman she knows among the people pouring down the steps. Beatrice, the woman from Nonna's farm in whose care she left Cecilia.

Chiara calls out. Beatrice hears her name, looks sideways at Chiara and stops dead, so that the people behind her have to quickly sidestep. There is too much tumult to make themselves heard. Beatrice points in the direction of a side street and Chiara nods her assent.

As they thread through the crowd, Chiara relives the night they left the farm. How Judas was in her mind and she didn't kiss her sleeping sister goodbye. How they knocked up Gabriele and he harnessed the donkey for Daniele to ride and accompanied them down as far as the road. How she wanted Gabriele to say, 'Don't worry. It will be fine,' but he didn't.

They make their way across the road, down a side street and into the vestibule of a little church, where it is quieter. Outside people are whooping, children blow horns, male voices sing 'Avanti, Popolo' in a bold, manly way, but Beatrice talks quietly and is kinder than Chiara remembered.

She tells her that she and Ettore are back in Rome now. That on a night not long after Chiara left the farm, Cecilia arose from her bed when all were sleeping, walked out in her nightgown and bare feet into the dark fields, climbed the hill into the olive grove and beyond, and never came back.

Cecilia must have had a fit out there in the dark by herself, with no one to fish her tongue out of her throat or arrange her limbs.

Gabriele has been missing, eventually presumed dead, ever since the night Chiara and Daniele left.

Chiara has an urge to fling herself to her knees on the stone church floor but knows there is no solace to be found here and no forgiveness.

A horrible conjunction comes to her unbidden: Cecilia lying in the ditch and Daniele caught in a moonbeam there on the hill, baying like a little wolf.

She made a choice. It is not his fault.

That is what Simone says to her.

'It's not your fault. She could have had a major fit at any time, whether you were there or not. You told me she had been going downhill for a while.'

'I abandoned her,' Chiara says.

She wishes she were a believer and then she would go to confession in a church where she had never before been and she would say, 'I killed my sister.' But, anyway, even if she believed, there would be no point because she doesn't want absolution.

Often, afterwards, Chiara will think of Gabriele, alone on the night path, being seen before he saw. But the image of her sister, face down in a puddle on the hillside, her arms flung wide, her long hair trailing in the mud, she carries with her for ever.

TWENTY-ONE

Her own doctor held her feet, and the visiting American audiologist – 'Mr Hennessey, call me Charles' – held her upper body. Between them the two men lifted Chiara into the air as if she were gossamer.

Charles, an inner ear specialist, was en route to a Japanese university and only in Rome for the briefest of sojourns to deliver a paper. It was he who directed operations in a kindly drawl.

'Hold her there, wait, keep her still, now, like this, gentle and slow, slow, slow as she goes,' he said, as if she were a ship that they were guiding into harbour.

They tilted her this way and that, tipping her almost upside down so her eyes swivelled up into her skull. Her head was held and cupped; she was dangled in a position that she hadn't been in since childhood. She handed over her body and experienced an extraordinary sensation of weightlessness, a desperate intensification of the spin, and then it was over, and they laid her back on the treatment bed, moved her head gently into a central position and left her to rest.

When she got up she discovered that the world had been restored more or less to its rightful place, and the sick dizziness that had accompanied her for weeks had gone. More than that, she realised as she set off home, swinging her now-redundant cane, a general fuzziness had lifted. The shop windows she passed gleamed as if they had just been polished. The sky was a radiant and unrelenting blue. The fountain in the piazza tinkled, and the water glistened as it fell.

Everything was sharp and bright and clear. The bells of St Cecilia rang out, loud and insistent. And suddenly she was hurrying. An urgency had come upon her. A desire to talk to Maria, because it couldn't wait. Whatever reason there was to delay was as nothing compared to the compelling reasons for speaking out. Not telling Maria the truth was putting a big, entirely unnecessary obstacle between her and the beloved girl, and she couldn't tolerate it a minute longer.

The apartment was empty. Maria was not there.

The phone rang, and Chiara jumped but it was only dear Simone to say she was back.

'You sound distracted,' Simone said. 'Are you all right?'

'I can't talk,' Chiara said, 'I'm expecting a call.'

Simone said she had plenty to do anyway, unpacking, having a deep bubble bath and then Umberto was going to give her a massage, but how about meeting at Babington's for afternoon tea tomorrow?

'I can't tomorrow, I'm busy. I have to go,' Chiara said.

She didn't know why she had said that about expecting a call, but something was coming, she could feel it in the air, an expectancy, a storm brewing. She paced up and down the passageway. She went out twice onto the communal landing. From the front window she looked down onto the street. Perhaps Maria had had an arrangement with the girls from school and had told her she would be out. She searched her memory. She paced some more. She poured herself a glass of wine. She must stay sober in case there was an emergency. She tipped the wine down the sink.

After an hour, she phoned Simone.

'Sorry,' she said. 'To be so brusque earlier.'

'That's all right,' Simone said. 'I know your ways. I didn't take offence.'

'It's just I'm worried about the girl. She's gone missing.'

'What girl?' Simone said.

'Maria, Daniele's daughter,' Chiara wailed.

She waited for the ceiling to fall around her ears or the floor to erupt, but nothing happened. She became aware that Simone was speaking. 'What?' she said.

'Pour yourself a glass of wine. Get a cushion and the stool and make yourself comfortable. I will phone you back in five minutes and you can tell me everything.'

Chiara did as she was told. The phone rang.

'That wasn't five minutes,' she said.

'*Zia*,' Beppe said. Aunt.

He told her Maria was going to stay on their sofa because she had accidentally got a bit drunk and emotional, but he would make sure she was up in time for school in the morning.

'I thought she was out with the girls from school,' Chiara said.

'Well, she must have lost them, because she was on her own when she turned up here,' Beppe said. 'Don't worry about her, *Zia*, we'll look after her.'

Simone phoned back. 'I'm just going to listen quietly,' she said.

Chiara told her the whole story.

'How absolutely lovely,' Simone said when Chiara had finished. 'What a very, very lovely thing. Daniele had a daughter. And she has found you. Oh, I am bowled over.'

She started to sniffle, and Chiara did too. Chiara began to think that perhaps things might be all right after all.

'Does she look like him?' Simone said.

'As soon as you see her, you will know. Her hair is much lighter than his, and she has blue eyes but otherwise she is like a female version of him, aged sixteen.'

'What I don't understand is why Antonio dictates the timing,' Simone said. 'I mean, what's it got to do with him? She's your granddaughter. Not his.'

'Goodness me.'

'Hadn't you thought of that?'

'I'm a *nonna*!'

She phoned Beppe back. 'Tell Maria that I will be making a special lunch tomorrow and to come straight home after school.'

'I thought I'd had a stroke,' she said the next morning.

She and Simone were in Babington's at the bottom of the Spanish Steps. Chiara had been reluctant, but Simone had insisted on her coming out, said she would only fret if she stayed in. It was Simone's treat.

Simone was wearing a floor-length caftan with broad gold and purple stripes, a present from Algeria. She wore a purple clasp in her hair and orange beads around her neck. She reached across to wipe a stray crumb from the corner of Chiara's mouth and chucked her cheek with the backs of her fingers.

'You're far too young for a stroke. And you're not the type. You're thin. Thin and young,' she pronounced.

She took her hand away, flapped it dismissively in Chiara's direction and picked up another cake, looking out of the window as she consumed it in such speedy little bites that it was hard to imagine afterwards that the cake had ever been there.

'Look at that,' she said, indicating with a nod a man on a bicycle pulling an empty rickshaw on wheels. 'Is that for tourists? It won't catch on.'

'I'm not too young. There was a man in the papers this week who was only thirty-eight. He had a massive stroke. He can move only his left eyelid,' Chiara said.

'What man?' Simone said.

'A man here in Rome,' Chiara said. 'I don't know. Haven't you read any newspapers recently?'

'He was thirty-eight?' Simone said, bringing her full attention to bear.

'Yes,' Chiara agreed. 'Thirty-eight.' Daniele's age.

'I don't think you've had a stroke,' Simone said. 'There are no indications. Your speech is normal. There is no drooping.'

'I know I didn't have a stroke. I said I thought I'd had one, that's all.'

'What were your symptoms?'

'A sudden, dreadful dizziness. Something fizzled in my head, and I couldn't speak for a while. It kept happening. I had to be very, very careful not to make quick movements because, if I did, if I swung my head to the right, then everything would spin. It felt as though the world had become unsafe. Uncertain.'

'Have you only just discovered that?' Simone said.

There was one cake left on the plate.

'I could eat that but I won't,' Simone said, virtuously. 'But then it's a shame to waste it,' she added. 'And it is my day off.'

She meant from her diet, which involved taking some potion that stimulated the production of amino acids, which in turn speeded up digestion or metabolic rate or something.

'You don't want it, do you?' she said, eyeing the cake, and then looked up. 'Oh, Chiara. It's serious, isn't it? Why didn't you tell me last night? Oh, you were so caught up in worrying about the girl you forgot to mention that you were ill.'

Her face sagged, and her great age, normally disguised by the bonhomie that pulled up the skin and flesh, the splendid bone structure, the languid bounce, was revealed, undeniable.

'I knew there was something dreadfully wrong,' she said in doomed, bereft tones.

'No, no, no,' Chiara protested. 'Not at all. I'm better. Look, I'm cured.'

She turned her head to the right. Outside, a portly middle-aged couple were negotiating with the rickshaw rider.

Simone seemed unconvinced. She picked up the last cake and dejectedly munched it.

Chiara set about a lavish description of the treatment, making it into an old-fashioned laying-on of hands, a calling-up of ancient wisdoms to banish the rogue, chalky substance from the canals of her inner ear.

'At one point,' she said, 'I was thinking about that marble floor and hoping they wouldn't drop me.'

'They were hardly likely to drop you. A child could lift you,' Simone said. 'So you're cured, are you?'

'Until the next time,' Chiara said. 'It was as if I were inside a tornado. Isn't it amazing, that a microscopic fragment out of place can so distort one's notion of reality?'

'What's more amazing is that hanging you upside down can rectify it,' Simone said. 'Do you think if the members of the government were all hung upside down, it would correct their interpretation of the world?'

'Well, it worked with Mussolini,' Chiara said.

And they both sniggered, like schoolgirls at a dirty joke.

Simone wanted to go for a ride in the bicycle rickshaw, but Chiara demurred at such a pointless extravagance. As soon as Simone had two pennies to rub together she liked to spend them.

'It's because you weren't brought up in penury,' she told Chiara. 'That's why frugality has an appeal to you.'

'It's not that,' Chiara said. 'I just want to get back. In case.'

'It's only ten o'clock,' Simone said. 'Let's at least have a little walk first.'

They climbed the Spanish Steps, weaving their way in between the tourists and hippie types, the vendors selling beads and painted plates, the artists who would execute your portrait or do your caricature for two thousand lira.

As they set off along the road at the top, Chiara told her about the outing with Dario Fulminante. It seemed to her almost like a dream, that afternoon. The bubbling waters of the river, the apparition of the peasant man among the bulrushes, the film-maker who had been her companion in that brief moment out of time.

'Dario Fulminante,' Simone said. 'That sounds like a stage name. Does he make porno films?'

'Oh, I don't think so.' Chiara had a sudden vision of the creepy financiers in their suits and sunglasses. 'Documentaries, he said.'

'Perhaps there'll be a role for me. You must keep in touch with him.'

'You wouldn't take part in a pornographic film,' said Chiara.

'Well, I don't mind taking my clothes off for a good cause,' said Simone. 'And I had years of practice as an artist's model. I can hold a pose.'

She paused, propped herself against the parapet, flung an arm on high and leant backwards an inch for Chiara to admire her upturned head in profile. Beyond the low wall that edged the pavement, Rome spread off into the hazy middle distance, with its trees and greenery, its roofs and roof gardens, its domes.

'Ha ha,' Simone laughed at herself as they resumed their stroll. 'It would depend. If it were an arty film or not. If it had a political message.'

They turned into the park and plumped down on the first unoccupied bench, sitting in silence in the general shade of the high umbrella pines and the more particular shade of an overhanging myrtle shrub. An incongruous and stumpy olive tree grew out of the gravel. Opposite was a children's play area. A donkey pulled a cart containing small children. Bigger kids shot past on roller skates.

Chiara looked at the little olive tree. It was not a good place to grow, in the shade of the pines. It would never get enough light. But it had to make the best of it, send down its own gnarly roots through the gravel and stone, in between the roots of bigger trees to find some sustenance, and at the same time it had to stretch itself upwards and aspire to bearing fruit. She thought about the olive grove above Nonna's farm and the ancient tree, the Mago, where Daniele one moonlit night, as he had later told her, had wished that he would go to sleep and never wake up. Then her thoughts leapt to the oak tree that he used to climb near the Anita Garibaldi monument and she remembered she had left a note for him there, not that long ago. How foolish she was.

'Would you like a caramel?' Simone said, shifting next to her on the bench and proffering a tube of boiled sweets. 'The lemon ones are the nicest.'

'No, thank you.'

'What's the matter? You're sighing.'

'Simone, do you think he might be alive? That he's out there somewhere?'

Simone looked at Chiara and opened her mouth as if about to speak. Then she closed it again and gazed straight ahead. She might have been watching a tottering infant who was chasing the pigeons, arms held wide, hands cupped. She put her arm over Chiara's shoulder and squeezed her upper arm as she spoke.

'I think if he doesn't want to be found, he won't be found. He is capable of disappearing and melting away. Of hiding right under your nose. We know that. He could be anywhere. He could be down the road. Or he could be in America. But, in all honesty, I think he would have been in touch.'

Chiara got to her feet. 'Shall we go?' she said.

Simone stood up too and gathered Chiara into her arms. 'I'm sorry, Chiara,' she said. 'Can you bear it?'

Chiara allowed herself to be held.

'What are you going to make us for lunch then?' Simone said in the cab.

'I'm going to do pasta with walnut sauce. With mascarpone. I've got all the ingredients already because it's what I was going to make for dinner last night but didn't. It's quite rich and creamy but then we'll have a very light main course. Just a green salad and some fish. Do you know that method where you fry the fish quickly in oil first and then marinade it?'

'No,' Simone said, a fond smile on her face. 'Tell me.'

'Well, that's what you do. So I fried it all up last night and put it in a marinade. Oil, white wine, garlic, parsley and mint.'

They had reached the house.

'Why don't I go and get some ice cream for dessert? We'll put it in the top of your fridge. What flavour does she like?'

'Get strawberry,' Chiara said. Then, 'Is it going to be all right?'

'It's going to be more than all right. It's going to be fantastic,' Simone said.

'You don't know,' Chiara said and she clutched at her friend's arm. 'I did such a terrible thing.'

And she tried to tell Simone, there on the doorstep, the thing she had never told anyone, that only she and Daniele knew, because suddenly the idea that her dear friend didn't know was unbearable, but Simone kept interrupting.

'Oh, I remember when you got that document,' Simone said. 'I said what does this mean, and you said something like, it means he's mine. But of course it also meant that all his family had been wiped off the face of the earth, and so that had to be dealt with too.'

'Will you let me get my words out?' Chiara said. 'I have to confess the terrible thing I did. The unforgivable thing. You might not want to be my friend when you know.'

'I already know,' Simone said.

'You don't know what I'm going to say.'

'I do. I half guessed it at the time. One minute you were going every week to the Israelite Community Office, standing in those interminable queues, and the next, hey presto, you're allowed to be his legal guardian and all obstacles have been removed. It all happened too fast. So you don't really need to tell me, except for the purposes of self-flagellation, of course. I know that does always have a pull for you.'

Chiara stared at her friend, who looked steadily back at her. 'I cut him off. I severed his only possible connection.'

'You saved him from more upheaval. No one could have loved him more than you did or cared for him better,' Simone said. 'There comes a point in a person's life, when whatever

354

has happened, whatever suffering he or she has had to bear, she has to shove it all into her backpack, pick it up and carry it, walking her own path.'

'Simone,' she said. 'Are you telling me it's time I grew up?'

'Impudent lady, aren't I?' she said. Then she kissed Chiara on both cheeks. 'I know I've told you this a thousand times, but I do adore you, Chiara Ravello.'

TWENTY-TWO

'Let me see,' the man behind the desk says, as he always does. 'Levi, Levi,' he mumbles and he starts shuffling through a pile of files and folders on the desk beside him. A foul-smelling cigar hangs from his mouth, and his eyes are half shut against the smoke.

It is the same rigmarole every time. Nothing ever changes except that the mountain of papers and folders and box files, stacked haphazardly here and there on the floor, on the shelves and covering a long table at the back of the office, grow higher. But Chiara is hopeful, more than hopeful, in a state of excitement and anticipation, because this time they are going to stamp her docket. On her previous visit, after an episode she cringingly thinks of as 'bribing the rabbi', although he wasn't a rabbi and it wasn't a bribe but a donation for which she received a receipt, she was given to understand as much. It is quite unrelated to the money that changed hands. It is above board and entirely to do with the fact that there is hard evidence that all Daniele's family perished at Auschwitz, as well as the amount of time that has passed, nearly four years.

Since the war ended, people have started to return: imprisoned soldiers from Russia, partisans from up in the mountains, prisoners of war from their camps in North Africa or Britain or wherever they were, Jews who had been in hiding. But nobody from Daniele's family.

There had been news of an old lady who might have been his paternal grandmother, but it transpired that it was some other family named Levi. His father had had a sister, but of her there was no trace. But still information keeps coming in and has to be collated, checked, cross-referenced and added to the piles.

'Good news,' the man says. 'Something came in. There's a file marked with a note telling the clerk to contact you.'

'Me?' she says.

'Did they contact you?'

'No,' she says. She shakes her head for emphasis. 'No one has contacted me,' as if by tripling her denials she can eliminate the fact of there being something worthy of notification.

'We don't get through it all,' he says, puffing on his cigar and looking round at the stacks of files. 'It piles up. But it is so important, this work.'

'What was it?' she says. 'What is it?'

There are loose folds of skin around his jowls as if he had been a very fat man who had suddenly became radically thin, and the skin, in a state of shock, has remained where it was, empty, waiting for the flesh to return.

'Perhaps I've got this wrong,' he says. 'Levi was the name, wasn't it? So many Levis. I thought it had been put out here with the green files for action.' He lifts the top file and riffles through the ones underneath. 'We had a letter from a lady in Genoa who might be the boy's aunt. She is married now and about to emigrate and she wanted to make sure before she went ...'

And he is telling her now about how they had heard from

this woman before but they hadn't connected it with this particular case. Chiara can see that in fact he has two files in his hand, that the second has attached itself – via the clip holding the note in place – to the top one.

She puts down on her side of the desk her neatly typed document, which she needs to have stamped and signed, and she smooths her hands over it. Bile rises in her throat, and she wonders whether she might be sick.

It is over. He is going to be taken away. Not across Rome to a *nonna*'s house where she might visit, but to an aunt who is going to remove him from the country. She will never see him again.

'Dorotea,' the man calls out, replacing the files on the counter, and a woman with hair so black it is almost blue appears from a back room and stands in the doorway. 'Do you know where the Levi file has been put?' he says, twisting around. 'The one with the note on it.'

Chiara looks expectantly across at the woman too. At the same time she slides her hand forward, plucks the note from the file and puts it in her coat pocket, all in a single movement.

'Was it Levi or Levante?' the woman at the door says.

'Oh,' the man says, turning back to Chiara, 'perhaps I made a mistake.' He shuffles quickly through the files in front of him again.

'Can you stamp my document then?' Chiara says.

'Do you know?' he says congenially. 'I'm not at all sure I can. Let me check.' He gets up and goes into the back room.

Chiara reaches across for the stamp. She moves only her arm, keeping her body very still so that the person behind her in the queue will suspect nothing. She rolls the stamp in the inkpad and presses it onto her document. There are voices coming from the back room. Chiara rolls the document, slides it up her sleeve and grips her cuff. She sneezes. She lifts her shopping bag up onto the desk and opens it wide to fish out her handkerchief. The man reappears at the door but then turns to answer a question. She picks up the Levi file, drops it into the bag and blows her nose.

'Husband's name Durante, that's right,' the man says as he walks back in. 'It appears my colleague remembers the letter too. The file has temporarily been mislaid. It might be that my superior has taken it up himself. We will write to you as soon as we have located it. We will make this a priority because the person in question is intending to leave the country soon.'

'You have my address, don't you?'

'Well, it's in the file, so when we find that, yes, we will have. But it was Via dei Cappellari, wasn't it?'

'Oh, no,' she says, 'that's not right. Please erase that one from your records.' She gives him a different address.

On the first Friday of every month, whatever the weather, Chiara and Daniele walk up the Janiculum hill to the Anita Garibaldi monument. Each time Daniele brings a new note and sticks it in the same spot, on the bas-relief at the back, in the crook of Anita Garibaldi's elbow. He doesn't ask where the previous note might have gone, nor does he give any indication that he expects a reply. They always sit for a while on one of the patches of grass around the statue or on the plinth steps.

Today, no sooner has he put the note in place than the heavens open. They sit on the steps huddled under an umbrella with the rain sheeting down at their feet.

'I don't look like my mamma, do I?' he says.

'Yes, you do,' she says, 'quite like her, except she had curlier hair.' He doesn't seem to notice the past tense. 'Your eyes,' she says quickly, 'your eyes are very like hers.'

360

'But her hair is like this,' he says, twisting to look at Chiara, drawing around his head with his hands the shape of a short, straight-cut bob. The shape of Chiara's own hair.

'No,' she says. 'Curlier than that.'

He turns away. The rain tumbles down in front of them out of a thunderously dark sky. They can't see even as far as the fence five metres away. Daniele stares into the blinding rain.

Chiara thinks of his mother as she was that day, the dark green coat and the way her hat sat on the back of her head, the earrings. But this is her memory of the woman, not his.

'You do look like her. That's why you are so handsome,' she says. She looks at him sideways. She might as well be talking to the statue.

Now, she thinks. It is time.

'Hold this,' she says, nudging him, and she passes him the umbrella.

She moves down to the step below and kneels at his feet, looking up into his face. For a moment his eyes meet hers, and then he looks beyond again, over her shoulder, blankly. The rain is beating down on the backs of her legs, filling her shoes. She puts a hand on his knees, bunching them in her palm. Still he doesn't look at her. She reaches farther and takes his chin in her other hand.

'Natalia Ferrara Levi,' she says, 'your mother, was the bravest woman I have ever met.'

The feel of his knees like hard fruit, like apples bunched in her hand.

'She loved you more than life.'

The squeeze of his cheeks, the delicate line of his jaw, the dark eyes.

'She is not coming back,' she says.

The swell of her heart.

'Davide Levi' – his father – 'Giuseppina Levi, Enrichetta Levi' – his two sisters, 'they are not coming back.'

She lifts her hand from his face and touches it to her own breast. She swallows.

'Chiara Ravello,' she says, 'not going anywhere. Ever.' She waits.

Then he seems to fall forward and into her arms.

TWENTY-THREE

'There won't be anyone in,' Assunta said to her grandson. 'But we'll ring the bell just to make sure.'

Maria answered, sounding sleepy. 'Assunta!' she said through the intercom. 'I didn't know you were coming today. Have you forgotten your key?'

'I've brought Marco,' Assunta explained, 'my grandson. He's going to clear some furniture for the signora.'

'She shouldn't be home,' she said to Marco. 'She should be at school.'

Then Assunta concentrated her energy on hauling herself up the stairs. They weren't getting any easier.

The girl stood at the door, rubbing her eyes. Her hair was tousled, her big creamy breasts spilling out of the top of her low-cut nightie.

'Oh,' she said when she saw Assunta wasn't alone. 'I wasn't feeling very well,' she said. 'I've got a headache. So I didn't go to school today.'

Marco had blushed beetroot red.

'Marco has come to clear the *ripostiglio* and see what furniture can be got rid of,' Assunta said.

'*Ripostiglio?*' Maria said.

Assunta explained what it was but could tell the girl didn't understand. Her Italian was improving fast, but still she didn't get everything. Assunta fetched the key from a jar in a kitchen cupboard, came back out to the hallway and lifted the hanging that concealed the junk-room door. Maria was making little surprised noises and comments in her own language. The door bulged outwards, as if something heavy was pushing against it from the other side. Assunta put the key in the lock. It was stiff and wouldn't turn.

'Let me,' Marco said.

She moved out of the way down the hallway, the girl by her side. Marco leant his weight against the door, pushing it back in. They heard a noise, a tinny musical note. He held the door in place, turned the key and leapt smartly out of the way as the door burst open. Out shot the pianola, crashing into the opposite wall, followed by various debris, all with a tremendous clatter.

The pianola was entirely blocking the hallway, Assunta and Maria on one side and Marco the other.

'I'll get this out of the way,' Marco called. 'Hang on. It will only take me a minute.'

Assunta and Maria went into the signora's room to wait. It was either that or the bathroom. They sat on the bed.

'I didn't even know there was a junk room,' Maria said.

'Mmh,' Assunta said.

She wasn't entirely comfortable sitting on the signora's bed. She never came in unless she was cleaning.

'I've got a new picture for you. St Crisogono,' Maria said.

Assunta thought for a moment. Crisogono.

'Beheaded,' she said. 'Thrown into the sea to feed the fishes. But his body was washed ashore, and an old priest found him and gave him a proper burial.'

'Amazing,' Maria said. 'You know them all, don't you?'

Assunta felt as though she should do a bit of tidying now but she had been the day before, and nothing needed doing. And it wasn't one of her days.

The girl was fiddling with something on the bedside table. She swivelled back to Assunta and laid in her lap a photo of a young man.

'Do you know who this is?' she said.

Assunta examined him. 'No,' she said. 'But I've seen that jacket before. I'll show you.'

By now Marco had pushed the pianola into the salon out of the way. Assunta picked her way along the hallway over the bits of broken furniture and sewing machines strewn about, Maria following.

'Some of these pieces, the big ones, I mean, like the pianola and that big cupboard thing, will have to be lowered out of the front window,' Marco said, emerging from the salon. 'I'm going to run round to that antique shop in Via di Monserrato and see if he might give some advice. Because if they're going to be junked, then I can smash them up here and cart them out myself, but if there's anything that has a value . . .'

He was a good boy.

'See you in a minute then,' Assunta said. 'I won't stay long myself. I've got some shopping to do for the little ones' tea but I'll wait for you to come back.'

She was thinking she had better encourage Maria to make herself decent before she left the two of them together. He was a good boy, but easily distracted.

Once he had gone, she rummaged through the coats hanging in the hallway and there, right at the bottom of them all, with its sleeves pushed inside the sleeves of another coat, was a leather jacket identical to the one in the photograph.

'Oh,' Maria said. 'What does that mean?'

Assunta didn't say anything. She didn't know how a jacket was supposed to mean something.

The girl put the jacket on over her nightie. It was a man's jacket. Much too big. She was still holding the photograph.

There was the sound of a key in the lock, and the signora walked in. All the colour went out of her face and she looked at them as if she had seen a pair of ghosts. It couldn't be the sight of her, of Assunta, on a Friday rather than a Thursday that had shocked her so.

Instinctively, Assunta stepped forward in between the signora and the girl.

Stricken, that's what she'd call it.

'Signora,' Assunta said. 'Can I have a word with you? Excuse us, Maria.'

She tugged at her employer's sleeve, led her into the kitchen and pulled the door to.

The signora stood in the middle of the kitchen. She picked up the wonky trivet on which she always put the coffee pot and held it as if someone might be going to snatch it away. Assunta took out the book of saints. She saw that it was the feast day of St Barnabas, who was nicknamed 'son of encouragement' because he encouraged others to live their lives bravely. She pondered that.

'Signora,' she said.

She did not feel it was her place to tell the signora that she needed to face whatever she feared with courage. She saw, though, that the signora was waiting for her to speak and wanted to be given guidance.

Assunta ran her finger down the page, looking for wiser words than her own. She read out loud, 'If you are silent, be silent out of love. If you speak, speak out of love.'

The relevance of these words to the present predicament, and even what the predicament was, remained a mystery.

'St Augustine said that,' she added.

'Thank you, Assunta,' the signora said. 'Out of love. You are right.'

She put the trivet back on the table, patted Assunta's hand twice and left the room, closing the door behind her.

Assunta stayed where she was, reading some more of Augustine's maxims. She discovered that only to those whose hearts were crushed did the Lord draw close. For a minute she worried that her heart might be insufficiently crushed, but then she remembered her dear Federico passing, and how hard it had been to raise the children alone, and she thought it might be enough.

She had the little grandchildren coming after school today for tea and she was going to make them apricot tart. She took out of the book of saints the piece of paper with the recipe and unfolded it. It was printed in big black letters but still unmistakably the signora's handwriting. She ran her finger slowly down the list of ingredients. It was the vanilla sugar that she needed. She closed the book and put it away.

She stuck her head around the door of the salon, which, she noted with a pang, was in turmoil again. It didn't take much. The pianola had rucked up the carpet. Half the contents of the junk room were piled up next to the window. They were sitting opposite each other, the signora and Maria, and the signora was holding both the girl's hands in hers.

They looked up at her. They had both been crying, she saw. She blinked at them.

'Assunta,' Maria said. She freed one of her hands and held up the photo. 'This is my *babbo*.' She smiled at Assunta through her tears. 'And the signora is my *nonna*.' They put her in mind of sunshine after the rain, the two of them. 'She's told me the whole story.'

'Oh,' Assunta said, wondering what story that might be. The signora had never mentioned that she had a son. 'That's nice,' she said.

She should probably mind her own business. Vanilla sugar, she thought.

'I was just coming to say to let Marco in when he gets back, and I'll be off now.'

'Marco?' the signora said.

'You remember? My grandson. We arranged for him to come and sort out the old furniture.'

'Oh, yes,' the signora said. 'Marco.' And she beamed at Assunta.

The doorbell rang.

'That'll be him now,' Assunta said. Speaking into the intercom, she told Marco, 'It might be better to come back another time. There's a lot going on here.'

'Assunta,' a woman's loud, ringing voice exclaimed. 'Are you trying to send me away as if I'm the bailiff?'

'Oh, Madame Simone. Excuse me!' Assunta said.

When Simone appeared at the top of the stairs, huffing and puffing, Assunta said, 'The signora is in the salon. With Maria.'

'Goodness,' she said. 'Have they started without me? Could you be a darling and put this in the freezer section?'

Simone swept past Assunta into the salon, leaving her standing in the vestibule, holding a box of strawberry ice cream.

'Oh God, you do look like him! Exactly like him. Oh my word and so beautiful,' Assunta heard Madame Simone say.

She was never one to think twice about taking the Lord's name in vain, Madame Simone. She wondered what Maria would think of her. They had something in common to be getting on with, both wearing their nightdresses in the middle of the day.

She took the ice cream to the kitchen and put it away.

The doorbell rang again. 'Hello,' she said suspiciously into the intercom.

'Nonna.'

'Oh, Marco,' she said. 'I think you'd better come back another time. I'll check with the signora when would be convenient. There's all sorts going on in here, and we'd best keep out of the way.'

'OK,' he said. 'Shall I wait for you?'

'Wait for me in that bar on Vicolo di Gallo,' she said. 'I'll buy you a coffee.'

She went back into the salon. Madame Simone was standing with her back to the window, her loops of honey hair silhouetted against the light. The other two were where they had been before, but, if anything, closer together.

'Assunta,' Simone called out. 'Would you be an angel and make us a cup of coffee?'

She looked at the three of them. It was her day off and she had her grandson to meet, as well as a tart to make. For some reason, she thought of rainbows and of what someone had told her once: that even on a dull day, up above the clouds, the sky was blue.

'Of course,' she said.

She went back to the kitchen, reached the big pot down out of the cupboard and filled the bottom part with water. She tapped the coffee into the filter and screwed it all back together. She lit the gas.

The doorbell rang. 'I'll be ten minutes,' she said into the intercom.

369

'It's Father Antonio,' a man's voice said, 'I'm expected.'

She pressed the buzzer. It was like Termini station in here today.

She wasn't used to seeing Father Antonio outside of church, where she did the flowers and cleaned the sacristy. She thought he was looking rather sickly.

'Assunta,' he said, when he saw her, 'what on earth are you doing here?'

'I work for Signora Ravello,' she said.

'Oh,' he said. 'I didn't know that.'

'They're all in the salon,' she said. 'And I'm just making them coffee. Would you like one too?'

'Yes, thank you,' he said. 'I know my way.'

It would be hard not to know your way from the front door to the salon, Assunta thought, seeing it was only two paces.

She went back into the kitchen, got down the best cups and saucers with the gold rims, and put four of each on a tray. She didn't know why but she felt it was some sort of an occasion. The girl liked milk in her coffee, even when it wasn't break-fast time, so she put some milk in a little jug. She thought biscuits would be nice, but the signora wasn't one for biscuits, so she didn't bother looking. When the coffee was ready, she placed it on the tray to carry through.

Father Antonio was still standing in the hall outside the salon door, turning his hat round and round in his hands. He had a haunted look.

There was laughter now coming from the salon. It sounded as though someone was doing an impression of a chicken.

'Are you all right, Father?' Assunta said.

'It might be better,' he said, 'if I just slip quietly away.'

'But isn't the signora expecting you?' she said.

He nodded, then shook his head. He didn't seem to know

what he was doing. 'I've never had a child of my own, you see,' he said.

'I should think not,' Assunta said.

The priest didn't move. He was looking at her appealingly.

She rested the tray on the hall table and fished out her book. What a day this was turning into. She thumbed through to the passage she'd read out to the signora earlier. The recipe was there as a bookmark.

'Those are wonderful words, Assunta,' Father Antonio said. 'Yes, love and silence. Of course. It would be kinder not to say anything, wouldn't it?'

Priests were only men, she reflected.

'I don't know, Father,' she said, 'but I do know that the truth never hurts as much as the lies.' She had heard that on the radio.

'Oh,' he said, and he put his hand to his heart. 'It wasn't a lie. Not exactly a lie. It was more that I didn't . . .' He shook his head and blew out his cheeks.

She took the hat from his other hand and hung it on the stand.

'Come on, Father,' she said and, picking up the tray, she led the way into the salon. 'Father Antonio is here,' she announced.

There were introductions and exclamations and hand-shakings, and somehow Assunta found herself squeezed on the little sofa next to Maria. That was where she sat while the priest made his speech.

It seemed that the signora's son had got into bad ways, and Father Antonio had sent him away, but that then – unbeknownst to the signora or anyone except the priest himself, because he had kept it a secret – the priest had helped him. He had gone on helping him, and the son, Daniele, had been living just down the road in Ostia. And every time Daniele went off the rails, the priest would go and sort him out. And he went on going off the rails. The way Father Antonio told it, he sounded as though he had something of the saint about him. Assunta tried to give him a look to remind him about truth and lies, but he avoided her eyes.

He was still talking when the signora suddenly jumped to her feet and clapped her hands together.

'What are you saying? That Daniele is in Ostia? Ostia!' she cried. 'I can't believe it.'

'What is it?' Maria was saying. 'What does that mean?' And she swung her head about, looking from one to the other.

The signora was staring at the priest with such an imploring, expectant sort of expression that it gave Assunta a peculiar sensation. She had never been in an aeroplane but she thought this was how take-off might feel.

'No, no, no,' the priest said in a squeaky voice and cleared his throat. 'No, I'm sorry, Chiara, no.' He shook his head, holding both hands up, palms outward, at chest height. They shook too. 'He's not there any more. I've been looking for him ever since you told me about Maria.'

He turned away from Chiara to look at Maria, letting his flapping hands fall to his sides and giving Maria a sorrowful smile. 'I don't know what happened to him,' he said. 'We lost contact.'

The signora sat down again and put her face in her hands.

'I am sorry to be the bearer of bad tidings,' the priest said, his voice returning to normal. 'But I fear that Daniele took up with drugs again.'

There was a silence. The plane had come back down to earth. Then they all started talking at the same time, and the signora burst into tears.

If the priest was the hero of this story all along, she didn't know why he had been in such a state in the hallway.

'Father Antonio,' she said, half standing up, and caught his gaze.

He looked at her, and she thought for a horrible moment that he was going to cry.

'Yes,' he said, then raised his hands and lowered them again, almost as if he might be going to bow to her. 'All right,' he said.

Madame Simone had drawn up a chair next to the signora and was speaking to her softly. The priest, who had lowered himself to his knees at the signora's feet, started beating his breast.

'*Mea culpa*,' he was saying. He was making a confession.

'What's going on?' the girl was saying. 'What's going on?'

And Assunta, who had a job following it all herself, took the girl's hand in hers and gripped it tightly.

TWENTY-FOUR

'Help me, Ma,' he says and then he passes out.

He is lying across the threshold. Half in and half out, his legs protruding onto the communal landing.

She drags him the rest of the way in, her hands in his hot, damp armpits. It takes her a few heaves. She grunts as she does it, and he half wakes.

'Is that my little ma?' he says. 'My little ma,' and he reaches up to her with fluttering hands, but before they connect, they fall down by his side. She lays him out in the entrance hallway. He is too heavy to take farther. She brings water. She puts a cushion under his head.

She thinks about the first time she saw him like this, so out of it that he could hardly form a sentence. He was only a boy. Fourteen or fifteen. It was after she had shown him the Levi file.

'I did it for us,' she said, 'for you and me, so we could get on with our lives.'

And he said, 'There is no us.'

There was a kind of sweet smell around him.

She removes and pockets his keys, which were hanging in the lock. There are kick marks in the door, the imprint of his boot, a dent in the wood, a splintering. What a battering he has given it. But better the door, she thinks, than someone's face.

Why did he try to kick the door in when he had his key?

She lifts his head. 'Drink,' she says.

She must keep him hydrated. Watch over him to make sure he doesn't fit or choke on his own vomit. Wake him hourly.

'Have you taken something? What have you taken?' she had said that first time, seeing that his pupils were dilated.

'Don't worry, Ma,' he had said. 'It's all under control. It's good for me.' He had nodded at her. 'Good for the thing.'

'What thing?'

'You know,' he had said, 'the sadness thing.'

She sits next to him, on the floor in the entrance hall, under the coat rack.

Help me, Ma.

She has the alarm clock beside her in case she should fall asleep and she sets it for one hour's time.

The clock ticks. He has his mouth open, lying on his back, slack-jawed, and he breathes noisily.

She touches the birthmark on his outflung hand. It has grown and stretched over the years, become paler and more amorphous. From this angle, it looks like the faint image of an uncoiling snake; a small patch within it of darker pigmentation could be the snake's eye. Funny how sometimes she used to think that because he had this horseshoe birthmark, a talisman of good fortune imprinted in his skin, he carried his luck with him. How she persisted in thinking it was luck that had saved him when the rest of his family had perished, and not, as he seems to want to demonstrate to her, its opposite.

'I don't blame you, Ma,' he has told her more than once.

'So why are you so intent on throwing your life away?' she has asked him, but he doesn't seem to have an answer.

376

'This is where we are come, my darling boy,' she says now.

His quiff has fallen forward, and she nudges it back from his forehead. His hair is stiff and slimy with the grease he combs through it. His skin is clammy, like uncooked pizza dough. She has the impression she could push her thumb into it and make a mark. Reshape it. Like putty. She dips a sponge into the bowl of water and gently wipes his face.

He always acts as if he has a hard shell, like a snail or a tortoise. Or an egg. She remembers the first egg Cluck laid, a globule that made no sound as it landed on the floorboards. Something barely contained, the line that divided the world from it and it from the world imperfectly delineated.

He used to love to roam the hills, climb trees, swing and jump, camouflage himself in mud. His eyes sometimes shone when he did those things, but now it is only in that briefest of moments, just after the needle has gone in, that his eyes brighten in the old way. As if it is the wildness calling to him. That's what they buy him, these drugs, something that is like freedom.

She remembers him, a switch in his hand, or a fallen branch, and he was swishing it through the grass and leaping about, near but not too close to the one sheep with its autumn lamb. She feared that he would lash out at the lamb as he passed, but he didn't. He never did. He would never hurt an animal. It is himself he hurts. All his rage goes inwards.

She puts her head on his chest and listens to his fast-beating heart.

She says, *Help me.*

TWENTY-FIVE

The view from the junk-room window was of tubes, vents, overflow pipes, ducts, waste pipes, wires: the hidden outlets and inlets that kept the building functioning, the grubby backside of things. But if Maria put her chair under the window and laid her head on the sill, she could look up at the sky.

In a minute she will go out into the mess of the apartment, where everything now was being shifted and sifted, thrown away or refurbished, and she will sit in the kitchen with the signora, Nonna Chiara, and they will work together on Keats's letters. After that they will have their conversation session, which has now become a kind of history lesson, both in the smaller, domestic sense – Daniele's favourite meal, how he played the trumpet at a school concert, his night-time drink – and the wider context of fascism and war and social upheaval. And she will try to grasp a bit more about the place where the two intersected and who he was, her pained and handsome father. Heartbroken and a heartbreaker, one of those boys girls think they can tame.

About all of it Maria was insatiable. However, she was also soon sated and had to retreat for a while to this quiet, white-washed little place that was her own. The false ceiling had been taken down and all of Daniele's possessions, stored up there for years, sorted through. She had hung his trumpet on the wall next to the photograph, and placed in her bedside cabinet all the notes he had written to his real mother, which Nonna Chiara had kept in a box. It was nice to have her own room, but it meant she was next door to Nonna Chiara's and she could hear her crying at night. Sometimes that would set her off too, even though most of the time, caught up in the glory of her new Italian life, she wasn't really sad.

'That ring you gave me,' she told her mum on the phone, 'used to belong to Nonna Chiara's father, and the initials stand for Alfonso Ferdinando Ravello.'

She knew now that at his lowest point Daniele had taken all of Nonna Chiara's jewellery and pawned it to pay for his drugs, but she didn't feel that was something her mum needed to know. This ring was the one piece that was rightfully his.

Her mum had wept when Maria had said that even if Daniele was alive, no one had any way of tracing him. That the chances were he would never be found, and was probably dead.

'Nonna Chiara is going to take me to the place where Daniele used to leave letters for his mum,' she said, 'and I am going to write him a message and leave it there. I thought perhaps you might like to write one too. To say goodbye,' she said.

Tommaso was coming to visit in a week or so, when the work on the apartment would be finished. He was going to sleep in her old spot in the salon.

'So it turns out I'm half Jewish as well as half Italian,' she had told him when he called.

'Blimey O'Riley,' he had said, affecting an Irish brogue, 'and you a Catholic.'

Later still she and Nonna Chiara will prepare their evening

meal or they will go out to eat in the trattoria on Campo dei Fiori where Maria had tasted smoked mozzarella, cockles and clams but had turned her nose up at rabbits' brains. Afterwards the alarming Simone, who frequently gathered Maria in her arms and crushed her against her cushiony, perfumed breasts, might take them to a show or a happening. Or she and Nonna Chiara might go to the cinema in Trastevere where they showed films in English.

Or she might go out promenading with Beppe and Carmelo. Once or twice, when it was really late, she had pretended she was going home but instead she had run, by herself, through the night-time streets to Piazza Costaguti in the heart of the ghetto where Daniele Levi's family home had been. She had stood alone in the darkness in the empty square and reached for it, the huge, cavernous absence of the family she would never know, the horror of their fates, but she couldn't somehow seem to feel it properly. It was all very sad, and she sort of missed him. Daniele Levi, her biological father, the person she most closely physically resembled and whom she would never now meet. But she didn't know him and, anyway, she already had a dad.

She lay with her head on the sill, looking up at the limitless sky.

TWENTY-SIX

It is August, the hottest month. Chiara waits in the relative
cool of the entrance hall. The red Murano bowl, one of the
objects to survive the cull, the great emptying and winnow-
ing that the apartment has undergone, catches her eye. She
takes the bowl from the shelf, balances it in the palm of one
hand, feels its weight, the perfection of its dips and contours,
the smoothness of the glass. She lifts it with the other hand
and uses her fingertip to find and touch the hidden flaw, the
tiny fissure in its base. She imagines dashing it to the ground,
the shock of its shattering, ruby shards and splinters scattering.

She raises it to her eye instead and peers through at the
world stained red. She steps sideways and through the bowl's
lens she looks down the length of her newly spacious hallway
to the place at the end where two ancient pieces of furniture
used to stand but where now a mirror hangs. She sees herself,
a small figure in black, with a Cyclops eye of burning red, like
a little devil.

Maria emerges from her room halfway down the hallway,
sees Chiara and smiles.

'Rose-tinted glasses?' she says.

Maria doesn't see her as a devil. She doesn't know the violence inside.

'You need a blouse with that,' Chiara says.

Maria is wearing a pleated pale-green crêpe de Chine skirt from Chiara's collection and one of her own tight black tops that puts Chiara in mind of a man's vest that has shrunk in the wash. Her arms and shoulders are bare.

'The skirt is lovely,' Chiara adds.

'Nobody wears blouses,' Maria says, sashaying down the hallway as if it is a catwalk.

'Nobody,' Chiara says as she replaces the bowl. The monster in her subsides.

'I mean nobody my age. You look nice in them. Anyway, you haven't got the full effect yet. It's going to look fab.'

Maria, next to her now, reaches down Daniele's old leather jacket from the coat rack and shrugs it over her shoulders.

'See?' she says. 'Eclectic chic.'

'You're going to roast,' Chiara says. 'It's like an oven outside.'

'I don't care,' Maria says. 'I'm wearing it.'

'Let's go then,' Chiara says.

The carved handle of the walking stick protrudes from the umbrella stand next to the door and on a whim she takes it.

If Maria asks why she is taking a cane when she is supposedly cured of her head-spinning malaise, she will make some joke about how it befits her new grandmother status. She will put on a croaky, old-lady voice. Maria, however, is more interested in telling Chiara a story about a man on the bus who had been staring at her.

As they walk along, Chiara swings the cane and reflects that the comfort of it lies not in the support it offers but in its capacity to transform into a weapon. A cudgel.

Ever since Antonio's revelation, she has been in turmoil. She

384

wants him defrocked, excommunicated, paraded in shame through the streets, her erstwhile friend. She wants him tarred and feathered, struck down by a thunderbolt. A savage rage burns through her. She is surprised that no one can see it from the outside. That they say, 'You look tired,' or 'Nice haircut,' when they should be saying, 'You look dangerous,' or 'You look nasty.'

Rage has replaced grief, and it is ugly beyond redemption. When first it came, like a gargoyle within her, it felt bigger than she was, pushing at her seams and bursting through her pores. It spoke through her mouth. When Simone reached out her hand to Antonio as he knelt at their feet, it said, 'Don't touch him.' It is more contained now but still it presses against her forehead from the inside, like a migraine. She has told Antonio by phone that she is not ready to see him yet, but that she understands that he was not motivated by malice.

'So when stamping on his foot didn't work, I started shouting,' Maria says as they wait for the lights to change at the crossing on Lungotevere.

'You what?' Chiara says. She has not been paying full attention to this dramatic tale.

'This gross man, groping me on the bus. How do you say "grope" in Italian?'

'Oh dear,' Chiara says, 'tell me that part again.'

Sometimes it seems to her that it is only the presence of Maria in her life that stops her from running amok with her cudgel, frothing at the mouth, smashing and breaking things, laying waste.

They pause in the middle of Ponte Sisto, facing upriver towards the dome of St Peter on the horizon, and Maria finishes her story.

How she shouted out, *Quest'uomo* – this man.

And then again louder, 'This man, this man!'

How no other words came to help, but it was enough, because she was shouting in her new Italian voice, which was richer and stronger than her English one. The cry was taken up by the women of the bus.

'Driver, stop the bus,' they shouted.

The man was manhandled off, dumped on the pavement, shouted at and cursed.

'Shame on you,' they cried.

She had been going to give him her supercilious look, but the bus had pulled away.

'You coped with that very well,' Chiara says. 'Show me the look.'

Maria turns to face her. She is already flushed in the heat, and they haven't started to climb the hill yet. She tilts her head so she is looking down her nose, half closes her eyes and raises one eyebrow.

'Very effective,' Chiara says, remembering a little boy with no defence other than a hooded gaze. She takes a tighter grip on the handle of her stick as the monstrous fury wells up in her again. It is as if she were pregnant and big with it. It makes her quiver.

'I love this bridge,' Maria says. She is looking down at the water swirling past. 'I think it might be my favourite because of the way, with the reflection, the arches make perfect circles.'

As they continue on their way, she prattles on about the relative merits of bridges, and Chiara finds herself arguing in favour of the splendour of the St Angelo one. They call in at the basilica of St Cecilia's to light a candle for Cecilia and so that Maria can see the likeness of the saint, her trailing hair, her outflung, dimpled hand. Then they weave through the little streets of Trastevere to Via Garibaldi, from where they climb first one and then another set of stairs that cut off the twists and bends of the road, carrying them steeply up the hill.

They emerge opposite the fountain of Acqua Paola.

'Wow,' Maria says, 'wow,' exclaiming at the great baroque façade and the water cascading out of the basins set into the pillared walls, the shallow bowl it falls into and the aquamarine colour of it against the white marble.

But Chiara doesn't speak. She has turned to look at the panorama of Rome laid out at their feet. As she gazes across the expanse of the city to the other side bounded by the mass of the Castelli hills, she experiences again that old sensation of rising above the rubble, the pettiness and the empty noise, to a quieter place.

She understands that at the heart of all her hopes for Daniele – that he might be alive, that he might even be well and alive – when all those layers had been peeled away and discarded, there at the innermost core one minuscule hope had remained: that Daniele, wherever he was, would at least know that he was loved. And now that hope is dead.

She understands that the monstrous rage that fills her hasn't replaced the grief. It *is* the grief.

She becomes aware of Maria standing quietly at her side. Maria has taken off the jacket, and the freckled skin on her shoulder glistens.

'I'm sorry you're so sad,' Maria says. 'What can I do?'

'You're already doing it,' Chiara says.

They continue onwards and upwards, past the Giuseppe Garibaldi monument and along the path lined with white-painted busts of Garibaldi's followers until there she is, Anita Garibaldi on her rearing horse.

'Daniele,' Chiara suddenly says, 'really liked coming up here. He liked high places. He loved climbing things, scrambling up trees and over walls and out of windows. He was a nimble and agile boy. He had a sort of grace. He was a wonderful dancer.'

She wonders whether this is quite true, whether she is rewriting him. Then she remembers a thing he did, his party piece.

'He could do this extraordinary thing,' she says. 'He called it the flagpole. He would place his hands in a certain way, like this.'

She hangs the walking stick over her forearm to have both hands free to demonstrate, bending her knees and stacking her hands around an imaginary pole.

'And then he would unfurl his body at right angles to the pole, like a banner. He was so strong.' She unhooks the cane and looks at Maria. 'How could he believe that I didn't want to see him?' she asks.

'Perhaps he didn't,' Maria says. 'I wouldn't believe anything that came out of that creepy priest's mouth.'

She climbs up the steps at the back of the monument to place her note.

'There's one already here,' she says.

'Oh,' Chiara says, 'I forgot.'

The futility of this ritual hits her like a blow to the breast-bone. She breathes out heavily.

'I left one to tell him about you. It must be that.'

'It's addressed to Ma,' Maria says.

Chiara leans on the stick and stares up at the girl. Her heart is hammering, and there is a rushing noise in her ears like the fast beat of wings as a thousand birds take to the air. She can see Maria's mouth move but she can't make out the words. Something hideous and irresistible is going on inside her body. The noise and the swirl and a dark fog all try to claim her, and she staggers, but she has the sturdy cane and she plants it in the earth.

It is a blastingly hot day, but Chiara is shivering. Maria places the leather jacket around her shoulders. They sit together on the steps of the monument and read.

Dear Ma,
All those years I left notes for my mother and finally she replies! Wait where you are because I'm coming to find you.
Love
Daniele

Later they will discover that he has been clear of drugs for three years. That after his last meeting with Father Antonio he took himself in hand, knowing that the choice of whether to live or go under was his alone. That word reached him that Father Antonio was looking for him again and that he came here to their special place to find the note Chiara had left him.

In a week's time, Chiara and Maria will catch a bus to Porta San Paolo, then the train to Ostia, and then another bus along the coast road, and he will meet them there at the bus stop. He will lead them into the thick Mediterranean scrub of the hunting reserve where he lives and works, with the wild boar and the deer for company, amid the holly oaks and the pines. He will show them the trees where the buzzards roost and make them tea on the stove in his shack.

But right now Chiara sits holding Maria's hand, in the shadow of the monument, with the letter on her lap, waiting for her lost boy to come home.

ACKNOWLEDGEMENTS

Philip Hensher, generous friend and mentor, for reading and commenting on an early version of the manuscript; fellow writers Sally Flint and Jane Feaver for their support and wisdom; Kate Smiley, reader extraordinaire, for instantly rising to the challenge at a critical juncture; insightful editors Ursula Doyle and Judy Clain and all those at Virago/Little, Brown who worked on this book; my brilliant agent Nicola Barr, her colleagues at the Greene & Heaton agency and Grainne Fox in New York; my family – both in the UK and in Italy – and my friends for their unstinting love and fellowship and enthusiasm for my writing.